FAMILY REUNION

His name was officially Peter Bentley. His
nationality was legally American. There was nothing
to tie him to his grandfather, Buonaparte Sartene,
or to the international crime empire Buonaparte
Sartene ruled.

Nothing, that is, except blood.

Nothing except honor—honor that required
avenging a murderous betrayal.

And blood, honor and vengeance were enough to
join Peter Bentley with his grandfather . . . as the
ways of the old world and the ways of the new
united to wage an underworld war in Southeast Asia
even more savage and sinister than the war the
U.S. Army was waging—in a shared killing ground
of violence and deceit, passion and
perversity. . . .

THE CORSICAN

"EXOTIC INTRIGUES AND BETRAYALS . . .
A DEADLY DANCE OF DEATH IN A
MULTI-GENERATIONAL THRILLER."
—*Publishers Weekly*

The Best in Fiction from SIGNET

"I won't take from any man
anything that my family does not need
to survive. And if he tries to take
from me, I will stop him."
—Buonaparte Sartene,
known as THE CORSICAN

THE CORSICAN

A NOVEL BY

William Heffernan

A SIGNET BOOK

NEW AMERICAN LIBRARY

PUBLISHER'S NOTE

This novel is a work of fiction. Names, characters, places, and incidents either are the product of the author's imagination or are used fictitiously, and any resemblance to actual persons, living or dead, events, or locales is entirely coincidental.

NAL BOOKS ARE AVAILABLE AT QUANTITY DISCOUNTS
WHEN USED TO PROMOTE PRODUCTS OR SERVICES.
FOR INFORMATION PLEASE WRITE TO PREMIUM MARKETING DIVISION,
NEW AMERICAN LIBRARY, 1633 BROADWAY,
NEW YORK, NEW YORK 10019.

Copyright © 1983 by William Heffernan

This is an authorized reprint of a hardcover edition published by Simon and Schuster.

SIGNET TRADEMARK REG. U.S. PAT. OFF. AND FOREIGN COUNTRIES
REGISTERED TRADEMARK—MARCA REGISTRADA
HECHO EN CHICAGO, U.S.A.

SIGNET, SIGNET CLASSIC, MENTOR, PLUME, MERIDIAN and NAL BOOKS
are published by New American Library,
1633 Broadway, New York, New York 10019

PRINTED IN THE UNITED STATES OF AMERICA

ACKNOWLEDGMENTS

I would like to thank Alfred W. McCoy, who together with Cathleen B. Reed and Leonard P. Adams wrote *The Politics of Heroin in Southeast Asia*, a masterwork of journalism that saved me much research time. I would also like to acknowledge the support and help of Martin Poll, Herman Gollob, Linda Grey, Lawrence S. Freundlich, and, as always, Gloria Loomis-Miller.

A special thanks to Russell Bintliff, whose past military and intelligence work in Southeast Asia were the basis for portions of this novel.

"But how meager one's life becomes when it is reduced to its basic facts . . . And the last, most complete, reduction is on one's tombstone; a name, two dates. This man was born, and died. And few ask why."

The Venetian Affair, Helen MacInnes

BOOK
ONE

Un Vrai
Monsieur

Prologue

The road began on the outskirts of Vientiane, then followed the Mekong River west, away from the garish lights of the city. At the edge of the bush it seemed to disappear, taken by the sudden blackness of the tropical forest. There the road changed from steaming black macadam to cracked, heat-hardened earth that left the bordering vegetation covered in thick brown-black dirt, cleansed only when the monsoon rains came in spring.

Even at night the heat along the road was oppressive. The forest rose on each side, then closed above it, keeping out the slight breeze that came off the river at sunset. The forest seemed to swallow everything. Only the incessant sounds of insects appeared undisturbed, their steady beat filtering through the dense, impenetrable growth, mixing there with the occasional scream of a dying animal.

The road continued for nine miles, following the sharply winding course of the river. Over the last three miles the road narrowed slightly, and there back in the bush sentry huts were set at regular intervals. Beside each hut, small, intense men squatted in silence, their eyes concentrating on the road, their presence undetectable to any who passed. Each man had an automatic weapon, and nearby a field telephone; the vegetation in front of them had been cut into gradually widening swaths that opened onto the road, offering a broad killing ground.

At the end of the nine miles the road ended abruptly, replaced there by two divergent paths, each wide enough for only a single vehicle. The northern path continued for a half mile to a small dirt airstrip. The southerly path ended where the jungle gave way to a broad plain. There the river dipped south, then turned back

again before continuing west, leaving behind a narrow jut of land
on which a dock had been built. Along the dock two motor
launches rode idly in the water, partially obscured by the heavy
ground mist that came each evening. There was another sentry at
the end of the dock, an automatic weapon slung over his shoulder,
his eyes scanning the white mist for any shadows that would
reveal the movement of men.

As it always did, the mist began in the high hills above the
river, moving in isolated patches through the dense vegetation to
the plain below, then out across the water to the opposite shore.
In the center of the plain, one hundred yards from the river, a
large white house stood above the mist, its lighted windows
illuminating much of the surrounding ground. The house was of
a solid European design, built far back from the river to protect it
from the flooding monsoon rains, and at night it seemed to float
on the mist, its encircling veranda resembling the deck of some
misplaced ship. On either side of the house, lone mangosteen
trees rose thirty feet until level with the roof, the thick branches
refracting the light from the windows, casting strange patterns on
the mist.

At the rear of the house was a Japanese garden, visible now
only in sections as the mist moved toward the river. A pond at
the garden's center gave off flashes of light from the house as the
patches of mist moved above it, and along its edges the sounds
of insects played against the steady cacophony of the bush.

The garden began at the foot of a wide stairway that rose
steeply to the veranda. There, another sentry stood next to a set
of open French doors, an automatic rifle cradled in his arms, his
flat oriental face and squat body hidden in the shadows. Beyond
the doors, an old man could be seen seated behind a heavy teak
desk. He was in his early seventies, but his sharp European
features and thick gray hair disguised his age. On the wall
behind him there was an equestrian portrait by Meissonier of
Napoleon leading his troops to Montmirail, his right hand thrust
into his greatcoat, his dark eyes, like the old man's, staring
straight ahead.

The man seemed deep in thought, then suddenly turned his
attention to an interior door across the room, as if anticipating
something. There was a knock on the door and another man
entered carrying a tray. He was approximately the same age as
the man behind the desk, but he too seemed younger. He was
dressed in a white jacket and together with the tray it made him

look like a servant, but he was not, and he bore himself without a trace of servility. His name was Auguste.

"I brought you some dinner, Don Sartene," he said. There was a deliberate humor in his voice.

The man at the desk noticed the formality of the title and raised his finger to his long curved nose and shook his head.

"You're too old to play nursemaid, Auguste," he said.

"And you're too old to need one."

They spoke in the Corsican dialect they always used with one another. Short staccato sentences that snapped back and forth.

Sartene waved his hand in a gesture of surrender and waited as Auguste placed the tray on the desk. His nose wrinkled at the food, but there was a faint smile on his lips.

"When are you going to learn to speak with respect, Auguste?" He was continuing the game the other man had begun, but each knew it was only a way of avoiding the subject they feared.

"I'm like you. I'm too old to learn anything new." Auguste's hard face softened and he gestured toward the tray. "You should eat," he added seriously. "You haven't had anything all day."

"Has there been any word yet?" Sartene asked.

Auguste lowered his eyes. "Nothing. But he's young and strong. And he's also Corsican. He'll survive."

Sartene's dark, vulpine eyes warmed to the man standing before him. He drew a deep breath. "Youth and strength and nationality haven't shit to do with life and death," he said softly.

He leaned back in his chair and stared at the ceiling. Above him a fan turned slowly, circulating the dank, humid air. "That damned fan. It squeaks when it moves," he said, dismissing the subject.

"It's like us. It's an old fan," Auguste said.

Sartene smiled, revealing uneven teeth, the gift of an impoverished youth. "How long have I put up with you now?"

Auguste turned his palms upward, thinking with them. "Twenty-one years here. Before that five years in France, during the war. But I'm not sure who did the putting up."

Sartene nodded. "We've changed, haven't we?" he said. "Now we have wealth and power and this damned foolish house that we built to remind us of home." He grunted to himself. "At least in France we killed the Boches and anyone else who deserved killing." He waved a self-deprecating hand in front of his face. "Look at what I'm doing now. You have me talking like an old woman. Get out of here."

Auguste walked to the door, then turned as he opened it. His eyes hardened again, like a schoolmistress preparing to scold a child. "Eat," he said. "Even in this godforsaken heat the food will get cold."

He watched as Sartene waved his hand again, then stepped out and closed the door behind him. As he did, the hardness he had fought to keep on his face disappeared.

Outside Sartene's study, fine paintings hung above the ornate tables and chairs that lined the walls, making it seem more like the corridor of a museum. The hall, like the house, was empty and quiet, and Auguste's heels echoed against the hardwood floors as he walked back to the kitchen. Once there, he took a bottle of wine from the sideboard, poured a glass and seated himself at the long table that dominated the room. He grimaced, then opened his jacket and removed a large automatic pistol from his waistband and placed it on the table before him. He sipped at the wine, hoping it would quell the uneasy feeling in his stomach. It was hard for him to think of Sartene as an old man. True, he knew it as well as he knew that he too was old. He had admitted his own age to himself. But never before had he heard Sartene do so, except when he was joking. And he knew why he did it now. It was because he was afraid. A man admitted he was old only when fear forced him to.

"But not for himself." Auguste spoke the words to his wineglass. He's afraid for Pierre, he thought. Afraid to lose the one thing that means more than life to him.

He drank the wine and poured another glass, looked at it for a moment, then pushed it aside. Remain alert, he told himself. Even though the others aren't Corsican, they're still dangerous. He stood and walked to the window, cupping his hands over his eyes as he stared out across the plain to the edge of the dense forest. He knew where each of the sentries should be, but he had to stare a long while at each place before he could see them. But that was as it should be.

He walked back to the table. Twenty-six years, he thought. A long time for two men to serve each other. Buonaparte Sartene and Auguste Pavlovi. Through so much. He smiled to himself, thinking of 1946, the beginning of their second year together in Laos. Little Pierre, only six then, watching, mystified, as the house was built, when he saw his first tiger, his first python. Auguste laughed, thinking of the trip they had taken in the old surplus jeep. Along the canopied forest path, where the squat female ape had stepped suddenly out of the bush, curious about their presence, refusing to move. The child's wide eyes and open mouth, trying to understand the "big monkey," as he had called it.

He rubbed his hand across his forehead, then down his face, feeling the growth of beard already there. They were all gone now. Sartene's son, his daughter-in-law, even his own brother, Benito. And the other one too, the friend who had proved himself a pig. Worse than a pig.

There had been a vendetta then, but not as complete as it should have been. The North Vietnamese had not allowed it. This time it would be, no matter who objected, especially if . . .

He stood abruptly and walked to the heavy black telephone that connected the main house to the hut where the radio transmitter was kept. A voice answered in Lao.

"Have you had any word from the Meo?" Auguste asked in French.

"*Je n'en ai pas,*" came the reply.

"Has there been any from the men along the road?"

"*Non,*" the voice answered.

"Let me know as soon as you hear anything."

He returned to the window and stared into the dark beyond the plain. Out of habit he began rubbing the scar of an old wound on his chest.

When he returned to the study an hour later, Sartene was not there. Auguste glanced at the tray of food, noting that it had not been touched, then walked out to the veranda, where Sartene stood, staring into the Japanese garden.

As he heard Auguste's quiet step behind him he turned. "Is there some word?" he asked.

"None. But there will be. The Meo have been alerted, and they're good at this sort of thing," he answered.

Sartene turned back to the garden. The mist had cleared somewhat under a gentle breeze coming from the distant hills, and more of the garden was now visible. In the distance a Theravada Buddhist shrine could be seen across the pond, something Sartene had included in the garden out of respect for the Laotians who worked for him.

"The orientals say it takes several generations for a garden like this to be perfected." He spoke without looking back at Auguste. His voice, as always, was near a whisper. "They always understood that a man creates for those who come after him. They're very much like the people of Corsica in that way.''

Auguste leaned against the railing beside him. ''There's nothing we can do now but wait,'' he said.

Sartene clasped his hands together and began flexing his thumbs. His eyes were sharp and piercing even in the darkness. He was several inches taller than Auguste; there was no stoop to his shoulders despite his age, and he had the same sense of command that his friend had first noticed years before in France.

''I should have never dealt with those American bastards,'' he said softly, still looking into the garden.

''If you hadn't, someone else would have. The result would have been the same,'' Auguste said. ''This way, at least, we know more about our enemy. Don't blame yourself, Buonaparte. It's just that now we're forced to wait. That's always difficult.''

Sartene turned and walked along the veranda, his hands behind his back. After a few yards, he stopped abruptly.

''We'll wait. But we'll also act,'' he said. He turned and walked back to Auguste and placed a hand on the smaller man's shoulder. ''You've done much for me all these years. Now I have to ask you to do one thing more.''

Auguste's eyes did not move from Sartene's. He would do what was asked; there was no need for words between them.

Sartene slid his arm around Auguste's shoulder and guided him back to the study, speaking softly as they walked.

''You must go to Saigon and gather the information that we'll need when all this has ended,'' he said. ''They may think we're no longer strong enough to fight them and they won't be expecting you, but you'll still have to be careful. There are very few friends there we can still trust. But it's necessary. When this is over, no matter how it ends, I'll want to strike quickly.''

They stopped in front of a bust of Napoleon that sat atop a pedestal near a wall of books.

''It will be hard with all the powerful people involved.'' Auguste's words held no resistance to the request. It was a simple statement of fact.

Sartene nodded. He was staring at the bust. ''As my namesake once said, the situation doesn't require victory, it only forbids surrender.''

''What will you do while I'm gone?'' Auguste asked.

Sartene smiled at him. ''Are you afraid I won't take care of myself?''

"In part." He avoided Sartene's eyes, not wanting to see the pain he knew he would find there, despite the humor in his voice.

"I'll wait for word and . . ." Sartene gestured toward a table across the room, then walked to it. The table held soldiers, horses, cannon and the various miniature accouterments of battle, arranged to show strategies used in campaigns of the past. Sartene picked up one of the five-inch wooden soldiers that dated back to 1792. He turned it in his bony fingers, his hand trembling slightly with age. "As my son used to say, I'll play with my toys," he said. "And I'll study."

He pointed to the battle scene that lay before him. It depicted the Leipzig Campaign of the autumn of 1813. The soldiers had been placed to show the position that had existed just prior to Napoleon's march on Dresden.

"The allied army under Schwarzenberg delayed its attack on the city and, in doing so, lost the battle." He was speaking more to himself than Auguste, and he continued to stare at the table. "War is an art, like music or pure mathematics. It's disciplined. While I wait, I'll study it and I'll do the things that must be done here."

Chapter 1

The cell was dark, and even during the day the narrow slit of a window near the ceiling gave just enough light to let them make out each other's darkened features.

It had been that way from the first. When the heavy steel door had swung open, the light from the corridor had blinded Auguste and he had not been able to see the face of the man who was pushed inside.

You can always tell French prisons by the stink. Those had been the first words Auguste had heard him speak in his Corsican-accented French.

"You're lucky you arrived when you did," Auguste had said. "They just emptied the piss bucket. Later it gets worse."

They remained together for over two months in the dark sweating stench-ridden hole, talking about their homeland, their beliefs, their friends and families back in Corsica; everything except the actions, committed separately, that now brought them together. Often they spoke about women, because doing so made it easier to be without them. Sartene spoke of his wife back in Corsica, of their first meeting, their formal courtship and the birth of their son. He spoke more with a sense of reverence than passion, but in his words it could be seen that passion had been there as well. For Auguste the conversation was different. There was no wife, only the available women of Marseille and Bastia and the other seaport towns and cities that had taken up his youth.

Together they fought off the loneliness and despair with their words. And with their hands and feet they fought the rats that came out to compete for the dry meat and tasteless soup that was

20

pushed through the narrow opening at the bottom of the cell door each evening. Sartene said there were five rats, insisting he had learned to distinguish them by the sound of their movements and methods of attack. The smallest and most devious he had named Napoleon, recalling that the king of Austria had once called the French emperor a Corsican gutter rat and had then given him his daughter for a bride.

Sartene's knowledge of military history had amazed Auguste at first; his discussions of battles and strategies seemed endless. Auguste had not been sure if the stories were accurate, but he had listened to them and discussed them, fascinated, like a small child hearing Bible stories told by nuns. And he had grown to respect the man's quiet sense of dignity. Despite the misery of the cell, he had never heard Sartene complain, other than expressing his contempt for French authority. He had simply accepted what had been forced upon him with the knowledge that he had the ability to endure.

It was June 21, 1940, when the cell door swung open again, blinding them. They were led down a long stone corridor, feeling their way with their hands, stumbling on the stone stairs that led up to even brighter light. Ten minutes passed before their eyes began to focus, the pain that had seared them fading into a mild throbbing in their temples. They were in a large stone-walled room, furnished only with a long writing table and a chair placed behind it. A French officer stood next to the chair, but they ignored him, staring instead at each other, two men who in the past months had become as close as brothers, clearly seeing one another for the first time in full light.

They were both filthy, their faces and hands crusted with dirt, their beards tangled with bits of food. Sores covered their faces and necks, and between the dirt and the pustules the fragments of skin showing through held the gray pallor of death.

Sartene was slightly more than average height, but he seemed taller. His lean, raw-boned body stood erect, and his severe dark eyes were accented by a classically curved nose. His hair, matted and knotted, showed flecks of gray through the filth, but his beard was dark and youthful, even though he was clearly in his mid-forties.

Auguste was shorter by several inches but had the same hard body, the same sense of physical strength common to the people of their island. His hair was thinner than Sartene's and small patches had fallen away from poor nutrition, but it was still dark even though he too was well past forty.

He looked at Sartene and smiled. They were opposites in appearance. Sartene's features were sharp and aristocratic, while his were the flat wide features of a peasant. The same was true of their hands. Sartene had the long slender fingers of a pianist. His were wide and stumpy, a butcher's hands. Yet despite the physical differences, they were the same in spirit. And they both smelled bad.

A faint smile formed beneath Sartene's ragged beard, almost as though he were reading Auguste's thoughts. "You need a bath, Auguste," he said.

Auguste nodded solemnly, then glanced at the French officer, who took a step back to the window, opened it, then remained there, away from the stench.

Sartene noticed the movement and stepped toward the desk. He was immediately followed by Auguste.

A look of displeasure flashed across the officer's face. He was a colonel, dressed in full uniform, the blouse heavy with the ribbons of past decorations. He was tall, also in his mid-forties, with a long, skinny neck, and his head was pear-shaped, ending in a receding hairline that made it look as though it came to a point.

He drew a deep breath, then seemed to regret that he had. He seemed nervous and embarrassed, and he opened the conversation with a stiff abruptness.

"I have called you here because the government of France is prepared to grant you each a pardon in return for certain services. I assure you they are services that any true Frenchman would be honored to perform." The colonel spoke the words as though struggling to overcome his uneasiness.

"We're not French. We're Corsican," Sartene said.

"Corsica is part of France," the colonel said, his voice softer.

"Only according to the French," Sartene said.

The colonel drew a heavy breath and then winced as if trying to remind himself not to do it again. "The point is moot," he said. "Perhaps you're not aware of certain events—"

His words were cut off by Sartene's laughter. "No, colonel, I'm afraid we are not."

The colonel colored, then drew himself up and turned to the window. It was all becoming too much for him. The army, his army, had crumbled within days. The cowards within it were handing France to the Germans like a Christmas package. And now these new orders. Recruiting these men to fight for France. These filthy arrogant thieving bastards.

"Perhaps you could tell us the latest news, my colonel," Auguste said. He had widened his eyes, feigning deep interest.

The colonel raised his chin. He allowed himself to look at them down the length of his nose. "Today," he said, struggling for dignity, "traitors within the government and the army of France have signed an armistice with Germany. Those traitors, led by Marshal Pétain, plan to establish a separate and illegal government at Vichy. But the fight against the Boches goes on. It is for this that I'm asking your help." The final word seemed to catch in his throat.

Sartene turned to Auguste and shrugged. "I wasn't aware that France and Germany were at war. Since I've only been here a little more than two months, it must have been an unusually short war," he said.

The muscles along the colonel's jaw danced against the bone, and his left eye fluttered in a nervous spasm. "As I said, the war continues and *will* continue until France is free."

"I've heard Corsicans speak those same words all my life, colonel," Auguste said. "It seems to have changed very little. As always, the big fish eats the smaller fish, only in turn to be eaten by still a bigger fish. Perhaps we're reaching the final result in Europe. Bouillabaisse, with a German chef."

Sartene's laughter broke the silence that followed. "I, for one, never cared much for German cooking." His cold eyes found the French officer. "But then I always found that French cooks were like French politicians, a bit overbearing. Why don't you tell us what kind of stew *you* have in mind, colonel?"

The colonel looked into Sartene's eyes, then glanced away, uncomfortable with the cold hardness he found there. He reached out and took two sheets of paper from the desk, looked at the first and then across the desk at Auguste. The document seemed to give him some sense of confidence.

"According to the records provided by the warden, you, Auguste Pavlovi, can expect to spend the next ten years in this not too pleasant place." He switched the papers, then, pursing his lips, looked back at Sartene. "You, Monsieur Sartene, are expected to be the guest of the government for the next seven years." He hesitated, eyeing the report again. "There's also a footnote, however, indicating that Buonaparte Sartene may not be your true identity and that if another suspected identity could be proved, that sentence would be greatly increased." He smiled at Sartene, trying to appear friendly. "If I'm not mistaken, Sartene is the name of a small, rather insignificant village in the south of Corsica, is it not?"

"Everything that isn't French is insignificant to Frenchmen," Sartene said. "But you're not here to discuss geography, colonel, you're here to *get* something from us." There was a faint smile on Sartene's lips that contrasted with the look in his eyes.

The colonel shuffled the papers in his hands, then returned them to the desk, folded his hands behind his back and turned toward the window. His left eye had begun to flutter again.

"The government of France is prepared to offer you each a full pardon for all past offenses under any identity, if you agree to lead resistance forces in an area north of Marseille."

"Which government of France are you speaking about?" Auguste asked.

"The government of Free France," the colonel said, ignoring the insult. "You will be expected to lead partisans who would attack both Nazi and Vichy forces, as well as Italian troops that are presently preparing to occupy the Alpine zone along the Italian border."

"And for this we get pardons that may be useless if Germany continues to occupy France." Auguste shrugged. "Perhaps Buonaparte and I should wait to hear what Vichy has to offer," he said.

The colonel turned on Auguste, his voice harsh for the first time. "You may regret such a choice," he said.

Auguste stuck out his lower lip and nodded. "What will you do, colonel?"

Sartene raised his hand, watching the colonel struggle with the humiliation he felt. "Why is it when governments despise certain people they always try to make their actions sound generous when they find they need those same people? If I'm not mistaken, colonel, you simply need men who can act violently and then hide from the authorities. Now, I don't mind killing Germans rather than remaining here," he said. "The possibility of killing *wayward* Frenchmen also doesn't offend me." He paused to smile at the colonel. "But I won't do it just for a pardon. In addition to some piece of paper that says my so-called crimes no longer exist, I want one thing more."

The colonel stared in disbelief. "And what's that?" he asked.

"I'll expect to be paid for my services," Sartene said. "Not in money, colonel." He paused to smile again. "I trust the French franc has lost its value of late. What I want, in writing of course, is the right to emigrate from France after the war, to the French colony of my choice. And," he added, raising his hand again, "I want this permission to extend to my wife and the family of my son, Jean."

"That's all?" the colonel asked, watching as Sartene nodded. "And where are your family and your son's family now?"

"They live in an *insignificant* Corsican village," Sartene said.

The colonel sighed, then stared at the floor, shaking his head. He looked up. "And you?" he asked Auguste.

"I would accept the same offer, my colonel. And I'd like it to include my brother, Benito."

"And where is he?"

"He is the guest of another French resort in Bastia."

"Agreed," the colonel said. "Although I must tell you honestly that it's doubtful you'll live long enough to collect your payment." He paused, smiling to himself at the madness of it all, then continued. "I understand your bitterness and your belief that you're being used. I can only say that it's not easy for me to ask for your help. Unfortunately there's no choice."

He was struggling now for some degree of dignity. Quickly, he opened a drawer in the writing table and removed a large rolled map and spread it on the table. "You will select your men from among those presently here," he said, speaking with clipped authority. "You may also recruit people in the countryside as you choose. Weapons and supplies are something you will have to procure for yourselves, I'm afraid." He jabbed his finger at the map. "You will establish a base of operations near Mount Ventoux. The nearest town of any size is Carpentras, and you will find men there loyal to France. You will have papers identifying yourselves to them, as well as your initial area of operation, which will extend west from Mount Ventoux to the Rhone, from Avignon in the south to Montélimar in the north. Are there any questions?"

"Yes, colonel," Auguste said. "What's your name?"

The colonel flushed. "Martin," he said. "Why do you ask?"

Auguste smiled. "I want to remember the name of the one Frenchman who wanted to let me out of prison, instead of put me in one."

Chapter 2

The base camp was in a dense pine forest at the two-thousand-foot level of Mount Ventoux. It was autumn, and already the fast approach of winter could be felt. From the summit, four thousand feet above them, the snow had already begun to move down the mountain. Auguste sat across a campfire from Sartene, hugging himself against the cold. He could see the frustration in his friend's face; his fists were clenched and he was flexing his thumbs. It was a nervous habit he had developed in recent months.

"Soon we'll need warmer clothing for the men, Buonaparte," he said.

Sartene nodded, then looked to his left, watching the approach of a stocky dark-haired young man in his late twenties, slightly older than his own son. "I'll ask Francesco to arrange it," he said.

Francesco Canterina squatted in front of the fire. Despite the chill in the air the sleeves of his sweater were pulled up above his elbows, exposing his heavily muscled forearms. His handsome face seemed impassive beneath a black beret, tufts of wavy black hair protruding from its sides, the dark, cruel eyes detracting from otherwise pleasant features. A cigarette dangled loosely in the corner of his mouth. Almost mechanically, he produced a long, slender knife, tested the blade with his thumb, then began sharpening it against a whetstone. He seemed about to speak when Sartene broke the silence.

"You know the Vichy military warehouse in Avignon?" Sartene asked.

Francesco nodded. "The one along the river," he said.

"We'll need warmer clothing soon," Sartene said. "Shipments should have arrived there. I'd like you to take four men and see if you can appropriate enough for us."

"How many men do we have now?" Francesco asked.

"Fifty-three." Sartene watched him sharpen the knife. He was good with a knife and he treated it with the reverence of a craftsman.

"I'll try to get more. So we can equip any new men who join us," Francesco said.

Sartene stared into the fire. "If you can," he said, thinking of how few men had joined them in the past month. "If not, we'll do the same as with the weapons. Allow the dead to provide for the living."

Francesco paused as if deciding how to continue. "I was just about to tell you," he said. "Word has come from Carpentras. Troops from the Boche garrison at Montélimar executed twenty this morning. Many were old men. Others were only children."

"Did the pigs give a reason?" Auguste asked.

"Payment for our last raid," Francesco said. "I'm told they placed a notice on each of the bodies before they withdrew."

"How is it with those who are left?" Sartene asked.

Francesco drew heavily on the cigarette, then threw the butt into the fire. "It's mostly women who are left now. Mothers and grandmothers and small babies. They just wish everyone would leave. The Boches, Vichy, even us."

Sartene ran a hand along his face. He was clean-shaven now, and his sharp angular features were more visible, adding to the fierceness of his eyes. "Pick your men, Francesco," he said. "You should leave now."

He watched the fire as Francesco moved off to a group of men seated beneath a large pine. Each wore the wide-brimmed, cowboy-styled hat common to the region of Provence. Several moments passed before Sartene looked up again at Auguste. They had been in the mountains only a few months, but already he had learned to hate the senselessness of the killing. He seemed tired and older. "Let's take some men to Carpentras and help the women bury their dead," he said.

"The Vichy will have troops there," Auguste said, "guarding that little pig of a mayor."

"The troops can dig the graves," Sartene said. "And when they finish they can dig their own as well." He withdrew a letter from his pocket and held it out before him.

"I received this yesterday," he told Auguste, his voice shaking like his hand. "It's from my son. He sent it through the underground a month ago. His wife has borne him a son. Another child for the Boches and the Vichy to butcher."

"What have they called him?" Auguste asked.

"Pierre," Sartene said. "They named him Pierre in honor of my adopted father."

The bodies had been left in the town square, flesh ripped by machine-gun fire, blood already coagulated in dark, sticky pools. Sartene stood in front of the body of a young boy. He had been no more than seven and had stood at chest height to the men on either side of him. The left side of his face no longer existed. It had been replaced by a gaping black hole filled with dried blood. Sartene's hand shook as he stood over the child.

At the opposite end of the square, across from the bodies, a small fat man dressed in a formal coat stood with the nine surviving members of the Vichy contingent. The fat man was trembling as he glanced at the ragged armed men who surrounded them.

Sartene stared across the bodies at the mayor and his remaining bodyguards. From his right a slender gray-haired priest approached. He was dressed in a simple black soutane, and he too seemed frightened. Sartene looked at him briefly, then down at the bodies again.

"Have you given them absolution?" He asked the question without looking at the priest.

"Yes, I have," the priest said. "I only wish now to beg you . . ."

Sartene cut him off, ignoring him as he spoke to Auguste. "Have our men take the bodies to the cemetery, so the Vichy can begin digging the graves. I don't want them to touch the bodies of these people." He turned back to the priest. "The church linens. We'll need them for shrouds," he said.

"The church?" the priest said, his jaw trembling. "Certainly bed-linens from their homes can be used. The church linens and the candles are the only things the Germans haven't taken."

"The families have given enough already, priest," Sartene said. He turned back to Auguste. "Send some men to the church to collect what's needed." He studied the priest again. The fear that had filled his face was now mixed with confusion.

"I think God will approve, priest. Now get your breviary.

You'll have final prayers to say for these others soon." He
motioned his head toward the mayor and the nine Vichy soldiers.

"There must be no more killing," the priest said. "I beg you
in God's name."

Sartene's mouth tightened. His voice, as always, was soft.
"Tell me, priest. Did you rush out and tell that to the Boches?
Or did you hide under your bed until they left?"

"This is wrong," the priest said, his voice convulsed. "It
only makes you the same as those you fight." The priest's voice
trembled, unsure of the reaction his words would produce.

Sartene exhaled heavily. "Sometimes there isn't a choice between good and bad. Sometimes there's only a choice between
horrors. Now get your damned breviary."

FRANCE, MARCH 1944

It was spring and the melting snow had swollen the mountain
stream, and at regular intervals rivulets broke off and ran their
own course until they formed shallow pools amid the wide
patches of wild flowers that covered each area of level ground.
From one such area Sartene and his men watched a German
column move along the road fifty yards below. To the right of
the column was the river, to the left the steep rock-strewn
foothills of the mountain. The troops were moving toward Italy
to strengthen the Nazi forces that had replaced Mussolini's army
and were now struggling to stave off the Allied advance. At the
head of the column two heavy tanks led the convoy, and two
hundred yards to the north two more tanks could be seen bringing up the rear. In between, assorted troop carriers and ammunition and supply trucks, trailing field artillery, made up the long
line of march.

It had been almost four years now since Sartene and his men
had taken to the mountains, and again spring had come bringing
its new life amid the endless killing. Across the river the pastel
blossoms of orchards could be seen, and everywhere there were
flowers showing through the new growth, and the trees on the
mountain swayed gently with the pale green of new leaves. The
only sounds intruding on the day were the tanks and the trucks
and the men singing in the troop carriers.

Sartene looked to his left, then back to his right. Far off in each direction, large camouflaged piles of stacked tree trunks could be seen perched at the edge of rock shelves that stood above the road. He nodded to Auguste, who was stretched out beside him, then stared at the troops moving along the road as Auguste raised his rifle to his shoulder.

A soldier in a troop carrier directly below was picked up and thrown forward as the report of Auguste's rifle echoed across the river. To the south and the north a great rumbling came as the denuded trees crashed toward the road, dragging rocks and dirt with them, blocking each route of escape. Then the mortar and machine-gun fire; the roar of the bazookas disabling the tanks and the screams of men dying as they scrambled from the trucks.

The Germans fought from behind the trucks, firing blindly at the spits of fire that flashed above them. To the right and left others assaulted the steep rocky slopes, firing their weapons as they ran, then dying before they advanced more than ten yards from the road. The explosions came in fiery orange bursts, followed by billowing black smoke as the ammunition trucks burst into hot shards of steel. The troops retreated toward the river, screaming in panic as the first of the mines that had been placed there sent bodies hurtling into the air. Those who survived then turned and ran back to the road, where the automatic-weapon and mortar fire poured down, chewing everything in its path.

The fighting lasted for twenty minutes, and then it was quiet and the spring air was filled with the smell of cordite and blood and burning flesh. Sartene moved down the hill, slipping on the loose rocks, righting himself, then sliding again. On the road the moans of the wounded could be heard amid the sounds of the flames, and there was the occasional shot of a partisan rifle ending individual torment.

He walked through the killing ground without speaking. Auguste was a few steps behind, his eyes searching the bodies for any sign of life. At the edge of the road where the high grass dipped down to the river, a German soldier lay on his side. His eyes were staring wildly at his hands, his gray-white face showing the final horror of his young life. The twisted bundle of gray intestines protruded between his fingers as he fought to keep them within the gaping hole in his belly. Tears streamed down the boy's face, and his jaw and lips trembled uncontrollably. He looked up at Sartene, and his body began to shudder. A gagging sound rose from his throat as he tried to speak, followed by a reddish-green mixture of blood and bile. Auguste withdrew a German P-38 from a holster and shattered the boy's forehead.

Sartene stared across the river to the orchards. "Another child, Auguste." He looked up at the black smoke blotting out the bright morning sky. "I wonder how many more children we'll have to kill."

"Too many," Auguste said. "Unless we're unlucky and they kill us first."

They walked back through the forest on the layer of pine needles that stretched out before them like a soft brown carpet. The smell of the fighting was gone now, replaced by the sweet scent of the trees and the sound of the birds; the only memory of the fighting was the sight of the men marching ahead, carrying the captured weapons.

They moved five miles through the gently rising forest before they reached the camp and were able to rest. Sartene slid to the ground, allowing his body to fall back against a large boulder. Others in the camp began preparing a meal, but he could not bring himself to think of food.

"How many men did we lose?" he asked. His voice was weary and even softer than usual.

"Only five," Auguste said. "It was a great victory. Except for the five."

Sartene struggled with his backpack and placed it on the ground beside him. He reached inside and withdrew a well-worn book, Emil Ludwig's *Napoleon*.

"I was reading this last night," he said. "Let me read you a part of it. It deals with an argument between Metternich and Napoleon, and it begins with the emperor shouting at the German.

" ' "You are not a soldier. You do not know what passes in a soldier's mind. I grew to manhood on the battlefield. Such a man as I does not care a snap of the fingers for the lives of a million men!" He flings his hat into a corner of the room. Now, there is nothing assumed about his anger, and what he has just said is the revelation of an innermost truth. The man who turns pale at the sight of a dying horse, who cannot bear to see a human being pass away, remains and must remain impassive when, in his army lists, he adds up the figures, shifts the hundreds of thousands from column to column, and erases the myriads of slain. Is not war made with human lives, and does it not end with corpses? What is the use of reproaching a craftsman for using the tools of his trade?' "

Sartene closed the book and placed it in his lap. "Sometimes I wonder why I spend so much time studying war. I don't enjoy it, I only learn about life from it. That's strange, isn't it? That a man learns about life by studying suffering and death, by reading about the lives of men who forced those things upon so many throughout history." He shook his head slowly. "It's different when you do it for yourself or your family. Somehow when that happens, it seems justified. But this is just killing for the sake of politicians. It puts nothing in your pocket."

Auguste picked up the book and held it in his hands. His face was drawn and haggard, and there were deep circles beneath his eyes, and he had not shaved for several days. He offered Sartene a half-smile.

"You wouldn't be a man if you didn't understand the difference and still accept the fact that you have no choice," he said.

Sartene returned the slight smile. "You must be getting old, Auguste."

"Why is that?" Auguste asked.

"Because you're becoming wise."

Francesco approached them slowly, then stopped in front of Sartene. He appeared uncomfortable; his dark eyes seemed to have lost some of their cruelty. Because of the battle, Sartene thought.

"An American captain from OSS just arrived, Buonaparte," he said. "He brings news from Corsica, from your son." He looked away. "It's your wife, Buonaparte. She's dead. From some illness."

Chapter 3

In the months that followed, Sartene left the others when he could to be alone with his thoughts and the mountain. There was new pain now, behind his eyes, but he did not speak of it, nor did the others. Once, in a small village to the north, Auguste noticed him staring at a woman gathering water at a fountain. She was a sturdy woman with the strong face of one who had endured much without complaint, and for a moment he thought Sartene might speak to her. When he had felt Auguste's eyes on him, Sartene had turned to him and nodded, then looked away. No words had been spoken.

The American had remained with them, fighting at their sides and reporting back to London by radio about troop movements to the south. His name was W. C. Peters and the French partisans laughed and teased him about his use of the initials, telling him that his parents had named him for a shithouse. But Peters took it well, and he joked about the wide-brimmed hats favored by the men of the region, accusing them of trying to be French cowboys. Most of them seemed to enjoy his boyish sense of innocence. He was always grinning; it was something different for them.

Sartene did not question why he stayed in the hills with them. It was not the Corsican way. To question a man's intentions was like questioning his past. It was an affront to his honor. It was enough that Peters fought well and was providing information to London. But the naiveté of the man disturbed him. He had met Americans before, working on the docks as a boy. He had learned English from them, and in conversations he had been surprised by their apparent innocence. Peters was like that. He did not seem capable of thinking beyond the orders he had been given; there was something sheltered about him, and that was disquieting, in the midst of a war. It made Sartene wonder if the man had the pragmatism needed for survival.

It was June 1 before Peters explained the reason for his continued presence. It was night and they sat off by themselves, Sartene, Auguste and the American, a large map of Europe spread between them. Peters beamed his flashlight on the map as he spoke, and Sartene listened closely as he translated for Auguste.

"Within the next couple of days or weeks an Allied force will invade northern France. The troops are already poised in England, and when they get the green light it'll be the biggest damned invasion force this world has ever seen." Peters paused to grin at the Corsicans, then waved his flashlight back and forth across northern France. "It'll be a big push, straight through to Paris, then north and west right into Germany." He directed the flashlight to the south, stopping it in the center of Italy.

"Within days," he continued, "Allied forces are expected to take Rome and then begin the push north. For the present the Germans will be pouring in troops to reinforce their men there. Our first job will be to disrupt that flow as much as possible. But once Rome falls and the invasion of France is underway, and the Russians begin pushing in from the east, we expect resistance to begin to crumble in southern France." He paused to let his words sink in, rather than to await any questions.

"Then it's almost over?" Auguste asked Sartene, who translated the question to Peters.

"Not quite, old buddy," Peters said, shaking his head and grinning again. "The Krauts can still be expected to put up one helluva fight. But once Paris falls, London expects a general pullback for a last-ditch effort to keep us from crossing the Rhine. London also expects that at that point a lot of high-ranking Jerries are gonna take a hard look at the big picture and that quite a few of them may suddenly lose interest in protecting the fatherland."

He beamed the flashlight at the border between the provinces of Burgundy and Savoy a hundred miles to the north. "Now if that happens, London feels this position here will become strategic. Since the Rhone flows from Lake Geneva in the north to the Gulf of Lions in the south, and since any Jerry officers on the run would probably head for Switzerland or Spain, that kinda puts it at a crossroads."

"The Boches will find it difficult to move through the

countryside," Sartene said. "The French will want to avenge what's been done to them."

"Well, Buonaparte, the kind of Kraut we're worried about should be moving with a pretty heavy guard. And that kind of a Kraut should be pretty valuable from an intelligence standpoint if we can grab him."

Peters waited, as though trying to decide whether to go on. Then he grinned at them. "Those Krauts also could be carrying a lot of loot with them. Gold, jewels, paintings. Anything they can use to feather their nest with, wherever they expect to end up. And we don't want to help the Frenchies free their country and then have them find out they got nothin' left but an empty cookie jar."

Sartene shook his head and smiled at the younger man. "Sometimes I think the Americans are the only English-speaking people who have never learned the language." He patted Auguste's leg and translated as literally as possible. "Did you understand our friend, Auguste?"

"Except for the cookie jar, I think so," he said.

Sartene turned back to Peters. Even in the dim light of the flashlight he could see the color in his cheeks. "You can count on Auguste and Francesco and me and the few other Corsicans who are with us," he said. "As far as the French partisans are concerned, I can't promise you anything. Many will want to return to their homes and families, and who can blame them? But there should be enough who will stay. But there is one thing you must understand, captain. These men may want to keep any valuables they find. They have lost a great deal and may want something for themselves now."

"I'm afraid that can't be done," Peters said. The grin was gone from his face. "The orders are very clear."

Sartene smiled. "We'll have to see," he said. "But there's also something you must do for us."

"Anything at all. You just name it and if I can do it, it's done," Peters said.

"Good," Sartene said. "Auguste has a brother in the prison in Bastia. You must use your influence to see he is freed and allowed to join us after the liberation. Also my son in Corsica. He must be contacted and told to join us too, with his family. You see, I have a grandson I've never seen, and soon he'll be four years old."

*   *   *

It was late August before Paris fell to the Allies and German resistance began to crumble. The German retreat was speeded by a second invasion on the southern coast of France, and when it began, Sartene and his remaining men moved north to Lyon, where the Rhone turned south in its meandering journey from Lake Geneva. It was a different war now. No longer was it necessary to hide in isolated mountain camps; no longer did his men have to depend on captured Nazi supplies. They went out regularly now from Lyon, traveling in groups of four or five, following the path of the Rhone west and then north to the town of Bellegarde, which sat in the foothills of the Jura Mountains nine miles from the Swiss border. Peters was still with them, directing the search for fleeing Nazis, and Sartene and Auguste worked with him, knowing that any intelligence gathered from those captured would speed the liberation of France and their own liberation from the war.

He had come to know Peters better during those months, but the familiarity had only intensified his earlier opinion. The young captain was indeed naive; he had no understanding of the people with whom he fought, no feeling for what it meant to them to have their home occupied by foreigners. They, like the Germans, were equally foreign to Peters, and he understood them only in terms of the rules he had been given to wage war by, never realizing that the concepts of rules and war were contradictions in themselves. Peters, he had learned, came from a large midwestern city and therefore lacked any understanding of country people. But what was most surprising to Sartene was the young captain's lack of interest in acquiring that knowledge. He would go through the fighting, risking his life, and gain nothing from it.

It was September 2 when they came across the bodies of the Germans outside a small farmhouse a mile north of Bellegarde. The French partisans had not left much. Those who had survived the initial attack had their throats cut, and the one officer among them had been tied to a tree, masculated, and allowed to watch his life drain away.

Sartene stood before the dead Nazi, noting the contortion of his face, the look of horror that had frozen there when death finally came.

"Helluva way to go. Having your prick cut off like that." Peters had come up beside him. He stood with his hands on his hips, the sun glinting off the skin that showed through his closely cut hair. He had continued to wear civilian clothes, even though the uniform he had brought with him would have been safe now, and it confused Sartene, given the rigidness with which he followed orders.

"I've seen it done before, at home in Corsica," Sartene said. "But it was usually reserved for those who had violated a man's wife or daughter or sister. But then the French have always thought of their country as a woman."

"Still pretty cruel," Peters said.

Sartene's thoughts wandered back. *The man on the ground inside a tent, his arms and legs spread-eagled, tied to stakes. One hand slipped the point of the knife beneath the man's eye. The man on the ground screamed as the knife twisted, popping the eye and sending it along his cheek, where it dangled on a cord of tissue.*

Peters was still staring at the Nazi.

"These peasants understand cruelty," Sartene said. "They live with the cruelty of nature, and they learn from it."

"Was it like that in Corsica?" Peters asked.

Sartene nodded.

"You miss Corsica, don't you, Buonaparte?"

"No, not Corsica. Only my family," Sartene said. "Corsica is a conquered land, and like all conquered lands it's only fit for the conquerors."

"You won't go back then?" Peters asked.

"Only to visit my wife's grave, while my son makes arrangements with the French for us to go elsewhere."

"Your son, is his name Sartene too?"

He turned to the stocky square-faced American, his hard, vulpine eyes showing a momentary contempt for his crude attempt at cunning.

"I only asked because I heard the men talking about its not being your real name," Peters added. He was grinning.

"A man's name is like his life. It's what he chooses it to be." Sartene turned away from the dead Nazi and started toward the cluster of trees near the house where Francesco and Auguste sat in the shade. Peters walked with him.

"What were you in prison for?" the American persisted.

"For offending the French," Sartene said. He stopped and squared himself in front of the American. "I'm a simple man, captain. And like most simple men I've learned never to dwell on the past. My concerns are for the future, for my family and our life together.''

''I thought you Corsicans were big on vendettas. That involves the past, doesn't it?'' There was a smirk on Peters' face.

Sartene placed his hand on the American's shoulder as though dealing with a foolish child. ''A vendetta comes from a lingering pain in someone who has been offended. The pain is of the present and the justice it demands is of the present.''

He turned abruptly and walked to the others. Auguste had removed one of his boots and was gently massaging the ankle he had turned an hour before. His eyes followed Peters as he entered the house.

''Is it worse?'' Sartene asked as he sat beside Francesco.

''Five years ago I wouldn't have noticed it,'' Auguste said.

Sartene nodded. It was true, the fighting had taken its toll. Auguste, like himself, was now fifty. He removed his beret and ran his hand through his hair. It was still thick, but what had once been a touch of gray had intensified in the past four years. He looked at Francesco. The additional years showed on him as well, even though he was still young.

''Tell me, Francesco. What will you do when all this has ended?'' Sartene asked.

Francesco shrugged his thick shoulders. ''Probably rob a bank and retire,'' he said. He withdrew his knife from a sheath strapped to his calf and began stroking it against a whetstone.

Sartene laughed softly as he watched the younger man sharpen the blade of his knife. The knife was like an extension of the arm, he noted. And he was constantly sharpening it as though it gave him some inner comfort to do so.

''Stealing from banks is a poor profession, my young friend,'' Sartene said. ''It's better to own the bank and steal by charging high interest. A clever man always finds something that others want and then finds a way to control it. That gives him wealth and it also gives him power.''

Francesco nodded; his eyes appeared to focus on something distant. ''Is that what you'll do when it's finished?''

''Yes. If I'm as clever as I hope I am.''

''How will you do it?'' the younger man asked.

''I've been thinking about going to Southeast Asia. It's easier to find that sort of thing in a place that isn't developed and where customs aren't completely foreign. I'm told there are many Corsicans there already.''

"Perhaps I'll go with you, Buonaparte," Auguste said. "And perhaps I'll ask Benito to come too. This war has made me lose my taste for Europe."

"I'd like that, my friend. You've been like a brother to me these past years." Sartene nodded toward Francesco. "And in many ways you've become a second son. I'd like you with me too, Francesco."

"Perhaps I will, Buonaparte. They tell me oriental women are very desirable."

Sartene wagged a finger at the younger man. "You're Corsican. Stay with your own blood. Your own blood can always be depended upon."

Peters marched noisily up beside them. It amused Sartene. He had never been able to understand how a man in Peters' profession had never learned to walk quietly. "I was just going through some papers that Kraut officer left in the house," he said. "I think I came up with some good stuff." He glanced around at the bodies of the dead Germans. "These Krauts are already starting to stink," he said. His face was unusually solemn.

Sartene followed Peters' gaze. The bodies were already swollen and covered with flies, the hot sun having done its work, but there was no great odor yet, except for the excrement the dead had given up in a final offering. He stared up at the American. He seemed agitated.

"Look, why don't you fellas go back to Bellegarde and see if you can hire some people to come out and bury these Krauts, before it gets any worse. They dumped their field packs and there was only one shovel in their truck." Peters glanced around at the bodies. "I want to stay here and see if I can find anything else on the other bodies."

"Francesco and I will go," Sartene said. He raised his chin toward Auguste. "You'd better stay here and rest your ankle."

"Look, you can take their truck," Peters said. "Then Auguste can have a doctor take a look at the ankle back in town."

"The truck's no good," Francesco said. "I checked it before. The partisans took what they could from the motor. They'll probably sell the parts to your army when it arrives." He smiled at Peters, enjoying the mild insult. Peters seemed not to notice it.

"It's better if Auguste stays with you anyway," Sartene said. "The partisans might come back and they might not wait to check your nationality. Auguste can keep watch. Anyway, he speaks the language better than you."

Sartene and Francesco stood and slung their machine guns over their shoulders.

"How long do you think it will take you?" Peters called after them.

"One hour. And whatever time it takes to find men with shovels," Sartene called back. "We'll find a truck too, so my friend's old legs don't have to walk him back."

"They're no older than yours, Buonaparte. You remember that," Auguste called after them.

Sartene and Francesco walked in silence for ten minutes. The narrow country road was deserted, and the only sound came from the large crows that dominated the abandoned fields on each side of them. Sartene stopped suddenly, taking Francesco's arm.

"Tell me something, Francesco. Am I being suspicious, or did our American friend seem anxious to be rid of us?"

"He seemed nervous," Francesco said. "But I assumed it was because of the bodies."

Sartene shook his head. "He's seen death before. It's no stranger to him." He stood quietly for a moment. "You go on to the village," he said finally. "I am going back. There's something about this that bothers me."

Sartene was two minutes away from the place he had left them when he heard the shot. He broke into a run, pulling back the bolt on his weapon as he did, so it would be ready to fire. When he neared the place he veered to his right, taking advantage of a dense line of trees for cover, then slowed his movements and crept forward, crouching low to the ground.

When he reached the clearing, he could see Auguste's body sprawled beneath the trees outside the house where they had sat talking. Sartene looked around the clearing, checking the other bodies. Peters was not among them.

Quietly he moved forward, his body flat on the ground, propelled by his knees and elbows. When he drew near Auguste he reached out and gently took his arm. Auguste opened his eyes.

"He shot me," he said. "The bastard shot me."

"Peters?" Sartene asked.

Auguste nodded his head. His breath came in gasps and it was difficult for him to speak.

"Where is he now?" Sartene whispered.

Auguste shook his head from side to side, his breath coming even faster with the effort.

"On the second floor of the house, I think." He reached out and held Sartene's arm with surprising strength. "There's a fortune in there, Buonaparte. Paintings, gold, jewelry. The Boches had started to hide it under the floor before the partisans came. I found Peters trying to finish the job and . . ." He began to cough.

Sartene covered his mouth with his hand to hide the sound. "Be silent. Rest," he whispered.

Auguste squeezed his arm again, and Sartene removed the hand from his mouth.

"I told him we could share it," he whispered. "He said no, it had to go to the authorities. The fool. I tried to stop him, brought him out here at gunpoint, but he was too quick. We fought and the bastard shot me."

"He's back up there now?" Sartene asked.

Auguste nodded; his eyes fluttered. "I think so."

"I'll be back," Sartene said, touching his shoulder. "Lie quietly."

He moved to the doorway and listened. Above, to his left, he could hear the sound of someone moving. Slowly, crouching low, he moved up the stairs, placing his feet gently on each step. The noise grew louder as he entered a small hall on the second floor, still moving cautiously, taking care to avoid anything that would give him away. Through an open door to his left, he saw Peters. He was on his knees, over a hole in the floor; he was refitting the planks, using the German field shovel when necessary to force the boards into place. His rifle was five feet away, leaning against the wall.

Sartene stepped into the room and leveled his weapon at the American. Peters froze with the movement. His eyes darted quickly toward his rifle, but he didn't move. It was too far. He looked back at Sartene. Fear filled his eyes; his lips trembled.

"I didn't expect you back," he said. He looked into the hole. "You found Auguste?"

Sartene nodded.

"It's not what you think. It's not ours, Buonaparte. I tried to explain that to him, but he wouldn't listen. I had to stop him. It's orders. The stuff has to be turned over. Dammit. Why didn't you take him with you like I said?"

Peters' hands had begun to tremble, and as Sartene shifted his feet and adjusted the stock of the machine gun more securely against his body, Peters' eyes suddenly widened.

"Look, I didn't want to kill him, but he was gonna kill me."

"You didn't kill him," Sartene said.

Peters exhaled heavily. "Then it's okay. Look, it's yours. You can both take it. You can do anything you want with it. You'll have enough money to start a whole new life. It's like you said before. You're entitled to something after all this." He wiped his mouth with the back of his hand, leaving a trace of dirt on his lips. "You can do just what the Krauts planned. Hide it here, then come back for it after the war. Then you can sell it and take the money into Switzerland. The Swiss never ask where money comes from. I won't tell anybody. Nobody at all." He grinned nervously.

Sartene shook his head at the grinning figure. "Fool," he said. "How could I ever trust you?"

Peters' body rose off the floor and flew back like a rag doll as the machine gun erupted in Sartene's hands. He kept his finger on the trigger, watching the American's body bounce across the room until the weapon jammed. He walked forward and stopped in front of the hole. The partially uncovered rolled canvases lay next to boxes that would contain the gold and jewels. He knelt and pried open a box with a knife and fondled a heavy diamond necklace. He dropped the necklace back and pulled the floor-boards across the opening, then walked over to Peters' body and reached down, grabbing him by the shirt. The top of his head had been ripped away, and as he dragged the body toward the door, bits of brain and bone fell to the floor. He dragged the body from the room, down the stairs and out the front door.

Auguste was still conscious when he reached him. Sartene opened Auguste's shirt and probed the wound. "The fool's dead," he said, as he gently wiped the blood away. "Fortunately, he also had the aim of a fool. But I must get you to a doctor. You're losing too much blood."

"Why did he do it?" Auguste whispered. "We could have shared."

"He was a fool."

"You must hide it," Auguste said. "Someone will find it. Hide it first, then take me to a doctor."

"It's hidden well enough for now. If someone finds it, he finds it. There will always be more. First I'll take care of you, then I'll come back and find a better place."

He picked Auguste up in his arms, staggering slightly under his weight. "Have I ever told you that you eat too much?" he said. He looked down at him. Auguste was smiling through the pain.

"You're just weaker than you used to be," Auguste said. His head fell against Sartene's shoulder and he fainted.

Sartene walked toward the road, carrying his friend tightly in his arms.

Chapter 4

The child ran across the open field, his straw-colored hair flying wildly about his head. He called out to himself as he ran, wrapped up in his own private game-world, paying no attention to the two men who watched him from the veranda of the house.

Sartene's eyes were soft as he followed his grandson's movement. His son, Jean, standing beside him, smiled and shook his head.

"He plays like a little wild man," he said, without looking at his father.

"He's happy to be out of the city and the small yard he has to play in," Sartene said. "It's good for a child to know this sense of abandon. You were the same. You had so many cuts and bruises as a child your mother always feared the other villagers would think we beat you."

Jean glanced at his father and smiled to himself at this uncharacteristic sentimentality. He was a large, boxlike man in his late twenties, with a thick neck that seemed part of his shoulders, and the smile appeared out of place on his square dark face.

He was dressed in the same manner as his father, in a shirt and tie, and the linen jackets of their suits were laid side by side over the railing of the veranda. But the similarity ended there. Sartene's features, his manner of standing, of speaking, reflected the intrinsic cunning that was so much a part of his being. His son had the look of a gentle brute. He had his father's dark, piercing eyes, but they were set in a peasant's face, giving them a softness that did not exist in the man. To Jean, cunning was

45

something that was used only when violence was not possible, a time-consuming process that should usually be avoided.

Behind them the sound of workmen echoed through the empty house and out across the veranda, as the final detail work on the interior neared completion. The house had been under construction for almost a year, delayed, as all things were, by the annual monsoon rains. Sartene had come to the house several times each week during its construction, more as an excuse to have an outing with his grandson than to inspect the work.

He had designed the house himself, making sure there was enough room for his son's family and for Auguste and Auguste's brother, Benito. The house in Vientiane, which he had purchased upon his arrival in Laos, would be kept as an office and to house Francesco, who would handle business matters in the city.

The choice of Francesco had angered Jean, but he had not challenged it. When he had first met the man, more than a year ago, he had told his father that he did not trust him, but his father had only smiled and said it was wise never to trust someone not of your own blood, until years of association had proved that trust was warranted. Jean did not know whether this meant his father's years with Francesco during the war had proved him trustworthy, or if he was still withholding judgment. Yet he knew, now that the decision had been made, he had no right to question it. But he did have a right to question Francesco, at least in his own mind. And he knew that it was not that he feared him as a rival. He simply questioned his loyalty to his father.

The child ran toward the veranda, stumbled and fell, got up and ran again with even more abandon than before.

"Grandpère," he shouted as he reached the house and stared up at them. "Come play with me, Grandpère."

Sartene grunted in a feigned harshness and shook his head. "I'm too old to play in this heat," he said.

The child held a long stick in one hand and waved it back and forth frantically. His eyes were a deep blue, and they implored his grandfather to do as he wished. He had the face of an angel, Sartene thought. Very much like his French mother.

"What's that you have in your hand?" Sartene asked.

The boy looked at the stick and his small face became very serious. "It's a gun," he said. "If we see a tiger I'm going to shoot it."

"Ahh, I see. You want to hunt tigers today." Sartene moved

past his son and started down the steps of the veranda. "I think it's too hot to hunt tigers," he said. "They will all be asleep under a nice shady tree. But if you like we can go for a walk."

The boy extended his hand, and Sartene took it, then turned to Jean. "Would you like to come with us?" he asked.

"No, I think I'll go in the house and see how my wife is terrorizing the workmen. If we're not careful she'll change everything."

"Let her change what she wants. Don't be fooled by the myth that men are masters of their homes."

The boy was pulling at his arm, eager to go on. They moved away from the house, toward the river. Sartene walked slowly, taking into account the child's smaller legs. But the child's exuberance was too great, and he pulled away, ran ahead, then turned and ran back to his grandfather, urging him to hurry.

Sartene ruffled the boy's blond hair, then squatted and took him by the arm.

"You must learn to take your time, Pierre," he said. "A man who moves slowly and steadily has time to look about him. Eventually he gets to the same place as the man who rushes ahead. But he knows more about where he has been and what lies behind him. So he's wiser than the man who hurried."

He held on to the child's arm, keeping his face toward him. "What's behind you now?" he asked.

The boy twisted his head and looked back over his shoulder. Across the plain, at the edge of the dense forest, a Laotian man stood next to a large, low-hanging nipa palm, its leaning trunk and feathery leaves offering both concealment and shelter from the sun. There was a rifle slung over his shoulder.

"That's just Lam," the boy said. "He's always there." He turned back to his grandfather and shrugged his small shoulders, as though the fact was of no consequence.

"But you didn't see him, because you were in such a hurry."

"But I *know* he's always there." The boy raised his eyebrows as he spoke, as if he were being patient with his grandfather.

Sartene repressed a smile at the precocious six-year-old. "But what if he wasn't there? What if a tiger had come and frightened him away?" He emphasized the word "tiger" and watched, amused, as the child's eyes widened. "Because you hurried, you would not have noticed that he wasn't where he should be and that there might be danger."

The boy freed himself from his grandfather's grasp and turned toward the forest, raising the stick to his shoulder like a rifle. "If a tiger comes I'll shoot him," he said.

Sartene stood and took the boy's hand again and started again for the river.

"I know you would," he said. "But you must always be sure you see the tiger before he sees you. And to do that you must always take care to see what goes on about you."

They walked on toward the river and the wide twenty-foot dock. Along the dock a large motor launch sat motionless in the flat still water. An identical launch was kept in Vientiane. The launches were used by the family only when the monsoon rains made the road to the house impassable. At other times the boats carried merchandise integral to Sartene's business interests, trips that normally occurred at night.

"Grandpère, can we take the boat back to the city today?" the boy asked.

"Why, Pierre? Don't you like the car?"

"I like the boat better."

"If you wish. Someone else can drive the car back."

Sartene ran his hand across the top of his head. The midday heat had reached its zenith, and he knew they should not remain out much longer. Across the river the air shimmered, making the opposite bank look as though it were being viewed through badly made glass.

"Look, look," the boy shouted, pointing off to his right.

Out toward the center of the river a slender green form glided smoothly just below the surface of the water.

"A snake," Sartene said. "Very bad and very poisonous. Even the crocodiles don't eat them."

The boy lifted the stick to his shoulder again and made shooting sounds. "If any crocodiles come I'll shoot them too," the child said.

Sartene ruffled the boy's hair again. "You're very bloodthirsty today, Pierre," he said.

He looked back, into the field. The Weimaraner he had imported from Germany for the boy came out from behind the house and loped into the field, its nose close to the ground. The dog moved in one diagonal, then switched course, following another, sweeping the ground with its nose like a living vacuum cleaner. At a large rock it stopped to sniff, rejected it, then moved on to another, where it lifted its leg and urinated, its mouth open with satisfaction. When it had finished, the dog trotted back to one of the mangosteen trees standing on each side of the house and settled down to the comfort of the shade.

Sartene took a handkerchief from his pocket and mopped his head. The dog has more sense than I do, he thought. He took the boy's hand again and pointed to the large ghostly gray lump of fur that was now the dozing dog. "Let's go play with Max," he said, knowing it would be the easiest way to cajole the child out of the sun.

Pierre freed his hand and burst ahead, running at full speed toward the dog, which, hearing his calls, jumped to its feet and began prancing excitedly in place.

Sartene had brought the dog from Germany at considerable expense as protection for the child. The area, like all of Southeast Asia, was infested with snakes, and while most of the many poisonous varieties remained in the bush, the Asiatic cobras often ventured into the open and were occasionally found near occupied dwellings. The Weimaraner was a classic hunting dog, a pointer used most often to hunt birds, and when in the open its nose was always to the ground seeking out the scent of other creatures. It was a relatively new breed, intended originally to hunt elk, yet mixed with the Spanish pointer to ensure gentleness. The end result had been an animal of extraordinary fearlessness and exceptional loyalty to its master.

Sartene smiled to himself, thinking about the animal now. Its striking gray color and stark, amber eyes gave it an eerie look, and despite its playfulness the Laotians who worked for Sartene were in awe of the creature and referred to it as the devil dog.

When he reached the mangosteen tree, Pierre and Max were involved in a tug-of-war over the stick, the dog wanting it to be thrown in a game of fetch and the boy resisting. Pierre laughed hysterically as the ninety-pound animal yanked him about.

"Give him the stick, Pierre," Sartene said. "He will bring it back to you."

The boy released the stick and the dog raced away with it clamped between its jaws. Twenty yards out into the field, Max stopped abruptly and spun around, waiting for the boy to follow. Sartene took the boy's hand again and held him. The dog began to prance in place and whine for action.

"Let's go to the back of the house and see how the work on the garden is coming," Sartene said.

"Make Max come," the boy demanded.

"He'll come. Don't worry."

They started around the side of the house, the dog raced by them, the stick still fixed in its mouth. When it reached the rear of the house it skidded to a halt, spun around and repeated its prancing, whining demands. At the rear of the house, they climbed the steps to the veranda and seated themselves in two deck chairs. The dog followed, then, realizing its chance for a game had ended, dropped the stick and settled itself at the boy's feet.

Before them, workmen moved about preparing the ground for what would soon be a Japanese garden. A few yards from the veranda a half-dozen Laotians worked inside a large irregularly shaped cut in the earth, mixing and spreading clay.

"When will they finish the pond?" Pierre asked.

"Very soon now."

"Then we can put fish in it?"

Sartene nodded.

"Big fish?" Pierre's voice went up an octave at the thought.

"Little fish that will become big fish," Sartene said. "Like you."

"Why can't we have big fish right away?" Pierre insisted.

"It's easier for the little fish to get used to a new place to live."

"Oh," the boy said.

Sartene glanced at his grandson. Like a little old man, he thought. But like a little fish he too had quickly adjusted to his new home, almost as though there were no difference between Corsica and Laos. For his son, Jean, and his daughter-in-law, Madeleine, it had been more difficult. Also for himself, and it had been a full year before he stopped yearning for the cool evenings in the hills and the dramatic rock-strewn beaches of his home. Now this was home, or soon would be. Still he had brought touches of Europe with him. The structural design of the house, which should have been made of stone, if stone existed. The furniture now stored in a Vientiane warehouse. The paintings. The hundreds of classical records and more than three thousand books, all of which would be used to educate the child seated next to him.

Pierre jumped up from his seat and went to the railing, laying his forearms on top of it, then resting his chin on his hands. He stared across at the oddly shaped structure being built on the other side of the soon-to-be pond, tilting his head to one side, then the other.

"Grandpère. What is that little house for?"

"When it's finished it will be a Buddhist shrine."

The boy turned and stared at him, wrinkling up his nose. "What's a Buddhist shrine?" he asked.

"It's like a small church, Pierre. The people here are Buddhists, most of them anyway. It's their religion, and shrines are very important to them." Sartene, as he always did, spoke to the boy in simple language. There would be time later, in the years to come, to explain the complexity of matters to him.

"Does that mean we're Buddhists? Mama said we were Catholics. Are we Buddhists now because we live here?"

Sartene laughed quietly. The child's logic was flawless. A year ago he had taught him to play chess, and his mind had proved to be mathematically precise. "No, Pierre," he said. "We are still Catholics."

"Then why are we building a Buddhist church?"

"A shrine, Pierre," Sartene corrected. "It is not for us. It is for the Laotians who work for us."

"You mean like Lam?"

"Yes, like Lam."

"I don't like Lam," the boy said. His jaw had become firm and determined.

"Why not, Pierre?"

"He never laughs and he doesn't like Max."

"He's just afraid of Max," Sartene said. "He's never seen a dog like Max before, and that frightens him. Lam is from the mountains, and they are very superstitious people there."

"I still don't like him," Pierre said. "Why do you have to build a church"—he hesitated, then corrected himself—"a shrine, for him?"

"It's not just for Lam, Pierre. It's for all the Buddhists who work for us."

"But why can't they build one for themselves?"

"They can, on their own land. But I chose to build one for them on my land. I do it out of respect for their beliefs, so they can pray here if they wish."

The boy's brow furrowed, and Sartene made a circular gesture with his hand that brought the child to his side. He placed a hand on Pierre's lower back and patted it softly.

"A man should always honor his friends and those who work for him," he said. "He does this by speaking their language and respecting their customs and beliefs. It's a sign of respect. Some men try to force those people to change their ways, to accept new ways of doing things, new beliefs. But they're fools to do that, and they never have the loyalty or the friendship of the people they try to change. You should learn this and remember it all your life. You must give respect if you expect to get loyalty from others.''

Pierre stared at his grandfather. His face was serious, and Sartene could almost see his mind working as he tried to understand what he had been told.

''You mean like how I call Auguste and Benito and Francesco 'Uncle,' even though they really aren't my uncles,'' the boy said at length.

Sartene smiled and his eyes brightened with pleasure. ''Yes, exactly, Pierre.''

He had patted the boy's back a little harder, and Max jumped to his feet and pushed his body between them. He raised his head, using the top of it to push Sartene's hand away.

''Max thinks you're spanking me,'' Pierre said, giggling. ''He doesn't like it when anyone hits. Watch.''

Pierre struck out violently at his grandfather, stopping his hand before it touched him. The dog became excited and pushed him away from his grandfather with his snout and nipped lightly at the arm causing the blows. Pierre giggled uncontrollably.

''Pierre. Stop that or that foolish dog will bite Grandpère.'' Madeleine had come through the rear door and stood staring down at her son, her arms folded severely across her bosom. She was tall and slender, with long blond hair and blue eyes like her son, and despite her voice there was no severity in her delicate features.

''We're only playing, Mama,'' Pierre said, still laughing.

''That's not playing. That's teasing. Now take the dog and play out in the grass with him.''

''Yes, Mama.'' The boy pouted and looked to his grandfather for intervention. Sartene only shrugged and inclined his head to one side, and the child let out a long sigh, then picked up his stick and marched noisily down the stairs. Max followed him happily.

Madeleine sat next to Sartene. She withdrew a delicate handkerchief from the pocket of the sun dress she was wearing and reached over and patted his brow. She shook her head. ''You let him wear you out,'' she said in a mildly scolding voice.

''He could wear out the devil himself,'' Sartene said.

"And you spoil him," she added.

Sartene nodded. "Yes, but he has many years ahead when he will not be spoiled. You think I spoil him too much?"

"No, Papa. Not too much for him. Too much for you." She looked at him with warmth as he waved his hand, rejecting her argument. She had called him "Papa" from the first, at his request, and although she was slightly intimidated by him, there was also a deep and honest affection between them that had grown out of a mutual love for her son.

"How is our home coming?" Sartene asked, more to escape her pampering than to seek information.

"It will be very beautiful, Papa. All except your study. I wish you'd let me do something there. That heavy paneling will make the room so dark it will be like a grave."

Sartene wagged a finger at her. "The house is yours to do with as you wish. The study is mine. I'll keep the door closed so it doesn't offend you."

She rolled her eyes, then stood and walked to the railing. "Now I know where Pierre gets his stubbornness," she said.

Sartene ignored her and joined her at the railing, and together they watched the boy play wildly with the dog.

Behind them Jean lumbered out onto the veranda, and Sartene turned with the sound. His son's large frame moved heavily. Thank God the child has his mother's grace and her looks, he thought. His son, though he loved him deeply, had the heavy, dark features of his maternal grandfather, and with it the dour expression of the mountain people of Corsica. Madeleine was from Marseille and had the delicateness of the French, something she had passed on to Pierre. He had not approved of his son's marriage to a non-Corsican at first, but his grandson's birth had taught him he was wrong.

Jean glanced at his wristwatch. "It is two-thirty, Papa. We're to meet the American in Vientiane at three."

"Yes, I forgot. I promised Pierre we would take the boat back today. You and Madeleine can drive back in the car, and then you and the others can entertain our guest until I arrive."

Jean nodded, and Sartene looked hard at his son before continuing. "Discuss no business with this man until I arrive," he added. "Our friends in Saigon tell me he's with the OSS, and my experience with those people has not been good."

Madeleine turned to go with her husband, and Sartene took

her arm, stopping her. He reached out and touched her cheek. "I promise I won't spoil him on the trip back," he said.

She withheld a smile and raised her chin slightly. "You'll promise, but you'll spoil him anyway," she said.

The house in Vientiane was old and spacious and had once belonged to a wealthy French exporter who had been executed by the Japanese during the war. The office where Sartene conducted his business was in the rear of the house and opened onto a walled garden. Had it not been for the boy, the house would have suited his needs. But the garden was small, and within a few blocks of the colonial quarter where the house was located, the filth and stench of the city were overpowering.

The others were gathered in the office when Sartene entered. He had put on his suitcoat and, despite the trip in the open boat, appeared cool and refreshed. The American, an OSS colonel named Matthew Bently, was seated by himself in a leather wing chair. There was a drink on the table next to him, and Sartene noted that it appeared untouched. The others had seated themselves opposite Bently, and when Sartene entered they stood. Bently followed suit, stepped forward, and extended his hand.

"Monsieur Sartene, I'm Matt Bently. Thank you for agreeing to meet with me."

Sartene nodded, shook Bently's hand, then motioned for him to sit. Jean stepped away from the chair directly opposite Bently, where he had been sitting, yielding it to his father, then walked to the large desk in the center of the room and leaned back against it. Auguste, Benito and Francesco returned to their chairs after Sartene was seated.

"I'm very sorry I was late," Sartene began. "We were out looking at a new house I'm building, and my grandson wanted to return by boat. His mother says I spoil him, and I'm afraid she's right. I hope you'll forgive the rudeness."

"Your son was a fine host," Bently said.

Sartene studied the man closely. He was tall and muscular, with hard gray eyes and a face that seemed steeled by the harsh life of a professional soldier. He was dressed in civilian clothes, but that was not uncommon these days. What Sartene had learned from friends in Saigon spoke well of the man, even though he was part of the same organization as the other American, the fool he had fought with in the mountains of France.

Sartene placed the fingers of one hand against his lips, then moved the hand forward toward Bently.

"You said in your letter you had some business you wanted to discuss with me."

Bently glanced at the others in the room, then back at Sartene.

"In business matters I trust these men completely and seek their advice," Sartene said.

Bently smiled. "It's merely a question of witnesses. Normally my organization avoids that whenever possible."

Sartene nodded. "I respect that. But you don't have to worry about that here. You have my word. We're all Corsicans and we serve as witnesses for no one. Any breach of trust would be an offense against me, and I assure you that won't happen."

Sartene's words had an icy chill about them, and Bently noted that the others in the room had averted their eyes as he spoke them.

"I accept your word, of course," Bently said. He leaned forward in his chair. "As I'm sure you're aware, sir, I took the liberty of inquiring about you prior to my request, as I'm sure you inquired about me, following it."

Sartene gestured with both hands. "A wise man always knows who he's speaking to."

The statement made Bently uneasy. He felt like a child who had stated an unnecessary fact which had required a patient reply from someone older and wiser. Bently was thirty-two, only a half-dozen or so years older than Sartene's son, he guessed. He had been through much during the war in the Pacific and even more since its end. He had attained the rank of lieutenant colonel, and yet in this man's presence he felt inexperienced, almost immature. He knew of Sartene's wartime background, and earlier he had noticed the extensive volumes on military history in his study. None of it helped.

Nervously he brushed at a speck of dirt on the knee of his tan cord suit, then reached up to his neck, checking the position of the knot in his tie.

"I only say that as a preamble to something else," he said. "I'm here because my government feels you can do us a service, which will be of great benefit to us and, I hope, to you as well."

Jean emitted a low grunt, and Sartene looked at him sharply. He turned back to Bently and smiled, nodding his head for him to continue.

Bently glanced at the others in the room. They all were

strangely silent. It was like going to church to confess and finding five priests staring at you, he thought.

"As you know," Bently began, "the communist forces here, who were our allies during the war, have begun an all-out effort to control the region. For obvious reasons we don't want that to happen. We believe they would be as dangerous to the west as the Japanese, and would eventually produce the same result."

Sartene nodded, but said nothing.

"The key to their control, to anyone's control, really, involves the region's major resource. Opium. The communists know that if they control its growth and distribution they'll have the loyalty of the hill people who produce it and the government officials who profit from it. And they know they'll also have a source of income that could finance their effort to take over the region."

Bently paused, awaiting some response from Sartene. When none came he continued.

"At present our intelligence tells us that the communists both in Laos and Viet Nam are trying to work a deal with a countryman of yours in Saigon, Antonio Carbone. We also believe he has close ties with a gentleman in Marseille by the name of François Spirito, who is suspected of having collaborated with the Nazis in France. We're also told that you have a long-standing friendship with the Guerini brothers, who are the dominant faction of the Corsican *milieu* in Marseille. What we hope is that you'll agree to compete with Mr. Carbone for control of the opium and in doing so deal with people not aligned with the communists. There would be substantial profit in this for you and you would operate under the tacit protection of my government and the colonial government of France. We're well aware that you have the facilities to move quantities of merchandise, primarily gold and currency, and feel that adding opium to these items would not be difficult for you."

Bently gestured with both hands to indicate he was finished and sat back in his chair. He had rushed through his preliminary proposal in a clipped military way, a sign of nervousness that had not been lost on Sartene.

Sartene smiled, rose from his chair and walked to the French doors that opened onto the rear garden. He stood there for a full minute, his back to Bently.

The young man had seemed nervous, but he had spoken well, choosing his words carefully, avoiding any insult. He had spoken of the Corsican *milieu*, the loosely knit organization of his countrymen involved in supposedly illegal activities. He had not called it the Corsican syndicate or criminal gang, terms so common in the French press. He had mentioned his *friendship* with the Guerinis, not his business connections. And he had spoken of his importing and exporting of gold and currency, not smuggling, which of course it was. He liked the man's tactfulness. He was not sure he liked his proposal.

Sartene turned back to face the younger man, clasping his hands behind his back and rocking slightly on the balls of his feet.

"When I came to Laos more than a year ago, I had the option of dealing with this merchandise you speak of," he said. "At that time I chose not to do so. It's a substance that has caused great harm to the people of this region for centuries. So much so that it's probably an irreversible thing." He shrugged. "So be it. That's the way of things. No one man can change history. But he can choose not to be a part of a thing he finds wrong. So far I've found other ways to earn my bread for my family and my friends." Sartene paused, looking at the others in the room. "I'm also a man who realizes that he must adapt to the realities of the world. But such an adaptation can follow many paths. As I'm sure you know, my new home will be part of a sizable rubber plantation which will have the benefit of contracts with a large French concern. This together with my other interests will provide me and my friends with more than we need to be financially secure, even if we are eventually forced to leave our new home. If I choose to accept your offer there will be more wealth, and, if your government is successful against the communists, there is also the possibility that our position here will be more secure." Sartene raised one finger. "But only the possibility," he added.

Slowly he walked back to the chair and sat down. "Now," he began again. "If we agree to your proposal we must place ourselves in direct conflict with Don Carbone. This doesn't concern me greatly. We have never been friends and each of our friends in Europe have never been friends." He paused, clasping his hands in front of him, then gesturing with them together. "What you do not understand is the Corsican way of doing business. We have always believed that each man has a right to earn his bread in whatever way is available to him. We also believe that no man has the right to deny another that opportunity. Perhaps, as you say, Carbone has friendships with men who worked with the Nazis. I fought with the French. But you're wrong to emphasize this difference. I chose the French side, at least in part, because I believed the Nazis would give Corsica to the Italians and I believed we had a greater chance to one day free ourselves from the French than from the Italians and the Nazis, together. Others disagreed. Perhaps they believed Corsica would always be under someone's control and that anyone would be better than the French. Who knows what they thought?'' He shrugged his shoulders, indicating the argument was of little value. "Still, I would never stop one of my peers from earning his bread because we disagreed about politics. We Corsicans believe we are each a government to ourselves. If I were to deny Carbone or any other Corsican this right, it would only be because it involved the survival of my own organization.''

Bently drew a deep breath. "I think a takeover by the communists would mean an end to your organization. Probably an end to Mr. Carbone's as well. The communists are not very enamored with free enterprise.''

Sartene laughed quietly. "That's the argument we will have to think about,'' he said, almost like a teacher speaking to a slow student who has suddenly discovered the root of a problem. "I'll send word to you, perhaps within a day, certainly no more than a week. If my answer is no, I assure you I'll do nothing to interfere with your efforts, provided you do nothing to interfere with mine.''

Sartene was smiling at him, and Bently was forced to smile in return. He had spoken of Sartene's importing and exporting of gold and currency and had asked him to add opium to his stock in trade. If he agreed he had promised the quiet support of his government and the French. The implication that problems for his other businesses might develop if he refused had been there as well. Sartene had now responded to that veiled threat with a warning of his own.

"I understand that leaders within the *milieu* carry a gold medallion used for identification among each other and that a holder of that medallion is referred to as *un vrai monsieur*. I think I now understand the meaning of that title.''

Sartene stood and extended his hand. Bently rose and took it. The others in the room who had been seated also rose.

"During the war I worked with a member of your organization. He was a fool. I'm pleased to see that there are wiser men in your ranks as well.'' He patted Bently's arm, then extended his hand toward the door.

"I'll look forward to hearing from you, Don Sartene," Bently said.

Sartene nodded and smiled. The formality pleased him.

When Bently had left, Sartene seated himself behind his desk and motioned for the others to be seated. He placed his palms on the edge of the desk and leaned back in his chair. "Now tell me what you think." He looked first at Auguste. The man had not changed since they first were together. He seemed ageless. Sartene suspected he always would.

"I don't like this drug business," Auguste said, making a face to emphasize his displeasure. "It's a dirty business on the other end. The opium goes to Marseille for processing into morphine. That's all right, because it's controlled by Corsicans. But after that it's sold to Sicilians, who take it to Sicily to make heroin, and then to the American Mafiosi. They're pigs and they're greedy. Eventually they'll want to control the morphine processing, and after they have that they'll want to control the exporting. They'll never be happy with having only part. They'll want all. Someday they'll come here and we'll have trouble we don't need."

Sartene's eyes were fixed on Auguste's face, noting every expression that emphasized the depths of his beliefs. He was quiet for several moments, only nodding his head in response.

"And how do you feel about doing business with this drug?" he asked at length.

Auguste shrugged his shoulders and raised his hands at his sides almost to shoulder height in an emphatic flourish. "I have no problem with that, Buonaparte. To me it's the same as a farmer who grows corn even though he knows it will be used to make liquor that will be bought by men who drink too much. You can't stop men from being fools. If opium isn't the source of their foolishness, they'll find something else to make fools of themselves with."

Sartene smiled at his friend. His view was very Corsican and one he held himself about mankind, although with some reservations.

"And this man Bently? What about him?"

Auguste made a similar gesture, only this time keeping his hands near his lap, allowing them to rise and fall. It was a less emphatic gesture, less certain.

"He spoke well. Handled himself well. He offered us a business opportunity and gave us a little warning also. But he treated us like men. My question is not with the man himself. He's not a fool like the other one from his organization that we knew in France.'' Auguste looked directly at Sartene and rubbed his chest lightly, then gave him a small smile. ''But I still don't trust the Americans. One American promises one thing and then another one higher up says it can't be done. It's the way they do business.''

Sartene rubbed his chin, then swiveled his chair toward Benito, Auguste's brother. He was seeking their advice by order of their age, honoring the wisdom that went with their years.

Benito waited patiently, his hands clasped across a protruding paunch. He bore no resemblance to his brother. He seemed plump, but the layer of fat covered muscle, and his triple chin hid a neck as bull-like as Sartene's son's. His face was round and gentle, the features appearing to fall away from a flat, fleshy nose, and the only hair on his head was a two-inch band above his ears that decreased to one inch at the back of his head. He was fifty, but looked ten years older.

Sartene looked at him for a moment, still digesting Auguste's words, then nodded for him to begin.

Benito's face was always jolly when he spoke, his mouth always forming a smile, even when he was angry. Only his brown-black eyes showed his true emotion. Now they were pensive.

''I agree with my brother,'' he said. ''But I think these problems can be overcome if you decide it's a good thing. What worries me is Carbone and what he'll do.''

''You think he'll make war on us.'' Sartene spoke the words as a statement, not a question.

''Eventually,'' Benito said. He began to move one hand in front of him in a circular gesture, as though it helped him find the proper words. ''He's a man who has a big opinion of himself, and even though we have a right to seek business, I think because we didn't go after opium when we first came here, he'll think it's his private thing. I don't think he'll care that we're only after the noncommunist business. He'll want it all. First he'll just try to stop us from getting a supply. But if we already have the supply before he knows we're in it, then sooner or later he'll come at us.''

There was no fear of a conflict in Benito's words. Sartene recognized that. He also recognized, with pleasure, Benito's subtle warning that if they chose to move ahead, they should guarantee their supply before allowing Carbone to know their intent. He turned his chair again, this time toward Francesco, and nodded to him.

The time in Laos had been kind to Francesco. The business suits he now wore gave him an elegance that had not been present in the mountains of France, and it softened his hard but handsome features. He had also given up the practice of playing with a knife, sharpening it constantly almost as though it were a part of his being. But the knife was still part of his nature, and there was always one in the pocket of his well-tailored suits.

Francesco, now thirty-five, had only touches of gray at the sides of his hair, and it added to his good looks, and provided instant popularity with the French colonial ladies of Vientiane.

Now, in this matter of business, he seemed to revert slightly back to his days in the mountains. His eyes hardened almost contemptuously, and there was a cigarette in the corner of his mouth.

"Everything that's been said is true, Buonaparte," he said, pausing for effect. "Except about Carbone and the Americans." He waited for some response from Sartene, but there was none. "Carbone is nothing. He has men and power but he doesn't know how to use them. He lives in his little world of grandeur. He struts around in his big white hat like he is some kind of king. It's not enough for him to be considered *un vrai monsieur*, a respected leader in the *milieu*. He wants people to think he is a *paceri*, one of the biggest, who can impose his discipline on all." Francesco gestured in disgust. "It's you who hold that right. We all know that. Everybody but Carbone. When we came here less than two years ago, he was the force in smuggling, in currency. Now we are. We own more bars than he does. Soon our real estate holdings will be bigger. He is only dominant in opium because we haven't touched it." He smiled wickedly. "There's a lot of money in this thing. More, maybe, than in everything else combined. But why should we give Carbone any of it? Why do what the Americans want and compete with the communists? That's only to their advantage. Why not deal with both? The American puppets and the communist puppets? Then we have twice the profit and complete control." He sat back in his chair and took a long drag on his cigarette, indicating he was finished.

Sartene swiveled his chair in a semicircle to face his son, who was now seated next to Auguste. He gestured with his hand for him to begin.

Jean slumped down in his chair, making himself look like some rocklike concentration of muscle. He was the youngest man in the room, and Sartene's decision to seek his advice last was no slight.

Jean gave a sideways glance at Francesco. He was not nearly as eloquent as this man he could not make himself trust, and knew he never would be. He spoke in choppy, distinct sentences almost as a defense against the flaw.

"I agree. There's much money and we should have part of it. But to deny Carbone a chance to earn his bread is wrong. If he fights"—he shrugged—"then that's a different matter. But to take something from a man is one thing. To take something from him and then to cheat him also is wrong. It's not the Corsican way. It's not our way."

Jean stopped as abruptly as he had begun. He could feel the anger emanating from across the room, from Francesco. A small, almost indiscernible smile formed on his lips. There was nothing that pleased him more than annoying Francesco.

The antagonism was not lost on Sartene. But he dismissed it in his mind. It was something he considered the natural order of things. Two young bucks competing. It had never gotten out of hand out of respect to him, and until it did he would not interfere.

He pressed his palms down on the desk and pushed himself up, walked around his chair and stopped. He stared out the French doors into the garden for several minutes, offering a profile to those around the room. "As always, each of you offers honest advice," he said without looking at them. "Now let me give you my thoughts, based on that advice."

The others in the room sat quietly, knowing that Sartene's "thoughts" would really be a decision on what would be done.

"Unlike Auguste, I have concerns about this opium thing. This very profitable but dangerous thing that comes from a beautiful flower." He spoke slowly, still staring out the window. "When we first came here I made myself learn about it. Because of the profit involved and because I thought one day we might have to decide if we would deal with it."

Sartene turned and walked back to his chair, seated himself, and folded his arms on the desk.

"It's a thing that's brought great wealth to many men. And

it's also brought suffering to the people of this region." He began drumming the fingers of one hand on the surface of the desk, his eyes staring past the steady rhythmic movement. As always his mind was flooded with historical fact that seemed to synchronize with the problems of the present in his mind. He was a self-taught man, and as such relied heavily on that which he had forced himself to learn. History, especially, was a near compulsion with him.

For a moment his mouth moved soundlessly, as if trying to find the needed words. "The Arabs brought this here in the fifth century. But the Chinese saw its dangers and only allowed it to be used for medicinal things. Later, in the fifteen hundreds, the Portuguese came and began selling it like tobacco. Then the Dutch did the same in all of Southeast Asia in the sixteen hundreds. And finally the British came two hundred years after that." Sartene snorted, then looked at the others. "You know the Chinese banned the import of opium then because they felt it was destroying their people. Once their government even raided British ships in Canton Harbor and threw thousands of kilos into the sea. For that British warships shelled the Chinese coast for three years in what the Chinese historians call the Opium War." He shook his head again and shrugged slightly. "Of course, the British won. And now we have the French. And finally today, the Americans."

Sartene stared at each of them in turn and jabbed one finger at the desk. "When men like you and me do these things we're called criminals. Even if we do it because they ask us to, they still call us criminals." There was an uncharacteristic sneer on Sartene's face now. He spit the next words out almost as though they produced a foul taste in his mouth. "When the governments of Portugal and Holland and Britain did this thing, it was an act of commerce," he said, waving one arm in a broad, expansive gesture. "Now for the French and the Americans it's diplomacy." He paused. "But for us it will always be something wrong, something criminal."

He folded his hands in front of him and seemed to stare past them for a long time. Auguste nodded his head, sensing Sartene's mood.

"Then we will do it, Buonaparte." It was a question spoken as fact.

"We have no choice," Sartene said. "And people will suffer no matter what we do."

He sat back in his chair and offered a look of resignation to Auguste. "The American was right about one thing," he said. "If the communists control the region it will be the end of our business." He swiveled his chair and stared at Francesco. It was a look of admonishment, and Francesco's face tightened under it.

"And this is why we don't deal with both sides," he said. "What Jean said is true. You can take from a man, especially a stranger, or a *man* like Carbone." He said the word "man" almost contemptuously. "But if you take from him you shouldn't cheat him as well. But the better reason is that if we deal with the communists and they're successful, we lose."

Francesco began to speak, but Sartene raised his hand, cutting him off. "I don't mean that we go home as beggars with holes in our pockets." He leaned forward, his face severe. "But I didn't come here to make money and then go home to Corsica to live like some fat *padrone*. I came here to establish a life for my family and my friends. The *milieu* here is our *milieu*, no matter what that fool Carbone thinks. It's for my son and his son and yours when you choose to have one. And for Auguste and Benito and their families, if they come here and join us." His voice had become almost strident. "That's what the *milieu* is. We have no country, no government. All that's been stolen from us. We only have what we take for ourselves. To hell with the Americans and the French. We use them as they use us. And we take the money and we become stronger."

Sartene stopped almost as if composing himself. No one spoke. "If there are problems with Carbone they'll be of his making." He waited again, looking at each of them. "Now, I know something about the man who is the leader of these heathen poppy growers to the north. He's called Touby Lyfoung and he's something of a fool. I'm told he's very impressed with authority and for many years now has tried to get the colonial government to give him some military title he can hang around his neck. We'll arrange for this through the Americans. They can have the French make him general of the poppies for all I care. But only if he deals with us and no one else."

Sartene turned to his son. "You handle this opium business for me," he said. "But I want you to work closely with Auguste." He wagged a finger. "He'll teach you patience. Anyway, it's time you had more responsibility."

Jean's face exploded with pleasure, and for a moment

Sartene questioned his choice. He disliked displays of emotion in business matters, believing it was something that gave advantage to a potential adversary.

He turned to Francesco. His face was impassive, even though Sartene knew he was seething over the decision to give the opium business to Jean.

"You'll continue to handle our other business matters for now," he said, offering Francesco some hope for the future, as well as issuing a warning to his son.

"Benito," he said, turning to face him, "I'll need you to help me arrange things in case there are"—he made a circular gesture with his hand, searching for the proper word—"difficulties with Carbone. I also want you to go to Saigon and meet with this American. Ask him to come to see me to work out the necessary arrangements. And tell him to bring someone in higher authority. Tell him I don't want to make an arrangement and have someone higher up change it the next day. He'll understand. He knows I've dealt with his government before."

He leaned forward, elbows on the desk, fingers steepled in front of his face. "If there's any disagreement we should discuss it now," he said. When no one spoke he separated his hands, then brought them back together. "Is there anything else?" Again there was silence. "Good," Sartene said, ending the meeting. "Jean," he said, looking at his son, "tell Pierre to come and see me. Francesco, I want you to stay here a moment."

As the others left the room, Sartene came around the desk and placed his hand on Francesco's shoulder. His eyes were penetrating and he looked directly into Francesco's, knowing he would see the man's true feelings there.

"I don't want you to misunderstand my reasons in this matter," he said. "I need you to do what you're doing now. And I also need you to do something else."

There was a glint of suspicion, perhaps even resentment, in Francesco's eyes. But that was to be expected.

"I want you to have someone keep a close watch on Carbone," Sartene said. "And I want you to do it the same way I would. You shouldn't discuss this with the others. Only with me. But it's even more important than the other arrangements we'll be making." Sartene inclined his head as though they were sharing some secret between them. "Someday you'll be leading men the same way I am now," he said. "Then you'll understand the need to divide authority. Right now I only ask that you trust my judgment and know that we'll all profit equally from this thing."

Francesco shrugged. "I just think I could do this better than Jean," he said.

There was no resistance in his words, only opinion. Sartene nodded, neither agreeing nor disagreeing. "He has to learn too," Sartene said, sliding his hand around Francesco and walking him to the door. As Francesco opened the door, he patted his back. "Like Jean, you too must learn patience," he said.

When he returned to his desk, Sartene sat heavily in his chair and allowed his mind to question the wisdom of his decision. This thing would mean trouble with Carbone, he had no doubt of that. So far his business interests had produced little bloodshed. But this time it would be different. In the short time since he had arrived in Vientiane he had made himself stronger than Carbone, both in manpower and in the businesses that excluded opium. Now he would move into opium as well, and it would leave Carbone with so diminished a status that he would either have to resist or risk losing many of the people in his organization. It would leave him little choice, of that Sartene was certain.

The matter of his son also bothered him. He had hoped that Jean would learn to think with the mind of a rapier, not a bludgeon, but such was not the case. At first he had considered sending him to work with the Guerini brothers in Marseille, but had decided against it. Perhaps he had been wrong. He only knew now that he wished his son were more like Francesco, and that too bothered and annoyed him.

Slowly he withdrew from his pocket a set of keys that was attached to a gold chain that hung from his belt. Selecting one key, he opened the middle drawer of his desk and withdrew a rectangular gold medallion. On the face of the medallion was a shield. Across the top of the shield the word *Corse* was engraved into the metal; below, the profile of a man with a bandanna tied across his forehead. Atop the shield there was an eagle perched with its wings spread.

Staring at the medallion now, he wondered if one day he would be able to pass it on to his son. A man can only do his best, he told himself. He can't control the accident of nature.

Almost on cue, the door to the office opened and Jean stuck his head in.

"Papa. Pierre is taking his nap," he said.

Sartene grunted in acknowledgment. "Tell him when he wakes up," he said.

Jean paused for a moment. "Papa," he finally said. "Thank you for your trust in me."

Sartene nodded abruptly, then looked hard into his son's eyes. "Don't fail me in that trust," he said.

As the door closed Sartene placed the medallion back in the desk and locked it. He would wait and see, he told himself. He sat back in his chair and drew a deep breath, realizing he was disappointed his grandson was asleep.

Madeleine sat before the mirror providing ritual strokes to her hair with a long-handled silver brush. In the reflection of the mirror she could see her husband seated on the edge of the bed, drawing heavily on a cigarette. He seemed deep in thought, as he had through most of the evening. When he had come to her after the meeting in the office he had been bursting with pleasure. Then later, for no apparent reason, his mood had changed and he had been pensive, almost nervous. She continued to watch him between glances at her own image to make sure the brush strokes were having the desired effect.

She was pleased with the way she looked, and she recalled now how she had been frightened six years ago that the birth of her son would change her into the frumpy, sexless mother her own had become. She drew a deep breath, watching her breasts rise and fall beneath the thin beige negligee she was wearing. It had not happened, would not be allowed to, she told herself.

She watched as Jean stubbed out his cigarette, then, without noticing, lit another. He was like an anxious child tonight, she thought. It must have something to do with their business, and though she wanted to know why he was disturbed, she did not want to know about their business. She had told herself many times it was easier to love them if she did not know what these Sartene men did.

She stood and walked to the bed and sat next to him, the thin negligee moving against her figure with an inviting sensuality that pleased her as much as it did her husband. She kissed Jean's shoulder lightly, then rested her head against it. "You seem very bound up in things tonight," she said, in her native French.

At first there was no response, the only sound coming from the rotating ceiling fan above their bed, a constant buzzing that always reminded her of the sound a moth made when it was trapped against a window struggling to reach the light beyond the pane.

"I have a lot on my mind," he said finally.

She ran one hand inside his pajama top and stroked his chest. "Do you want to talk about it?" she said, knowing he would either decline or speak in such vague generalities it would not matter. He was quiet for a long time, and she surrendered again to the sound of the fan above her head.

Jean looked around the large bedroom. It was the largest in the old house, one that rightfully belonged to his father, but Sartene had insisted it go to his son and Madeleine. Instead, he had taken a small room across from Pierre's, saying it was enough for a man who slept alone.

It was his nature to do those things, Jean thought now. All his life, or at least as much as Jean had witnessed or had been told about, his father had always provided for his family first, his friends second, and then, when he was satisfied all had been cared for, himself. He was like that with everyone within the small, intimate group he held so closely to himself. Beyond that group it was different. His acts of apparent benevolence were done to produce a loyalty necessary to his business. Like the building of that Buddhist shrine at the new house, Jean thought. It was a simple act—"to show I understand and respect their needs," his father had explained—that would provide payments in loyalty that could not be bought.

Now his father had given him a great responsibility—a test, really, of his worthiness—but still something that could affect the organization badly if he did not do it well. And there would always be that bastard Francesco, waiting in the background, hoping he would fail.

"It's just that my father has asked me to do something that's very important to our business," Jean said, as though the long silence since Madeleine's question had not occurred.

"And you're worried?" Her voice was soft, intentionally soothing.

"I can do it," he said abruptly.

She stroked his chest again.

"I suppose I am," he said at length. "Not that I can't do it. Just that so much depends on it. And I want to do it in a way that pleases him, the way he would do it."

"You can only do things the way you do them. You can't be a copy of your father," she said.

He nodded his head, more as an acknowledgment of her words than in agreement. "That bastard Francesco can," he said.

He was right about that, she knew. Even from a distance, her distance, she was able to see the similarities between Francesco and her father-in-law. They had the same quiet, threatening way about them. Only Francesco's was more open, more obvious. Buonaparte's seemed veiled, perhaps because he was older.

"Francesco still worries you, then?"

"I don't trust him," Jean said, his voice soft but gruff at the same time. "He respects my father, even fears him. But he doesn't love him the way I do, the way Auguste and Benito do. He only uses him, and if he ever gets strong enough, or if my father is weakened enough, he'll go against him."

She thought about Francesco, the feeling of discomfort she experienced when he was near. There was an animal cunning about him that came through his good looks, perhaps even intensified them in an unpleasant way. She had caught him looking at her on occasion, when no one else could see, and she had suspected what was on his mind. Her father-in-law had the same sense of cunning, but in a less malevolent way, or at least she had never seen the malevolence manifested. But with her he was gentle. No, not gentle. Considerate, really. The only person he was truly gentle with was Pierre.

"Why don't you talk to your father about it, about your concerns?" she asked.

"He'd think it was jealousy. And maybe he'd be right. No. I just have to prove myself to him and make sure Francesco never gets strong enough." He nodded to himself, as if approving his own decision.

She continued to stroke his chest quietly, urging him to leave his thoughts. It was so like him. Barging straight ahead forcefully. It was a simple honesty, and she loved that about him. But she also knew it was not the way his father would act. He was right about that.

He looked at her for the first time. "You know, even talking to you like this. It's something my father would never approve of, never do himself. He would think it wasn't the Corsican way."

"In our bedroom you don't have to be Corsican," she said, smiling.

She watched him look at her in a new way now, with a sudden understanding that she wanted to be with him. His face became one large smile, making him look so much like the little boy he was at these times. He reached out to her gently.

"I must look in on Pierre, first," she said, still smiling.

She stood and slipped into a robe that matched her nightgown, still watching him. Pierre's room was next to theirs, across the narrow hall from his grandfather's. When she reached the door she could see light coming beneath it, and she opened the door quietly, suspecting the child had fallen asleep with his bedside lamp on.

Standing in the doorway now she saw the true reason. Pierre lay atop his bed, his eyes fixed on his grandfather's face, as the older man read to him from a book.

"Papa," she said in a gentle admonishment. "He's supposed to be asleep."

Both sets of eyes turned toward her, each reflecting a sense of guilt that seemed suddenly comical. Two children caught in the act of disobedience, she thought, trying but failing to withhold a smile.

Sartene shrugged. "He couldn't sleep. I thought I would read to him for a bit."

"Ahh," she said, "I see." She moved toward him and looked down at the book. "And what bedtime story have you chosen? I see," she said, leaning down and looking into the open pages of the book. "The Battle of Craonne. Of course. That's the story where Napoleon and Hans Christian Andersen defeat the goose who laid the golden egg, is it not?"

"Mama, it's a good story," Pierre insisted.

"Yes, I know it is, my darling. But now you must go to sleep." She emphasized the word "sleep," casting an amused glance at her father-in-law as she spoke it.

Sartene shrugged and rose from his chair. "Your mama is right, Pierre," he said. "We'll finish the story tomorrow."

The child stuck out his lower lip in a pout, as his mother tucked the light sheet about his body and leaned down to kiss his forehead. His grandfather followed suit, winking at him and causing the child to grin.

Two little conspirators, Madeleine thought. As Sartene started to leave the room, she noticed he had left the book on the nightstand next to the bed. She picked it up and looked at it, shaking her head. All these things about military history that he filled the boy's head with, she thought. Sometimes it made her wonder if he was entertaining the child or training him for battle.

"Papa," she said. "You forgot your book."

Sartene turned and took the book from her. "We'll finish our story tomorrow, Pierre," he said, repeating himself. He raised his eyebrows and inclined his head toward Madeleine by way of apology.

Chapter 5

Sartene had first met Antonio Carbone during his first week in Southeast Asia. It had been a courtesy visit to the massive house on the outskirts of Saigon that Carbone had decorated like the palace of some gauche little prince.

Sartene had always despised ostentatious displays of wealth and power, believing it invited curiosity where none was needed. But he had expected little else from Carbone, based on what he had heard of him during the man's days in Corsica and Marseille.

They were contemporaries, but had never met. Carbone had come to Saigon in 1943, after his brother, Paul, a leader in the *milieu* during the 1930s and 1940s, and a collaborator with the Nazi SS, had died. His brother's successor, François Spirito, had bankrolled his move to the east, and for Sartene, the fact that Antonio had not succeeded his brother spoke enough in itself about the man.

When Carbone had received him in a large study, overflowing with Louis XIV furnishings, Sartene had realized that the two brothers could easily have been twins. They had the same round fleshy face, the deep-set eyes beneath heavy brows, and the thin mouth that seemed to turn up at the edges as though trying to hide some great and humorous secret. Only this Carbone was fat, a fat that came from overindulgence in all things. From what Sartene had already learned, the man even indulged himself with the prostitutes who worked in his bars and nightclubs.

During that first meeting, Carbone had ensconced himself in a gilded, carved chair that sat like a throne behind his equally gilded desk. He had extended both hands in a gesture of welcome as Sartene had entered, but had not risen, simply indicating a chair instead.

"So you come here to earn your bread," Carbone had begun.

"The war has been hard on Europe," Sartene had said. "I hoped the opportunities here would be better."

Sartene's words had been spoken softly, almost humbly. He had found during his life that there was a great advantage to playing the innocent before a man like this. He would learn later that he had been deceived, but until then it was better to offer no sense of threat.

Carbone had toyed with his wide flowered necktie for a moment, then had reached out for the gold medallion on his desk. It was Sartene's, given at the door of Carbone's home as a means of introduction.

"You have done well for yourself, my friend," he had said. "Of course, I had heard you were coming to my region from friends in Marseille. I understand you are friendly with the Guerini brothers. Very noble men. Tell me, do they give you financial support to earn your bread here?"

Sartene had remained impassive. Carbone would have known of any financial arrangements through Spirito. The remark had been intended as a condescension.

"No," Sartene had said. "I'm afraid I don't have the advantage of a benefactor. As I said, things are not good in Europe now."

"Do you come to me for financial help, then?" Carbone had asked.

Sartene had shaken his head. "I found a bit of good fortune toward the war's end," he had said. "It will be enough to help me earn my bread in a modest way. I'm here as a courtesy to you and to express my hope that if matters of mutual advantage come my way, we might do business together."

Carbone had extended his hands in a benevolent gesture. "I am always willing to help a fellow Corsican," he had said. "Especially if it profits me as well. Will you stay here in Saigon?" His eyes had narrowed slightly as he asked the question.

Sartene had shaken his head again. "I am going on to Vientiane. There's more opportunity there to work without great competition, and at present my plans are small by your standards."

Carbone had smiled and nodded his approval. He was unaware that Sartene had already purchased business properties in Saigon and would undoubtedly remain ignorant of it for a long time. Too long for his own good, Sartene had thought.

Carbone had heaved his heavy body from the chair and walked around the desk, still holding the medallion in his hand. Sartene had also risen, and as Carbone had reached him he had taken Sartene's elbow and begun guiding him toward the door.

"I want you to know, Don Sartene, that you can always come to me if you need my help. We're alone here among these yellow heathens, and if we don't help each other they'll swallow us up like so many crumbs on a table. But fortunately for us they're a stupid people, easily taken advantage of. They work and die for pennies."

When he had opened the door he had seen Francesco sitting in a chair in the hall. Sartene had brought Francesco with him so Carbone would know there were hard, young Corsicans beneath him, just in case he was cleverer than he appeared and decided to react harshly.

"And who is this?" Carbone had said, raising his eyebrows.

"Francesco Canterina," Sartene had said. "One of our countrymen who has come with me to earn his bread."

Carbone had looked at Sartene closely. "And how many of you are there?" he had asked.

"Only myself and my son and three others," Sartene had said. Not too many, but still enough, he had known.

"It's good," Carbone had said, still wary. "A man should have countrymen around him he can trust."

Carbone had taken Sartene's hand, returning the medallion with it as they shook farewell. He had waved his hand in an expansive gesture. "If you're going to stay in Saigon a few days, go to any of my restaurants, any of my bars, and you'll be my guest," he had said.

"You're very kind," Sartene had said. "Everything that I've heard about you is true."

When they had left Carbone's house, they had walked silently for several minutes.

"Is he as much a donkey as he seems?" Francesco had finally asked.

Sartene had nodded. "But donkeys have a nasty kick," he had said. "We'll let this one slumber in its stall for now. Later, when he wakes up, he'll find his farm has been sold while he was asleep."

*   *   *

Over the next few months Carbone had made various inquiries about Sartene's activities and had found little with which to concern himself. Sartene, in fact, had done little in those months. He had purchased a small bar in Vientiane, arranged some modest currency transactions with contacts in Hong Kong and established an insignificant protection network with some small Laotian gambling dens. All of it had been the work of a small-time operation, exactly as Sartene had intended it to appear. When Carbone's interest had waned, however, Sartene's activities had increased. Within a year these interests had grown to an extent that rivaled Carbone's, and six months later had surpassed them.

During that later six-month period the donkey had awakened and some subtle but definite resistance to Sartene's smuggling and currency operations had developed. What followed had been a minor conflict, in which several of Carbone's Vietnamese employees had simply vanished from the face of the earth. Carbone had been upset, but not enough to risk a major confrontation. His main business, opium, had not been threatened, and until it was he could afford to live with the fact that he had been duped. But from that moment on he had watched Sartene closely.

Even though he had no respect for the man, Sartene did have respect for Carbone's large force of manpower, which could not be discounted. His own force had grown as well. Laotians who had fought the Japanese during the war—men who would instinctively hate Carbone, who had been treated well by the Japanese because of his brother's ties with the Nazis. Carbone also was strong with Viet Nam officialdom, which flagrantly peddled its influence. Sartene too had developed strong political alliances, in both Viet Nam and Laos, and he knew the Vietnamese would not welcome war between the two Corsicans, simply because it would reduce their graft by half. He knew too that a war would have been treated harshly and that such resistance would have caused difficulties for both groups. Now, with the support of the Americans, it would not. Still, it was a situation Sartene had tried to avoid. Conflicts like that only provided danger to those close to you, and he had always felt there was enough danger in the world without courting more, except when it could not be avoided. He had not foreseen that such a time would come, but it had.

*　　*　　*

As a young man in Corsica there had been other things Sartene had not foreseen. He had been sickly as a boy and had been left thin, lanky, and pale by the time he had reached adolescence. He had grown up in the small village of Calvi, which sat on the northwestern coast with the massive bulk of Mount Cinto rising nearly nine thousand feet to the east. Because of his sickly early years he did not lead the life of a normal Corsican child, and his father, a traveling wine merchant, always returned home, true to his middle-class standing in the village, carrying books to occupy the boy's time. Since there was little money for school and little energy for play during those formative years, the boy, whose name then was Bonaventure Marcosi, lived much of his life in the pages of histories and French novels, so much so that his peers in the village made jokes about his virility.

When he was fifteen his father died, leaving his mother and sister without support, and young Marcosi took a job on the docks, unloading fishing boats when they returned with the day's catch. To everyone's surprise, including his own, the work seemed to agree with him, and the fishermen joked that the smell of dead fish had returned him to health. In fact it had. By the time he was eighteen he had gained twenty pounds and had begun to spend his Sundays hiking in the mountains with other young men his age.

Now his life seemed set before him. Hard work; someday a marriage and children and continued life along the beautiful rugged shores and in the mountains of his homeland. It was what most had, and he saw no reason why it should not suit him as well. In the evenings there would still be his books and the life he lived within his mind. He had learned from his books that a man should content himself with the boundaries of his prospects, that to do otherwise led to misfortune. He had also learned that a man must live up to his responsibilities. And his were to his mother and his sister. His mother was a simple, strong peasant woman with the bulk of a small ox. His sister, Carmela, was entirely different, however, a delicate beautiful creature, who caused the eyes of young men to risk too long a look as she moved past. She was his closest friend, partly because of his inability to play with other boys as a child, but mostly because of her devotion to him. At night she would sit for hours and listen to everything he had learned from his books that day.

Carmela was sixteen, two years younger than he, on the day she was killed. He had found her body near the edge of the town. She had fought the men who had raped her and had been beaten for her efforts. They had left her there with her skirt still pulled up over her face, the underpants they had ripped from her body still stuffed into her mouth. She had choked on the cloth and they had just let her die. But she had also identified them in dying. Next to the body he had found a French army insignia, ripped from the collar of one of the men, and in the dirt around her were the footprints of at least five.

Two days earlier a squad of five soldiers had camped outside the town. They were the advance unit of an army force that would engage in one of the regular sweeps of Mount Cinto in another vain effort to locate a group of Corsican bandits.

On the evening after his sister's funeral, Marcosi gave his mother all but a few francs of the money he had saved and told her she would leave that night for his uncle's home in the village of L'Ile-Rousse, ten miles to the north. At first his mother objected, knowing what he would do. But one look into those dark, piercing eyes told her she was no longer dealing with a child, and it also told her she would not see him again for many years.

The Frenchmen slept in three tents, snoring deeply from the large amount of wine they had drunk the night before, the sound obscuring the young man's movements as he went from one tent to the other shortly before dawn. It was simple and quick for the first four, a hand over the mouth and a quick slash of the throat severing the jugular vein. In the last tent was the sergeant. Marcosi had gone to that tent first, but when he saw the insignia missing from the sergeant's tunic he had decided to save him for last.

He had knocked the sergeant unconscious as he slept, then tied his hands and feet, spread-eagled, to the four stakes of the tent. When the man regained consciousness he lit the kerosene lantern in the tent. He wanted to see this man, but even more, he wanted the sergeant to see what would happen to him.

Slowly he opened the sergeant's trousers as the man screamed for mercy. Marcosi did not speak. His eyes told the sergeant the reason. He pulled the man's genitals from his trousers as his body bucked violently, fighting to escape. The knife moved in three quick motions and the blood spurted from the severed arteries as he placed the prize on the man's chest. Now he worked even more quickly. The blade of the knife slipped under the socket of one eye and with a quick twist of the wrist the eye popped forward and dangled on a cord against the sergeant's cheek. Within seconds the other eye followed. Marcosi pulled the gray egg-shaped testicles from the severed scrotum and placed one in each empty socket. The sergeant's screams were deafening, turning into a muffled gagging sound as Marcosi forced the severed penis down his throat with the blade of his knife. The sergeant choked to death on his own member before he could lose consciousness from a loss of blood. The man suffered and died just as his sister had.

Marcosi sat staring at the dead man for several minutes, then tore open his tunic and, with his knife, carved a message on his chest, knowing it would be found by the French army unit that would discover the bodies. It was a simple message. *In memory of Carmela Marcosi. Murdered at the hands of French pigs.*

When the Guerini family found him in the mountains a week later, they had already heard of young Marcosi's vengeance. It so impressed Papa Guerini that he adopted the boy at once and told his two sons that from that moment they would consider him a brother. But he was not given the Guerini name, which Papa insisted would be as dangerous as his own for the present. After two weeks of thought, Papa renamed him Buonaparte Sartene. The first name, Papa explained, was owing to his love of history and Corsica's great hero. The second was the name of a village far to the south. The French, he had said, thought all Corsicans were ignorant, and because of that if they discovered his new name, they would look in the area of that village. If he remained in the north he would be safe.

But safety came from another source. Within months, World War I erupted, and for the next three years he lived in the mountains with the Guerinis, relatively safe from Frenchmen occupied with war. Papa Guerini was truly a father to him during that time, teaching him the ways of the mountains and how to earn his bread despite the enslavement by the French. Throughout that period travelers along the coast lived in fear of Guerini raids, and banks in the larger villages repeatedly suffered the indignity of unauthorized withdrawals.

Papa, who never used his given name, Pierre, was a large jovial man with a full black beard and bald head that was constantly covered with a black beret, even when he slept. He carried a thick cane that had been fitted for a sword, and a *lupara*, the short-barreled shotgun common to the mountains.

His sons, Antoine and Barthélemy—known as Mémé—were several years older than Buonaparte, but quickly took him under their wing and taught him all they knew. In exchange, Buonaparte would spend his evenings by the campfire teaching them Corsican history and filling them with his endless stories about Napoleon.

They were still in the mountains when the war ended in 1918. The news was brought to them from Bastia by Papa's favorite niece, a surprisingly self-possessed girl of seventeen whose raven-black hair and soft dark eyes immediately attracted young Sartene. He had seen her before in Bastia, but only briefly. Her name was Maria Guerini and she was the daughter of Papa's only brother, who had been killed by French police when she was only a child. There was a simple peasant beauty about her and a great deal of the mischief that was in Papa. She was more like him, in fact, than were either Antoine or Mémé, who were dour and serious most of the time.

He did not speak to her during the two days she remained with them, except when normal amenities required it. But he watched her almost constantly. Mémé and Antoine noticed and teased him about it in private. He suspected that Papa had noticed as well, although he gave no outward indication. She was just so beautiful Sartene could not help himself. And she was strong and healthy, the way Corsican women were expected to be. Not like the frail, delicate, washed-out women who came to the island for the sun, or to recuperate from some imagined illness. He had seen those women since he was a child and could never understand why men found them attractive, with their small breasts and narrow waists. They could not serve a man as a partner through life, he had decided. They could only be one added burden.

Maria was different. Her dark olive skin was soft and rich and she moved gracefully yet with an undeniable strength. And she was not awed in the presence of men. She kept silent on matters she knew nothing about, but freely told them what she thought, when she felt she did. And her loyalty to Papa reminded him of his own sister. That, and other things as well.

The evening of the day she left he approached Papa as he sat alone before their campfire and, with great nervousness, asked formally for the right to court his niece.

Papa listened to the words solemnly, stroking his bushy beard with one hand. He did not speak for several moments, then looked up at the sky, rotating his head along the horizon. "Funny," he said, "I've not seen any lightning in the past two days. How is it you were struck then?"

Buonaparte stammered helplessly, and Papa burst forth with a roar of laughter, then slapped him on the back so hard he almost tumbled forward into the fire. He reached out and took Buonaparte's face between his hands, pulled him close and kissed him on the forehead. Then he held Buonaparte's face away in his bearlike grasp, and his eyes filled with tears. "Buonaparte, nothing would give me more joy. But are you sure?" he added with a growl.

"Yes, Papa. I'm sure."

"Good," Papa roared. "Then it is done. Later in the week, when we've gotten you some decent clothes and some gifts to bring with you, we'll go to Bastia and I'll speak to Maria's mother."

Papa looked at him for a long time, his eyes still warm, but with an added touch of seriousness. He held his hands in front of his chest, as if in prayer, then shook them up and down.

"But before I do, you must tell me about your future, what you plan for your life. This is an important decision you make, this decision to marry. And it means great responsibility. No longer will you be able to worry just about yourself. There will be a woman, and one day, God willing, there will be children."

Buonaparte's brow knitted; he stared deeply into Papa's face, searching for some clue. "I don't understand?" Papa roared. "Your life, you donkey. What will you do with your life?"

Buonaparte's eyes seemed bewildered. "I planned to stay here," he said. "I planned to work with my family. With you, and Mémé, and Antoine. The French would never let me have any other life."

Papa leaned forward, his eyes coming hard from his bearded face. "And if they would? Would you then choose another life?"

Buonaparte thought for several moments. He stared into the fire, his mind searching out his own feelings. He looked back at Papa, the hint of a smile on his lips. "Yes, I would, Papa. I would like very much to be respectable. I would like very much to do good, honest work, and earn my bread and come home to my family at night, and not worry about the police coming to my door. But here, in Corsica, I have only two choices. To be what I am, or to be a victim of the French. And I don't want to be any man's victim."

Papa sat back and pulled on his beard. He stared at his boots, then back at the young man seated before him. When he spoke his voice was soft. "You have learned much these past years," he said. "And you have spoken a great truth, something that many men never learn their whole lives." He leaned forward and placed his hand gently on Buonaparte's knee. "A man can only be what fate allows him to be. True, there are different paths he can follow, but even those paths are chosen by fate. When I say this, I don't mean that a man can't become rich or powerful or respected because fate won't allow it. Any man can do this if he has the courage. But he must know where to find the path." Papa squeezed Buonaparte's leg and smiled through his ragged beard. "I'm a simple man, and in understanding life, I've always thought of each man being surrounded by a circle. Some men have very big circles, some very small. But within each circle are the paths. It's the man who seeks a path outside his circle who fails." He raised one bearlike hand and let it fall. "For us it is a very small circle. The French have seen to that, and they will continue to see to it. A Corsican who wants to earn his bread with honor will always be so much shit to them, a criminal to be spat upon, to be hated." He paused, bringing one hand up in a massive fist. "But also to be feared and respected." The fist fell away and he smiled again, his head nodding slowly. "And fate will condemn men like that to remain criminals in their eyes. The French and their kind will never understand our need for honor, our need to give more to our families and our friends than they would allow us."

Papa stopped speaking, taking time to look deeply into Buonaparte's face. "Is this, then, the life you choose?"

Buonaparte's lips formed a soft, understanding smile. "Yes, Papa. It's the life I choose. I'll help you make the French regret they made our circle so small."

Papa threw back his head and bellowed like a wild bull. "Good," he shouted. "Fuck the French, then, if they have no sense of humor."

The courtship was an arduous and nerve-racking process for the would-be bride and groom. They were allowed to meet only on Sundays and then only when the family was present, and on those occasions it was not considered proper for them to speak directly to each other. Instead, Maria spoke to her mother, who repeated the words to Buonaparte. He, in turn, followed the

same ritual, using Papa Guerini as his intermediary. After a
month had passed, they were allowed to go for walks and speak
directly to each other, but always within the view and hearing of
relatives who followed closely behind. Touching of any kind was
forbidden.

They were married in January 1919, in the small village of
Cervione, twenty-five miles south of Bastia, at the home of a
friend of the Guerini family. It was a safe village for the Guerinis,
one that would provide adequate warning of movement by the
police. But as usual the police lived in blessed ignorance of the
Guerinis and the wedding feast continued past midnight without
interruption.

During the feast Papa and Antoine became very drunk. It was
a great day for each. Antoine had married a year earlier, but his
wife had been forced to remain in Bastia, because she would
have been left alone and unprotected at their camp when the men
were away on business matters. Now, with Maria there as well,
Antoine could have his wife and the one son she had already
borne him with him at the camp. For Papa it meant the presence
of his grandson, a fact that so pleased him he was drunk by
midafternoon and dancing so wildly that his beret had fallen
unnoticed to the ground.

Buonaparte and Maria left the feast late in the afternoon by
donkey cart for the long, slow journey back to the encampment
on Mount Cinto. When they arrived they found the family had
built them a small thatched hut, like the one used by the men. A
short distance away was a third hut, which would be occupied by
Antoine and his family after the newlyweds had been given
adequate time to learn about each other.

The first night together surprised and pleased Sartene. He had
expected his wife to be frightened, timid, and he came to her
gently as they stood inside the hut.

She pushed him away. "First you go to the cart and get the
sheet I brought for the bed," she said.

He reached out to her again. "The sheet isn't important to
me," he said, misunderstanding her meaning.

"It's important to me," she said, pushing him away again.
"Tomorrow my mother and aunts will come to take the sheet
back to the village. They would be ashamed if a bloodstained
sheet was not given over to be washed."

He smiled at her, embarrassed by his naiveté, and went quickly
to the cart. When he returned she spread the sheet carefully on

the bed, then, keeping her back to him, asked him to help her undress. As the clothing fell away, exposing her smooth olive skin, she turned to him, her eyes fired by passion. This time when he reached for her there was no resistance, only a pressing of their bodies, so uncontrolled it both thrilled and frightened him.

It was an excitement that remained with them in the months to come, and by the following November, one year after they had first met, she delivered a son. But the delivery was cruel, the child much too large, and the doctors in Bastia warned that another birth would certainly mean her death.

From that time on Sartene practiced abstinence, except for the few days of her menstrual period. She had come to mean too much to him, and he knew that his obligation as a man was to protect her and his son above all else.

With the end of the war, black-market goods became the lifeblood of Europe, and the Guerinis changed with the times and made smuggling their primary business activity. Buonaparte, now in his early twenties, quickly became a major part of that effort. His knowledge of the seacoast and of boats overcame a major drawback for the mountain-dwelling Guerini clan, and Papa jokingly dubbed him "admiral" of his navy.

Within a year, business grew beyond all their hopes, and Marseille became the base of the Guerinis' new operation, its rough, violent docks a new training ground for Sartene and his "brothers." Like most Corsicans, the Guerini clan lived in the Corsican ghetto near the docks, a series of narrow streets lined with tenements, each building connecting to the next like an elaborate network of tunnels that thwarted the periodic searches of the police.

"When the hound has a cold, the fox can hide most easily under his nose," Papa had proclaimed, adding that the large noses of the French were "always filled with snot. If their pricks could smell we would be in trouble," he had explained. "It is the only part of his body a Frenchman pays attention to."

And he was proved right. The French never found him. Death found him first.

In 1921, Papa Guerini lay mortally ill and the *three* Guerini brothers gathered at his bedside to receive his final benedictions. Antoine and Mémé were now in their early thirties; Buonaparte was twenty-seven. All three had matured into hard young men, nurtured by the mountains and then seasoned by the cunning and cruelty needed to survive the endless bloodbath that was Marseille.

Lying in his bed, his face a pale gray with the approach of death, Papa Guerini still possessed the impish joviality that had always filled his eyes. His now gray beard lay on his chest outside the covers and his black beret was fixed firmly on the top of his bald head. Next to the bed, leaning against a nightstand, the sword cane and *lupara* were within easy reach.

Standing there, Sartene looked down at the weapons, then back at the old man he had learned to love like a father. Papa caught the movement of his eyes and smiled weakly through his beard.

"Just in case the police beat the devil to my door," he whispered.

"Maybe St. Pierre, your namesake, will come instead, Papa," Sartene argued.

Guerini's eyes flashed with mirth. "You think so, Buonaparte? Then I will still need them. God will pay a heavy ransom to get that rascal back."

His laughter ended in a wheezing cough, but he motioned them away as they moved closer to him to help. After several minutes the wheezing subsided and his face became serious.

"Tomorrow morning you will take me back to the mountains of Corsica and put me in the ground," he said. "Now I just want you to listen." He was breathing in shallow gasps, and the strain of his words showed in his eyes. "We've had a good life in the mountains and here in Marseille," he said weakly. "We didn't get rich, but we didn't live under the heel of anybody's boot. But things are different now. The days of the bandit are gone. Now everything is done by bigger and bigger organizations, like this one Paul Carbone has here." A coughing spasm rocked his body, then stopped abruptly, almost as though the dying man had willed it. He cleared his throat and looked at each of them. "You have a wife now and two children, Antoine. And you too, Buonaparte, have a son. If you're men, you must work the rest of your lives for them, not for yourselves. Mémé, when you marry, it will be the same, and you should start to plan for that now."

"How, Papa?" Antoine's voice was choked and his eyes were brimming with tears.

A faint smile crossed Papa's lips. "I spoke to this man, François Spirito, who works for Carbone. He's agreed that you can each work in his group." He saw displeasure flash across Mémé's face and waved his hand at him for patience. "It will be a good thing for now," he said. "But don't do it too long. Just until you learn, however long that takes. When you've learned and have money, then you should start your own group. Never trust these Marseille Corsicans. They're more French than anything else. But use them now." Another coughing spasm seized him, but he fought it off as he had the last. "And while you work for them, make money of your own. This thing now they have in America, this law that says a man can't drink. There's money in this thing. If you take wine and cognac from the French, these thirsty Americans will make you rich men." He jabbed a finger at Sartene. "Listen to my admiral. He'll know how to get it there." He smiled. "You're Antonio's admiral now, Buonaparte. He's the head of our family now. You and Mémé must help him, as good brothers should."

Papa Guerini was true to his prediction, and the following day they began the long journey back to Corsica to bury him in the foothills of Mount Cinto. He was buried still wearing his beret, with his sword cane and his *lupara* lying next to him in his coffin. For the first time in many years, Buonaparte Sartene wept.

The work for Spirito was difficult, often degrading. Papa had been right—these Marseille Corsicans were much like the French. They looked upon the Guerinis as simple bandits, ignorant peasants from the hills, who should be used only for the simplest of tasks. Antoine was assigned the duties of an enforcer, dispensing violence to those who resisted the black-market and smuggling activities of the *milieu*. Mémé and Buonaparte were assigned to hijacking and the menial distribution of stolen goods. To Antoine and Mémé it was an insult, both to themselves and to the memory of their father. Only Buonaparte accepted it with pleasure, knowing the best way to learn a thing was at its roots.

He explained his reasoning to his brothers one Sunday afternoon, when the wives had taken the children out into the streets after the family meal was finished. The three men sat at the large kitchen table drinking wine, Antoine and Mémé expressing their anger over the two years they had worked for Spirito with no sign they would ever be given more authority within the *milieu*.

"You forget Papa's words," Sartene said softly. "We are dealing with Frenchmen who call themselves Corsicans. Now we only have to learn how they do what they do, and earn enough money to do it for ourselves someday." He gestured broadly with his hands. "Last year we made thousands of francs in our dealings with the Americans. This year we'll sell even more liquor to them, and the year after that even more. Spirito knows of our business and he knows it's our right as long as we do our duty to him. What he doesn't know is how much money we're making. We still live poorly and he thinks we're peasants. He has no idea we save this money for our future." He smiled at Antoine, whose burly, flat face was red with wine and anger. "Papa once told me that when the hound has a cold, the fox hides best right under his nose."

"But how long do we have to hide?" Mémé growled. He was smaller than Antoine, with a craggy face and fast-receding hairline that made him look more like a store clerk than the truly violent man he was.

Sartene shrugged. "What's time, Mémé? Each day my stomach tells me the time. Breakfast. Dinner. For more complicated things, my brain tells me."

"My brain tells me we should strike out on our own now," Antoine snapped. He stood and began pacing the small kitchen, his movements and bulk seeming very much like Papa's at that moment.

"We could do that," Sartene said. "And if you, my brothers, decide, I'll be with you." He waited, watching the words calm Antoine.

Mémé, to whom he was much closer, watched him intensely, knowing more was yet to come.

"If we do this, Spirito will cut us off from his protection with the police and the politicians. Right now we don't have the money to buy our own, so anything we do will be small. If we wait until we have the money, we don't have to worry about that. If Spirito wants to stop us then, he'll have to use force, and that would violate all the principles of the *milieu*. Right now, we're like the ten-year-old boy who picks up the gun and seeks vengeance for his father's death. What he does is right. But if he waits until he is grown, remembering all the time what he must do, then his vengeance is more certain."

"Buonaparte is right," Mémé said. He stood and walked to his older, larger brother and placed a hand on his shoulder. "I don't like it either, but he's right."

"But how long?" Antoine asked, staring angrily at Sartene.

"How long do we swallow our pride for these *Frenchmen?*" He used the final word as an ultimate insult.

"How long is long?" Sartene asked, smiling. "If I said one year, that would seem too long. If I said ten, that would also seem too long. Last week I read in the papers about an Irish writer named Joyce. He spent seven years writing a book. The paper said the book was very difficult to understand and that this writer says people who read it should spend seven years doing so."

"So he's crazy, like all writers of books," Antoine said.

"Maybe so," Sartene said. He looked at Mémé. "Your new wife is pregnant," he said. "When the child is born, will we expect him to walk the very next day?"

Mémé began to laugh. He looked up at his older brother. "How do we fight our little admiral?" he said. "He always makes too much sense."

Antoine shook his head and lumbered back to his seat, sat heavily and cradled his face in both hands. "I know you're right, Buonaparte. In my heart I know it. It's just that these fucking *Frenchmen* make me so damned mad."

The question of "how long" in fact did become ten years. It was 1933 before the Guerinis broke from the Spirito faction of the Carbone *milieu*. Even then it was a year or two earlier than Sartene would have preferred. But prohibition had been repealed in the United States, drying up their outside revenue, and to wait longer, they had decided, would be of little practical value.

The decision to break away caused initial difficulties with Spirito. At first he simply withdrew his protection, as they had expected. But when he realized they had bought their own with hidden resources, he became angry and sent men against their business interests.

The Guerinis reacted calmly. Spirito's men simply disappeared. This was Sartene's doing. Antoine had been in favor of open warfare. Buonaparte, with Mémé's support, argued that scattering the landscape with corpses would only bring the police to everyone's door. So the violence was handled quietly, and within a year it had not only brought Spirito to his senses, but had also brought many men into the newly formed Guerini faction.

But the *silent war*, as it came to be known within the Corsican community, also produced personal hardships for Sartene and his brothers. As a simple matter of protection, they had sent their wives and children back to the quiet, protected village of Cervione. This was especially hard for Antoine and Buonaparte, whose sons were sixteen and fourteen, respectively, ages when they should be at their fathers' sides, learning valuable lessons for the future.

For Buonaparte it also meant a bitter separation from Maria, and despite his frequent trips to Corsica, it made him even more reclusive than he was by nature.

The years that followed were prosperous for the Guerinis and for Sartene. Antoine and Mémé became known as men of power within the Corsican community and began to assume the life-styles that went with that power. Buonaparte, by comparison, shunned any recognition, preferring to live and work quietly, so much so that his brothers had jokingly dubbed him "the monk."

The coming of World War II brought an end to prosperity for the Guerinis and other factions within the *milieu*. In the years to come it would devastate their resources, which would not be reclaimed until the postwar period. It also brought imprisonment for Buonaparte Sartene, when he was caught late in 1939 running guns to Corsica, which he believed would soon fall victim to an Italian invasion. The French, however, believing all Corsicans would always side with anti-French forces, dealt with the matter harshly. After a perfunctory trial, the following spring he was sentenced to seven years in the prison at Marseille.

Maria Sartene entered the small, cramped, sterile room with her chin high, seemingly unaffected by the humiliating search to which she had just been subjected. She was thirty-eight now, with touches of gray in her deep-black hair, but she moved with the same strength and grace that had first attracted Buonaparte in the mountains of Corsica twenty-one years earlier.

Buonaparte had been allowed one request before beginning his sentence, and had asked for time alone with his wife. He had not asked to see his son, Jean, who was now twenty. The less the French knew about him the better, he had decided. Now, watching his wife enter the room, he was filled with pride. They can kick us, he told himself, but they can never make us weep.

The room was on the first floor of the old prison, and the walls were made of stone and it was cold. Maria moved quickly to him, and he could feel her trembling slightly as they embraced.

"Are you cold?" he whispered, still holding her.

"No," she answered. She stepped back, her hands resting on

his chest. "Seven years," she said. Her eyes became suddenly fierce. "The bastards."

He guided her to a long wooden bench against one wall, then sat next to her, holding both of her hands in his.

"The suffering doesn't bother me," he said softly. "I can deal with it as it comes. And I know you will be cared for by Mémé and Antoine. What bothers me is this damned war that's racing down on us." He looked at her firmly. "I don't want Jean involved in this. I don't want him to be used by the French. They spit on us until they need us to bleed for them. Then, when we're through bleeding, they spit on us again. I don't mind their spit. To men like that we're criminals, and always will be. Fate has condemned us to that. But I will not let my family be used by these bastards."

"If there's fighting, Jean will want to fight." There was no resistance in Maria's voice. It was purely an observation about her son.

"He can fight with Corsicans if the island is invaded. But you tell him I said he must not let them take him into their army and use him like so much garbage." He squeezed her hands. "There are business matters that will have to be looked after while I'm in this place. Let him do some of these things. But guide him. He doesn't have your wisdom." He released her hands so he could make a circular gesture with his own. "Let him think he's making these decisions by himself. But point him in the right direction. Counsel him. Right now he's so busy with this young Frenchwoman he wants to marry, he won't even notice." His voice had taken on a tone of distaste as he mentioned the woman.

"She's a good woman, Buonaparte," Maria said.

"Yes, but she's not strong. A strong man needs a strong woman. Only weak men need the other kind, so they can have someone to dominate."

"What would you know about it?" she said. "You married the first peasant girl you saw in the mountains." There was a slight smile on her face. "A little movement here, a little movement there, and you were like some poor goat, being led to slaughter."

"But I was lucky. At least you knew how to cook," he snapped.

"Cook!" She snorted. "In those first years I could have fed you sheep droppings and you wouldn't have known the difference."

He laughed softly, then leaned to her and kissed her forehead, allowing his hand to run gently along her cheek. "The time will pass," he whispered. "Then there will be many years together."

"Who knows?" she said. "Maybe the Germans will come and set you free."

"All that will mean is that our faces will be washed by German spit instead of French spit," he said. He gripped her hands again. "This is why you must keep close watch on business matters. We will need money when this war is over. I want a new life for all of us then, and I have plans for it. But you must be careful of the police. They'll be watching you."

"The police always watch, but they never see anything," Maria said. She stroked his cheek. "Don't worry, my Buonaparte. Everything will be cared for." She smiled. "Don't forget, I also learned at Papa's knee."

Chapter 6

VIET NAM, OCTOBER 1946

Matthew Bently ran one hand along his close-cropped, military-styled hair. He looked about his sparsely furnished office, which was located at the ground-floor rear of the same building that housed the International Restaurant and Bar, one of colonial Saigon's favorite watering holes. The street door to the small office identified it as Tiger Export Ltd., one of the many fronts being used by the OSS during its ongoing transition into the new Central Intelligence Agency. Inside the office he could still smell the heavy cologne that had surrounded Benito Pavlovi as he sat before his desk a few minutes before. So this is how it would be now, he thought. The same shady deals in peacetime that had existed during the war. He glanced at the stainless-steel Rolex on his wrist, noting that he had an hour before he met Pavlovi in the bar upstairs to confirm the meeting requested by this man Sartene. He reached out and pressed a button on the square wooden intercom on his desk. A gravelly voice responded with a terse "Yes, sir."

"Mike, get me Charlie Metcalf at the embassy," he said. He released the button without waiting for a response, then pushed himself up from the small, square military desk. Big covert export company, he thought. They paint a sign on the door and then furnish the damned place with GI-issue furniture. He walked to the window and stared out into the narrow street that ran along the west side of the building. Except for the door to the office, the entire ground floor of the building was filled with open-air shops, selling everything from seafood to clothing to jewelry, and each, as he well knew, had a back room where the more desirable black-market goods were proffered.

The buzzer on the intercom snapped him back, and he returned to the desk and pressed the button.

"Mr. Metcalf is on the line, sir," the gravelly voice announced.

"Thanks, Mike," he said, releasing the button and picking up the telephone receiver. "Hi, Charlie. How are things in the world of the living?" he said.

"You call this living?" a thick voice came back.

They had been out together the night before, and the severe hangover Metcalf was now certainly suffering hung in his voice.

"I've heard back from our friend in Vientiane," he said, following the procedure of not using names over telephone lines they all knew the Vietnamese monitored. "He thinks he can handle our order, but wants to meet again there to iron things out."

"So?" Metcalf groaned.

"There's one hitch. Seems he's done business with us before, so he wants someone higher up along who can agree on terms. Just so the game isn't changed halfway through."

Metcalf grunted. "I wish I could get that for myself," he said.

"So what do I tell him? He wants to meet in two days at his place."

"Tell him yes," Metcalf said. "I'll talk to the boss and find out who we can send along and get back to you in ten minutes. You'll be going, right?"

"Right."

"Okay, talk to you in ten."

Matt replaced the receiver and remained standing by the desk. A few inches from the telephone was the letter he had received from his father two days before. The South Dakota return address on the envelope still gave him a sense of warmth, even if the contents of the letter had not.

His father was pressuring him to return, to "take up his role," as he had put it, in their Pierre banking concern. A nice office overlooking the wide, murky Missouri River, he mused. Listening to the endless arguments that the Missouri was the true course of the Mississippi and if it had been so mapped, it would be the longest river in the world. As if anybody really gave a damn.

He had written back, tried to explain how he wanted to see the OSS through its transition. To make sure the nation had a decent intelligence system, never to be caught unprepared again as it had been in 1941. The argument sounded good to him, but he couldn't help wondering what his strait-laced father would think if he knew his son's major task at the moment was setting up an opium network. For the benefit of God and country and a few million addicts.

He walked back to the window and looked out into the narrow, filth-strewn street. To his left a large black hearse drawn by a black ox came into view. As it passed, the windows on its sides revealed a flower-covered casket within. Behind the hearse, Vietnamese mourners, dressed in the traditional flowing white funeral garments, walked with eyes lowered. Right on cue, he thought. Divine fucking prophecy. Just what the hell I needed.

The door to his office opened and a skinny, hawk-faced man entered and dropped a handful of papers on his desk. "Mr. Metcalf is on the phone again, colonel," he said.

"Mike. How many times do I have to tell you we don't use rank? I'm just a nice American businessman, peddling Vietnamese goods."

Mike nodded. "Right, sir." He pointed to the papers he had just placed on the desk. "Those are the bills of lading for some of the shit we just bought."

Bently shook his head. "Get out of here, Mike," he said.

As the door closed behind Mike, Bently picked up the receiver and glanced at his Rolex. "You're a man of your word, Charlie. Ten minutes on the dot."

"I hope you like the rest of the conversation, boyo," Charlie said. His voice sounded as though his hangover had intensified.

Bently felt a tightening in his stomach. "Go ahead, Charlie. Tell me how you're gonna fuck me this time."

Charlie cackled through his obvious pain. "The man upstairs has informed me that Malcolm Wainwright Baker, Yale, class of 1920, and our distinguished first counsel, will accompany you to Vientiane." There was a long silence. "Are you there, my good man?" Charlie said, doing his best imitation of Baker.

"That's wonderful, Charlie. The biggest asshole presently in the far east and you manage to get him just for me."

"Always try to please, old man."

"Fine. You tell Lord Ha Ha that our friend has a private airstrip at a new house he's building outside Vientiane and that we're going to meet there. It can handle small aircraft, so if he can arrange for one, we'll leave day after tomorrow at nine A.M. and have him back in time for tea."

Metcalf made a scolding sound. "You know his lordship hates to fly."

"Fuck him. The man we're seeing wants us to come and go unnoticed. So unless his lordship wants to go incognito, wearing a dress, we'll have to oblige our Corsican friend."

"He might like that idea, actually," Metcalf said.

"Just tell him not to wear his fucking Yale Club tie, Charlie. It's going to be hard enough to pass him off as it is." He replaced the receiver with the sound of Metcalf's laughter still flowing across the line. "Malcolm Wainwright Baker," he said aloud. "Wonderful."

Forty-five minutes later he slid into a booth in the International Bar, across from Benito Pavlovi. The heavyset man was smiling at him, and he couldn't help wondering if he would still be smiling when he met Baker.

"All set," Bently said. "Our first counsel, Malcolm Baker, will be coming along."

Benito nodded and began to look casually around the bar.

"Nice place, isn't it?" Bently said.

"Yes. I always liked it," Benito answered.

"Oh. You've been here before."

Benito nodded. "I was here with Buonaparte when he bought it last year."

Bently stared across the table. "Sartene owns this place?"

Benito nodded again. "He owns the whole building. You might say he's your landlord."

Bently laughed. "We're a great intelligence agency. I was told some Paris consortium owned it."

"Buonaparte does business under many names," Benito said. "The only name he never uses is his own."

Chapter 7

The World War II surplus jeep bounced down the narrow dirt road that led from the airstrip to the house. With each rut Malcolm Baker groaned and threw angry glances at the stone-faced Lao driver, who he was certain was making the short drive as unpleasant as possible. From the rear of the jeep Benito and Bently observed Baker's performance: Benito with amusement, Bently with disgust. Throughout the flight, Baker had moaned his displeasure. Halfway through it, his normally tanned patrician face had taken on a gray tint that matched his neatly trimmed hair. It was only now beginning to return to its normal color.

And the silly bastard *was* wearing his Yale Club tie, Bently thought, realizing for the hundredth time that day how much he'd like to strangle him with it.

"We are almost there," Benito said to the back of Baker's head.

"Thank God," Baker sighed as he was tossed to the side by another jolt.

Benito smiled. "I'm afraid Mr. Baker is not used to the jungle. You weren't in the war, Mr. Baker?"

Baker twisted in his seat but did not turn to face Benito, speaking instead into the side of the driver's head. "I was in the diplomatic service during the last war," he said. "During the Great War I was at university."

Bently rolled his eyes. *At university,* he thought. Now the asshole was even playing the anglophile. He looked at Benito and shrugged helplessly, hoping it would disassociate him from the fool. Benito smiled reassuringly.

95

The jeep entered a sharp turn that almost threw Baker from his seat, then broke suddenly out of the cover of the forest and into a broad plain where the already oppressive heat immediately intensified. Bently and Benito had earlier removed their jackets and loosened their neckties. Only Baker had remained fully clothed, in a lightweight blue pinstripe that now looked as though he had showered in it.

"Is that the house?" Baker called back, pointing to the massive white structure two hundred yards distant.

"That's it," Bently snapped.

The jeep groaned to a halt a few feet from the Japanese garden. Within a large cut in the earth at the garden's center, Lao workmen were spreading a layer of clay.

"Come up to the veranda where it's cool," Benito said. "I will go and find Buonaparte."

Baker watched Benito move heavily up the stairs and disappear into the house. As Bently moved past him, he reached out and took his arm. "What in heaven's name is that?" he asked, indicating the garden with his chin.

"I'm told it will be a Japanese garden," Bently said.

"And the hole?" Baker asked with a slight smirk.

"A pond, I imagine."

Baker smiled indulgently. "Fits in with the house. A bit pretentious, this Corsican, eh?"

Bently's eyes hardened. "I think you'll find Buonaparte Sartene to be many things, Malcolm. But I don't think pretentious will be one of them." He motioned with his eyes toward their driver, who was still seated in the jeep. "I also understand that many of the people here are bilingual, Malcolm."

Baker pursed his lips. "I hadn't realized," he said. "But a word to the wise."

They climbed the stairs to the veranda, Bently fighting to control his anger, Baker looking over his surroundings with a sense of aloof superiority.

Twenty feet down the veranda, behind a bay window, Sartene and Benito looked out at the two men. They stood well back from the window, out of view, Sartene studying the man he had not seen before.

"What do you think of this man Baker?" he asked Benito.

"A pompous little clerk, who thinks quite highly of himself," Benito said. "But still a clerk."

Sartene nodded. "And Bently?"

"I like him," Benito said.

"Do you trust him?"

"I'm like you, Buonaparte. I trust no one who hasn't proved himself."

Sartene nodded again. "Let's talk to this clerk. We'll see if his brain matches his look."

They were seated in deck chairs around a low table at the corner of the veranda that offered a slight breeze off the river. The introductions had been formal and stiff, and as refreshments were served by a Lao servant, Sartene noted that Bently seemed uncomfortable.

Baker dominated the conversation, praising the house and its location and inquiring into Sartene's plans to grow rubber in the surrounding jungle. As he spoke, Sartene noticed that his lips remained pursed, barely moving to form the words. It was an affectation he had observed among so-called British aristocrats, one that had made him dislike them immediately.

And Baker fit the mold perfectly, he thought. High cheekbones, patrician nose, a touch of arrogance in his blue eyes. He was tall and slender, in his late forties, and his suit was of good quality, even though it was rumpled now by the heat of midday. At least we know he sweats, Sartene thought, recalling the great pains the British upper classes took to avoid revealing that human function. The jaw was neither weak nor strong. But the mouth was pure weakness. And as he knew, only weak, uncertain men required affectations.

Sartene leaned forward in his chair, clasping his hands in front of him. His eyes were as hard as their color. "I appreciate your compliments to my home, and my land and my agricultural plans," he said. "But before we discuss those things further I'd like to talk about our business together."

The abrupt dismissal of his ivy-league niceties threw Baker off stride. "Certainly," he said, offering a weak smile and fondling his club tie. "Actually," he went on, "I'm really just here to affirm Matt's previous conversation with you." He nodded toward Bently as if indicating he would continue from there. Bently remained silent.

"What do you know about these people, the Meo, that might help us do what you ask?" Sartene's eyes had remained on Baker, hard and unrelenting; his voice, in contrast, was soft and even.

Baker continued to fondle his tie. It was dark blue with a

pattern of white "Y's." "Well, they're a bit primitive," Baker said, uncertain of his ground. "What we really want to do is make them see they're better off doing business with our friends, rather than the other side. We thought we'd leave the methods up to you, actually."

Sartene sat back in his chair, still staring at the American diplomat. "Methods vary, just as people do," he said.

Baker extended his hands, palms up, at his sides and smiled.

Bently drew a deep breath. "I think my office can give you some help in that area, although I can't guarantee the complete accuracy of our information," Bently said. "A good deal of it comes from French intelligence gathered prior to the war."

Sartene placed the fingers of one hand against his mouth, then tipped the fingers toward Bently, indicating he would listen to whatever he knew.

"Baker's right to a certain degree," Bently began. "The Meo are primitive by our standards. But at the same time they have a strong sense of their own history and customs, and their sense of loyalty to others only lasts as long as they see advantage in it. The tribes are divided into what they call 'little kingdoms,' each with their own aristocracy and hereditary leaders, whom they call 'little kings.' "

"The kaitongs," Sartene said.

Bently suppressed a smile, knowing now that he was offering Sartene no new information. He was merely being allowed to compare knowledge. Being tested, really. "Precisely," he said.

A gust of hot wind came off the river and cut across the veranda. Behind Sartene an eight-foot khoai-sap plant swayed wildly at the edge of the Japanese garden, its massive leaves, shaped like elephant ears, banging together in dull slaps.

Sartene watched Bently's eyes narrow and move with the sound. Baker appeared to hear nothing.

"There are two major clans, each with their own kaitong, at present," Bently said, returning his attention to their host. "The Ly clan, now headed by Touby Lyfoung, and the Lo clan, which has Lo Faydang as its little king. Faydang is actually Touby's uncle, but the two clans, though never waging war on each other, have been enemies since the early twenties. Faydang's older sister, May, married Touby's father, Ly Foung. He was considered a brilliant man by Meo standards. Quite powerful and quite ruthless. Apparently that ruthlessness involved his wife as well. Four years into their marriage, after giving birth to two sons, she committed suicide by eating a fatal amount of opium. Her father, Lo Bliayao, who was then kaitong of the Lo clan, immediately banned the Lys from his territory. It's a rift that's never been mended, even though all those directly involved are long dead.''

Sartene nodded. ''Vendettas last a long time among some peoples,'' he said. ''What about the present?''

Bently drew a deep breath. ''That's where it gets a bit fuzzy. It involves certain diplomatic decisions made by the French, and as you know, diplomats often justify their mistakes with one-sided information.''

Sartene watched Baker twist uncomfortably in his seat, but just nodded for Bently to continue.

The hot breeze crossed the veranda again, hitting Bently like a sauna. He took a handkerchief from his pocket and mopped his forehead.

''Lo Bliayao died in 1935, and in the four succeeding years before Ly Foung's death, the Ly clan virtually pushed the Los into obscurity. It was supposed to have something to do with better management of local tax collection for the French, but I suspect it was more likely a better payoff on opium protection.''

Again Baker twisted uncomfortably in his seat, this time throwing a harsh glance at Bently.

Bently either didn't notice or didn't care, Sartene observed. ''I'm familiar with the corruptibility of the French,'' he said.

Bently returned the comment with a slight grin. ''In any event, Ly Foung was made chief of the Keng Khoai district for the French, a job traditionally held by the kaitong of the Lo clan. It's a position that carries a great deal of power among the Meo, as long as the person holding it is strong enough to enforce his will.

''After Ly Foung got the job, Lo Bliayao's younger son, Lo Faydang, took control of the clan from an inept older brother, and immediately sought out and got the support of a very important Lao aristocrat, Prince Phetsarath. The prince then interceded on behalf of Faydang with the French, other Lao aristocrats and Ly Foung, and reached a rather clever agreement that when Ly Foung died or became incapacitated, Faydang would take over as district chief of Keng Khoai.''

Bently mopped his face again, then leaned forward as if ready to impart some secret. ''The French went back on their word, of course, when Ly Foung died in 1939, and gave the post to

Touby. Both Touby and Faydang had been prepared to present themselves to an assembly of Keng Khoai village headmen for election to the job—a mere formality, really. But the French suddenly announced that Faydang was barred from the election, without giving any explanation."

"What were the reasons?" Sartene asked.

Bently smiled, sure that Sartene already knew the answer. "We believe the French decided they wanted someone of proven loyalty who would guarantee the opium harvest to them and keep the amount diverted to smugglers at a minimum. Faydang, it seems, has strong ties with the Lao nationalist movement, the Pathet Lao. He was actually pushed into their hands by the French. And so was Prince Phetsarath. The French believed they would divert much of the opium to the communists who run the movement. Personally, I think Faydang could have been brought back into the fold if he hadn't been stabbed in the back that way. But that's really moot. There's no question he's vying with Touby for control of opium in the region now, and will divert everything he can get to the Pathet Lao. And he's very strong among the hill people of the region."

Sartene stared silently toward the river for several moments, then nodded to himself. "To what degree can the French be expected to satisfy our needs in taking care of this problem?" he asked at length.

"Completely," Baker said, his voice exuding confidence.

Bently glanced at him, then lowered his eyes. "We feel we can pressure them and keep pressuring them to live up to any commitments given. But we also understand that you too have influence there that would have to be applied as well. They're up to their asses right now, trying to keep the Pathet Lao in line, and they're spread pretty thin in doing it. I think they'd welcome any help in resolving this problem. As far as their keeping their word afterward, I think we'd both have to keep the pressure on to ensure that."

Sartene studied Bently's eyes closely. He was pleased with his honesty, and the answer to his question did not surprise him. He had already been aware of the realities of the situation

"I think I can find a way to ensure that," he said. "But I have one more concern." He waited, allowing the curiosity of both men to peak. "When the French are driven out there will be a void here that your government will undoubtedly be forced to fill, unless the area is to be surrendered, in which case everything becomes academic. I believe your government will find it impossible to abandon the region, because of your past problems in the Pacific. What I want is your guarantee that when that happens, *you* will live up to our arrangement.''

Baker blustered forth immediately. ''I assure you,'' he said, ''the French have no intention of giving up Southeast Asia.''

Sartene looked at him coldly. ''I'm sure they don't,'' he said. ''But it will happen anyway, and I *will* require those assurances.''

''Monsieur Sartene,'' Baker said, offering his most indulgent smile, ''the French forces here are quite capable of keeping this rabble in line. General de Gaulle certainly has no intention—''

''Monsieur Baker. The French have not been able to accomplish anything militarily in many years.'' Sartene had cut him short, both with his words and a piercing, almost malevolent stare. ''General de Gaulle is a man who ran a make-believe army from the safety of Great Britain during the last war. He is a politician who makes political decisions, not military ones. So please don't tell me about his intentions. Either you give this assurance to me, along with Colonel Bently's later confirmation that documents stating the fact have been filed with your government, or we can end our discussion now.''

''You have it,'' Bently said. He turned to Baker. ''Malcolm?''

Baker stuttered, then caught hold of himself. ''Well, of course. If that's what you require. I see no problem.''

''Good,'' Sartene said, pausing and looking both men in the eyes. ''I assure you, gentlemen, I have the ability to know if those documents exist or not.''

Bently smiled. ''I don't doubt it one bit, sir.''

Sartene stood abruptly and smiled coldly at Baker, gesturing, as he did, toward Benito. ''Since you have such great interest in my house and my agricultural plans,'' he said, ''Benito will give you a tour of what we are doing here, while Colonel Bently and I discuss details of this matter with my son, Jean.''

Baker rose, confused. ''Well, thank you, I, uh . . .''

''Don't thank me at all,'' Sartene said. ''It's my pleasure.''

He turned abruptly and walked into the house with Bently behind him. As they entered the hall that led to the front of the house, Sartene glanced at Bently and smiled. ''I thought a nice walk in the jungle would be good for him,'' he said.

Bently stifled his laughter. ''He'll love it, sir,'' he said.

They returned to the veranda through the front door, on the opposite side of the house. There Jean waited with Auguste, his hard flat features and muscular frame a sharp contrast to the older man's almost frail body and cagy eyes. The comparison struck Bently immediately, and he wondered if their ways of conducting *business*, this business, would be equally different.

Introductions not being necessary, Sartene simply gestured to his son and explained that he, with the help and guidance of Auguste, would deal with the problem of the Meo.

They took chairs, arranged in a semicircle on the veranda, Sartene flanked by his son and Auguste, Bently to Jean's right.

Sartene's face was solemn, almost as though he questioned the wisdom of what he was about to say. Auguste noticed his change in demeanor and wondered if it was due to his lingering doubts about the opium business they were about to enter. He saw that Bently appeared to notice as well.

"We will take three steps at first," Sartene said to Bently. "Each is needed to take a firm grasp on the situation, and in each, to a small degree, we're going to need your assistance."

Bently nodded but remained silent. Sartene opened his hands and held them at his sides, palms up, in an almost saintly gesture.

"First we have this prince, this Phetsarath. I understand he lives in his ancestral home in the Lao royal capital of Luang Prabang, and that the house, like the one I'm building here, is on the banks of the Mekong River."

"That's true," Bently said.

"I will need to know if he is there now, and how many men he has guarding him."

"Our information is that he's always there this time of year and usually has between twelve and fifteen men, including servants, at the house. But I can reconfirm that within twenty-four hours and keep a running surveillance on the house."

"Good," Sartene said. He rested his elbows on the arms of the chair and steepled his fingers in front of his lips, gesturing with them by moving his wrists as he spoke. "The second thing I'll need is a commission in the colonial French army for Touby Lyfoung, and I'll need you to present it to him. He's an egotistical man, and I think since you are a colonel, we should make him a colonel as well. Within the next two weeks my son will visit him, and I would like you to go with him when he does so. While you're there an action will also be taken against this man Faydang, and while you won't have to be personally involved in that, I'd like you to be present in the area when it happens."

Bently turned uncomfortably in his chair and began stroking his chin absentmindedly, something he did only when worried. "Monsieur Sartene."

Sartene raised his hand, stopping him. "Please call me Buonaparte. I like informality with people who have close business dealings with me."

"Buonaparte," Bently began again, still nervous. "I'm going to have to know a little more detail about this. I'm going to be asked about it, and while I assure you I'll give out only limited information, I have to be able to cover my own butt."

"I understand," Sartene said, pleased again with the man's honesty. "What I plan is very simple, yet very forceful, and will involve the smallest amount of violence possible." He smiled at Bently. "No matter what you've heard, I'm not a bloodthirsty man. But I'm also a man who knows that force is respected by forceful people." He extended his hands to his sides again in that saintly gesture. "What I'll do is very simple. First, a force of my Laotians, led by one of my fellow Corsicans, will attack the home of this Phetsarath. He will not be killed. He'll be allowed to escape. And being a sensible man, seeing an attack by Laotians, led by a European, I think he will do the wise thing and leave the country. His ancestral home will then be destroyed as a warning not to come back." Sartene shrugged his shoulders. "It's unfortunate, but necessary, since Faydang's power in this country comes largely from this man.

"Next, one of his men will be captured and given a message to take to Faydang. It will be a simple message, suggesting he also leave Laos. Now, the royal capital is about one hundred twenty miles from the Meo country, and the roads there are difficult. So it should take about five days for the message to be received. We will give a week to be sure. Then my son and you will visit Touby Lyfoung, along with the men who raided the prince's home. Touby will be given his commission, provided an agreement is reached with us, and the following day Faydang's village will be attacked by Lyfoung's men, along with those led by my son."

"Don't you think Faydang will be forewarned and ready for just such an attack?" Bently asked.

"Of course he will," Sartene said. "If he's as clever as I believe he is, he'll have spies in Touby's inner circle. He'll then know of Touby's commission, which will imply French backing for what is happening. And he'll know that you're there, and will assume there is American backing as well. He'll also know of the prince and of the very similar force in Touby's village."

"And so he'll protect himself against attack?" Bently asked.

Sartene nodded. "But he doesn't have the men available to meet that type of attack with force. That I already know. So he'll hide and wait to see what happens. And then, being sensible, he'll leave and hope to be able to regroup and come back. I don't want to kill this man Faydang, or this prince. They believe in what they're doing, and they only fight to get what they think is theirs."

"And if they come back?" Bently asked.

Sartene shrugged again. "Then we have no choice."

Bently leaned forward in his chair. The manner in which Sartene talked about general mayhem was chilling, but he could not help admiring how the man's mind worked, and his somewhat warped—at least to Bently—sense of morality.

"It's very clever," he said at length. "The prince and Faydang running with Touby and his supporters at their heels; the military commission; the appearance of an outside force—all of it should make Touby very powerful among his people. And he'll owe that power to you."

Sartene smiled for the first time since they had begun talking. "And he'll know that power will continue only as long as he follows our arrangement."

Bently sat back in his chair, shaking his head. "I have no problem with it," he said. "I only wish I'd thought of it." He paused a moment, his eye catching the movement of two figures walking toward the river. One was a child, small and active. The other was a woman, and although he could not make out her features, the grace with which she moved convinced him she must be quite beautiful. He brought himself quickly back. "Outside of being there and handing over the commission, what role would you like me to play?" he asked.

Sartene too had noticed the movement toward the river and took time to watch his grandson run wildly ahead of his mother. He was concerned the dog was not with him, as it should be. "A very minor one," he said, looking back at Bently. "I would like you to show a certain respect for my son and an interest in the arrangement they're seeking. A quiet show of support, nothing more. Any part you want to take in the attack against Faydang is up to you."

"Will Jean also lead the attack on the prince's home?"

Sartene shook his head. "Francesco, whom you've met, will do that. It will be very fast, hit-and-run as you Americans like to say, and Francesco's training as a partisan is well suited for that." Sartene did not look at his son. He also avoided mentioning his own belief that involving Francesco to some degree was needed to avoid future problems.

Bently noticed Jean's jaws tighten almost imperceptibly as his father spoke of Francesco. There's a rift, he thought. Maybe a serious one. "You'll need transport for your men?" Bently asked Sartene.

"Only to the Meo country. There's a landing strip at Phong Savan on the Plain of Jars. Lyfoung's village of Lat Houang is in the valley below. He can provide the transportation to Faydang's village. We have to let him do something," Sartene said.

"Do you think it would be better to have a French official deliver the commission? It might seem more authentic."

"No," Sartene said. "I don't want to involve the French any more than necessary. Besides, the Meo aren't stupid. They recognize real power and they know the French have none."

"All I'll need to know is the date, then," Bently said.

"As soon as you confirm the information about the prince, I can give you that."

Sartene's eyes flashed back toward the river, where Madeleine and Pierre now walked. "Come," he said to Bently. "I'd like you to meet my grandson." He stood and clapped his hands several times. From the rear of the house the hulking Weimaraner appeared, running full out.

They started down the steps. "We'll take the dog," Sartene said to Bently. "It's a foolish beast, but I bought it because nothing on the ground escapes it. We have many snakes here, some dangerous, and the dog is supposed to be with Pierre, my grandson, when he is out. My daughter-in-law must have forgotten. You see, I'm overprotective of my grandson, and even though I know it's a weakness, I can't help myself."

Bently smiled to himself, pleased to find the man had a weakness.

Madeleine and Pierre were standing on the dock when they reached the river. They were watching the water. Sartene and Bently moved quietly, something each had learned from the war, something they had not forgotten and never would.

Madeleine and Pierre did not hear them until Sartene spoke. As always his voice was soft, a conspirator's voice, Bently

thought, and the sound did not startle them. The dog had remained behind on the shore, obeying a hand signal from Sartene,
and upon turning and seeing the gray hulk twisting there anxiously,
Pierre ran past the men and began playing with it.

Madeleine smiled, taking the time to study Bently closely. She
was as beautiful as he had assumed she would be, long and lithe,
yet ample in a pleasing way, and her eyes were a stunning blue,
like the child's. He felt both an immediate admiration and envy
toward Sartene's son.

"Madeleine, I'd like you to meet Monsieur Bently. He's an
official of the American government and is here discussing some
business with us," Sartene said.

She inclined her head in greeting. "I met the other American,"
she said.

"This one is different," Sartene said.

"That's good, I think," she said, smiling slightly.

Bently found it difficult to speak to the woman. It made him
feel slightly foolish, like a goddam high school kid, he told
himself.

"Good day," he said. It was all he could manage, except for
a small smile.

"And this," Sartene said, turning and gesturing toward Pierre,
"this wild man is my grandson, Pierre. Pierre," he called.
"Come meet the gentleman."

Pierre left the dog and walked toward them, with what Bently
considered a great deal of forced dignity for a little squirt in short
pants. The child stopped in front of him and extended his hand.

"Good day, sir," he said in English.

"You speak English very well," Bently said.

"It is something we feel is important," Sartene said. "Something that always served *me* well. Little Pierre speaks our own
language, of course, along with French and English. Gradually
he's learning the languages of this area." His voice had a teasing
reprimand in it, as though the boy had not been studying the new
languages as hard as he should.

"I'm very impressed, Pierre," Bently said, still looking down
at the child.

"Thank you, sir," he said. He had ignored the gentle reprimand.

There was a bit of the old man in him, Bently thought. And a
lot of the mother. He ran his hand over the boy's silky blond
hair. "That's some dog you have," he said, gesturing toward the
Weimaraner with his chin. "We have a lot of hunting dogs

where I come from in America, but not many are as handsome as he is."

"He can catch snakes," the boy said, acting like a child for the first time.

"I'll bet he can," Bently said.

"Oh, the snakes," Madeleine said. "I forgot, Papa."

Bently turned to the sound of the woman's lilting voice, realizing even the sound was exciting to him.

She looked away from Sartene and spoke to Bently. "I'm afraid I'm supposed to take the dog with us when we walk. But as usual, I forgot. Are you very annoyed with me, Papa?"

There was a teasing quality to her voice. She used her beauty even on Sartene, Bently noticed, And it left him defenseless, as it would any man.

"It's here now," Sartene said. "Besides, the boy enjoys the dog."

She smiled, realizing he was defending his protectiveness. "Do you have children, Monsieur Bently?" she asked, turning to the American.

"Please, call me Matt," he said. "And no. I'm afraid I never married."

"That's too bad," she said. "They can be a joy. And so can their grandfathers," she said, offering a smile to Sartene.

Sartene shook his head. "Perhaps we should go back to the shade now," he said. "It's very hot."

She laughed. A beautiful laugh, Bently thought.

"Yes, Papa," she said, taking his arm.

They walked slowly across the open plain, the boy and dog running far ahead, Bently trying awkwardly to make casual conversation.

In the distance he could see Malcolm Baker and Benito with the others on the veranda. From the way Baker sat in his chair, Bently could tell he was exhausted. He would undoubtedly bitch about it the entire way back. He sincerely hoped Baker would become ill during the flight.

Chapter 8

When the Manchu dynasty began an extermination campaign against China's rebellious Meo tribes in 1856, the numerous Meo clans fled south by the thousands. The majority of the Meo burst into northern Viet Nam's Tonkin Delta like an invasion of locusts, only to be driven back into the Vietnamese highlands by the Vietnamese army's elephant battalions.

Three Meo kaitong escaped that disaster by fleeing China's Yunnan and Szechwan provinces and turning southwest for the Nong Het district of northern Laos. The three clans, the Lo and the Ly—who would later struggle for dominance of opium—and the warlike Mua, lived, at first, in relative harmony. Throughout the latter half of the nineteenth century the Mua were clearly dominant, primarily because of their reputation as the fiercest of Meo warriors. But it was a dominance that would not last. Led by kaitong who were militarily strong but politically weak, the Mua were pushed aside by the Lo and Ly clans at the turn of the century, so much so that they fell into relative obscurity.

Offered little more than a beggar's role among the stronger clans, the young warriors of the Mua drifted throughout Laos, offering their skills to those who needed them, often as not ending up as free-lance mercenaries for the French.

It was the Mua whom Buonaparte Sartene employed, and it was they who taught him their history and the intricacies of tribal customs. From him they received respect and honor, and in return Sartene enjoyed the fierce loyalty of a forgotten clan, which gradually grew in number as Mua scattered throughout Laos learned they had at last found a unifying force.

Sartene recognized, and as a Corsican understood, the feelings of a people who had been denied their birthright, and it was something he used to the ultimate. When the Mua were told of the coming attack on Prince Phetsarath, and the subsequent move into Nong Het to seize control of the Ly opium dynasty and to drive the Lo clan from the region, they knew they had at last found a kaitong worthy of leadership. It did not matter that he was a European.

The raid on Prince Phetsarath's ancestral home was executed with brutal force. Located on the banks of the Mekong outside Luang Prabang, the attack came from the river under the cover of the predawn mist. Francesco Canterina, who led the assault, had been told by Sartene to avoid a bloodbath if possible. It was an order Francesco chose to ignore, and only the prince and a few servants were allowed to escape the brutality of the Mua onslaught.

Seated in the prince's ornate study, surrounded by a priceless collection of Chinese and Laotian art, Francesco knew he would have little trouble explaining away the *unavoidable* need for violence. He had little respect for life, especially oriental life, and he knew the Mua, pleased with the vengeful bloodletting they had been allowed to enjoy, would never contradict him. Besides, Sartene's interest in limiting violence was self-serving, intended to allow *him* to consolidate his power in the future among both the victors and the vanquished. It was something that did not fit into Francesco's plan, the execution of which was still years distant. Like Sartene, Francesco Canterina understood the value of patience, and the need to plan quietly for the future.

But today he was not in a patient mood. He was murderously angry. He had been used, was being used and would continue to be used to help establish Sartene's son, Jean, as the *milieu*'s leader in this new opium business. Jean was being groomed to succeed his father. And that being the case, he, Francesco Canterina, was being pushed aside.

Francesco leaned back in the delicate, gilded chair that dominated the center of the study like some imperial throne and studied the collection of Ming vases that littered the room, deciding which he would take with him as prizes of combat, and which lesser pieces he might bring back to Sartene as a gesture of respect. It was fitting. He had not personally shared in the wealth that had been found in that French farmhouse years ago. No one had. Not even Auguste, who had been there. Francesco grunted, thinking of it now. Payment in return for his life. The gesture of a fool. Sartene had said then that the money belonged to the new *milieu* they would form and as such would be enjoyed equally. But he had become the head of that *milieu*, and that wealth had helped *his* power to grow until now, without question, he was *paceri* of the region, the biggest of the big, who now with the move into opium would become even more powerful. And after him, his dull-witted son.

Above all others Francesco despised Jean most of all. Jean had never proved himself in his youth, had never been required to do so. Still he had everything *he*, Francesco, wanted. And one thing more. That woman, that wife, that Madeleine. Francesco wanted her as well. That Frenchwoman, whose father had been a shop-keeper, but who carried herself like some rich bitch, like the daughter of some baron. He would teach her someday as she lay beneath him. He could tell she wanted him to, even though she ignored him. There was always that slight look of fear when their eyes met, that sense of discomfort in his presence. Yes, she wanted it as much as he did. He smiled to himself, wondering if she ever thought of him when she was making love to that brute of a husband. Absentmindedly he took his knife from his pocket and pressed the small lever that sent the stiletto blade shooting up through the shaft. He held the knife loosely in his hand, allowing his thumb to alternately feel the sharp edges on each side of the long, slender blade.

The time will come, he told himself. Years from now. But it will come. And with it everything I want. *Everything*.

The door to the study swung open and two of the Mua pushed a trembling guard into the room. Francesco returned the knife to his pocket and sneered at the cowering little man, who stood now with a rope tied around his neck, the end of it held firmly by one of the Mua.

They were like bugs on the ground, all of these people. Slowly he lit a cigarette, keeping his eyes on the guard. He was dressed in the uniform of the prince's household, a bright, brocaded jacket that went to mid-thigh, plain baggy black trousers and brocaded slippers. He looked like some ethnic doll sold in the shops of Vientiane. The only difference was that he was trembling with fear.

Francesco exhaled a shaft of smoke toward the small, middle-aged man. "You will take a message from us to Lo Faydang. Do you know where his village is?" he asked in formal but broken Lao.

The guard nodded, afraid even to speak. The fear made Francesco smile.

"If you do not do as I say, you will be killed," he added, watching the trembling intensify. He stood, allowing his greater size to tower over the guard. "I'll know if you fail to do this," he added, waiting to let the threat settle in the mind of this bug. "I want you to tell him what happened here. And I want you to tell him that he is next, unless he follows your brave prince and runs like a frightened dog. Also tell him he can never return. Do you understand?"

The small guard nodded his head, still afraid to speak.

Francesco turned to one of the Mua, the one holding the rope. "Take him outside and after he sees us set the house on fire, put him on the road that leads to the hill country," he said. He beckoned the other Mua to him, as the first jerked the rope harshly and pulled the guard from the room.

He smiled at the remaining Mua, bowing his head slightly as a gesture of respect for their part in the victory. "You will follow this guard," he said. "Be sure he does as he was told. If he tries to run, you take him to the edge of Faydang's village. Later, after he delivers the message, find him alone and kill him. Then join your people at Lyfoung's village."

The Mua bowed and left the room. Francesco returned to his chair. The first part of the instructions to the Mua warrior had been Sartene's. The second had been his own. He wanted to be sure that in years to come this guard would not be able to identify him as the one who had led the raid on the prince's home. He smiled to himself. You're a clever man, Buonaparte. But so am I, he told himself.

He looked about the study one last time. It was too bad they would burn the house to the ground. It was a house worthy of an important man, like Carbone's house in Saigon, only bigger still. He walked to the window and looked out. The grounds were beautiful too, sculptured and cared for in a way that emphasized the importance of the man who owned them. He had not understood the Japanese garden that Sartene had included in his new house, but now he thought he did. Things should emphasize the power and the importance of a man. It was necessary.

He turned, his back to the window, and looked about the room again. A long road from the hard seacoast village where he was born. Longer still from the docks and narrow back streets of the Corsican ghetto of Marseille and the filthy French prisons. He drew a deep breath. In a way he missed those streets and the teeming docks. He thought of the massive Cathédrale de la Major that looked out into the Joliette Ship Basin, only four hundred yards from that place on the Rue de la République where, at eighteen, he had killed his first man. The whores on the Rue Colbert, and the ones who worked the Boul' Charles Livon on the Quai de Rive Neuve, across the old port where the City Hall watched them without concern. His mother had been one of those whores, forced into that life by the French. Frenchmen like that first man he had killed, one of his mother's customers. He would go back one day, he told himself. But not for many years. Not until he had what he wanted. Not until he had all of it.

Chapter 9

The unmarked, hulking, gray C-47 transport slowly circled the Plain of Jars as it prepared to land at the primitive airstrip at Phong Savan. Below, the grassy plain jutted out of the surrounding mountain jungle like a natural fortress, the massive clay jars that held the remains of the dead clearly visible, giving the plain more the look of some marketplace for unseen giants than of the cemetery that it was.

The door of the transport swung open as the plane lumbered to a halt at the end of the dirt runway and Matt Bently got his first look at Touby Lyfoung, standing at the head of a Meo reception committee. The Meo standing behind Touby were dressed in the typical dark pajama-type clothing worn throughout Southeast Asia. Some wore traditional bamboo hats, some skullcaps, a few wide-brimmed western hats. Like their heads, their feet were covered with everything from homemade sandals to French military boots, and each carried a ragtag assortment of weapons; the only thing each man had in common was the traditional long Meo knife that hung in a sheath from his belt.

In contrast, Touby was resplendent. He was dressed in the uniform of a French army officer, minus any indication of rank, complete with necktie and brass buttons; his trousers were stuffed carelessly into a pair of non-uniform Wellington boots, and atop his head he wore a pith helmet that made his short, round body seem more squat than it was.

Bently, who had worn his own uniform for the occasion, glanced back at Jean, who had on the purloined uniform of a French army colonel.

"This thing is turning into a fucking masquerade," Bently
said.

Jean grunted an attempt at laughter. "Let's hope there are no
surprises when the masks come off."

He's tight, Bently thought. Has been throughout the trip. He
wants it to go well, needs it to, so he can show his old man he
has what it takes. He wondered if Sartene realized the kind of
pressure he had placed his son under. The kind that makes
people screw up. He would have to try to help him, he decided.
During the trip he had found he liked this big, hulking Corsican.

They deplaned, followed by thirty-nine Mua warriors, all
armed with automatic weapons, all dressed identically, a sharp
contrast to the bobtailed assortment of the "superior" Ly clan.
Standing before Touby, Bently and Sartene offered a sharp
military salute in unison. Touby fought back the glee that quickly
spread across his oversized mouth, pressing his lips shut, but
unable to keep it from his eyes. He returned the salute, then
stepped forward and greeted them in perfect French, his eyes
passing over the Mua with a trace of nervousness.

He looks like an oriental chipmunk, Bently thought, forcing
himself to remember the man was important to his country's
interests. He controlled one of Indochina's most productive opium-
growing areas, twenty tons a year, with a potential of ten to
twenty more if properly managed.

While greetings were exchanged, another Mua warrior stepped
from behind the gathered Meo and walked toward his fellow
tribesmen. Jean's eyes caught the movement, and he looked hard
at the dark-clad figure. The Mua nodded almost imperceptibly,
indicating he had completed his task. The prince's servant had
delivered the message to Faydang. What Jean did not know, and
would not, was that the servant's throat had been cut within
hours after the message had been received.

"We are greatly honored to have you here," Touby said, his
eyes moving back and forth between Bently and Sartene. "Our
life here is humble, but I think you will find it interesting."

"I'm sure we shall," Bently said. "I'm already very impressed with your command of French."

Touby smiled enthusiastically. "I was very fortunate," he
said. "My father understood how much the French valued a
good colonial education. I was graduated from the Vinh *lycée* in
1939, the first Meo ever to attend high school."

"Your father was a wise man," Bently offered.

"Indeed," Touby said, nodding his head.

"It will make matters easier for us," Bently added. He gestured toward Jean. "Colonel Sartene has much to discuss with you. Matters of great importance to his government, to mine and, of course, to your people as well."

The transition had been made, as planned. It was clear now that Jean was in charge of the negotiations and that Bently was there in support of his position.

Touby picked up on it immediately, turning his attention to the younger Sartene. "If you will come with me to my village we can talk in comfort," Touby said. "I have a vehicle for us. My men will follow on foot. Unfortunately the number of vehicles we have is limited to one."

"Is the route secure?" Jean asked. His eyes were hard, his manner very military.

Touby waved his hand in a broad, expansive gesture. "It is not far and I have men all along the route. We have no fear of Faydang's people here." He spoke the last sentence louder than necessary, for the benefit of his own men and the Mua.

Sartene nodded, then turned and motioned to the Mua behind him. Two stepped forward. "These men will come with me," he said. His voice had a command to it, and the gesture was intended both to let Lyfoung know these were his men, who followed his orders, and also to instill pride in the Mua as well. His father had cautioned him to make sure his men knew they were valued more than the Ly clansmen.

The gesture was not wasted on Touby, and Bently noted a slight discomfort enter and then leave his eyes. Touby forced a smile and gestured toward a battered Japanese staff car fifty yards from the runway. Where the hell did they get parts to keep it running? Bently wondered, as he fell in three paces behind Sartene and Lyfoung. The proper distance to trail royalty, he told himself. The new kings of opium. No, only princes. The king was back in Vientiane, probably playing with his grandson.

The route from Phong Savan to the Ly village of Lat Houang was an indirect route of nearly ten miles, traversing two of the worst rock-strewn roads Bently had ever seen. Parts for the Jap car obviously weren't available, he told himself. Certainly not where the suspension system was concerned. He smiled to himself, suddenly wishing Malcolm Baker were with them.

The terrain was lush and beautiful in a primitive yet threatening way. Virtually impassable without a machete, Bently mused.

And the opposite of any norm. Traveling *down* from a plain into mountains. Incredible. But everything about Laos was different; the people were as variegated as the terrain was chaotic. No one even knew where the term "Laos" came from, he recalled. Local legend held that it evolved from "Lwa" or "La-Wa," the name of the tribes who supposedly held the land prior to the fourteenth century when Thai warlords staged a series of successful invasions. But there was another legend also, one that claimed the entire Lao people came out of two large gourds, or *lawus*. He thought of Touby seated behind him now in the car, and of the way he had waddled slightly when he walked, the way most fat men did. They would have to be damned sizable gourds if his ancestors were anything like him, he told himself.

The road, twisting and turning, continued to drop to the mountaintop. Geographically, Laos had five distinct types of regions, he recalled. The rice-growing lowlands through which all rivers flowed, the Mekong; the two plateaus, the Plain of Jars here, and in the south the Bolovens Plateau; the massive Annam Cordillera mountain range to the east, its continuous line of eight-thousand-foot peaks separating Laos from Viet Nam for over five hundred miles, yet passable only at three points in the south; and finally, the wavelike ridges in the far north, which seemed to flow down from China's Yunnan Province. Bently shook his head. And each of its five tribal groups had chosen a different terrain in which to live. Virtually one atop the other. You could literally travel upward through tiers of different peoples. The Lao majority in the lowlands, then up to the next belt in elevation to the villages of the Kha Mou, which then gave way to the White or Black Tais. And higher still, the Lolo Kha Kho, until finally, at the mountaintops, the settlements of the Meo, perched precariously on the edges of cliffs and limestone walls. The place where the poppies grow, Bently reminded himself. Along with just enough corn to sustain the inhabitants.

When the car rumbled and creaked into Lat Houang a few minutes later, Bently found the village identical to others he had read about. It was little more than a shantytown of hootches, gathered together on a sheer cliff that looked dizzyingly down into the steaming forest below. Touby's hootch, larger and covered with a layer of plaster, sat nearest the edge.

Inside, the hootch was primitive but comfortable; scattered about the center of the lone room were heavy pillows serving as chairs. There was a low table, laden with delicacies, each succeeding one spicier than the last, clearly reminiscent of the tribe's former life in Yunnan and Szechwan. Bently quickly gave up on the food and gulped tea to ease the burning in his mouth. Settling back, he studied the photographs that covered all four walls. Touby with generals. Touby with diplomats. Touby seated at a long table, as the only Meo on the Opium Purchasing Board. And, of course, Touby's high school diploma. Sartene had been right, the man was egomaniacal. And soon he would carry the rank of colonel in the colonial army. He'll piss in his pants, Bently thought, again marveling at the insight of the older Sartene.

They chatted socially for the first half hour, Jean following the oriental custom of never rudely rushing straight into business matters. The conversation covered Jean's family, Touby's and Bently's bachelorhood, policies of the French government in Vientiane, and the subtle but gradually deepening American involvement in the region.

"The communists are much worse than the Japanese," Touby intoned. "The Japanese at least were foreign slavemasters. The Pathet Lao would enslave their own people. We are grateful to have strong nations here to help us drive them out."

A slight smile flickered across Jean's face as he picked up the cue for business to begin. "That's why we are here," he said, waiting, as his father often did, to let the effect of his words sink in. He took the lapel of his uniform between his thumb and index finger and pulled at it. "This uniform is only for show, only for the benefit of your followers and, more especially, for the followers of Lo Faydang." He raised a finger for emphasis. "But it's a uniform I wear today with the approval of the French government. And to prove that I've brought you a commission in the colonial army. The rank of colonel, which you will wear if our meetings are successful." He smiled, watching Touby's eyes dilate with pleasure, followed by a quick bow of his head.

The donkey and the carrot, Bently thought. The kid's not bad. He doubted that the old man could have done better, and he made a mental note to tell him how well Jean had handled himself. At least to this point.

"I'm part of a Corsican business group headed by my father, of whom you may have heard," Jean went on. "We have been approached by the French"—he nodded toward Bently—"and the Americans, to try to resolve this communist threat to opium production."

"Yes, yes," Touby said, nodding his head rapidly.

Jean raised his hand, reminding Bently again of Buonaparte. "We all know the communists want to *use* your people's opium crop to finance their interests. But their interests aren't *our* interests," he added, raising his voice for the first time as he made a circular gesture with his hand to include the three of them. "So the solution is simple. We must drive the communists out and guarantee that opium only goes to those who support *our* interests." Again the circular gesture of the hand.

"That is not easy," Touby said. "The mountains and the forest offer many hiding places."

Jean smiled, genuinely this time, Bently thought.

"You've heard of Prince Phetsarath's decision to suddenly leave his ancestral home?" Jean asked.

Touby nodded, his eyes questioning the information.

"The same men who arrived here with me today were the men who sent the prince running like a dog."

"The Mua?" Touby said, eyes wide again, but this time fearful.

Jean raised his hand again. "No longer think of them as Mua," Jean said with a reassuring smile. "Think of them as the army of my father, of Buonaparte Sartene." He waited, allowing the nervousness to remain in Touby's eyes. "We have already sent a message to Faydang, suggesting that he follow his prince and never return." Jean extended both hands, palms up, at his sides. "But the day after tomorrow, if we agree on matters here, we will attack his village and drive him away. Or kill him. I would be pleased if you join forces with us. It would be a great victory to have as your first act as a colonel in the colonial army." He smiled again. "The French and the Americans appreciate victory even more than they appreciate education."

Touby looked numb, slightly uncertain, and more than a little fearful. But he had been offered a potent carrot. "What would you want my humble clan to do?" he asked.

"Not much more than you have been doing. With a few minor changes," Jean said. He waited, playing out the ensuing silence. "The opium crop, *all of it*, will come through my organization. The French are too busy now, their resources spread too widely fighting the communists, to control things properly. *We* will control them. The opium will go to the French through us to be used against the Pathet Lao. You will simply have to manage production. Increase production, as well. You will continue to collect the opium tax for the French, plus an additional tax for us. The tax is now three silver piasters a year per grower. We suggest you raise it to eight."

"The people could never gather together eight piasters a year," Touby said.

"We're not greedy men. We don't lack understanding," Jean said. "They can pay the additional tax in opium. In increased production of opium. Otherwise it will have to come from the opium you regularly hold back from the French for yourself." He let the words fall like a great tree, and an eerie silence followed the crash.

It's the old rock and the hard place for you, Touby, Bently thought. Even juicy carrots cost. Sartene gets rid of your competition and you goose your people to higher production or lose some of that precious bankroll you've been squirreling away on the sly. And Sartene gets more than one and a half times the taxes the French government gets, plus all the opium he holds back.

"But one more thing," Jean added, narrowing his eyes and leaning forward so his sheer bulk added to the threat. "Any smuggling, any transactions with anyone else, will be dealt with as an offense to us. You must warn your people of that. And then you can sit back and become a rich man."

"I will have to persuade the other village headmen," Touby said. "I am district leader, but . . ."

"If you can't persuade them, you are of no use to us," Jean said. "But we're confident of your abilities. Otherwise we would have gone to some other leader, even to Faydang."

It was rare to see an oriental blush with shame or embarrassment, but Touby did so now. The threat was so blatant that Bently wondered if Jean had overplayed his hand. The bull charging ahead.

"You must understand that I must show the village headmen the respect to speak to them. But this does not mean I will not insist that they follow my decision. If you will give me some time to think, I will give you that decision. Tonight, at dinner."

Touby stood and smiled nervously. Bently momentarily wondered if he would leave and gather his men for an immediate attack. No. He had been too nervous about the Mua, and they were still outside, better armed than Touby's men, and already instructed about the possibility of conflict. Most, he thought, hoped it would happen.

Touby bowed to Bently and Sartene. "It is just that this was most unexpected," he said. "As an educated man, I must think it through. But only for a short time. During my absence young women of my village will bring you more food and will entertain you with music and their charming ways. Dismiss any who do not please you."

He had smiled again before leaving. Just saving face, Bently decided. He has no choice and he knows it. If he's smart. But he doesn't want to jump at it, acknowledge that he's being bullied into it, even if he is.

There were five young women, dressed in formal Meo clothing, obviously prepared to entertain Touby's guests in advance. They were small and delicate, their long black gowns hiding all but the fact they were frail. The gowns had V necklines, but the white blouses worn beneath guarded their modesty. The necklines and cuffs of the long sleeves were trimmed in red, and each wore a wide gold sash around her waist, tied in the front, the ends hanging down to indicate her unmarried state.

Bently looked the women over, then glanced at Jean. "Something for the outer man, no doubt," he said.

Jean looked at the women. "I wonder what we'd catch." His brow furrowed.

"We mustn't be rude," Bently teased.

Jean shook his head as though he hadn't heard, then looked back at Bently. "How do you think it went?" he asked.

"I think our friend Touby is about to become a colonel in the colonial army."

During dinner Touby's makeshift uniform did indeed have a new addition, and throughout the meal his hands repeatedly drifted to the patches that had been hastily pinned on, assuring himself they were still in place. The newly appointed colonel had agreed on all points, insisting only that the new taxes not be retroactive, thereby saving face and guaranteeing that his personal bankroll would not be affected.

Bently could see that Jean was delighted, even though he maintained his hardened exterior for Touby's benefit. The earlier tightness reappeared only when the conversation turned to the attack on Faydang's village. It was the final part of the mission his father had entrusted to him, and Bently knew he wanted to return home with a perfect score. During the trip up they had briefly discussed the raid on Prince Phetsarath's home. It had been an unqualified success, although more brutal than Sartene had wanted. But he had accepted it as an inevitable part of fighting. "People fight and people die," he had said. "I wish I could make it different. But I'm not God." To Jean, Bently saw, it meant simply that Francesco had again pleased his father, and even though the raid benefited him as well, Francesco's continued success clearly worried him.

Now he too had to prove himself in combat. Bently decided that even though he had the option to remain behind, an option his embassy wanted him to exercise, he would go with Jean, help him where he could, guide him as much as he would allow.

It was eleven o'clock and the house in Vientiane was dark and quiet. Sartene was upstairs, reading to Pierre, and Madeleine moved slowly along a shelf of books in the library, searching for one to take to her bed.

She had left the door to the library open and did not hear him enter. Francesco stood in the doorway behind her, watching her move along the far wall, intent on the titles of the books. She was dressed for bed, with a silk robe over her nightgown, which, though covering her fully, accentuated every line of her body. He fantasized about taking her now, forcibly if necessary, and his lips curved into a small, satisfied smile.

He wondered if she knew he was there, behind her, watching her. She seemed to be moving with an excess of sensuality, delicate and graceful, a way he was sure women moved only when men were watching them. The line of her body pressed against the silk, struggling to be free of it. It would tear so easily, leaving behind that delightful soft flesh he knew was there. She'd fuck with abandon, he thought. Her kind always did. He wondered if there was anything he could do to her, make her do to him, that would be humiliating, that would make her pull away in fear. It would be fun finding out. But not now. Not yet.

The books were grouped in sections according to the nationality of the author. She stopped before the Russians, reaching out and taking a leather-bound copy of Tolstoy's *War and Peace*. Her father-in-law had urged her to read Tolstoy, telling her how the man had devoted his entire life to the achievement of greatness, consciously writing books that would live long after he was dead, guaranteeing himself immortality. He seemed to admire the man's thought, his plan for his life. Madeleine shook her head slightly, returning the book to its shelf. Farther down she withdrew a book by Chekhov. She remembered reading somewhere how Chekhov had said that every story should be locked away in a trunk for seven years, then taken out and read again, to see if it still had meaning. A sense of pleasure flickered through her eyes. She turned, stepping away from the bookcase, then stopped short, gasping and pulling the book to her breast.

"Oh. You frightened me, Francesco."

"I'm sorry. That's what I was trying not to do. I just stood here, because I was afraid if I spoke I would frighten you."

He was smiling. A handsome, leering smile. There was something about him that was so strange, threatening really. She thought it came from his eyes. They seemed to signal death. "I was just getting a book," she said, annoyed at her own nervousness.

"Can't sleep?" He walked toward her, noticing that she took a slight step back, then he stopped at a bowl of jackfruit on a low table in front of the sofa. He reached down and took one of the yellow bulbs of pulp, raising it to his nose and smelling the sweet scent of pineapple and banana. He bit into it, then gestured toward the bowl. *"Mit?"* he asked, using the Lao term for the fruit.

She shook her head. "I'm not hungry, just tired."

"But not sleepy." He grinned at her. "Otherwise you wouldn't need a book, would you?"

"A book always helps me sleep," she said.

"You must read very bad writers." He took another piece of fruit. "Or are you just lonely for your husband?"

"I'm always lonely for Jean when he's away," she said. She was getting ready to move past him, but he seemed to sense it and stepped to the side, blocking her way. You're being silly, she told herself. You're seeing threats where they don't exist.

"I never like to sleep alone either," he said. He shrugged his shoulders. "But what can a poor bachelor do?"

"Oh, Francesco," she said, speaking to him as though he were a child. "Your reputation with the ladies of Vientiane doesn't make you a candidate for sympathy."

He laughed, but his eyes grew colder. "You shouldn't listen to gossip," he said.

"I never do."

She started past him, but he reached out and took her arm, stopping her.

"What are you reading?" He had cocked his head sideways, appearing intent on the book in her hand.

He was still holding her, the grip loose, but keeping her close to him. She moved her arm free, without any abruptness, and stepped back, holding the book between them.

"Chekhov," she said.

"Russian." He scowled. "I knew Russians during the war and I never liked them. They were filthy bastards." He placed the fingers of one hand against his lips. "Sorry," he said. "I forget one shouldn't talk that way in front of a lady."

The way he said the word "lady" annoyed her. There was a mocking sound to it, but he continued talking before she could say anything.

"Jean should be back day after tomorrow. If all goes well."

The final sentence seemed to imply something not said. She looked him straight in the eye. "Why shouldn't all go well?"

He shrugged. "You can never tell with these crazy orientals," he said.

She continued to stare at him. "Don't you want it to go well, Francesco?"

He laughed again, but not with his eyes. "Of course I do, my sweet Madeleine."

"I'm not your sweet Madeleine, Francesco. I'm not your sweet anything."

The harshness in her voice made him smile, truly this time. "Of course you're not. You're Jean's."

"I'm my own. I choose to be Jean's," she said, her eyes angry now.

"You make it sound not very permanent," he said.

"It's very permanent, because I want it to be."

Her breasts were rising and falling rapidly. He looked down at them, and she drew the book up, covering herself.

"You don't like Jean, do you?"

He laughed, now treating her like a child. "How silly of you to say that. He's like my brother. And Buonaparte is like my father. We're a family here, Madeleine. Even little Pierre calls me uncle."

"I'm very glad to hear that, Francesco." She moved past him without difficulty this time, saying goodnight as she did.

He watched her leave, her body seeming stiffer than it had before. He smiled to himself as she disappeared out the door. Patience is a terrible thing, he told himself. He put the rest of the jackfruit in his mouth, then spit the seed into his hand, finally dropping it into an ashtray on the table. He hoped she would take care of herself in the years ahead. Not let herself get fat and ugly. Just save herself.

He walked to Sartene's desk and eased himself into the leather chair behind it, extending his hands and allowing them to run across the smooth teak of the desk top. He leaned back and looked about the room. It was foolish to sit here. He knew that. If Buonaparte came in the vision would remain in his mind and fester. But he was upstairs with that spoiled brat of a grandchild. He smiled to himself. Little Pierre. No doubt the next in line after Jean. Emperor Buonaparte. He leaned forward and placed his hand on the middle drawer of the desk, testing it. Locked. He tugged gently at the lobe of his ear. Good fortune to you, Jean. Good fortune to all of you. Build up the opium business. Build it and build it and build it. But not for Jean. And not for that fucking little brat.

Francesco laughed softly, then stretched the muscles in his back. Bedtime, he told himself. Time for the sleep of the angels.

Chapter 10

By dawn sixty of Touby's men, augmented by the forty Mua warriors, had encircled the village of Xieng Khouang. Jean and Bently had spent the previous afternoon instructing the Ly force until they were satisfied they would follow the battle plan. Then they marched, under the cover of night, the twenty miles to Faydang's village. Throughout the march Touby had been a mixture of glee and self-doubt, keeping up a constant prattle, reassuring himself, Bently decided. He had argued that a warning should not have been sent to Faydang. That a massacre of the village would have been preferable. But he would settle, they knew, for Faydang's swift retreat into Viet Nam. Such a fearful retreat would give him even more prestige than an outright slaughter, even if it would not provide the sense of security he wanted. Buonaparte had explained that he wanted Faydang left unharmed. He was the only other strong leader among the Meo. And Touby was not immortal, and certainly not trustworthy. There could come a time when he would have to be replaced, and Faydang was the only option for the present.

Sartene's care in ensuring Faydang's survival had been excessive. Touby's uncle was a wily adversary, and his network of spies within Touby's ranks gave him adequate warning of any plan to move against him. Within hours of the arrival of Bently and Sartene, Faydang was apprised of the situation. He knew of Touby's elevation to the mock rank of colonel, of the planned increase in the opium tax, and of the Corsican interlopers' newfound dominance of the opium trade. As Touby's men trained for the attack, Faydang planned his own survival. The villagers of Xieng Khouang were told to sleep in the jungle that night.

And when the attack began at dawn, Faydang and his followers were already retreating, their only resistance coming from a handful of snipers hidden in trees outside the village, left there to die as a face-saving gesture.

Bently and Sartene were side by side when the gunfire erupted behind them.

"Merde," Jean grunted, spinning and firing his Thompson submachine gun wildly into the trees.

He jumped up and ran forward firing from the hip. Bently shouted at him, but his voice was obliterated by the gunfire. He raced after him, overtaking him within twenty yards, and threw his body at the back of Jean's legs, knocking him to the ground.

"Stay put," he shouted, then, rising up on one knee, opened fire with short bursts of his own weapon, until a Lo warrior fell spinning from a distant tree.

He sat back alongside Jean, breathing deeply as the gunfire gradually subsided around them.

"You've got to learn about jungle fighting, buddy," he said, grinning to ease the scolding. He stood, glancing about until he saw what he wanted, then walked to his left and picked up a rock the size of a football. "Come with me," he said. "But stay behind me."

He walked slowly, testing the ground ahead with his foot. After five yards he stopped short, turning his head back to Jean. "Now watch," he said. He hefted the rock, throwing it a few yards ahead of him, and watched as it crashed through the false layer of thin bamboo strips that had been covered with leaves. The covering gave way, exposing a hole six feet in diameter. At the base of the hole, heavy bamboo sticks had been driven into the ground, their sharpened ends pointing up in every conceivable direction, the knifelike tips coated in buffalo dung so even a scratch might prove fatal without medical treatment.

Jean exhaled heavily.

"Punji sticks," Bently said. "You'll also find those damned things tied in clusters and attached to long poles hanging in trees. They're set off by trip wires and come flying down, and . . ." He slapped the palm of one hand into the other for emphasis. "Very messy," he added.

In the distance a piercing scream came from the forest. Bently wasn't sure if one of his men had found one of the devices or was simply giving a *coup de grace* to a wounded Lo warrior. He doubted it was the latter. The Meo, like most Southeast Asians, preferred beheading, believing it forced the soul to leave the body prematurely, thereby denying entrance to heaven. Coming across a beheaded member of your own force had great psychological impact on an opposing army. The probability of beheading also made a man fight to the death rather than risk capture.

Jean took his arm, drawing him back. "You won't mention this?" he said.

Bently threw an arm around his shoulder and turned him back toward the village. "You're a helluva tough guy and a brave one, Jean," he said. "It's not your fault you haven't fought here before. Christ, during the war some of the best men we had got chewed up by those things. Jungle warfare's different from any other kind. There are just too many ways to kill somebody, outside of bullets and bombs and landmines. There's just too much cover."

Back in the village, Touby was holding court, strutting about in his uniform, basking in the praise of his men. When the fighting began Bently had not seen him, and he doubted Touby had been anywhere near it. He stepped forward and clasped Touby by the shoulder.

"Well, colonel. A great victory," he said, making sure his voice carried to Touby's men.

Touby nodded. "The frightened dog has run away," he said, then, *sotto voce:* "Let us hope he stays there."

Jean had come up beside him. "He will if he's smart. We'll be setting up radio contact with you. And we can be here in two hours if needed." Jean's eyes carried an intended warning, along with the reassurance.

"Now we'll burn his village to the ground," Touby said. "Just like the prince's house."

"Don't burn it," Bently said softly. "Occupy it. Then he'll have nothing to come back to, and you'll be closer to the frontier and have better warning if he tries to move back in force. You'll also be headman of two villages, not just one."

Touby bobbed his head, grinning. "Yes. And there'll be more opium," he said.

"And a place for your growers to live," Bently added.

"And more taxes," Jean said.

They laughed, and Bently had no doubt a bond had been formed, be it tenuous or not. He would report as much to his masters in Saigon.

They remained in Touby's village that afternoon for the cele-

bration that marked his victory, the first over Faydang that had
not involved mere political manipulations by the French. The
chubby new colonel was feeling very much his own man, calling
upon the young women to perform traditional dances, directing
special food to be prepared, and staging a knife-throwing tourna-
ment among his men. Jean had sent the Mua back to the airstrip,
not wanting them to become competitive with the men of the Ly
clan, not wanting to risk any confrontation between the hated
factions.

Bently admired his decision. Jean wasn't cunning, as his
father was; he lacked the shark's instinct so obvious in the older
man; but he *was* smart in his own methodical way. Bently also
liked the fact that Jean wasn't a carbon copy of his father. Knew
he could not be and accepted the fact, even though it bothered
him.

Over the course of the celebration, the same group of young
women were again presented to them by their host. Each had
declined the honor the previous day, but now, after the tenseness
of battle, Bently felt more inclined. He half-jokingly suggested
to Jean that they avoid offending their host and partake.

"If I went home with some disease, Madeleine would not be
amused," Jean said stoically. He raised his eyebrows. "I'd wake
up some morning and find a knife through my heart. She's not
Corsican," he added. "But almost."

The C-47 left the Phong Savan airstrip shortly before dusk, as
the sun slipped behind the jungle foliage, changing the lush
green to a rainbow of shimmering colors. Bently and Jean sat
together, behind the cockpit, Bently staring out the window,
enjoying the beauty that stretched out below them.

Beautiful but deadly, he thought. So different from South
Dakota, different really from anything he had previously known.
Yet he had been here so many years it was difficult to think of
this place as foreign. Southeast Asia grew on you, invaded your
being, much the same way the tropical forest swallowed up
everything. You could clear a piece of land, cut a road, but the
forest was always there, inching its way back, ready to reclaim
what had been taken away as soon as the usurper relaxed his
vigilance.

He turned to Jean. "How do you like it here? In Laos, I
mean?" he asked.

"It's good. I like it well enough. It takes time to get used to."
Jean thought for a moment. "It's a hard place," he said at

length. "But Corsica was a hard place, too. France also, after the war. Like you Americans say, war is hell." He chuckled over his small joke.

"I guess Europe got clobbered pretty bad," Bently said. "At least that's what I've been told."

"Yes. I saw some of it," Jean said. "But we didn't stay very long. My father went back to Corsica to visit my mother's grave. She died during the war. But from an illness, not the fighting. Then he spent a brief time in Marseille with friends, and then went on to Switzerland. He left me to make the arrangements for our emigration with the French authorities. I think he had enough of them during the war."

"He puts a lot of trust in you," Bently said.

Jean tilted his head to one side. "I wish he felt he could put more," he said. "But it's hard for him. He's used to doing things for himself, for others. He has difficulty letting people do things for him." Jean turned to face Bently. "He's a very strong man," he said. "I don't think he ever doubts himself."

"All men doubt themselves," Bently said. "It's human nature."

"Not Papa. His life has been a series of struggles. And he has always won those struggles."

Bently sensed that Jean would like to be more specific, but knew he could not. The Corsican belief in secrecy, of not speaking of personal matters to outsiders, was legend. "Were you close to him when you were a boy?" he asked. He felt safe with the question. They had been in battle together, fought side by side, and he knew from experience that that created a unique bond between men.

Jean shook his head. "He was away much of the time. But he tried to be with us as often as possible. When he was there it was good. But I would have liked it to be more. What about your father? Did you have a lot of time with him?"

"No. Business took up most of his time, and on weekends he had his country club, which was good for business, too." Bently glanced out the window trying to bring his father's face to mind. "He's a banker," he said. "Lately he's been writing me, telling me I should go back home and be a banker too."

"Where's home?" Jean asked.

"Pierre, South Dakota." The name was pronounced *pier*, and Matt explained the difference between the spelling and the pronunciation. "It's dead in the middle of the country, what we call the midwest."

"Pierre. Just like my son's name. It is a large French community?"

"No. But it was named by French fur trappers who once worked the Missouri River. One probably named it after *himself.*"

"That's just like a Frenchman," Jean said.

"Be careful. Your wife's French."

"She's a Frenchwoman. That's very different." He smiled at Bently.

It was a good smile, Bently thought. It softened him, let you see a little of what was inside. "She's very beautiful," he said. "I envy you."

"Most men do," Jean said. "She's very good to my son, also. And very loyal to my family." He paused, as if deciding whether to continue. "Papa was not pleased when I told him I wanted to marry her. He wanted me to marry a Corsican. Blood is very important to him. He's old-fashioned that way. But he was wrong and he knows now that he was. He never admitted it, but I can tell."

Bently laughed. "It's hard for men to admit they made a mistake. Fathers, I mean. I think they're afraid to let us know they're fallible. I think it's probably even harder if you're in business with them. I guess that's why I'm resisting going back."

"I never thought of it that way," Jean said. "But maybe you're right. Still, it's hard for me to think of my father that way. He dominates everyone. Even my son. Already, I think, he's closer to Pierre than I am. But that's not intentional. He just wants the best for him, and he thinks he knows best how to provide it." His face warmed again. "Anyway, how can you stop a grandfather? And it's good for him to have a small child to give his affection to, don't you think?"

Jean's voice seemed slightly rueful to Bently. "Yeah. I was closer to my grandfather than I ever was to my father. Maybe that's just the way things are when you have a successful father. Who the hell knows? Besides, I never had a kid, so how could I tell?"

"Why didn't you ever marry?" Jean asked. "You're older than I am, and Americans always seem to marry younger than Europeans."

"Afraid, I guess." He winked at Jean. "No, not really. I suppose I was just too busy playing the field, having a good time after college, and always looking for the one, special, untouched

THE CORSICAN   131

woman. But never really wanting to find her. Then it was the
war. God and country and all that crap. And now this.''

Jean held his palms together, rubbing his hands back and
forth. "I want to ask you something," he said. "It's something
that bothers me about this opium thing we're involved in. I know
it's on my father's mind too.''

"Shoot," Bently said.

"We both know that a lot of this opium is going to find its
way out of here and end up in heroin factories in Europe.''

Bently nodded.

"The biggest market for that heroin is going to be in the
richest countries. England, France, and especially your country.
It's going to be like a plague, because the more that's produced,
the more that's going to be sold. That's business. Now I know,
as my father says, that you can't stop fools from destroying
themselves. But if I thought that children in my village in
Corsica would be destroying themselves that way, I wouldn't
touch this thing. Fortunately they're too poor. But they're not
too poor in your country. I don't understand why your government wants to do this. It's like raising a poisonous snake for a
pet, even though you know that sooner or later it's going to bite
you.''

"I asked some of those same questions myself," Bently said.
"My government is communist-crazy right now. And this is one
way to keep the communists under control, keep them from
gobbling up countries they want to control. At least I think that's
the reason. I hope to Christ it is.'' He drew a breath and let the
air out slowly. "They tossed a lot of statistics at me when I
raised the question. Apparently the addict problem in the States
was practically wiped out by the war. The shit just couldn't get
in. Shipping it over was almost impossible, and border patrols
were really tight for the first time in our history. So most of the
addicts were forced into involuntary withdrawal. Right now they
estimate we have less than twenty thousand addicts in the country.
Back in 1924, when Congress outlawed heroin, there were over
two hundred thousand. I guess they feel they've got the problem
licked and can keep it that way. Either that, or they're not
thinking at all, or they don't give a damn. I don't know which
would be worse.''

"There's a lot of money in heroin," Jean said, letting the
accusation remain unspoken.

"I hope that's not it. But who the hell knows? They make the

decisions. I just carry them out." Bently grunted at himself.
"Sounds like what all those Krauts were saying over in Nuremberg,
doesn't it?"

Jean did not answer.

"Anyway, if you're right, and it does happen, there are going
to be a lot of people who ought to find it hard to sleep in their
old age. Myself included. What does your father think? Doesn't
he worry about the effect?"

Jean shrugged. "He draws very fine lines for himself. He's a
very moral man, in his own way. I know most people think of us
as criminals, and maybe we are. But we think, my father thinks,
only about providing for our families. And like most men, we
want to provide many things. As much as we can get. Corsicans
never had many chances to do that in Corsica. The French
controlled everything, and they made laws that suited *them*. But
they weren't laws that protected us, helped us, so we ignored
them. We made our own laws. Better in some cases. Fairer
anyway, to us. My father knows he can't control the world, all
the evil in it." Jean paused and smiled. "He'd like to, but he
can't. So he does what he has to do to earn his bread. If
powerful governments tell him they want this thing, he gives it
to them. At a price. You think that's any different from the man
who manufactures weapons? He knows they won't all be used
for target practice and parades, just like we know all the opium
won't be turned into morphine for hospitals. Tell me. If we
didn't accept your offer, what would you have done?"

"Probably have gone to Carbone and persuaded him to do it
our way," Bently said.

Jean nodded his head. "I like you, Matt. You're an honest
man."

"An honest dope dealer." He smiled at Sartene. "I like you
too, Jean."

Chapter 11

LAOS, 1952

The room was small and plainly furnished, located next to his father's large, paneled study, but Jean found it a comfortable place to work. The confined space seemed to help him concentrate, keeping distractions to a minimum. The room had originally been intended to house his father's collection of toy soldiers, but at Jean's request, Buonaparte Sartene had moved the antique miniatures to his study, where, his son had teased, he could play with his toys with greater secrecy.

During the preceding six years, opium production in the north had increased to thirty tons a year, and the elder Sartene had relinquished more and more control to his son. With Auguste's help, Jean had established a varied and complex transportation network, which included massive air shipments to Saigon with transshipment to Marseille by sea. Smaller quantities were moved by caravan to Bangkok for delivery in Paris by air, usually in diplomatic pouches. Opium kept exclusively for the Sartene *milieu*—some five tons a year—was shipped directly to business associates in Hong Kong, where the family firm, Southeast Asian Rubber, was a darling of British banking interests.

Jean had assumed the role of business executive with surprising ease and had grown in confidence with each year. He had learned to fly and regularly used his small single-engine war-surplus scout plane, obtained with the help of Matt Bently, to personally keep track of production and transportation problems, and to keep tight rein on the Meo.

There had been sporadic attempts by Faydang to reassert his influence, through the formation of the Meo Resistance League, which sought to recruit tribesmen by promising to abolish the

133

opium taxes administered by Lyfoung. But each attempt had failed, and Faydang was forced to remain in Viet Nam, where he and his men sought refuge with the Viet Minh.

There had also been trouble with Carbone in 1948, but that too was quickly resolved when his personal automobile exploded in the driveway of his home. The car had not been occupied. It had been intended as a warning from Buonaparte Sartene, and within weeks Carbone had traveled to Vientiane to meet with Sartene and resolve their difficulties. The resolution, as dictated by Sartene, had been simple. The Sartene *milieu* would not involve itself in opium production in the Tonkin region of northern Viet Nam, and Carbone would do the same as far as Laos, Burma and Thailand were concerned. It had left Carbone with little more than a saving of face and the guarantee that he would live to a ripe old age.

The money Carbone could derive from opium production in northern Viet Nam was minimal, and offered no threat to Sartene dominance. Following the war the French had made White Tai chieftains their opium brokers in northern Viet Nam, and Carbone was forced to deal through them. The Tais regularly cheated the Meo opium growers of that region, vastly underpaying them and forcing them into a close bond with the Viet Minh. To increase his own part in the opium trade, Carbone would have to subvert the Tais and deal with the Viet Minh, and this was impossible from Saigon, where French surveillance was intense. It could be done from Laos, where government controls were minimal, but that option had been cleverly closed off by Sartene. Carbone, in effect, had been left the crumbs, while Buonaparte Sartene enjoyed the feast.

The six years had also been kind to Jean Sartene in other ways. He had grown closer to his son, who was now twelve. And his friendship with Matt Bently had also grown. Together they hunted in the jungle for wild boar and barking deer. In the delta plains, Bently introduced him to the American passion for wing shooting, and the kitchen of the Sartene household was always stocked with jungle peacock, pheasant, partridge and quail.

Jean's relationship with his wife had also developed, and although she disliked his constant travel, she was pleased by the dwindling domination of the older Sartene. Jean had become his own man, and although Buonaparte was still the unquestioned leader of the *milieu*, Jean now consulted him more out of respect than need.

It was because of this that Madeleine felt secure in broaching
the subject of their son's education. Pierre had first been sent to
a colonial school in Vientiane. His Corsican heritage had become
the subject of cruel jokes by the French children there, and the
family had decided to spare him that indignity and have him
tutored at home. But the time was coming when private tutoring
would not suffice. There were other reasons as well. The child
had repeatedly asked to travel with his father, and his naive
interest in the family business had greatly concerned Madeleine.
Also, she wanted him away from the influence of his grandfather.

It was with this in mind that she entered her husband's study
one evening, in one of her rare interruptions of his work.

"I have been talking with Pierre's teacher," she said, taking
an upholstered chair opposite his desk.

"Is he having problems?" Jean asked.

Jean was in his mid-thirties now and his hair had begun to
gray at the temples, and together with his growing self-confidence,
it had given his face a gentler, softer appearance.

She smiled, pleased with his concern. "No. But soon there
will be. He's already far advanced of other children his age, and
his studies should be at the level of a good secondary school. A
tutor can't really do that, Jean, and I don't want to subject him to
the cruelty of the *lycées* in Vientiane or Saigon."

Jean's brow furrowed; he leaned forward. "What are you
proposing, then? It certainly wouldn't be any better in France."

"I was thinking of England, or perhaps even the United
States. I spoke to Monsieur Bently this afternoon. He went to
university at a place called Stanford in California, and he said
there are some very good boarding schools near there." She had
rushed on, seeing the pain in her husband's face as her words
assaulted him.

"Jesus, Madeleine. We'd never see the boy." His mind flashed
to his own youth, the absence of his father in years when he
desperately needed him. He shook his head. "God has seen fit to
give us only one child, and now you're talking about sending
him away."

"I'm only thinking about what's best for him." She paused,
deciding whether to be completely candid. "I want more for him
than all this. I want him to grow up to be a doctor or a lawyer,
anything but . . ." The look on his face stopped her.

"You mean you don't want your son to grow up to be a
Corsican gangster like his father and grandfather," he said. His

voice was rasping and cold, and his eyes seemed hooded and distant.

"Jean, you know I don't judge you or your father. I understand that you were both limited in what you could do. But Pierre isn't limited. Do you really want him living a life where a man like Carbone might decide to kill him someday? Or to deal every day of his life with men like Francesco?" She watched the anger drain from his face.

"I don't want to lose my son, either. I don't want him to grow up without a father. A boy needs that. He needs a mother too." He added the latter almost as an afterthought.

"We could all go," she said.

"Leave here? My God, Madeleine. How could we do that? We couldn't just abandon my father after all he's done for us."

"Jean, he could come with us. We've more than enough money. There's no need to stay. Auguste could handle matters, or even Francesco." She saw the reaction to Francesco's name and immediately regretted including it in her argument. "Certainly Auguste would be the one your father would want," she added quickly.

"He would never leave." Jean's voice was abrupt, almost curt. "He didn't create this thing we have so he could retire like some *padrone*. He's said so many times. A man builds for his family, and he doesn't abandon what he's built." He leaned forward again, his voice becoming softer. "Besides, there are still problems. And I couldn't just leave him while they still exist. Let me think about it, Madeleine. I know much of what you're saying is right, but it's all too sudden." He smiled at her. "Give me a little time."

"Of course, my darling," she said.

In bed that night, he held her close to him, her head resting against his chest. She was breathing softly, but he could tell she was still awake.

"There's going to be a meeting here in a few days," he whispered. "Lyfoung and some others will be here for dinner, and afterward we will discuss the business problems I mentioned to you. If we can find a way to resolve them permanently, then maybe we can talk to Papa about this thing with Pierre."

He was avoiding the term "leaving," unable even to say the word. She recognized it and understood the pain it gave him. But he was thinking about it, and that was a beginning, she felt.

"We have time," she said, reassuring him. "Pierre is only

twelve. It would be another year before he would have to enter a secondary school, especially in the United States. Perhaps in that time Papa will see the need for it. He loves Pierre as much as we do. I don't think he wants this life for him.'' She stroked his arm with her hand, deciding to say no more.

But she did fear what Buonaparte wanted for her son. His regular studies with his tutor had been augmented with military histories, Corsican history, all of which had been directed by Buonaparte. They spent hours in his study, using his antique soldiers to recreate battle strategies, as though they were part of some mystical religion. She feared he was training the child, preparing him for the future. And it was not the future she wanted for her only son. She had not wanted it for her husband, but she had not been able to exert her influence then. Perhaps it was too late even with her son. But she knew she had to try.

Chapter 12

He was tall and lanky, and often seemed awkward when he walked, but the burgeoning muscle tone that already showed along his body at twelve promised a lean and powerful young man would one day emerge. His blond hair was long for a boy his age, especially one living in a hot, humid climate, but it was a European tradition much admired by his mother, and one he preferred as well. He had learned years before that orientals held those with blond hair in awe, believing it was an indication of superiority, so he had decided it was an advantage he could use. He had found other similar advantages in dealing with orientals. The year of his birth, 1940, had been the Year of the Dragon, a sign—to them—of great power, and one, as his grandfather had explained, that was once an essential criterion for all emperors of China.

The orientals were crazy, he told himself, as he moved about the small roped-off circle he used each day for his karate lesson. Across from him Luc Vien, Lam's twelve-year-old son, feigned repeated attacks with his head, then moved out of reach. Luc was crazy too, he told himself. He had heard his Uncle Francesco complain repeatedly about the "crazy orientals," and it was something he repeated to himself whenever he was frustrated by them. And Luc frustrated him now.

Luc was smaller than he, smaller in every way. But he moved like a land crab and was almost impossible to hit squarely. They had grown up together, the last six years at least, and they were almost like brothers. He had always been better at everything than Luc. Better at swimming, better at running. Everything. And then his grandfather started the karate lessons and it all changed. It made him wonder sometimes if his blond hair had stopped working for him.

The noise came from his right, and he turned his eyes to it. Max was jumping excitedly at the edge of the circle. He felt the blow to his chest and his body spun sideways as he fell, face first in the dirt.

"That's not fair," he shouted, pulling himself to his knees. "I wasn't looking and you knew it."

He struggled to his feet and saw his grandfather standing on the veranda watching him. Their eyes met, then his grandfather turned and walked back into the house.

"Damn," he whispered.

"You must pay attention." The voice was sharp and military.

He turned to face his instructor, Lu Han. The short, squat man marched toward him, hands on his hips, his body swaying from side to side. Lu Han had been an instructor with the Kuomintang army before the communists had sent them running to Taiwan. Now he was here, brought by Pierre's grandfather, and every day, for two hours, he seemed to do nothing but yell at Pierre.

Lu Han growled at him in English, the only language he knew other than Cantonese. "If this were true karate, you be dead now. Why you look at dog when you not fighting dog?"

Pierre knew better than to answer Lu Han back and just hung his head and waited for the tirade to end. It had happened before with the dog. The dog was supposed to be locked in the house during his lesson, and he wondered if his grandfather had let the dog out to see if it would distract him. *Damn*, he told himself.

Lu Han stepped back and brought his palms together, signaling that the two boys should begin again. They circled each other. Pierre's eyes remained fixed on Luc's. He knew if he watched the eyes he would not fall victim to any feint, would know when a real blow was coming. He wanted to get Luc now, so that later he could tell it to his grandfather. He couldn't lie to him about it. Somehow his grandfather always knew.

Luc moved quickly to his right, feinted to his left, then struck out with his right foot. Pierre moved back to his own right and caught a glancing blow along his left knee, hard enough to send a sharp pain shooting up into his hip. Instinctively he struck out with the heel of his left hand, catching Luc on the forehead. The blow was not a strong one, but Luc was still off balance from the kick, and he fell back on the seat of his pants. Pierre recovered and went to him, but Luc spun up and moved to his right and was gone.

Lu Han clapped his hands once and they stopped. "Enough for today," he snapped.

The boys turned and bowed. Lu Han bowed in return.

Pierre let out a long breath. Lu Han turned and started up to the house. He would report to his grandfather now, Pierre knew. He looked angrily at Luc. "I'll get you for that," he whispered.

"For what?" Luc's flat, moonlike face remained passive, his eyes blinking, confused.

"You know for what."

Luc broke into a grin. "You shouldn't look at your dog," he teased.

"Damn you." He lunged at the smaller boy, but missed again.

Luc giggled, spun around and ran toward the river. Pierre raced after him with Max at his side. They practiced in cloths that were wrapped tightly around their loins like bathing suits, and when Luc reached the dock he dove into the water and swam out to the center of the river. Pierre dove in behind him, followed, after a moment of indecision, by the Weimaraner.

"You wait till I get you," Pierre shouted as he broke water.

Luc turned, treading water, then giggled again before diving. He was immediately invisible in the brown, murky water, and Pierre remained in place, waiting for him to surface. He heard Luc giggle behind him and turned. Luc had gone under him and had surfaced ten yards back toward the shore. Pierre started after him, but Luc reached the dock first, pulled himself up, and stood there kicking at Pierre's hands as he tried to get a hold. The dog swam next to Pierre in the water, barking.

"Oh, shut up, Max. You've caused enough trouble today," he shouted at the dog.

Luc laughed again, then leaned down and held out his hand. He pulled Pierre onto the dock, then fell down beside him. Each remained quiet, breathing deeply. After a few moments Pierre turned and punched Luc on the arm.

"Ahh. What you do that for?" Luc groaned.

"You know why." He turned his back on him. "You made me look stupid in front of my grandfather."

"I didn't know your grandfather was there," Luc said.

"You did too."

"No, I didn't. I was watching you . . ." He paused before adding: "Like I was supposed to."

Pierre turned and balled his fist again.

"Hey, stop it," Luc said, flinching away. Over the past six years of playing together Luc's French and English had become as good as Pierre's Lao. But mostly they spoke English; the tribesmen who worked for Pierre's grandfather understood only Lao and some French, and speaking English allowed the boys to have secrets that would not be reported back to the adults.

The dog ran up on the dock and began shaking itself, spraying both boys with water.

"Stop it," Pierre shouted.

"It was all his fault anyway," Luc said. "I thought you said you were going to keep him in the house when you practiced."

"Somebody let him out," Pierre said, thinking again how it was probably his grandfather, intentionally or not. "I don't know why everybody makes such a big thing about it anyway. It's just a sport."

"Not according to Lu Han," Luc said.

"What does he know? If he and his men were so good, why did they get thrown out of your country?" Pierre said.

"You got thrown out of your country," Luc said.

"I did not. We left because my grandfather wanted to. We could have stayed. Besides, my mother's French, so that makes me half French."

"You'd better not let Benito hear you say that," Luc said.

"I can say anything I want," Pierre insisted.

"I bet you won't say it to him," Luc said.

"If I want to I will," Pierre said, knowing he never would.

Pierre struggled to his feet. He didn't want to talk about it any longer. He knew being Corsican was important. It was important to all of them, especially his grandfather. "You want to swim some more?" he asked.

Luc shook his head. "Let's go get dressed and see if we can catch something."

Pierre grinned. "We could catch a snake and put it in my Uncle Auguste's room," he said. Auguste was terrified of snakes, never taking the time to see if they were poisonous or not. A month earlier the two boys had captured a baby python, no more than three feet long. When Auguste had found it in his room, he had panicked and taken a pistol to it, blowing a hole the size of a piaster in the floor.

Within ten minutes the boys were dressed and searching the edge of the forest that bordered the broad plain. Pierre had a burlap sack hitched to his belt to carry their prize back to the house. Max moved ahead of them, head sweeping from side to side, nose to the ground, occasionally breaking off when a rat or ground toad was flushed from cover.

After two hours they gave up on snakes and settled for a four-foot-long monitor lizard they found sleeping next to a rotting log. It took them fifteen minutes to subdue the angry reptile, mostly because Max kept interfering, trying to bite the frightened creature and getting slapped with its tail with each effort.

"We'll have to be careful going back to the house," Luc warned. "If any of my people see it, they'll take it away."

Pierre nodded. He knew the lizard was considered a delicacy among the Meo.

"I don't know how you people eat those things," he said. He had eaten lizard once, not knowing what it was. It had tasted like a cross between poultry and frog's legs, only chewier. When he had discovered what he had eaten, he had felt ill.

"It's good," Luc said. "Almost as good as snake."

They moved casually, as innocently as they could, across the plain toward the house. Pierre had tied a vine around the neck of the sack and now dragged it behind him in the knee-high grass, pushing Max away with his foot as the dog repeatedly tried to circle them to get at it. Ten yards from the house, where the grass was cut to ground level, they broke into a run, stopping at the mangosteen tree that stood along the side of the house.

Auguste's room was on the first floor, off the veranda, opposite the tree. Pierre placed a finger against his lips, then leaned toward Luc's ear.

"I'll lift you and you go and look inside and see if he's there," he whispered. "If he's not, I'll come up with it and put it inside."

Luc placed his hand over his mouth to suppress a giggle, then, with Pierre's help, climbed over the veranda. He was back at the railing in a moment, waving Pierre ahead. Pierre climbed over the railing, dragging the sack with him. The two boys tiptoed to the French doors outside the room, then crouched down. The door was partially open, and Pierre opened it farther, then poked his head inside. When he pulled his head out he was biting his lip and his eyes were dancing. Quickly he untied the sack, grabbed it at the bottom and swung it inside, shaking it until the lizard flopped out on the foor.

Each boy felt a hand grab the back of his neck at the same moment. Simultaneously they were lifted from the floor. When Pierre glanced over his shoulder he saw Auguste staring down at him. Auguste stuck out his foot and kicked the door open, just in time to see the lizard crawl under his bed.

"You," he said. "And it was you who put that damned snake in my room."

Pierre's eyes widened, not sure what would happen next. Auguste just stared at him, then at Luc, whose dark complexion had suddenly gone gray. Behind him Max began to whine his dissatisfaction, and Auguste released them, knowing the dog would not tolerate much more.

"We will discuss this with your grandfather," Auguste said. His voice was a growling whisper, and it seemed more threatening to Pierre than if he had been shouting.

The two boys stood before Sartene's desk. The study was imposing, threatening to a minor degree. It was intended to be so. It was foreign territory, even for those who had been there many times; very much the private terrain of one man. The dark paneled walls, even at midday, muted the light; the heavy teak desk was a distinct barrier. The paintings and books that lined the walls were very much the personal property, the individual taste of the occupant. Even when he joined his grandfather at the long table of antique soldiers and horses and cannon, Pierre often felt they were things he should not freely touch.

Standing in front of Sartene now, with Luc beside him, he felt a sense of boyish doom.

Sartene's face was grave, disappointed, as he heard Auguste's complaint, and he remained silent when his friend had finished, looking from one boy to the other.

"So, you don't like your Uncle Auguste. You want to harm him, or cause some poor ignorant beast to harm him. I understand that." He leaned back in his chair and gestured with one hand toward Auguste. "I've heard his complaint, and now I want to hear yours." He watched Pierre's lips move, then stop. "I couldn't hear you, Pierre," he said softly.

"I don't understand what you mean," the boy whispered.

Sartene nodded. "I see. I'll try to make myself clear." He leaned forward, his forearms on the desk, drawing closer to his grandson. "I assume Auguste has done something to offend you, and that you felt the need to avenge that offense. I just want to know what it was so I can understand who was in the right, that's all."

Pierre looked down at the floor, then sideways at Luc. He desperately tried to think of something Auguste had done. He knew there was no hope. "Nothing, Grandpère," he finally said.

"Nothing. Nothing at all." He sat back, raised his hands, then allowed them to fall helplessly in his lap.

"I'm sorry," Pierre whispered.

"Well, that's fine," Sartene said. "But now Auguste has a grievance against you, and I can't ask him not to do anything. His manhood may require it."

There was a long silence before Sartene continued. "But before we decide on that, we must deal with Luc," he said. "Your family serves us here, Luc. And so far they have served us well."

"Perhaps we should send him back to the hills," Auguste interrupted.

"No," Pierre said, his voice still a whisper. "It was my idea," he added, louder now.

A wave of trembling swept Luc's shoulders. "It was my idea too," he said.

"See," Auguste said. "They protect each other."

Sartene lowered his head, covering his mouth with the fingers of one hand. He looked up again, keeping his eyes from Auguste, knowing he had to if he was to avoid giving himself away. "Well, what will you do with them?" he finally asked.

"Since they didn't actually harm me, I don't feel I have to harm them," Auguste answered. "I'd be willing to accept some payment instead. Maybe that dog, Max. I always thought he was a good dog."

"No, Uncle Auguste," Pierre said.

Auguste continued to stare straight ahead. "Maybe just some service I need. I'll have to think about it, Buonaparte. But right now I want them to get that damned beast out from under my bed. And to clean up any mess it's made."

Sartene waved the back of his hand at the two boys. "Go do as you're told," he said. "Auguste will need time to decide how to deal with this."

Pierre gave him a pleading look. Sartene looked from one boy to the other.

"I can't do anything," he said, making sure each boy knew he was speaking to both. "If Auguste were my enemy, or an enemy of any in our group, then it would be different. Then I could protect you from him." He shrugged his shoulders in a gesture of futility. "But he is one of us, so I must respect his need for vengeance. So go. Go."

When the two boys reached the door, they found Pierre's father about to enter.

Jean ruffled Pierre's hair. "Where are you going?" he asked.

"I have to do something for Grandpère," Pierre said, rushing past his father with Luc at his heels.

Jean leaned out the door and watched them retreat down the hall, then returned to the room, closing the door behind him. "What's happened?" he asked, looking from his father to Auguste. Both men's eyes were dancing with pleasure.

Sartene raised a finger, then could contain himself no more. He and Auguste burst out laughing. Jean looked at them as if they had lost their minds.

"Those little bastards," Auguste said, before bursting into laughter again.

"What?" Jean said.

"I caught them putting a monster lizard in my room," Auguste said, struggling for breath.

"How big?" Jean asked.

Auguste stretched his hands apart, almost as far as they would go. "A damned dragon," he said. "If I'd found it in my bed tonight, I would have had a heart attack."

"I'm sorry, Auguste," Jean said, trying not to laugh. "I'll see that Pierre is punished."

Sartene waved his hand back and forth. "No. Give him a little hell, but let Auguste and me have our fun. We just had a trial here. I should have called for you, but I never thought of it. We were enjoying it too much. He thinks now that Auguste has the right to seek vengeance from him."

Jean shook his head. "Corsican games," he said.

"Let old men have their fun," Auguste said. "What harm can it do?"

"You know," Sartene said, "it reminds me of something that happened when I was a boy in the hills with Papa Guerini." He laughed to himself, warming to his own story. "Papa was asleep in his hut, and Mémé and I, we found this field mouse outside. Well, we snuck into Papa's hut, and we put the mouse under his blanket, then went outside to wait and see what would happen. All of a sudden the mouse starts to run up Papa's leg, headed straight for his balls. What a roar he let out. Then he comes running out of the hut and he sees Mémé and me. Christ, he chased us for half a mile, waving his sword over his head." He stopped, wiping the tears from his eyes. All three men were laughing.

"Well, at least we know where he gets it from," Jean said. Then: "Right now I have to talk to you about this meeting with Lyfoung."

"All right, all right," Sartene said. "Auguste, you go torture the criminals while I talk business with this humorless son of mine." Auguste started for the door and Sartene called after him. "Come back later and tell me what you did," he said.

The two boys sat on a log at the edge of the forest, each looking paler than usual.

"Do you think they'll send me away?" Luc finally asked.

"If they do, I'll go with you," Pierre said defiantly. "And he'd better not try and take Max either."

"I hope they don't tell my father," Luc said.

Thoughts of his own father crept into Pierre's mind. He would have to face him as well. He could see no immediate end to the punishments at hand.

"How come you didn't see him?" Pierre asked, hoping to affix blame on Luc.

Luc simply shrugged, too intent on his own inner visions of banishment to even notice. He looked up, and across the plain saw Auguste starting down the steps of the house. "There he is," he whispered, as if his voice would carry the entire distance and give them away.

"Let's get out of here," Pierre said, slipping off the log and stepping back into the bush. "Hurry."

They went ten feet into the bush, keeping their eyes on Auguste. "If we stay out of his way, maybe he'll just forget about it," Pierre said.

"You think he will?" Luc asked.

"Not really," Pierre said. "But maybe he won't be as mad later."

"Maybe he'll get madder if he can't find us," Luc said.

"Damn," Pierre whispered. He looked mournfully at the smaller boy. He seemed to have become even smaller. "Come on,'' Pierre said finally. "We might as well go and get it over.''

The two boys walked slowly into the plain and started toward Auguste. Max raced ahead of them, impervious to the dangers for which each boy was prepared.

Stupid dog, Pierre thought. It'll serve you right if he takes you away.

Jean had told Madeleine about Pierre's mischief and the game that his father and Auguste were now playing out. She had smiled, but had said nothing, and as he lay next to her now in the darkness of their room, Jean was troubled about the possibility of taking Pierre away from his father. He wondered if she truly understood the love the older man felt for the child. But he knew she was right too. Sending Pierre to the *lycée* in Vientiane or Saigon was no solution to his need for more education. He had come home bruised and battered from the colonial school he had attended years before, and had repeatedly been punished by the headmaster for starting fights with the children of the French officials who had taunted him. His father had likened it to Napoleon's school days in France, and had given Pierre a book to read that contained portions of the emperor's schoolboy diary and letters written to his brother in Corsica. Sartene had been angry about the abuse, but in some ways, Jean knew, he had almost seemed proud of the comparison. He drew a breath, thinking of it again, and Madeleine reached out and ran her hand along his chest.

"Is something troubling you?" she whispered.

He shook his head, then realized it could not be seen in the darkened room. "I was just thinking about what we talked about. About sending Pierre away. I understand the need for it, but the idea of taking him away from my father is hard. You should have seen them today, my father especially. The only time I see him enjoy himself is when he's with the boy.''

"All the more reason for him to come with us," she said. She knew the words were an unspoken confirmation that they would all leave. It was what she truly wanted if possible, but she also knew saying it openly would produce resistance. He was quiet again, and she feared he had noticed the implication. She stroked his chest again and drew closer to him. "There's time. At least a year," she said, remaining close.

Fifteen minutes later his breathing pattern had changed and

she could tell he was asleep and she allowed herself to relax. Earlier that evening she had overheard her father-in-law talking with her son. It had been about his karate lesson that afternoon, and she had heard her son complain that Luc had not fought fairly. Sartene's voice had been gentle with the boy, but again there had been the never-ending instruction. She recalled his words again.

"You should know two things about fighting," he had told the boy. "The first is to avoid it whenever possible. The second is that only the loser ever concerns himself about what was fair."

Madeleine rolled over on her side, her back to her husband now. It was not what she wanted her son to be taught, she told herself. It was not the life she wanted for him.

Chapter 13

The request for a meeting in Saigon had thrown Antonio Carbone into near panic. He was still the unquestioned leader of the Saigon *milieu*. He still earned an annual fortune from the illicit piaster-gold market between Marseille and Saigon, Saigon and Hong Kong. And he still maintained his control over the gambling and opium dens run by Saigon's Binh Xuyen river pirates. He lacked control only over the source of local opium and, because of that, remained a minor force when compared to Buonaparte Sartene. And as such, he continued to earn his bread at Sartene's indulgence. He had only to look out the window of his study and see the faintly charred remains of his once dynamite-blackened driveway to be reminded of the fact.

The request from Francesco Canterina had been straightforward enough. "A business meeting to our mutual advantage," it had said. And the place, the exclusive Continental Palace Hotel, which Carbone owned, had been a gesture of good faith. But still, perhaps, a trap, he told himself.

Francesco had arrived one day before the meeting was to take place, and had registered at the hotel under a false name. It had been another gesture, to give Carbone ample time to determine whether he had come secretly and alone. Yet there had still been concern. It could prove to be a test by Sartene, an excuse to take away the little that had been left to him.

They met in the late morning, in the large suite Francesco had taken. Carbone arrived with four aides, who remained outside the door. As always, he was resplendent in a white suit, set off by a garishly flowered necktie that seemed to rest on his large protruding stomach like a wayward garden. Francesco greeted

149

him warmly, respectfully, and noticed at once that his deep-set eyes were filled with suspicion, his thin mouth, usually curved up at the edges as if hiding some great and humorous secret, now even and tense. He smiled to himself, knowing he was dealing with a frightened man, even more frightened than he had expected.

They sat opposite each other in two straight-backed chairs drawn closely together. Francesco wanted intimacy, and he spoke quietly, only slightly above a whisper, to emphasize the fact.

"I came here to tell you my feeling that the day of Buonaparte Sartene is past," he began.

Carbone stiffened slightly, his suspicions heightened. He raised one hand, stopping any further words.

"Tell me, my friend, why I shouldn't go straight to a telephone and call my good friend and tell him what you've just said."

Francesco smiled. "You'll always have that option. You could listen to my proposal, even agree to it, and still pick up your telephone when I'm gone. You could even agree, wait to see if my plan works, and then, if it fails, join forces with Buonaparte and help him get his vengeance." He smiled again. "Or you could work with me and reclaim your right as *paceri* of all the *milieu* of the region. For now I only ask you to listen."

Carbone laughed, his fleshy cheeks shaking. The laughter stopped abruptly and his eyes narrowed. "You offer me the moon and the stars and no danger. You think I'm a fool?"

"If I thought that, I wouldn't be here. You think this might be some kind of trick by Buonaparte." Francesco shook his head. "Buonaparte doesn't play tricks. His strength is that he knows ahead of time what people will do. In the message I sent you, I asked you not to discuss this meeting with two men in your group. Did you keep it secret from them?"

Carbone nodded, his eyes becoming even narrower under his bushy eyebrows.

"They're Buonaparte's spies," Francesco said. "I give you this as a gift. You have ways of finding out if it's true."

"Go on," Carbone said.

Francesco leaned back in his chair and gestured with one hand as he spoke. "We both know that the opium growth in North Viet Nam is controlled by the Viet Minh. The French have allowed the Meo there to be cheated, and because of that they've lost the loyalty of the tribesmen. Even so, the amount grown in North Viet Nam is small compared to what's produced in Laos,

Burma and Thailand. Up to now, more expensive opium has been available from China and Iran. But as you know, since 1950 the Chinese have sealed off their borders. They're convinced the Americans will help the Kuomintang invade from the south. Two years ago, Iran exported two hundred and forty-six tons a year. But under pressure from the west, that has now dropped to less than a hundred tons, and is expected to go to less than half that within the next year or two.''

"So what does that mean, except more riches for Buonaparte?" Carbone said. "And if he gets rich, you get rich."

Francesco shook his head, his handsome face twisting with anger. "This is what Buonaparte thinks. And it's why his time is over. The Viet Minh use the opium from the north to finance their revolution. The French, even though they claim they're trying to abolish opium from the region, use it to keep their control, to finance their army and their mercenaries. But the French can draw from all Southeast Asia. The Viet Minh know they have to do that as well. Already they've joined with the Pathet Lao, and they're getting ready to move against the Meo in Xieng Khouang. After that they'll move into Thailand and Burma. Just enough to control the opium. That's all that's needed."

"Buonaparte will never let them," Carbone said.

"No, he won't." Francesco leaned forward, emphasizing the intimacy again. "But in time it will happen anyway. This is what Buonaparte doesn't understand. But the Viet Minh want it now, and they know if they can't succeed in Laos, they can't go beyond it. There would be no supply lines. Right now the French are spread too thin to do it themselves. They have to rely on Buonaparte to keep the area secure. But what if Buonaparte didn't exist? What if he and his son were to meet with an accident?'' He paused for effect. "An accident arranged from within his own group. Then the Viet Minh would succeed. And they would owe an obligation to the men who helped them. Even today, the generals and politicians here in the south buy opium from the Viet Minh to feather their nests; the French know it, and they know they have to let them buy it to keep their loyalty. You know it too. Your people buy what you can from the Viet Minh. But if the Viet Minh succeed, they would deal only with you, and the others would have to buy from you. And the Viet Minh would control all the opium, or nearly all. And then everyone would have to buy from you.''

"The French would never allow it," Carbone objected. "They

watch us like eagles. I'd be thrown out of the country, or worse, if I dealt with the Viet Minh that openly."

"Here in Saigon, yes," Francesco said. "But in Laos the French have less control. And I would be in Laos. And we would be partners." He looked hard into Carbone's eyes. "Equal partners."

Carbone squeezed the flesh of his double chin, massaging it with his fingers. "Why doesn't Buonaparte deal with the Viet Minh? He could handle this as well as we could."

Francesco smiled at Carbone's use of the word "we." *He wants to stay in this godforsaken country.* "He wants to build his dynasty and pass it on to his son and his son's son. He thinks of himself as some emperor." He laughed. "Like his namesake."

Carbone joined Francesco's laughter, pleased with the derision.

"Buonaparte thinks if he deals with these people, these communists, they will win, and he'll be thrown out, forced to leave as a rich man. I don't care about that, any more than the generals and the politicians here in the south care. Any more than I think you care. Besides, years ago Buonaparte attacked a Meo leader named Lo Faydang, the man the Viet Minh will use to lead the attack in Laos. And Lo Faydang would rather deal with someone else. He has been trying to regain his position with the Meo for years. Now the Viet Minh are supporting him as part of their latest offensive against the French."

An image of the slender aesthetic Meo leader flashed through Carbone's mind. He had seen his picture among wanted posters issued by the French, along with warnings that, like other Viet Minh, he often moved freely through the south. "But you think he'd deal with you," Carbone said.

"Yes," Francesco said.

Carbone shrugged, accepting the statement while expressing his doubt. "How would you arrange these accidents you spoke about?" he asked.

"Years ago, when Buonaparte drove Faydang from the region, he warned him he would die if he returned. Now he will have to make good his threat, and he'll send his son to do that. I'll make sure I'm with him. I'll also make sure he never comes back."

Carbone laughed. "Buonaparte will spend the rest of his life looking for you, if you do that," he said.

Francesco shook his head. "Only if he's alive," he said. "I have some men loyal to me within our group. The same day, at the same hour as his son dies, so will he." He raised his hand

and hurried on. "They'll do this, but only if they're assured I have your support. If you have men there with them to prove that support. Otherwise their fear of Buonaparte may make them wait. And that would be very dangerous."

Carbone folded his hands across his stomach and began tapping his thumbs together. "It's a nice story, my young friend. But it's only a story. To believe it, I would have to believe you have contacts among the Viet Minh that no white man has." He shrugged, dismissing the idea, and leaned forward, preparing to lift his bulk from the chair.

"Before you go, there's someone I'd like you to meet." Francesco rose and walked to a door leading to a bedroom.

Carbone froze. Despite his security precautions, someone else had been present. The words he had spoken raced through his mind as he searched for anything he had said that would now be used against him. He thought of running for the door, for his own men. But he knew it would be useless. If there was someone in the bedroom, his men would have been taken by now.

Francesco opened the door and stepped aside, allowing the slender oriental to pass. Carbone's mouth formed a circle, then changed into a smile. He stood and bowed his head to Lo Faydang.

Chapter 14

Pierre struggled to hide his fascination with the dinner guests, but his eyes kept returning to the three oriental men. His grandfather had told him never to appear in awe of another man, warning it was something that would be exploited. But he couldn't help himself, and he doubted if these strange men from the north would bother exploiting a twelve-year-old boy.

They were seated in the massive dining room, which his mother had furnished. He knew his grandfather did not particularly like the room. The ornate Louis Quatorze furnishings were not to his taste, and even though he had built the large, sprawling house, Pierre knew he would have furnished it simply. He disliked displays of wealth; Pierre had heard him say so many times. But his mother had been allowed to choose the furnishings and, according to his father, had gone mad with her love of beautiful things.

Throughout the house the walls were lined with paintings by French and Dutch impressionists, mingling with intricate tapestries, each seeming to compete with delicate oriental vases and jade sculptures. Rich oriental carpets, imported from Iran, graced the highly polished teak floors, and each room had a mantel of Italian marble, decorating fireplaces that were never used. She had told his grandfather she was seeking an eclectic beauty, but Sartene had told Pierre later that his mother simply needed something that reminded her of home. So he indulged her. Outside of his study, the only mark he had placed on the house was in the dining room, a portrait of Napoleon that hung opposite his place at the table.

Pierre recalled now how his mother had tried to talk him out

of it, claiming it struck a note of disharmony among the paintings by Manet, Degas and Monet that surrounded it. His grandfather had only smiled and told her that Napoleon had always been
considered out of place during his lifetime but that he could
never be so in the home of a Corsican.

His mind had been wandering; he had been thinking about the
house, and he had not heard the question directed at him in
French.

"Excuse me, I didn't hear what you said." The boy's face
took on a touch of pink.

Colonel Deo Van Khoun smiled and repeated the question,
asking how many languages Pierre spoke.

"Well, I speak Corsican, of course," Pierre said. "And English,
French and Lao. But my Lao isn't as good as it should be.
Sometimes I mix up the words and make people laugh."

The colonel laughed now, a high-pitched laugh that seemed
more appropriate for a woman. "It's a difficult language," Deo
said. "It has a little Thai mixed in, some Chinese, and of course
some Meo." With the last linguistic ingredient he gestured with
his hand toward the end of the table, where Touby Lyfoung sat
opposite his mother. "Fortunately, we all speak French in Laos.
Otherwise we would have to use sign language with each other,"
Deo added, giggling again.

"Fortunate for you," Matt Bently said. "My French often runs
into the same problems as Pierre's Lao. I once gave an order for
some Lao troops to advance, and they all put down their weapons and took off their shirts."

Everyone laughed. Pierre could not see Bently. He was seated
opposite Touby Lyfoung, to his mother's right, the same side of
the table the boy occupied. But he was grateful for the remark.
Bently always had a way of making the boy feel at ease.

"I often had the same difficulty during the war, dealing with
Americans," Buonaparte Sartene said. "I learned English as a
boy, working on the docks in Corsica and Marseille. But the
Americans we met during the war were always talking about
seeing the big picture, and worrying about the cookie jar being
empty. You remember, don't you, Auguste?"

Pierre followed his grandfather's gaze down the table to where
Auguste sat. Auguste smiled and touched his chest with one
finger.

"I remember well, Buonaparte," Auguste said. "But I never
understood what they were talking about." He gestured with his

head across the table, toward Francesco Canterina. "Francesco understood them. He learned it listening to the songs on the radio."

"The Andrews Sisters taught me everything," Francesco said.

Buonaparte shook his finger. "Just like you, Francesco. You learn everything from women."

"We all learn from women," Jean Sartene said.

Pierre looked across the table at his father. He was seated between Deo and Lyfoung, and his size seemed to dwarf both men. When Pierre had been introduced to the two men earlier, he had been surprised to find that at five feet seven inches, he was an inch taller than they. He was taller than most of the Mua, but somehow he had expected the two colonels to be larger, more like Bently, who was also a colonel.

Colonel Deo reminded him of a snake somehow, even in his Royal Laotian Army uniform, the left breast of which was covered with a rainbow of ribbons. He was a slender, delicate-looking man, with hooded eyes and high cheekbones and a flat nose that seemed to grow out of his black mustache. It was his long neck, Pierre thought. Or maybe the white silk scarf that protruded from his tunic, like the belly of a cobra when it reared to strike.

Colonel Lyfoung was different, funny even, he told himself. Like a big ball, even in his uniform, which had actual medals hanging from its tunic, not just ribbons. The third oriental, the Meo who stood behind Touby's chair, was supposed to be his aide, but his father had told him he was really Touby's bodyguard. He was the most fascinating of all, but he had not been introduced to anyone, which Pierre had thought rude.

The aide/bodyguard was dressed in the black pajama suit the Meo always wore. But his was elaborately decorated with red and gold embroidery, and from the gold sash around his waist a long sheathed knife hung. When he had been introduced to Touby, Pierre had stared at the knife and Lyfoung had ordered the man to show it to him. To Pierre's shock the man had cut the heel of his hand before returning it to the sheath.

"It is a Meo custom," Touby had explained. "Once a knife is drawn, it must always be bloodied before it is returned."

Pierre had stared at the aide's hand, noting the many scars that marked it, and he had decided that the Ly clan spent much of their time carving themselves up. He had also decided to ask Luc about it. He had never seen the Mua do anything like it.

Almost as though he had felt Pierre's thoughts, Touby suddenly turned and grinned at him. "What year were you born?" he asked.

"Nineteen forty, sir," Pierre said.

Touby nodded, still grinning, then turned his gaze toward Sartene. "A child of the Dragon," he said. "Someday he will rule here as kaitong."

"Only if he proves worthy," Sartene said, tossing a glance of mock seriousness at the boy. "He does well in most things. He is very good at catching lizards and snakes, right now," Sartene said, watching the boy's face turn scarlet.

"Do you eat them?" Colonel Deo asked.

"No, sir," Pierre said, praying silently that his grandfather would not elaborate on the story.

The colonel continued, saving him. "The Meo are very fond of these delicacies," he said. "It comes, I think, from the years their ancestors spent in China. Our Tai food is similar to theirs, only not as spicy."

"You need spicy food in a hot climate," Lyfoung interjected. "It helps you perspire, and keeps the body clean of evil spirits." He grinned, watching the boy's eyes widen. "There are many evil spirits in the mountains," he added.

"And most of them are Phou-Keo," Deo added, using the Lao term of contempt for the Vietnamese.

When the meal ended, Madeleine excused herself and Pierre, leaving the men to discuss business over brandy. Pierre had hoped he would be allowed to remain with the men; he had hoped his mother would relent this one time. He had been pleased by Lyfoung's reference to him as a future kaitong. He knew the Mua called his grandfather kaitong among themselves, and the idea that he would one day be like his grandfather pleased him. The only thing he didn't like about the term was that it meant "little king." He saw no reason for the word "little."

When the servant who poured the brandy had left, Sartene gestured to Colonel Deo. As scion to the feudal Black Tai chieftains, and as a field officer in the regular Lao army, he outranked Touby, and was entitled to the courtesy of explaining the difficulties in the north.

Deo leaned back in his chair, swirling his brandy glass in one hand, his hooded eyes fixed on the tablecloth. "We have learned that General Vo Nguyen Giap is massing his Viet Minh force near Dien Bien Phu to the north," he said. "The peasants there tell us he plans to move against the area by your Christmas. It is not well defended and it will fall if he does."

"The French know this," Bently said. "They're not concerned about it. They feel they can recapture the area quickly and limit the effect. There's even talk of starting to reinforce the area then, of bringing in artillery to form a large defensive hedgehog over the next year or two. They feel they can make it impenetrable."

"The French. The French," Sartene said. "They still think they can fight this war of theirs from textbooks. They don't understand that the Viet Minh are fighting a political war, not a military one." He waved one arm in a circle. "They take one village and then they withdraw and disappear. But each victory makes converts to a new nationalism. The French always thought they had conquered Corsica. But each time a bandit robbed a bank, the people cheered."

"What the French do not know is that the Viet Minh will join with the Pathet Lao after this, and then move on Xieng Khouang," Deo said.

"Already Faydang has been seen to the north of our region. I think he's preparing for this," Lyfoung added. "But he's been like a spirit. When we search for him, he's gone."

"I have plans for defending the region," Sartene said. "I've talked about it with some of the younger French officers, some Corsicans who understand the problem. But I'll explain that later. What I don't understand is why you suddenly find it difficult to locate Faydang."

Touby began to speak, but Deo interrupted. He obviously enjoyed this part of the unfavorable news. "Some of the Meo have been seeking conciliation with Faydang. They seem to feel it's necessary to ensure their next harvest, should the Pathet Lao be successful this time." He glanced sideways at Lyfoung, who had folded his hands and was nervously rubbing the palms with his thumbs.

"Why haven't I heard about this?" Jean said.

"I thought we could resolve it. I still think we can," Lyfoung said. He smiled at Jean, but the smile faded when their eyes met. "It is only a few, but they warn him and help him hide from us."

"A few grow into many, dammit," Jean said. "You should have told me so I could have stopped it immediately."

"It is not too late," Deo said. "I have learned who these peasants are. When the example is made, the others will realize who is in control. A few beheadings will serve us very well."

"We'll go tomorrow morning," Jean said, directing himself to Lyfoung. "And I hope I'm not going to find a bigger problem than you've described."

"Wait," Sartene said. "I don't want my son involved in these reprisals. He will have to carry out the new plans I spoke of, and it would be difficult if he made enemies in any of the villages." He looked down the table at Auguste. "You could do this, Auguste. But I'll need you here until Benito returns from Bangkok in the afternoon. We could delay this one day," he added.

"I could do it for you, Buonaparte," Francesco said. "I'd be happy to do this service for Jean, and since I'm not involved with the people in these villages it shouldn't harm any future plans."

"What do you think, Jean?" Sartene asked.

Jean stared across the table at Francesco, puzzled by his willingness to help. "I'm happy to have Francesco's help," he said. "How many of the Mua would you want to take?"

"None," Francesco answered. "I could use Touby's men. It would reinforce his strength there, and later when you went to these villages with the Mua, there wouldn't be any connection. Besides, Touby has good men." He looked across the table and nodded his approval of Lyfoung.

"Yes, it's good," Lyfoung said, eager now for some support.

Sartene glanced between his son and Francesco. The offer surprised him too, but he knew that to refuse Francesco's offer to help his son would only widen the rift that had divided them for years. He turned his attention to Bently. "Can you go with them, Matt?" he asked.

"Yes," Bently said. "I'd like to. It'll be my last chance to see the Meo country."

"Last chance?" Sartene questioned.

"I'm going home, Buonaparte. At the end of the month. In time for Christmas. I was going to tell you later."

"I'm sorry to hear this," Sartene said. "I knew someday you would leave, but it was something I always put out of my mind."

"I'm sorry too," Jean said. "But perhaps I'll come and visit you." He let the words drop, then changed the subject. He had decided to speak to his father about Pierre's schooling, about all

of them leaving, but that was for later, after the others left.
"Will you go with Francesco?" he asked.

"No. I've seen enough beheadings to last me a lifetime,"
Bently said. "If you don't mind I'll stay with you."

Deo leaned forward, taking his brandy snifter in both hands.
He had no interest in the American. "What is this new plan you
spoke of?" he asked Sartene.

Sartene took care to look at each man at the table. "It's very
simple, really, and as I said it has the support of younger French
officers who can provide the initial training we will need. The
other thing it will do is to move the hill people out of just a
military fight with the Pathet Lao, a simple holding on to certain
geography, and put them into the political fight." He turned his
attention to Lyfoung and Deo. "Right now your men work under
this Mixed Airborne Commando Group of the French, whenever
they need you to help their forces in your region. The rest of the
time you do nothing but keep watch on your own people to
maintain their loyalty. When you need money or arms you go to
Saigon and take what you need from the SDECE *caisse noire.* In
return they get their percentage of the opium harvest to finance
this war they're trying so hard to lose."

"It's the way the French have always wanted it," Deo said.
"We provide the opium and the fodder for the fire when it's
needed." He glanced at Touby with a hint of irony. "At least it
has made some of us rich," he added.

Sartene's eyes darkened, and he allowed them to carry their
full weight to the two men. His voice remained soft, but held an
undeniable threat. "The French may want it that way. But I
don't," he said. Sartene timed his words, as always. Waiting
before continuing, allowing for the full impact of his edict.
"Whether the French remain here or not. Whether they're replaced by the Americans or not. *We* will remain. To do this we
have to have the support of the people who concern us." He
spread his hands apart benevolently. "We've been fair with
them. We don't cheat them like those fools in the Tonkin region.
Maybe they think we tax them too much, but we provide them
with protection for those taxes. They have a market for their
opium, and that puts food on their tables. They have to understand that even if the French leave, they still have that market
with us." He jabbed one finger forward. "They also have to
understand that they have their independence with us, and they

will never have that with the communists. This independence is a fierce thing with these people, and it's our best weapon."

"I don't understand," Touby said. "How can we make our hold on the people stronger and make them think they are independent at the same time?"

"You think discipline and freedom can't work together?" Sartene asked. He smiled at Lyfoung, playing the teacher to the pupil. "During the war in Europe the resistance operated with great independence, and they were still the most disciplined fighters in the war. When they were needed somewhere, they were there. Because they *knew* it was in their interest to be there."

"I don't understand," Deo said.

"I think I do." Bently smiled down the table at Sartene. "You're talking about a *maquis*, a small, tightly disciplined counterguerrilla infrastructure."

Sartene's eyes warmed to his American friend. Over the years he had learned to appreciate the difference between this man and the fool he had known in the mountains of southern France. "We are going to miss you, my friend," he said.

"But how do we pick the right people, and how do we train them?" Touby asked. This new idea meant work for him, and possible expense. But even worse, he felt, it might also prove a threat to his authority.

"When you go back to the hill country tomorrow, you and my son will begin this thing." He noted Touby's concern, understood it and decided to deal with it directly. "You'll start in your own village. Later you can go to the others. In all we only need fifty men to start. They will report to you, and they'll owe their new opportunity to you."

Sartene stood and walked behind his chair, placing his hands on the back of it almost as though it were a lectern. "You'll need men who fight well, who've proved their worth that way. And some of these men should be ambitious." He wagged a finger at Touby. "Don't be afraid of ambitious men. To have a successful organization you have to have these people. Just make sure they're loyal to you and that they understand that their hopes for the future depend on your success. Besides, these people you choose will control very small numbers of men, so by themselves they won't be a threat."

Sartene returned to his chair and leaned forward, his palms pressed together, prayerlike. "You'll only need fifty men to start with, picked from all the scattered villages of your region. They will be sent to the French Action School at Cap St. Jacques for thirty or forty days of training, whatever's needed. The French officers I spoke of will do this for you in return for certain considerations." He smiled. "About three or four thousand dollars' worth of raw opium. A fortune back in France. They'll train the men in small weapons, counterintelligence, explosives and how to operate radios. After the training we will break them up into four-man groups. Each group will have a commander—the ambitious ones—a radio operator and two intelligence officers. The groups will have been trained to operate independently, so if one group is destroyed, the *maquis* still survives. And each reports to you, and through you to my son."

"But fifty men, just fifty . . ."

Sartene stopped Touby with a gesture. "When this first group returns, you will give them two tasks. First, they must gather information about Pathet Lao and Viet Minh in the area and report this back. Second, they must start to propagandize the villages. Remember, they'll be coming back with new weapons and radios; they'll have great stature and a certain closeness to you, their kaitong. In addition to their intelligence-gathering, each man will be expected to recruit two new men. Some will recruit three even, and all those men will then be sent off to be trained, at a cost to us of another nine thousand dollars in raw opium. But within about three months, well before the new planting must begin next March, we will have a *maquis* of forty different groups, each one capable of searching out Pathet Lao and Viet Minh and assassinating leaders and traitors, of finding camps and supply lines. Then, together with your warriors, they can drive them out, or disrupt them. And most important, they'll be independent. And that will produce pride in their villages." Sartene paused to smile, then jabbed his finger into his chest. "And they'll owe this to us. And they'll be loyal in order to keep what we've given them."

"Won't the French wonder about this new training?" Deo asked.

"Why should they?" Jean asked, taking up his father's plan. "The French are always training mercenaries, and they'll have nothing to do with the final way these men are organized. Besides, if someone from SDECE becomes suspicious, a little raw opium will satisfy him. Everyone here has a bank account in Hong Kong that needs filling."

Touby was fidgeting in his chair. He was still nervous, still concerned that he might lose control over his region.

Bently saw it and decided to soothe the fat little colonel. "This is a great opportunity for you, colonel," he said. "There were guerrilla groups like this in the Philippines during the war, and the people who ran them became national heroes and are running the country now." He caught a glimmer of contempt on Deo's face. The Black Tais had no respect for the Meo, considering them little more than ignorant peasants. Bently's manipulation of Touby seemed to confirm those beliefs. Bently decided to push Deo as well. "Isn't that so, Colonel Deo?" he added.

"Most definitely," Deo said.

"You must remember, Touby," Sartene added, "these men will be in contact with us by radio. And we'll have the power to take away what's been given to them."

"And that gives you even more power than you have now," Auguste added.

Touby nodded, trying to convince himself, satisfy himself there was no threat. Sartene watched him, knowing the man would talk himself into it, if given time. Touby's ego was such that he was able to convince himself that a defeat had been a victory, a criticism truly disguised praise. He believed he was kaitong of his region, even though he took his instructions from Jean and, therefore, from Sartene himself.

Sartene picked up a small crystal bell and rang it. The servant reappeared and refilled the brandy snifters. The only person at the table who had not joined in support of his plan was Francesco. The fact had registered. It was unlike the man not to assert himself, not to attempt to impress with his ideas and his loyalty. But he had offered help. Sartene would now have to see how that help was given.

When the three orientals and Francesco had departed, Madeleine remained in the sitting room with Bently. Pierre was already asleep. It was late, and Madeleine had been kept from her bed only by the need to bid them goodbye as their hostess. Her father-in-law and her husband were in the study, discussing still another trip Jean would make tomorrow. The meetings, the private conversations, seemed interminable, and she longed for an end to it all.

Bently leaned against the superfluous marble mantel, enjoying the natural grace of the woman. He wondered if he had stayed on so much longer than he had intended because he so much enjoyed being near her. A longing from afar, he chided himself. Like some hackneyed line from a nineteenth-century novel. A *stirring in his loins*. He smiled at himself. You read too much romantic claptrap as a kid.

"I'll be leaving here soon," he said.

"What?" She seemed to come back from a distance, drawn back by the statement that came without any preamble. "You're leaving?"

"It's time to go back home," he said. "It's long overdue, actually."

"I'm sorry to hear that, Matt. And Pierre will be heartbroken. He's become so fond of you."

He smiled, wishing she had said she would be heartbroken, not the boy.

"What will you do there?" she asked.

"Back to work in my father's bank, I suppose."

"In that city that is spelled like my son's name, but pronounced *pier?*"

She smiled at him, enjoying her small joke, but the smile was so electrifying he could only nod his head.

"Why is it that the sons of powerful men always have to work for their fathers?" she asked.

There had been a note of personal bitterness in her voice, almost imperceptible, but there. "You mean like Jean?" he asked.

"Or you," she said.

"Perhaps we just want to please them. Or maybe we're looking for the easy way for ourselves. It's not a bad thing, you know. Your husband has grown into quite a man these past few years. I've watched him. He's much stronger than he was when I first met him. Stronger in the ways that are important, I mean."

"Yes, I know," she said. Her mind seemed to drift again, and then suddenly she seemed to snap back. "Do you think he's happy in what he does?"

"That's hard to tell, Madeleine. I'm not sure I even know what being happy in what one does really means. I've done a great many things these last years that haven't made me happy."

"Then why did you do them?"

"I guess I felt they had to be done, were necessary. We're all taught to do that, you know. You remained up to say goodnight to your guests, even though they really weren't your guests.

They wouldn't have noticed. Maybe Francesco, but certainly not the orientals. But you've been taught to do it."

"I suppose," she said absently. Her eyes hit him squarely again. "Do you trust Francesco, Matt?"

"Why do you ask? I really don't know the man that well. My dealings with your family over the years have been mostly with Jean and Buonaparte. Sometimes Auguste and Benito, but almost never Francesco."

She shook her head. "It doesn't matter," she said. "There's just something about him that's always frightened me."

"That's not hard to understand, especially when he starts playing with that knife of his. He's a hard man, as we'd say in the army."

He watched her. Her mind seemed to move in and out of their conversation, drifting to her own concerns, then returning to what she was actually saying. He wished he could make her concentrate on him. Just this once.

"It's not that kind of fear I mean. It's almost as though he knows something no one else does, and that knowledge gives him a kind of power over the people he deals with. Buonaparte has that same sense about him. Don't misunderstand. I love my father-in-law. I know he wants only good for us. But he has that . . ." She hesitated, struggling for the right word, then giving up. "That *thing* about him. I don't know how to explain it. It's just something you can feel."

Bently knew what she meant. He had known military commanders like that. Men whose mere presence reassured their troops. Men who could stand knee-deep in bodies and make the survivors proud of what they had just gone through, instead of merely disgusted by the waste and senselessness of it all. He didn't know what you called that quality. He just knew that some men had it. He also knew that he did not.

"I'm going to miss you . . . all," he said.

She smiled again. That same electric smile. "I envy you, Matt. I wish we were going with you."

Sartene's face was as dark and cold as his eyes. His chest rose and fell rapidly, and he seemed ready to leap out violently at his son.

"It would be for the best, Papa," Jean said.

"What are you talking about, 'for the best'?" He mocked the words, his lips twisted as though they were something foul in his mouth. "All my life I've done what was best for my family. Now you come and tell me what we've done here is shit. That you want to take your son away."

"Papa, I didn't say that. I said the boy needs schooling. I said we could all go. What more can we get from this place?"

"Get. Get. All you can think of is *get*. There's more to life than just taking for yourself. A man builds, he doesn't just take nourishment. An animal does that."

He began to pace his study, then turned and jabbed a finger toward his son. "I thought you could succeed me, that you could take what we have here and build on it." He threw his hand aside in disgust. "I don't mean opium, I don't mean smuggled gold, or any of the things we had to do to be strong. All that will pass for us. They're a means to an end. We have a rubber plantation that is growing all around us. We have hotels and restaurants and bars." He closed his hands into a fist and held it before him. "We have political power, not just here, but in Europe, in Hong Kong. When the Americans take over here, which will happen, we'll have power with them too. Roads will be built here. Goods, legal goods, will be exported. We'll have a part of that. Not me. You. And even more important, Pierre."

"Papa, with the money we have, we can get anything we want. Anywhere." Jean's voice was soft, pleading, yet firm in its conviction.

"What?" Sartene spat out. "We can be *padrones*. We can sit in a fine house and drive fine automobiles, and produce nothing, leave nothing behind. You make me sick with that talk. What kind of man do you want your son to be? Some soft little fool, like that American who visited us from the embassy? Where do you get these ideas? I didn't raise you to think like this."

"Papa. The boy needs education. At the schools here they spit on him."

"So he spits back!" Sartene shouted the words, something rare for him. He caught hold of himself and took several deep breaths. "He can learn here," he said softly. "If we were in danger here, then it would be different. When you were a boy I sent you to Corsica because there was danger. It tore my heart to send you and your mother away." He shook his head. "I know you don't want to be away from your son. That's only natural. But he can learn here. We can teach him more than any school. And the *lycée* in Vientiane is not that bad. I can talk to the parents of these French children. They won't want to offend me.''

"Those people can't control what their children say and do," Jean said.

Sartene turned his back, so he was facing the high mahogany mantel that dominated the middle of one wall. He placed his hands on the mantel and leaned forward. He was tired of fighting. Tired of arguing against the logic of his son's words. Logic at least where Pierre was concerned. But the education Pierre needed was more than just the knowledge from books, he told himself. And Pierre could not get that away from here, away from him.

Jean came up behind him and placed a hand on his shoulder. "Papa. I didn't want to make you angry. And I don't want to take Pierre away from you. I know how much you love him. How much you want for him. We have plenty of time. More than a year. We'll find a way to work it out."

Sartene could feel the anger tighten his stomach and chest. He breathed deeply, struggling to calm himself. But when he spoke his voice was cold. Colder than he intended.

"You have something important to do tomorrow. That's what you should be thinking about now. The future of our group depends on it. And I expect you to do it well."

Jean allowed his hand to drop from his father's shoulder. He stood there for a moment, staring at his back, then turned and walked slowly out of the room.

It was a small, seedy bar in the red-light district of Vientiane. The bar was owned by a Laotian, who paid tribute to the Sartene *milieu,* but the bar was never frequented by the Corsicans who worked for Sartene.

Even in the early-morning hours the Laotian whores scattered along the bar eyed each prospective customer as he entered. The smoke from dozens of cigarettes was thick and hung near the ceiling like wispy clouds, reflecting the colored lights that flashed from the Wurlitzer jukebox that occupied one corner of the room.

Francesco Canterina and the two men from Saigon sat in a rear booth, the front of which was covered by a beaded curtain. The men were Corsicans. Carbone's men. They had been in the city for five days, hidden in a cheap hotel near the bar, awaiting word from Francesco.

One of the Corsicans had the thick body and flat face of a

peasant. He was young, in his late twenties, but he was already losing his hair, and it made him seem older. The second man was small and wiry, and his face seemed to come to a sharp edge along the line of his nose, giving his head the shape of a hatchet. They spoke quietly in Corsican, the hatchet-faced man glancing repeatedly toward the entrance of the bar.

"You sure he doesn't suspect anything?" the large man said.

Francesco smiled coldly at him. "Nothing. If he did, I'd be floating down the Mekong right now, food for the crocodiles. He's an old man, past his time, like I told you. All he wants to do now is play with his grandson. Meanwhile our *milieu* suffers. It'll be a kindness to him to put him out of his misery."

"And his son will be taken care of too?" the smaller man asked. "I've heard about him, and I don't want him looking me up later."

"That I do myself," Francesco said. Bently flashed through his mind. He hadn't anticipated his presence. It would require some diversion, something unexpected.

The large man rubbed his massive chin, which already showed the dark stubble of his returning beard. "I'm not sure of the airport," he said. "It's very open."

"He and Auguste Pavlovi will go there to meet Auguste's brother, Benito. His plane is due in at four-thirty in the afternoon, and Buonaparte always goes to meet him. They're very close, these three old men. The Mua bodyguards will stay in the car. Buonaparte doesn't like to attract attention by taking them inside with him. It's the one place he's most vulnerable. And the time is right. By that time his son will be dead." Francesco shrugged, confirming the logic of what he had said.

"What about these other two?" the smaller man asked.

"They're like him. They're old and their minds have gone soft."

"Will they have guns?" The smaller man was still pressing.

"Of course," Francesco snapped. "Listen, I didn't tell you I wanted you to take three old nuns. They'll have pistols, that's all. The Mua guards will have heavy weapons, but they'll be in the car. You take them inside." He snapped his fingers three times. "Just like that. You're making it sound like I'm asking you to fight some fucking army, instead of three old men."

"Look," the big man said. "Carbone told us no mistakes. We're just being careful."

Francesco looked at each man in turn. Carbone, the ass,

couldn't have picked two more likely assassins. Two hard young
Corsicans, dressed in rumpled cord suits. Sartene and the others
would recognize them immediately for what they were. "You
won't have to worry about anything," he said. "There's a
lounge in the airport. You'll both be sitting there, reading
newspapers. They'll have to walk right past you, but I don't
even want you to look at them. Keep your faces covered with the
papers."

The large man threw his hands up in a gesture of disbelief.
"How are we supposed to see them?"

"You won't have to, until just before you shoot." He grinned
at his own cleverness. "There's a Mua who works at my house
in Vientiane. He'll come rushing up, calling Sartene by name,
just as they reach you. Then you drop the papers and they're
right in front of you."

The two Corsicans exchanged glances. The larger one nodded
appreciatively.

"He's really gotten that careless?" the smaller man asked.

Francesco raised his eyebrows in a what-can-you-expect gesture.

"I'm not really surprised," the smaller man said. "Power
makes men overconfident. Don Carbone does the same thing.
Sometimes I think he's also getting too old for this kind of life."

Francesco laughed. "It happens to us all," he said. "Let's
have another drink. We'll drink to youth, and to tomorrow." He
extended his hand through the beaded curtain and snapped his
fingers for the waiter. He would buy each of these men a whore
tonight, he decided. He wanted them to be content. Especially
the one who thought Carbone was getting old.

Chapter 15

Jean Sartene swung the small observation plane in a wide arc prior to landing at Phong Savan. With each turn he and Bently studied the forest below, looking for any sign that a hostile force might be lying in wait. The jungle was still, a hundred different shades of green reflecting the early-morning light. The plane passed over the village of Lat Houang with its scattering of hootches, children playing in the dusty soil, old men squatting in the shade, buffalo standing idle, some already hitched to wooden-wheeled carts.

There was no one working the steep hillsides where the poppies were grown. The plants that remained from the previous crop where now scorched and brown and almost hidden by new growth waiting to be replaced by the new plantings that would be sown in late March, only weeks before the rainy season began. Looking out the window, Bently remembered the first planting he had witnessed, the primitive slash-and-burn agriculture common to all of Southeast Asia.

It had been a hot, dusty morning, just as it was now. The men, women and children of the village had gathered at the bottom of a wide, steep hill. For weeks, men of the village had been cutting the forest growth that covered the hill with single-bitted axes. The fallen trees and soft vegetation were now dry and brittle. Slowly the men of the village climbed the hill. At the top they lit torches, then turned and raced wildly down the hill, dragging the torches behind them. Flames shot hundreds of feet into the air, literally chasing them down the hillside, and within hours the billowing smoke rose two miles above the fields.

Later, when the fires ended, the field was covered with a thick layer of nourishing ash that sealed all moisture beneath the burned surface. Now when the hillside cooled the planting could begin, the scattering, by hand, of tiny poppy seeds. Three months later the greenish plant would stand three or four feet high, with a main tubular stem and six to twelve shoots, each holding a brightly colored flower. For a week the color on the hillside would be awesome, beautiful beyond description, then gradually the petals would drop to the ground, exposing a green seedpod, the size and shape of a bird's egg.

This was what the planters would await, moving through the fields then with curved knives, making shallow parallel incisions across the surface of each pod to allow the milky white sap to seep out. Then returning, when the sap had congealed, turned into a brownish-black, to scrape off the new opium with flat, dull knives. He had seen all of it, year after year now, up to the point the pungent, jellylike opium was gathered in bundles for shipment to the recently built morphine-processing plants outside Vientiane and Saigon. He had not gone to these plants, where the opium was cooked in water and lime fertilizer to extract the morphine, then molded into chalky white bricks, ready then to be shipped again.

He wondered why, why he had not. That part of it was the reality of it all, he decided. This was only agriculture.

The plane made its final approach to the ramshackle runway, at the end of which Touby and a small group of Meo warriors waited.

"We're here," Bently said over his shoulder, stirring Francesco Canterina from the sleep he had enjoyed throughout the flight.

Francesco yawned and looked out at the dirt runway that raced toward them. "I should have gone to bed early last night," he said.

"You say that every morning," Jean said. "And every night your prick keeps you awake."

The plane bumped along the runway, the metal shuddering, then skidded slightly to port as it came to an abrupt halt.

"What time did *you* go to bed?" Bently asked.

"They only taught me how to take off and fly this thing," Jean said. "They forgot about landing."

Bently pushed the flimsy square door with his shoulder and stepped out into the dust storm produced by the single engine of the plane. Through the dusty haze he could see Touby Lyfoung making his way toward him, his hand holding the rim of his pith helmet low over his eyes. The last time I'll see you too, colonel, he thought. Next month, Pierre, South Dakota; a new office overlooking the Missouri River; even a new president of the United States. He smiled to himself, wondering what Dwight David Eisenhower would think when he found out his new intelligence agency was in the dope business. If he ever did find out about it.

They gathered under the wing of the aircraft as the dust settled. Touby was still wearing his medals. He had flown back from Vientiane a few hours before they had left Sartene's airstrip to prepare for the day's work, and Bently wondered if he had decided not to remove the medals so he could better influence the men they would recruit for the new *maquis*. Everything in Southeast Asia was played out like a comic opera. But that was true in most of the world. You only noticed it more here, because the contrasts were so much more striking.

During the trip in the beat-up Japanese staff car Jean seemed more animated. Perhaps the poor landing and the joking about it had livened his spirits. During the flight he had seemed morose; he had hardly spoken. His father had not seen them off with his usual last-minute instructions and good wishes, and Bently wondered if the two had fought the night before. But now Jean seemed fine. He was confident and ready to do what had been asked of him, a far cry from the man who had first visited the Meo hills six years before. Behind them, seated next to Touby, Francesco was equally calm. Truly a hard man, Bently decided. Ready to go and lop off a few heads in the same way someone else would go to market to buy a freshly killed chicken. How much different was it, he wondered, than his own father marching off to his office to foreclose on some fledgling business? Maybe the only difference was that it was neater. You didn't get blood on your shoes.

Within an hour of their arrival in Lat Houang, Francesco was off with a contingent of Meo to spread his deadly message to the outlying villages. It would not take long, six hours at most, and then they would be airborne again, headed south, away from a primitive, innocent people who were the first link in a chain that often ended thousands of miles away in small dirty rooms where people filled their veins with milky fluid.

As Jean spoke to the men of the village, gathered together now to hear of the new *maquis* that would protect that vital link, Bently studied the dull, flat, undernourished faces. Accidents of fate, he told himself. Born to a life in a brutal jungle, sitting on top of a mountain, instead of in some dull suburb of an American city. Most of them, he knew, had never seen a city, not even Vientiane. Few had traveled more than twenty miles, unless they had been chosen to be part of the opium caravans that moved through the jungles after each harvest. *Only a few would be chosen,* Jean was telling them. The lucky ones, he told himself. Like the kids who had followed him into battle during the war, and who now owned small, exclusive pieces of land in places they had never heard of before. *But there would be chances later for a few more.* Bently studied the faces of the men, knowing immediately those who would be considered. Their eyes were eager. The others simply stood patiently, waiting for the talk to end, waiting to get back to whatever it was they would do that day to scratch out another twenty-four hours of existence. They didn't look like warriors, or even farmers. They looked like kids, small squat kids, who should be off learning to play baseball, or reading comic books in a local drugstore. Tiny people, with a life expectancy that seldom went beyond fifty in these godforsaken mountains.

Jean was outlining the training, the equipment they would be given, the important part they would play among all the tribes of the Meo. Sweet Jesus, Bently thought. Jean would have made one helluva recruitment officer back in the States, convincing young kids that they could have a chance to get their asses shot off, if only they proved themselves worthy.

Duty, honor, country. And a free wheelchair in the veterans hospital of your choice. It was time to go home. Now, before the next war started. *Colonel Lyfoung will decide who will be chosen.* He would leave the next war to those who wanted to fight it. There were always people who wanted to fight wars. And there were always people caught in the middle who had no choice. He looked through the faces of the assembled Ly clansmen again. Always people who never knew about the bank accounts in Hong Kong and Switzerland that make wars worth fighting.

They sat in the shade of Touby's oversized hootch and watched the fat little colonel move about among his men, assuring those who expressed interest that they would be considered for this new opportunity. The clincher Jean had delivered was that those chosen for the *maquis* would pay only a token opium tax of three piasters each year. Bently smiled, thinking of the cleverness of the offer.

"When did your father come up with this new tax incentive?" he asked.

Jean continued to stare straight ahead. "He didn't," he said. "It was something I thought up when I was talking to them. Most of them didn't look too enthusiastic."

Bently shook his head. "Jean, my lad, you should come back to the States with me and open a used-car lot."

"I just might do that. Sooner than you think." He was still staring out into the corner of the village. Touby had taken refuge under a chum-ngay tree, its long, slender pink pods dangling overhead, still not ripe enough to be harvested and cooked as a wild asparagus.

Bently didn't respond immediately, allowing his eyes to wander around the squalid village. Off to his left a group of women were turning and basting a wild pig that would soon be served to the men. On his last visit Touby had offered the prized flesh of monkey and porcupine. The porcupine had been tolerable, the flesh sweet and gamy. The monkey had been another matter. They had sat in a circle outside Touby's hootch. Before each guest a monkey had been buried in the ground up to its neck. The monkeys had chattered wildly, twisting their heads around, looking for some escape. The chattering ended when the guests cleaved into their skulls with machetes and began picking at the still-warm brains.

"Thank Christ they're serving pig today," Bently said.

Jean nodded, remembering some of his more exotic meals among the Meo, the flying bats and raw cockroaches. "Aren't you curious about my interest in your country?" he asked, looking toward Bently for the first time.

"I figure if you want to talk about it, you will. Does it have anything to do with why your father didn't see us off this morning?"

"Now I know why your army made an intelligence officer out of you," Jean said. "I talked to him last night about taking Pierre away for his education."

"You said 'taking,' not sending him away," Bently said.

Jean nodded. "I don't want to be away from him. I don't want to lose my son for all those years, the way my father had to lose his."

Bently let out a low whistle. "That must've been some conversation."

"I never saw him that angry with me," Jean said. He looked back into the village for several moments, then turned his body to face Bently. "Tell me, Matt, is it wrong to want what's good for Pierre?"

"You're asking the wrong man, buddy. I never had a kid, never felt what you're feeling now."

Jean waited as if deciding whether to continue. "You told me once how you tried to escape your father," he said at length. "First when you went away to university, then later to the army."

There was a pleading in Jean's eyes, and Bently didn't know precisely how to respond to it. He liked the man, liked the hidden gentleness that recently had begun to show through the brutal exterior. "That's different," he said. "What are we really talking about? Taking Pierre away to school, or you getting away from your father?"

"Maybe I'm talking about all of us getting away." He concentrated on Touby and the villagers again. It was almost as though he had wanted to say "getting away from him," but couldn't. "I suggested that he come with us, if we did go, but I knew he couldn't agree to that. If he had agreed I think I would have been disappointed. Dammit, it's not that he doesn't want what's good for us, it's just that there's never a chance to prove anything by yourself . . ." He seemed to have trouble finding the words. "For yourself," he finally added.

"You've done pretty well the past few years," Bently said. "I know. I've watched you."

Jean nodded, almost solemnly. "To some extent, yes." He faced Bently, his eyes imploring again. "But he's always been there. To correct the mistakes, to set things right again. A man needs a chance to fail too, doesn't he? Maybe I'll never have that chance now. But damn, I want it for Pierre. I want him to love his grandfather, to know him. He can learn a lot from my father. Good things. Things that will make him strong. But I want him to be independent too. I want him to have a will as strong as my father's, so he can make his own decisions, in his own way. And maybe I want that for myself too, even if it's just for a short time."

Bently felt the beating, bone-killing heat of the day. It had intensified, almost as if hell were pushing through the ground in this insane part of the globe. It must be what Jean was feeling, he thought, only it's coming from within him. "So you'll do it?" he asked.

"I don't know. I just don't. I want to, but I'm not sure I

can." He smiled weakly. "If I do, I'd like you to help me find a good school for the boy."

"Of course I will. You know that," Bently said. "I'm just glad it's not my decision. It's hard to leave what you were born to. Maybe that's why I'm going back now."

The food was served at three in the afternoon, after the sun had eased. The cool of the late afternoon in Laos, Bently mused. It was like high noon in Arizona. Even at midnight here you could stand still and sweat.

Throughout the meal, Touby Lyfoung jabbered like a schoolboy. He was ecstatic with the response of his men. Bently remembered the preponderance of flat, bored eyes while Jean talked, and he wondered what Touby was talking about. There had been some who had been interested, but only a few. But then, according to Buonaparte, only a few were needed.

They had finished eating by the time Francesco returned. He came from the wrong direction, from the airstrip and the plain above. He was alone.

"Where have you been?" Jean asked.

"I doubled back through the jungle, just to be sure no one was at the airstrip, waiting to pay us back for the day's work." He smiled, almost as though his actions were a rebuke, that he had thought of something that Jean should have considered.

Jean stared at him for a moment. New games, he thought. There were always two men, Touby's men, left to guard the plane, but sometimes they just sat inside and played with the controls like children. Perhaps Francesco was just being cautious. "Do you want to eat?" Jean asked.

"Just something quick," he said. "I have an appointment in Vientiane tonight."

"An appointment," Jean snorted. "Which of the French officials has left his wife unattended?"

"One never knows whose wife will be unattended," Francesco said. There was a leering smile on his face, almost a taunt.

Jean ignored it. "Where are the men who went with you?" he asked.

"I left some at the villages we visited, just to be sure our messages were received. And I left others at the airstrip, so we could get back to the plane more quickly, and not have to keep pace with a group of guards in a buffalo cart."

"You are in a hurry," Jean said. "I hope she's worth it, whoever she is."

"You're lucky I went there," Francesco said. "One of Touby's men was in the cockpit, turning dials and playing with things. I chased him out, and told them all to sit back near the jungle and protect the plane from there.'' He laughed. ''Someday they're going to fix your plane so it kills us all,'' he said.

''I always check everything first,'' Jean said. ''How did things go in the villages?''

Francesco shrugged. ''Five villages, seven examples. Some others ran away—that's why I left men behind. But I don't think they'll be back. The heads were hung from trees as a reminder. Touby's men will make sure they stay there. By morning there'll be nothing left but the skulls. The birds and the insects will see to that.''

Francesco stuffed bits of pork into his mouth as he spoke, making Bently wonder if the man ever lost his appetite, or any sleep over the things he did.

Francesco sucked the grease from each finger in turn. Bently stood and stretched. His shirt was soaked and clung to his back, and he felt as though he had lost five pounds just sitting there.

''We might as well start back,'' Jean said. He clasped Touby's arm. ''I'll talk to you by radio in a few days, and we can decide when I should come back. We should make the selection of the men an important occasion.''

Touby, grinning at the idea of a future ceremony, gestured to the warrior who had been trained to drive his car. Within seconds the engine of the Japanese staff car gurgled to life, sputtering and coughing until the buffalo began to strain at their tethers. They climbed into the battered vehicle, and the car struggled up the final hill that led to the plain, sending out a mixture of dust and thick exhaust fumes in a billowing rooster tail. The sound of the dying engine, the dirt and the fumes announced Touby's movements better than a brass band, Bently mused. Someday he would get his ass shot off because of it. But he knew Touby would rather lose one of his medals than surrender the vehicle.

The car ground to a halt thirty yards from the aircraft. In the distance, on the other side of the runway, Bently could see three of the Ly warriors leaning against a cluster of thien tue palms, the heavy, low-hanging fronds partially obscuring them from view. They seemed to be asleep with their weapons across their laps, but he knew they could never have slept through the noise the car made on arrival. They were just lethargic, like most of the Meo. Or perhaps angry they had been chased away from the plane. He squinted, trying to see them more clearly.

Francesco stepped from the car, stumbled and let out a cry of pain, distracting Bently.

"What's the matter?" Bently said, coming out behind him and grabbing his arm.

"My ankle, dammit. I twisted it."

"You want me to help you to the plane?" Bently asked. Francesco shook his head, grimacing in pain. "I'll just lean against the fender for a minute. I'll be all right. You go ahead."

"No, I'll wait with you," Bently said.

"You sure it's not broken?" Jean asked. He seemed amused by Francesco's pain.

"No. I'm sure," Francesco said. "I'll be all right in a minute. By the time the plane is warmed up, I'll be ready."

"I hope so," Jean said. "Otherwise there'll be a very disappointed lady in town tonight."

"Never," Francesco said. "I've been waiting for this one for years." There was a look in his eyes of something unspoken, then it seemed to submerge again. He bent over and rubbed his ankle.

Jean laughed quietly, patted Touby on the back and whispered something to him, then started toward the plane.

Bently allowed his eyes to wander back to the Ly warriors. Still they hadn't moved. He was about to ask Touby about them when Francesco groaned again and grabbed his arm. "Getting worse?" Bently asked.

"I just tried to put pressure on it. Maybe you will have to help me. Just let me rest a little longer."

Jean opened the door that led to the pilot's seat and climbed in, quickly scanning the controls to see what had been tampered with by Touby's men. Everything appeared unchanged. Unusual, he thought. Maybe they were learning to return things to the proper settings. Automatically he looked at the checklist taped to the center of the instrument panel.

Behind him, along the bulkhead above the rear passenger door, the Asiatic cobra slowly twisted its body, struggling to free itself. The lower third of the snake had been tied to the handhold above the rear door, and its body was drawn into a tight bundle of expanding and contracting muscle, making the oblong patterns of white along its gray-brown back appear to move with a slow rippling rhythm. The head of the snake snapped back, the hood expanding along the upper sides of its body, as the whine of the aircraft's engine roared into a steady throbbing beat.

The first strike caught Jean on the back of the neck, hitting with the force of a mildly heavy punch, the pain immediate, spreading quickly up the back of his head and down into his shoulder. He cried out instinctively and reached back, covering the wound with his hand. The second strike hit the back of his hand, and he screamed again. He turned his head toward the attack and the snake struck again, sinking its fangs into his cheek. Jean grabbed the body of the snake and pulled it away from his face, the force ripping one fang from its mouth, leaving it dangling from the gaping, blood-streaked puncture. He threw the writhing body across the cabin, slamming it against the far bulkhead. Already he felt the numbness surging through his body, the deadly toxic venom attacking the nervous system. His eyes clouded and he crashed his shoulder against the door, forcing it open, feeling none of the impact as his body fell to the ground.

He scrambled on his elbows and knees, fighting to gain purchase with his hands, then falling forward, his face sliding on the dusty ground. Again he struggled to right himself. He opened his mouth to call out, but only a rasping groan came from his throat. His bladder and bowels voided as the poison surged into his brain.

Bently looked toward the plane and saw him. Jean was crawling and falling, then struggling up again, his arms moving in uncontrolled spasms. Blood was streaming down his cheek. "Jean!" Bently screamed, alerting the others, and raced forward. He had covered two thirds of the distance when the bullet hit the upper right portion of his back, lifting him and throwing him forward.

The Ly warrior and Touby, each a few steps behind Bently, spun with the sound of the weapon. Francesco squeezed off two rounds in succession, watching as they exploded in the chest of Touby's driver, cartwheeling him back. He swung the weapon. His legs were spread in a classic shooting stance, the weight evenly distributed, the false pain gone from his face, replaced now by a slight smile.

Touby turned and ran to his left, throwing himself under the aircraft, then rolling out the other side. Three bullets kicked up dirt near his head. Then he was up and running, shielded by the fuselage of the plane, his voice screaming out to the men seated under the trees ahead of him. They didn't answer. Their dead eyes only stared blindly from heads tied to the trunks of the trees.

"*Merde*," Francesco muttered to himself, as he watched Touby's legs, the only part of him now visible, move toward the jungle. He was amazed the fat little man had been able to move so quickly.

Bently lay in the dirt, struggling for breath. A few feet away, Jean's face was lifted toward him, the eyes fluttering, the jaw trembling out of control, struggling to speak. Behind him, Bently could see the cobra. It had crawled to the edge of the cockpit. It hung half in the air for a moment, then fell to the ground and began to move away.

Francesco. The name assaulted him, as he lay there fighting to breathe. *Checking out the plane. Making sure it was safe. Men left behind to guard it. Sleeping men. Dead men.* Each thought hit his mind like a blow. Before him Jean shuddered, his body shaken by endless spasms. His cheeks began to quiver and vomit erupted from his mouth. His eyes fluttered again, and his tongue moved in and out of his mouth. Then his head fell forward into his own filth and he was still.

Bently twisted his body, ignoring the pain, pulling the .45 automatic from his shoulder holster. Twenty yards away Francesco was walking around the front of the car, moving to the driver's side. Bently extended his right arm, grasping his wrist with his left hand to steady his aim. Francesco turned and started down the side of the car. *Only seconds left now.* He squeezed the trigger, feeling the heavy weapon leap in his hand. Francesco staggered, one side of his body buckling, one hand grabbing the side of the car to keep himself upright. *Too low. Too damn low.* Bently leveled the pistol again. The ground erupted twice in front of him, throwing dirt into his face. A wave of dizziness came. It was like water washing over him. His face fell forward into the dirt.

The bullet had ripped through the back of Francesco's thigh, exiting through the front, and within the leg Francesco could feel the shattered bone as he forced himself behind the wheel of the car. He pulled the belt from his trousers and tightened it around his leg above the wound. It was ten miles to where Faydang's men would be waiting, then farther still to the radio he would use to contact Carbone.

Francesco felt dizzy from the pain. He had to move. Move away quickly. He was a target now that could not move well. A target even Lyfoung could hit. He threw the car into gear. The three bodies weren't moving. Run over them, he told himself. No. They're dead, get away. Get away.

They stood in the shade, watching the plane taxi slowly toward them. The sun was behind them, hidden by the old colonial-style terminal of Wattay Airport. The sun sank slowly toward the western jungle, yet it left behind its smoldering presence. Sartene took a handkerchief from the breast pocket of his lightweight suitcoat and mopped his brow and face. Auguste watched him, ignoring the rivulets that streamed down his own face. He was concerned about his friend. All day Sartene had been sullen and distant. It was as though he was seething with some personal anger, some pain he could not speak about. Auguste had asked what was troubling him, but had received only a gruff reply about terrible dreams the night before. Sartene would say no more about it.

The twin-engine Beechcraft, bearing the name Air Laos Commerciale, ground to a halt only yards from where they were standing. Even before the engines had come to a stop, the door to the aircraft swung away and Benito Pavlovi's bulky frame moved lightly down the few steps to the ground.

It had always amazed Auguste how lightly and quickly Benito could move. It was not just that his brother moved well for a big man. He moved better than most small men, better even than Auguste himself.

As always, Benito was grinning. For any other man it would have been a sign that his journey had been a great success. With Benito one could never tell. He had been sent to Bangkok to handle two unrelated matters. The first involved complaints from Thai police officials, who felt the level of their bribes was not commensurate with the service they provided. The second concerned Sartene's interest in taking over the small airline on which Benito had returned.

The three men greeted each other warmly, grasping each other by the arms and kissing each other's cheeks. As they turned back into the dankness of the Wattay Airport terminal, Sartene slipped his arm into Benito's, drawing him close.

"I'm glad you're back," Sartene said, his voice its usual near whisper. "I had terrible dreams last night and I was worried for you."

Benito laughed softly. "Things could not have been easier,"

he said. "The Thais agreed to our counteroffer without a murmur. But I think they'll ask for more again soon."

Sartene shrugged. "Everybody in this business is greedy, these days," he said. "You have to expect it. What about this airline?"

"That will be harder," Benito said. "The man Endobal, who owns it, says he doesn't want to sell. All his life in the French air force he wanted to have his own airline, he says. Now with his four little planes, he has it, and he wants to keep it that way."

"You offered him the fair price we talked about?"

Benito nodded. "I'm afraid this man isn't interested in what's fair. I even told him we would want him to keep running the business for us. Nothing would change his mind." Benito inclined his head to one side in a gesture of resignation. "I'm afraid we'll have to do it the other way."

Sartene shook his head. "Life would be so much easier for everyone if men were sensible," he said. "You found out what we have to know to accomplish this?"

"Yes," Benito said. "Every month they do what every small business tries to do. They smuggle one or two kilos into Viet Nam. It's just enough to keep the airline going, and they get very bad prices, because they have to deal with the Black Tais there. They use a small landing strip in the Central Highlands where they wait for a day or two to make contact. If we have the French arrest them, the Thai police will seize their other aircraft back in Thailand. Then, I think, Endobal will let us buy him out of trouble. He'll lose the planes anyway, and this way he'll avoid five years in a stinking Thai prison."

"What the hell is this?" Auguste said. He was watching the Mua move toward them. They were halfway through the terminal, and the Mua was weaving through the small clusters of people. He seemed excited.

"That's one of Francesco's men," Auguste said. "I don't like this. They know better than to come in here."

"Maybe something's happened in the north," Sartene said. He was searching for some sign on the Mua's face. He heard the approaching figure call to him.

"Buonaparte!"

Benito's shout brought Sartene back. Instinctively he ducked his body, moving slightly to the left.

The two men had been seated in the lounge area to their right.

At the sound of Sartene's name, they had dropped the newspapers they were holding and had begun to rise. The movement caught Benito's eyes immediately, and he knew, even before he looked and saw the guns rising up, why these men were here.

Benito felt Sartene's movement, and he reached out, grabbing his arm, pulling him back, moving his own heavy body in front of his as he did. Benito reached for the pistol under his left arm, and the first shot shattered his wrist, forcing him to bend at the waist in pain. The second shot struck the buckle of his belt, smashing the bullet, and sending small shards of lead into his lower abdomen. He forced himself to remain upright, stretching his arms back to keep Sartene behind him, not allowing him to move from the protection of his own body.

Before the second shot had come from the lounge area, Auguste had fired his own pistol. The shot caught the small, skinny man in the throat, and he stood there, his face filled with horror, both hands covering the gaping wound in his neck, the blood spilling between his fingers and down the front of his white shirt. He seemed to sway for a moment, then his body became disjointed, and he fell forward like a limp piece of rope. The second shot from Auguste's automatic hit the large man squarely in the chest, but he just stood there, the barrel of the gun dropping down, but still in his hand.

"Bastard," Auguste shouted, firing two more shots into his chest, then watching as the body flew back, crashing over the chair the gunman had been sitting in moments before.

Benito slumped to the floor, and was sitting there now, held in Sartene's arms. Auguste spun toward the Mua, who had stopped a few feet away, and swung the gun toward his chest.

"No," Sartene snapped. "I want to question him." He spoke in Corsican so the Mua would not understand him. "I want to know who." He barked an order in Lao at the Mua, telling him to help with Benito, then leaned over his fallen friend. Benito's face was a pale gray, but there seemed to be little blood. "Benito," he said. "How bad is it?"

"Very little pain," Benito gasped, fighting for the breath knocked from him by the impact of the bullet. "But I can't feel my legs. I can't feel anything at all."

Sartene looked across at Auguste. Tears were pouring down Buonaparte's face, mixing with the perspiration, and dropping in large blotches on his shirt. "We have to get him to the hospital," Sartene said. "Then we have to find out who."

"I know who," Auguste said. "Carbone. There's no one else."

"Someone helped him," Sartene said. "Someone had to help him. Otherwise I would have known his people were here in Vientiane."

Auguste stared across his brother's body. He understood what Sartene meant. "We must get to a radio and warn Jean," he said.

"Those damned dreams," Sartene said. "I knew it. I knew it."

Chapter 16

Bently's room was in an isolated wing of a large private hospital run by the Catholic church in the center of Saigon. The nuns who worked the floor had showered him with attention. He was something of an oddity. They did not get many bullet wounds, most of those going to the French military hospital near the airport, and like most nurses there was nothing they liked better than something unusual to challenge their skills.

The wound had collapsed his right lung, but the bullet had passed through his body, and the missionary who worked near Phong Savan had been well trained and was able to stop the bleeding. He was unable to do anything for Jean. He had lapsed into coma within minutes, and two hours later he had died.

Bently blamed himself. He should have known something was wrong. He was trained to sense these things. But Francesco had been clever, diverting his attention from the Ly warriors sitting under the trees. He hoped his own bullet had hit a vital spot. But he doubted it. The way Francesco's body had sagged, it had looked like a leg or hip wound. Now he would probably never know. He could only hope the bastard had bled to death somewhere in the forest.

You're lucky to be alive, he told himself now. When he had awakened in the hospital the first thing he had seen was the pale, almost heavenly blue of the ceiling. Hell of a color to paint a hospital room, he reminded himself. You wake up convinced the next stop is the pearly gates.

It had been three days since the surgery. He had not heard from Buonaparte. Not from any of them. He wondered if they blamed him for what had happened. If Francesco hadn't missed

Touby, he'd be dead too. And Canterina would be back in Vientiane claiming they'd been attacked by Faydang's people. It almost seemed preferable, except for the part about Francesco.

The small, young nurse burst into the room. She was the energetic one who worked in the evenings, the one who always moved as though someone were chasing her, her white habit swirling behind her, her beads rattling like a dozen miniature sabers. It made him tired just watching her, and the smile that was permanently fixed on her open, pretty face always made him want to say something obscene, just to see the horrified reaction it would produce.

She rushed to his bedside, pulling the covers back gently. "Time to change the dressing," she cooed in French.

"Speak English," he snapped, putting as much force in his weak voice as he could manage.

"We're very cranky today, aren't we?" she said in heavily accented English.

"I don't know what the hell *we* are," Bently said. "I know I'm feeling piss-poor, myself."

The nun closed her eyes and crinkled up her nose. It gave Bently the first feeling of pleasure he had known since he had awakened in the room. "You cannot shock me, monsieur," the nun said, opening his pajama top to expose the dressing. "I had three brothers and they were all quite vulgar."

Bently laughed, despite himself, then regretted it as pain shot through the right side of his chest. He slowed his breathing deliberately, trying to ease it.

"You see," the little nun said. "God punishes."

"Oh shit," Bently muttered.

The nun yanked the tape holding the dressing, ripping away the hair that had begun to grow back on his chest. Bently yelped.

"And so do his servants," the nun added, smiling down at him.

He started to object, but the nun raised a finger in warning. He clamped his jaws together.

"You have a visitor," the nun said, as she concentrated on the exposed wound. "Oh, this is looking very good," she added.

"Who is it?" Bently snapped.

"You will see as soon as we've finished here," the nun said, smiling again.

Bently let out a sigh. He hoped it would not be Malcolm Baker. The silly ass had come to visit him one day after his surgery, and had sat there babbling for almost an hour, impervious to Bently's pain.

He had been sent to the private hospital because of his cover as a businessman, Baker had explained. As if he gave a shit where he had been sent. He just wanted out now. Some R&R in Hong Kong or Tokyo. Then back to Pearl and finally the States. Just out of this fucking place once and for all. Four years of war and not a nick, he told himself. Not even a good case of malaria. Then you go and get yourself shot up in some shitty mountain village trying to protect the goddam opium crop. And just weeks before you're scheduled to be shipped out.

The nun finished replacing the dressing and rebuttoned his pajama top. Her eyes were dancing with the pleasure of her work, and he wished he could fill a bedpan to make her less pleased with herself.

"You're not going to tell me, are you?" he said.

"Tell you what, monsieur?"

"Who the hell is here to see me," he snapped.

"You will see," she said, turning quickly like a dancer and hurrying toward the door, habit fluttering behind, rosary beads rattling together.

Bently stared up at the heavenly blue ceiling. There were traces of mildew from the heat, where the ceiling met the wall, and he wondered if there would be mildew in heaven as well.

When Buonaparte Sartene entered the room, Bently was shocked at the man's appearance. Buonaparte was in his late fifties, but he looked older now, much older. His face was drawn, haggard, the eyes sunken in his head. He did not seem as erect as he always had, his shoulders seemed slightly stooped and his suit was rumpled. He walked slowly to the bed and took Bently's hand gently, then bent down and kissed his forehead lightly. When he stood again there were tears in Bently's eyes.

"I know," he said softly. "You mustn't blame yourself. There was nothing you could do."

"You know, then?" Bently said. "Tell me about it. All of it."

Sartene drew a chair up beside the bed and sat. He patted Bently's hand. "It was Francesco and Carbone," he said. "They tried to kill me the same day. But they only crippled poor Benito. He'll be in a wheelchair the rest of his life. And the doctors say it won't be a very long life, either. It was Francesco's plan, badly done by two fools who worked for Carbone."

"Where's Francesco now?" Bently asked, hoping he would hear that the bastard was dead.

"Somewhere in the north. With Faydang, we think. But we'll find him. If it takes the rest of my life, I'll find him."

There had been no harshness in Sartene's voice, no anger, nothing. The voice was just resigned, Bently thought.

"What about Carbone?" he asked.

"He's in hiding, somewhere near Hanoi. There'll be a war now between us. He'll ask others to help him seek a peace, but no one will. He'll die just as Jean died."

The memory of Jean's death flashed through Bently's mind, the agonized contortions of his face. It was the worst death he had ever seen. Tortured. "I wish I could be there to see it," Bently said.

"No, it's best that you go now. This war will be costly for all of us. It will take many years to heal the wounds." Sartene thought of the men, the Guerinis' men, who were already on their way from Marseille at his request. Much would change for the *milieu*, for all of them.

He smiled weakly at Bently. "Jean was going to leave, you know. He was going to take Pierre away to school. Either to Europe or America."

"No, he wasn't, Buonaparte." Bently listened to himself lie to the man, knowing he had to.

"What do you mean?" Sartene asked.

"We talked about it. Only a few hours before . . ." He didn't finish the sentence. "He told me about his talk with you. He said he'd decided it was wrong to leave you."

"He said that?" There were tears in Sartene's eyes now, as well as Bently's. He had never seen emotion in Buonaparte before, never even a hint that he was capable of it.

Bently just nodded.

"I argued with him the night before," Sartene said. "My last words to him. Angry words. When he left me I didn't even look at him. Then that night I dreamed. Terrible dreams. I should have known." He paused, staring down at the floor, gathering his words. "He was right about Pierre," he finally said. "Even more now. He must leave here."

He stopped again, looking up at Bently. "This opium thing is wrong. I knew it was wrong. I always knew. But I committed myself to it anyway. Opium is king here now. The true kaitong is that plant, not any man. It's good that you're getting away from it. It destroys everyone it touches."

"You should get away too," Bently said.

Sartene shook his head. He smiled slightly, and it seemed to emphasize the sagging in his cheeks. "I have obligations to people, and I can't let them suffer because I have been hurt. But there is something you can do for me, Matthew. You have no obligation to me. I want you to understand that. I ask you only as a friend, who will be indebted to you all his life, no matter what your answer is."

Bently knew he did not care what the request was; he knew he would do it if he could. The guilt he felt over Jean's death was real, no matter how hard Buonaparte tried to absolve him.

"Take Pierre to America with you," Sartene said. His voice was filled with pain at having to speak the words. "Take his mother too. And also Benito, if you can." He clasped his hands in front of him almost as though he were praying. "It will not be safe here for the boy, and this place is no longer good for Madeleine. I would like you to raise Pierre as your own son, if you can. Teach him to be a man. Help him. Benito can teach him about Corsica; he can continue what I've tried to begin. Then someday he can come back to me if he chooses. But only if he wants to."

"I'm sure he'll want to," Bently said, knowing he was not being truthful again.

"Perhaps," Sartene said. "But perhaps not." He smiled. "I know you care for Madeleine. I've seen it in the way you looked at her. And I know you've always dealt with those feelings honorably. She respects you and she knows you care for Pierre."

"Do you think she'll want to leave?" Bently asked. He was too weak, too surprised by the request for it to excite him. But he knew it would later. When it became real to him.

"I think she wanted it before, and now she'll want it more than ever."

"I can arrange the immigration matters," Bently said.

"Only for Benito," Sartene said. "I'll arrange papers for Madeleine and Pierre. They will show that she has been in your country for many years, and that Pierre was born there. I don't want my enemies to be able to find him. And I want him to have the benefits of your country. All the benefits. He speaks English well enough, and he will do as I tell him. You will have to explain this to your family and friends some way. But if you agree, I'll leave that to you."

"I agree, Buonaparte. Of course I agree."

"Good." Sartene looked at him for several moments. "Many of my assets will be transferred to your father's bank. The income from them will support my family." Bently began to object, but Sartene stopped him. "It's theirs as well as mine," Sartene said. "And I'll want to make other investments from time to time. Through you, if you want. Through others you suggest, if you feel you don't want to deal with money that comes from my businesses."

"I helped establish the worst of those businesses, Buonaparte. How could I object?"

Sartene stood and patted Bently's hand again. "Thank you. I'll make the arrangements, and then I'll come to you again. You can always come to me. For anything you ever need. Anything."

When Sartene had gone, Bently lay staring at the ceiling. He was tired, but he could not sleep. He understood what Sartene's final words meant, and he also knew he would never seek his help. Jean's words spoken in the dusty, squalid little village kept returning to him, playing over and over in his mind.

I want it for Pierre. I want him to love his grandfather. But I want him to be independent too. I want him to have a will as strong as my father's, so he can make his own decisions. . . .

"That I can try to do, my friend," Bently whispered to himself. I only hope to Christ I don't fail you in that too, he thought.

Madeleine had never been religious, but she had need of religion now. She sat in the dark, morbid, threatening study, the rosary beads balled tightly in her clenched fist. They had been in her hand constantly since the news came of Jean's death. They were in her hand when she finally forced herself to sleep each night, and they were still there each morning when she awoke. She had been praying to God that this old man would not also find a way to kill her son as well.

Listening to him now, her fist squeezed the beads more tightly, forcing the sharp edges of the crucifix deep into the soft flesh of her palm. But she could not feel the pressure or the pain. She could only feel the words slashing at her like knives; carried by that soft, rasping, torturous voice; hidden by the gentle expression in the eyes, the calm, imploring gestures. But the words had blood on them, and she could almost see them coming at her, coming for her son. The old man was talking about danger. Danger for Pierre. Why does he say those things? she kept asking herself. There is no danger for Pierre. There should never be any danger for Pierre. Pierre's a child, a child, a child. . . .

Buonaparte watched the glazed expression return to her eyes. She was drifting from him again, as she had each time he had tried to speak with her since Jean's death. There was no strength to the woman; her solution to the threat was to hide from it. He drew a deep breath, waiting for her to return. Auguste had urged him to be patient, to give her time. But there was no time. Not if Pierre was to be safe.

He had been standing in front of her, but now moved to the chair opposite the one in which she was seated. He drew it close and took her clenched fist in both of his hands.

"Madeleine." His voice was soft but jarring, intentionally so.

She jumped slightly, lips trembling, and looked at him. Slowly he opened the clenched fingers of her hand, allowing the rosary beads to fall into her lap. He stroked the palm of her hand, feeling the deep red indentations in her flesh.

"You're going to hurt your hand," he said softly. He held her hand between each of his and pressed softly. "You're going away from here. With Pierre," he said.

Her eyes blinked; her lips moved soundlessly. She looked at him, her whole face a question. "Away?" she repeated.

"Yes. You and Pierre and Benito. Colonel Bently is going to take you where it is safe. Where no one can harm Pierre."

"When, Papa? When?" She was back now and she was squeezing his hands as she had squeezed the rosary beads before.

"In a few days." She began to object, but he shook his head, stopping her. "But there are conditions, Madeleine."

The fear returned to her eyes again; her lips began to move uncontrollably. "Papa, I'll do anything. Anything, Papa. Pierre must be safe from these people."

"He will be, Madeleine. If you do as I tell you." He watched her nod her head. Like some foolish child, agreeing to anything to avoid a spanking, he thought. Her lack of strength annoyed him, filled him with concern for Pierre's future. "Now, listen to me closely," he began again. "Colonel Bently will take the three of you to the United States, to his home in South Dakota. It is one of the states in the center of the country." She was nodding her head again, eager for more information, eager for the place he was offering her to hide. "There will be no danger for Pierre, *if* you do as I say." He waited, allowing the suggestion to play through her mind. She was bobbing her chin like a child again. "He will take you there as his wife. You don't have to marry, unless you choose to. But everyone must believe you are his wife, and Pierre is his son. Otherwise there will be immigration problems. And there will be danger." He hesitated again, letting the final word settle in her mind. "No one must ever know Pierre's name is Sartene, or that you were ever in Southeast Asia. A believable story and documents will be arranged. All you must do, you and Pierre and Benito, is tell that story to anyone who asks. Money, everything you need, will be provided. But if you fail to keep your silence you will endanger Pierre's life. You must believe this."

Buonaparte's voice had grown cold, hard, and his eyes seemed to look through her, as if searching for some inner flaw he knew was there. She shivered uncontrollably.

"I'll do anything, Papa." Her mind kept repeating the word "anything," over and over, as if it was some talisman that could protect her son, keep him away from this man, away from his words and the blood on them.

Sartene looked at her, his face now impassive. "There is still the condition I must insist on," he said at length.

Madeleine's face twisted as though she had been kicked. She was breathing rapidly. "What?" It was the only word she could manage.

"Pierre must never forget he is a Sartene," he said softly. "He must never be told about our illegal business interests here, or the truth about his father's death. But he must never be allowed to forget he is a Corsican. Benito will see to that. It is why he is going with you."

He watched her recoil, her shoulders drawing into her neck, her lips trembling again, her fingers interlocking and squeezing together in her lap. He could feel the anger rise within him. He was giving up the one thing he loved, the one thing that mattered in his life, and now this Frenchwoman wanted it to be forever. For the first time in his life he felt as though he could strike a woman. He waited for the feeling to pass.

"Someday," he began, "if Pierre wants to return . . ." He paused, redirecting the thought. "When he becomes a man I want him free to choose if he will be a Corsican. I do not want him turned against us because of what he has been told. So you will tell him nothing. If you agree to this, he can be raised in the United States under Benito's guidance. If you violate this condition, I will bring him back here." He watched her eyes, watched the doubt grow there about his ability to keep his threat. He allowed a small smile to form on his lips. "The papers you will have will be false. You will be in the United States illegally. Any attempt you make to legalize your status there I will consider a violation of our agreement. And my people will come and take Pierre in any way they can. Don't doubt my ability to do this." Sartene's voice had remained calm and cold. He let his eyes play against her now. "You must also never tell Colonel Bently about our arrangement. That also would violate the agreement. For my part, I will not see Pierre again, unless he chooses to return to me. That is the pain I will carry." He stared into her face again, his dark, piercing eyes seeming like small dots coming at great speed from a long distance. "Do you agree?"

She heard the words, and felt her body convulse. She pressed her teeth together to keep her jaw from trembling. "Yes, Papa," she finally said. "I agree."

The boy was alone in his room with the dog. He was seated on the bed, his back against the headboard, his knees drawn up to his chin. The dog's head rested on the bed, its strange, eerie amber eyes staring up at the boy. When Sartene entered the room, the boy looked at him, then back at the bed. Sartene walked to the front of the bed and stood there until the boy looked up at him again. When he did, he smiled at the boy.

"How are you feeling, Pierre?" he asked.

"Why are you sending me away?" The boy's eyes were cold and hard, holding a strength and bitterness far too old for his years. Sartene had seen it often before, during his youth in Corsica. The young forced to bear too much pain too soon.

"So you can grow up to be an educated man," he answered.

"I can get educated here," Pierre said.

"It will be better in America. Better for you. The war here is going to get worse. In America you will be safe, and it will be easier for you to learn all the things you must know."

"I don't care about the war. I want to stay here with you."

"It is what your father wanted, Pierre."

"I don't care. Why'd he have to crash his plane, anyway?" His chin began to tremble as if he was about to cry, but he fought to control it.

Sartene felt the ache in his stomach. "He didn't mean to, Pierre. It was an accident. He loved you very much, and he wanted only what was good for you. Now I must see that his wishes are followed."

"Then why can't you come too?"

Sartene walked to the window and looked out into the plain. He kept his back to the boy, not wanting him to see the pain he knew his eyes would reveal. "There's the family business, Pierre. I can't abandon all the people who depend on us to earn their bread."

The boy said nothing, and Buonaparte continued to stare out past the cross pane of the window, his mind drifting back to his own youth, to his conversations with Papa Guerini. He had been right, Sartene told himself. Even then he knew the truth of the years to come. Fate has condemned us to be criminals. And those we love must live with that fate as well. For a moment he allowed himself to wonder if it could have been different, and if it could have been, would he then have been able to keep his grandson with him, or if not, leave with him, without having every police agency in the world watching his movements. Perhaps then he could even have told the child the truth about his father's death. Or perhaps there would have been no need. He forced the thought of Jean from his mind. Fate is such an uncompromising bastard, he told himself.

He turned from the window and walked to the bed and sat next to Pierre, reaching out and running his hand along his blond hair. "I only do what is best for you, Pierre. And I only do it because I love you."

Pierre's eyes brimmed with tears, and he fell against his grandfather's chest to hide them. Sartene stroked the boy's back and kissed the top of his head. "It's all right to cry, Pierre. There is no shame in tears, when they come from the loss of someone you love."

He eased the boy back and lifted his chin with one hand, forcing the child to look up into his face. The tears moved slowly along Buonaparte's cheeks. "I miss your father too, Pierre. We had too little time together over the years. There were problems when he was young, and then, later, there was another war that kept *us* apart. Sometimes I think God has a special vengeance against Corsicans. Perhaps our love for each other is too great for Him to accept." He smiled softly at the boy. "But just as your father and I were together again, so will we be. I promise you.''

The boy stared up at him, his eyes still filled with tears, then he fell back into his arms, sobbing. Buonaparte held the boy, rocking him back and forth.

"You will come back one day, Pierre. Now there is only us. You must never forget your life here, or your Corsican heritage. And you must always believe that one day we will be together again.''

The boy clutched at him. "I don't want to go, Grandpère. I want to stay here. I don't want Colonel Bently to be my father.''

He stroked the boy's head. "He won't be your father, Pierre. He's just going to pretend so we can escape the stupid American immigration laws.''

"I'll tell them when I get there, and then they'll send me back." Pierre's face was still buried in his grandfather's chest, muffling his voice, and together with the sobbing it made him sound much younger than twelve.

Buonaparte eased him back and gently brushed the tears from his eyes. "You are not a child anymore, Pierre. You are a young man, a young Corsican man, and you must act like one. Together we must do what is good for our family. You must learn and you must grow strong, so one day you can come back and help me with our businesses here.'' He smiled at the boy again. "Do you understand me?'' Pierre looked down and slowly nodded his head. "And you must do as I say, Pierre.'' He watched as the boy nodded his head again.

"When can I come back?'' Pierre asked.

Buonaparte felt the tightness return to his stomach. Too many years from now, he told himself. "When you are a man, and you have learned what you must know. You must go to a good university, and you must go into the American army. You must never let yourself become a part of that army. You must simply take what knowledge you can from them. Then when you come back you will be ready to learn from me, and together we will be stronger than ever before.'' He squeezed the boy to him. "We are Sartenes, Pierre, and we are Corsicans. Someday you will understand all that that means.''

"Will you come and visit me?''

The boy's question struck out at him, driving away the euphoria he had willed upon himself. If only I could, he thought. The irony of it assaulted his senses to a point that it almost seemed comical. I, he thought, who love you more than life. If I came to you it could destroy all your chances, perhaps even your life itself. Fate, you bastard. He stroked the boy's back, then began to pat it gently. "It's a long way, and I'm not as young as I used to be, Pierre." And the police, he thought, would follow these old bones anywhere.

"But what if you die before I come back?"

Buonaparte laughed softly, then kissed the top of the boy's head. "I won't die, Pierre. Not until after we are together again."

Pierre sat back and stared up at him. His face was confused, concerned. "But how do you know?"

Sartene took his face in his hands. "Have I ever lied to you, Pierre?" He watched as the boy shook his head. Buonaparte nodded his head abruptly. "Then I tell you it will not happen. I will not allow it. You have my word as a Corsican."

Chapter 17

The villa was small, and the garden was overgrown and neglected. The faded old house was located on the edge of Hanoi, in a part of the city not often visited by Europeans. For Antonio Carbone it had been a refuge for three months now, guarded by his own men; he had even refused offers by Faydang and Francesco Canterina for additional protection.

He had met Canterina only once during those months. He had asked then that they not meet again. He did not want to chance any breach in security that would allow Buonaparte Sartene to find him. And Francesco was hiding too. Deep in the hills.

They were everywhere now, looking for him. He could not even touch his money in Hong Kong. All he had was the gold he had taken with him. The gold and the few men who had not fled in fear. His only hope was to get Buonaparte before Buonaparte got him. Then he could seek peace with the others, and they couldn't refuse him. He had the right to survive; no one in the *milieu* could deny him that. Not even the Guerini brothers. Sartene was not their blood, even though they treated him as such.

But how? Carbone paced the large sitting room of the villa, trying to find some answer. The ceilings and walls of the room were cracked from lack of care. A hole to hide in, he told himself. Like a mouse hiding from a cat that waited outside.

He had lost weight over the months. His pants were loose around his waist and, like all his clothes, were baggy and rumpled. Can't even send my clothes out to be cleaned, he told himself. Because they'll be watching even for that.

There was a small Beretta in his right pants pocket. He had

not carried a weapon in years. A leader in the *milieu* never needed one. There were others for that. Now he had the small automatic with him at all times. *Un vrai monsieur*, he thought. Of what? He had even turned to religion. Always the rosary beads in his other pocket. And the damned trembling, it came so often now.

He walked to a small table where the bottles of liquor were kept and poured himself a drink. He was drinking too much, but it was the only thing that helped the trembling. Or maybe it made it worse. He didn't care. He slumped in an overstuffed chair that smelled of mildew and brought the glass, shaking in his hand, to his lips.

He jumped slightly when the knock came on the door. "Who?" he said, taking the Beretta from his pocket.

The door opened and one of his men, Philippe, entered. He was tall, wiry, with dark eyes that never seemed to blink, and a thin black mustache that always seemed as greasy as his slicked-back hair.

"I just got word that Sartene was seen in Saigon today," Philippe said.

"You're sure?" Carbone said.

"Good," Carbone added, responding to his man's assuring nod. "Soon we'll move against him. He thinks we're beaten, but we're not. I just let him think so. Then, when I move against him, he'll be like a sleeping child."

Philippe nodded again, and the agreement made Carbone feel better. He needed his own bravado. Even more, he needed to know where Buonaparte Sartene was. Sartene would want to be there to watch him die if they found him. He knew that. It would be expected of him. He knew too that as long as Sartene was far away, he was safe. At least for the present.

He slipped the Beretta back into his pocket. Philippe was still standing in the doorway.

"I'm tired now," Carbone said. "I think I'll go up to bed. When you talk to our people again, tell them to watch Sartene closely. It will be soon now."

Philippe nodded and stepped aside to let Carbone pass.

The upstairs bedroom, like the rest of the house, was dank and humid. Even at night the walls were wet, almost as though they were sweating from the heat.

He removed his shirt, leaving his trousers on, the Beretta still in his pocket. Sitting on the edge of the iron-posted bed, he removed his shoes and stockings, then fell back, swinging his legs up. He stared up at the ceiling. Even the fan was broken. There wasn't even the simplest of comforts. He drifted off to sleep with that thought of deprivation still running through his mind.

It was two hours later when the first of the Malayan pit vipers crawled out from under the bed. The snakes, twelve in all, had been placed there in an open cage; they had been drugged by a Hanoi veterinarian earlier in the day, and only now, with the drug dissipated, had they begun to unravel from their intertwined mass of tan and russet. The vipers were common to the lowland thickets and forests near the seacoast, and had excellent night vision. They were sluggish, almost comically so, but naturally aggressive, and required little or no provocation to strike. The bite of the three-to-five-foot reptiles was extremely painful, and produced immediate bleeding, swelling and discoloration. In severe cases victims lingered for several hours, suffering intense thirst, nausea and general hemorrhage, until respiratory failure finally produced an agonizing death similar to strangulation by the garrote. They were Buonaparte Sartene's final gift to Antonio Carbone.

The first viper to emerge lay extended on the floor next to the bed, its four-foot body curved into a large S, its head slightly elevated, moving back and forth, the tongue flicking out, testing the room for a sign of body heat. The reptile was hungry after its unexpected sleep, and annoyed to find itself in unfamiliar terrain. Slowly, it moved to the foot of the bed, found the heavy metal post, and entwined itself; slowly, almost lethargically, it moved up. The other snakes began to emerge, moving to separate parts of the strange new terrain, some coiling to lie in wait of prey, others finding objects to climb in search of food.

A light breeze floated in from the open window. The bars on the window, placed there years before for the security of long-vanished inhabitants, cast shadows across the plain wood floors that occasionally caught the movements of the vipers, giving them a broken, near kaleidoscopic effect.

When the first viper reached the foot of the bed, a movement beneath the sheet startled it, and it coiled instinctively, its spade-shaped head arched back over its body.

Antonio Carbone awoke slowly, his eyes blinking. He had been dreaming. Something unpleasant that he could not remember. His sleep had been fitful for weeks now. A few hours at a time, then awake again. Never any decent rest. He had to find a place that was safe, a place where he could rest. He let out a long, low sigh. His eyes were adjusting to the dark. He would be awake for hours, he knew. Something moved. Across the room. He stared, but there was nothing. He thought he had seen something on the small table near the closet. Just the light, playing through the bars on the windows. Bars, he thought. So like the French to bar themselves in to keep others out. The safety of the imprisoned. And now he was imprisoned, locked away like . . .

Something did move.

Slowly he reached for his pocket and withdrew his Beretta. He raised it to his chest and pulled back the slide, chambering a round. He pulled himself up and leveled the weapon. He screamed. The pain struck his calf and shot up into his knee. Shot, his mind told him. A silencer. He hurled himself from the bed and began to move away. He screamed again. Pain in his other leg. He jumped forward; his foot brushed something and the arch of the foot was engulfed in a searing, red hot stab. "Snakes," he screamed. "Oh my God! No!" He jumped, looking for some safe portion of floor, hopping from one foot to the next. There was movement near him. Again the pain. He screamed again, them jumped forward, reaching the door. He grabbed the handle and pulled. It moved a half inch but held. Something was holding it from outside. He pulled frantically. "Let me out! Let me out! Oh, Jesus, there are snakes in here! Let me out!" He reached out and twisted the small knob that operated the ceiling light. The light flashed on and he saw the blurred red-brown movement coming toward him from atop the dresser next to the door. The snake struck his shoulder, sending shards of pain up through his neck and down his left arm. Again he screamed, jumping back into the room. Another struck at his leg, buckling his knee. The scream became a wail, and his head darted side to side, searching for a safe place. They're everywhere! Oh, my Christ, they're everywhere! One moved sluggishly toward him. He raised the pistol, his hand shaking so the barrel wavered back and forth across its approaching body. He fired, missed, and fired again. Again and again, until finally a bullet ripped into the side of the snake's body, sending out a spurt of blood. The wounded viper's head snapped back at the gaping cut in its flesh, its mouth open, the long curved fangs ready to strike out at the unseen attacker. Carbone fired again, missing, then tried again, but the pistol was empty. He pulled the trigger three, four, five times, then stared at it, his eyes wide with terror.

Already he could feel the swelling in his legs and shoulder. His knees wanted to surrender to the pain, to buckle, but he inched his way back into a corner that was free of the rising, twisting bodies. He cringed there, trying to remain standing, feeling his legs turn to mush beneath him, then gradually sliding to the floor. "Help me! In the name of Jesus, help me!" he screamed.

"Don't you like snakes, Don Carbone?" the voice came through the door, slightly muffled but still clear.

"Help me, please!" Carbone screamed again.

"Help yourself, *paceri*. Make peace with your enemies."

Sartene's voice. Carbone recognized it now. The long, low wail began deep in his throat, then rose to an ear-shattering pitch, finally breaking into short, high-pitched bursts.

Outside, in the hall, Sartene, Auguste and Philippe stood listening. There was a heavy rope tied to the outside door handle of the room that stretched across the hall to the handle of another door.

Sartene placed a hand on Philippe's shoulder. "You've done well," he said softly. The only sound from the room now was a gentle whimpering, like that of a child suffering the agony of monsters in a dream. "Auguste tells me your name is Francisci. Are you any relation to the gentleman in Marseille?"

Philippe smiled, inclining his head to one side. "No," he said. "Unfortunately I have no powerful relatives in the *milieu*."

"Today you have earned yourself a powerful friend," Sartene said.

"I'm grateful," Philippe said. "I always hoped one day I could do you a service."

Sartene nodded. He did not like the man's mustache. It was too well cared for. A vanity. "Would you like to continue that service to me?"

"Very much, Don Sartene," Philippe answered.

"Good. You remain here and find any others of Carbone's men who feel the same. We will be in Saigon for several days. Come and see us there. You know the hotel I own, in the city?"

Philippe nodded.

"Come there and see Auguste. He'll give you another, smaller matter to arrange for me. If you prove yourself in that too, I'll have an important place for you."

A low whimpering moan came from the bedroom, followed by a sharp cry. Philippe glanced, unconcerned, at the door, then back to Sartene. "Would you like me to clean this up?"

"Don't dirty your hands," Sartene said. His eyes were hard, the gray iris of each appearing to glow with hatred. "Let him rot there, food for the rats that will smell him out." He turned abruptly and started down the stairs, Auguste at his side.

"I'm not sure I trust this man Philippe," Auguste said as they reached the bottom of the stairs.

"We'll find out," Sartene said. "He's done us a service, and deserves something. Give him this Air Laos Commerciale matter. If he handles it well, we can let him run the operation for us. We can watch him easily there. Right now we have one more pig to find. If it takes a week, a year, a dozen years."

They walked out the front door, down the overgrown pathway and out to the street. The air was cooler now. It was late March, and within weeks the rainy season would begin. As always, approaching rains could be felt, and the slight respite they would bring from the heat. The two friends walked slowly toward Sartene's waiting car.

"Did I tell you, Auguste, I got a letter from Pierre today?"

"No. Is he well?"

"He sounds a little confused, but that's to be expected. He's discovering all the mysteries of a new country. It must be very difficult for a boy his age. But he says next year he will enter a military school, and that he'll have to wear a uniform every day." Sartene smiled at his friend. "A little soldier, Auguste. A small soldier in a foreign land. Just like Napoleon."

END BOOK ONE

BOOK
TWO

The Stranger

Prologue

SOUTH DAKOTA, AUGUST 1953

The house was at the northern end of the small capital city of Pierre, and from his second-floor room he could see in the distance both the Missouri River and the boundless fields of wheat and hay and cattle that seemed to stretch into infinity across the broad, flat, wind-swept plain. It was summer now, hot and dry and dusty, and it left everything covered with a film of dirt, and Matt had told him that when winter came, the same flat land would also surrender to deep cold and blizzards that would gather the snow in huge drifts until it covered the tops of utility poles. He hated it now, and he was sure he would hate it then even more.

They had arrived in June, and now it was late August, but it had not taken him long to hate the place and its people. It was dull and flat and boring, and the people could not even pronounce the name of their city, his name. They called it *pier*, like a boat dock, even though Matt had told him it had been founded by French fur trappers, maybe even Corsicans. And like the land, the people were cruel and unyielding, and they laughed and mocked him for the slight accent he had brought with him. Even the children called him names, and he hated them most of all.

Standing in his room now, he stared out toward the river. It was the only thing about the place that gave him comfort. It was broad and muddy and it reminded him of the Mekong, of his grandfather's house, his home.

He reached up and touched the swelling along his left cheek. It was tender, and he winced as he ran his fingers lightly against it. It had been the same as always, only this time they hadn't stopped with the names. The other boys had gathered around

205

him, taunting him. Then they had grabbed him and the biggest one had tried to make him say he was a frog, and when he wouldn't he had hit him, again and again. He wished Luc were here. Then they could go and get them all. Every one of them.

There was a knock on the door, then it swung away, revealing the hulking mass of Benito seated in his wheelchair. He had two wheelchairs, one for each floor of the house, and he would move from one to the other by swinging his body onto the stairs and then, in a seated position, moving himself up or down, using only the great strength in his arms and shoulders. From the beginning he had refused any help.

When he entered the room, Pierre looked over his right shoulder, keeping his swollen left cheek from Benito's view. His uncle was smiling, as always, and he pushed the wheelchair forward until he was next to Pierre at the window.

"So. Why are you hiding here?" Benito asked.

"I'm not hiding. I just came up to my room to read for a while, and I started looking out the window."

"That's good. I thought you were hiding."

"Why would I be hiding?"

Benito eased himself up in the chair and leaned forward, as if looking down toward the ground for something. "I thought maybe you didn't want anybody to see the bruise on your face, that's all."

Pierre squeezed his lips together in exasperation and exhaled heavily through his nose. Benito was just like his grandfather. He saw everything, especially when you didn't want him to.

"Did you fall down?" Benito asked.

Pierre considered adopting the lie, but knew it would be useless. He shook his head.

"Then somebody must have hit you, huh?" He waited, watching Pierre nod his head. "Did you hurt your tongue too?" The boy stared at him; his nose wrinkled into a question. "Well, you keep nodding your head like some stupid doll. You're a man, Pierre. Use your mouth like one."

Pierre's face became sullen, and he looked back out the window. "Somebody hit me," he said.

"Why?"

"He didn't like the way I talked. He wanted me to say I was a frog."

"A frog?" Benito bellowed the question.

"It's what they call French people."

"Did you hit him back?"

Pierre shook his head, then caught himself. "No," he said.

"Why not? You should have hit him just for calling you French."

"There were too many of them."

"Oh." Benito pressed his lips together and slowly began nodding his head. "So they tied your hands, and your feet, and they taped your mouth so you couldn't bite them, eh?" Pierre looked to his left, away from Benito. The beating had been bad enough, humiliating enough. Now he could feel his stomach tightening under Benito's questions. "So what are you going to do?"

Pierre shrugged his shoulders, but did not look back at his uncle.

"What?" Benito said. "I couldn't hear you."

"I thought I'd just avoid them. Keep out of their way." Pierre's voice was almost a whisper and he kept looking away to his left. His body jerked to his right and was spun roughly around to face Benito.

"You're going to hide?" Benito's voice was soft and gravelly, but it came out like a soft bellow. His lips were curved up in his perennial smile, but his eyes were like coals and seemed to glisten with anger. He stared at Pierre for several seconds, then loosened his grip on the boy's arm. "Go sit on your bed. I want to talk to you."

Pierre swallowed hard and walked quietly to his bed and sat on the edge of the mattress. He was tall for his age, skinny and awkward, and when he sat his shoulders hunched forward.

Benito pushed the wheelchair toward him and stopped so close to the boy their knees were almost touching. Then he leaned forward until their faces were little more than a foot apart.

"Maybe you are French," he said.

The boy's jaw tightened, and he glared back at his adopted uncle. "I am not. I'm just as much Corsican as you are."

Benito raised a bearlike hand. "You get fresh with me, I'll give you a bruise to match the other one."

Pierre could feel the fear race through his stomach, and he tightened the muscles against it, and kept his eyes hard on Benito's.

A slight trace of humor seemed to play across Benito's lips, then disappeared. He sat back in his chair and folded his huge hands across his protruding stomach.

"I'm going to tell you something about Corsicans," he said. "Then we'll see if you understand it." His fingers were interlocked, and he began to tap his thumbs together, almost as if timing his words with each tap. "In Corsica," he began, "vendetta is a very important thing. If a man's honor is attacked, it is a very serious matter. And it requires a very serious action to overcome the offense. Otherwise the man who is offended is nothing." Benito unclasped his fingers and began gesturing with his right hand, using it like a backhand slap to emphasize his words. "Sometimes the offense is imagined. But that doesn't make it any less real. Then the person who is accused is also wronged by the accusation itself." He held one finger up in front of Pierre's face. "In Corsica, when a man learns that someone is coming to attack him, a certain ritual is followed. On the day the attacker is coming, the man rises from his bed, and he washes himself, and he shaves, and he puts on his best clothes. Then he walks into the square in his village and he waits for the person who is coming for him. And only one of them walks away from that square."

Benito sat back in his chair and continued to stare at the boy. Pierre's eyes were still firm; there was no fear in them. There's a lot of Buonaparte in this child, he told himself. And he thinks, too. Just like his grandfather.

"There always seem to be a lot of them together," Pierre finally said.

"They can't always be together," Benito said.

"The one who hit me, he's big. He's sixteen."

"In the garage there are some small lead pipes. The sides of the knees. The sides of the elbows. Big men can be made very small, very quickly." Benito grunted and pushed his chair back, then began to rub his stomach. "I'm hungry," he said. "I think I'll go downstairs and eat something."

Benito was seated in the small kitchen alcove, chewing on a piece of chicken. It was a half hour since he had talked to the boy, and now he heard him coming down the stairs and going out the door that led to the attached garage. Benito smiled when he saw Pierre walk into the rear yard, climb on his bicycle, and pedal toward the road. He was dressed in a blue suit and he had put on a necktie.

Matt Bently entered the kitchen in time to see Pierre pedaling away. "Where's Pierre going?" he asked.

Benito turned and smiled up at him. "He had some business

to take care of in town. I don't know what. But I don't think he'll be very long."

Matt laughed softly. "It must involve a little girl. He's pretty dressed up."

"Could be," Benito said, smiling again.

"Well, I hope so. The little guy's had a pretty rough time so far."

Benito grinned at him again. "I think things are going to get better very soon," he said. "Very soon. You'll see."

Madeleine came to the kitchen doorway and stopped. She had heard her son's name and Benito's voice, and the combination of the two had drawn her. She stopped in the doorway and forced any sign of concern from her face.

"Did I hear you talking about Pierre?" she asked.

Matt turned and smiled at her. "I just saw him going into town all dressed up." He nodded toward Benito. "Benito thinks our young man has discovered girls."

She looked down at Benito, noticing there was a slight smile on his lips, one that did not carry to his eyes. "Is that what you think?" she asked.

Benito shrugged and inclined his head to one side. "It is only a guess," he said. "Young boys can be very secretive."

Madeleine nodded, her eyes momentarily blank. "Yes, they can," she said. *Especially when they've been taught so well.*

September 12, 1953

Dear Luc,

I started military school this week, and so far it's been pretty good. We have to wear uniforms and march and do things like that, but most of the kids are pretty nice and nobody takes it seriously. Except the cadet officers, that is. They're older than we are, and they really like to scream and yell when somebody does something wrong. Like turning left when they're supposed to turn right. That part of it's dumb, but we have a lot of fun anyway. But it's still not like home. The land, at least this part of it that I'm in, is really flat. Even the woods are flat. No mountains or anything. But they have an awful lot of animals, and Matt says I can go hunting with him in a few years. They don't have any good animals, like elephants or tigers. But the deer are really big. A lot bigger than the barking deer that live around Grandpère's house. There are two kinds. White-tail deer that weigh almost two hundred pounds, and mule deer that are even bigger. Out west they're supposed to have mountain lions that are like tigers, only smaller, and really big bears, ten times bigger than the small bears in Laos. The only other big animal around here is a thing called a bison. It's like a water buffalo, only bigger, but they won't let you hunt it. It's really strange here. You have to have a license to hunt things, even birds. The people here have rules for everything. I told one kid here how Corsicans don't believe in rules, and he looked at me like I was the one who was crazy. Matt says I'll get used to it, but I'm really not sure. He and my friends even call me Peter now instead of Pierre. But it's really hard to be an American, and I have to make them believe I always was one, and that only my mother came from Corsica. I still wish we could all come back to Laos and live with you and Grandpère. Grandpère writes to me every week, but it's not the same. Don't tell him or Auguste that I said that, Brother Two. I think Grandpère would be upset if he thought I didn't like it here. I guess it cost him a lot of money to send me. He was right about one thing, anyway. The schools are better than the lycée in Vientiane. Those problems I had with some of the kids that I wrote to you about before are all over now, but I still wish we could be together.

Put another lizard in Auguste's room. If you don't you're a coward. Write soon, Brother Two.

Your brother,
Pierre

The shotgun was a 12-gauge, pump-action Remington with a full choke, a perfect weapon for the pheasants that abounded in the plum thickets and cornfields of neighboring farms, and a perfect gift for Peter's fifteenth birthday.

Standing with Matt in a field at the rear of the house, Peter ran his hand over the smooth walnut stock, feeling the high polish of the wood. Matt knelt beside him, adjusting the settings on a manual trap machine that would soon hurl clay targets out into the field.

"This is really a terrific shotgun," Peter said. "I hope we can go out and try for some birds soon."

Matt looked up at him and grinned. Peter was already five feet ten inches tall, and his large-boned frame carried 150 pounds of hard lean muscle, a far cry from the gangling twelve-year-old he had brought home from Laos. And there was a confidence about him now, something that had grown steadily.

"A new weapon takes time to get used to, and it's only terrific if you can hit something with it," Matt chided.

Peter grinned at him. It was an easy, boyish grin that seemed to imply some personal secret. "When we go out, you find them, and I'll shoot them for you," he said, looking down at the ancient shotgun that lay on the ground next to Matt.

Matt glanced at his old hammer-action double-barreled shotgun, then back at the boy. "You just remember, smart-ass, it's the shooter, not the weapon, that gets the job done."

Peter laughed softly. He enjoyed the man-to-man byplay that Matt now offered him, and the status of near equals it gave him. "No kidding, Matt. I really do appreciate the gun," he said.

Matt winked at him. "You earned it, tiger. The grades you managed this year were no small deal at that school of yours."

Matt made a final adjustment on the trap machine, concentrating on the angle of flight he wanted to produce. Over the past year, he had realized how much Peter had begun to feel like his own son. He had married Madeleine after their first year in the United States, a quiet wedding in a neighboring state, to avoid jeopardizing the cover story devised by Sartene. But it was only in the past year that the boy had warmed even slightly to him. Now they were friends, more like brothers really from Peter's viewpoint, but to Matt, very much the son he would have liked to have had.

"Get ready," he said.

He released the first clay target and it veered off to the right toward a nearby road. Peter's body pivoted in one fluid motion, the shotgun against his right shoulder, the barrel tracking the movement of the target. He lowered the weapon without firing, and looked back at Matt.

"Well, at least you know when not to shoot," Matt said. "Now if I can figure out how to adjust this damned thing, maybe we can find out if you can hit anything with that fancy new piece of firepower."

Matt grinned at him, then turned back to readjust the trap machine. There had been a look of disappointment in the boy's eyes when the target had flown toward the road, denying any shot. It was part of the intensity he seemed to give everything. There was still a great deal of the boy in him. But it was a great deal less than in most boys his age. And that, Matt knew, was due to Benito. They talked incessantly about Corsica and its traditions; about the need for Corsicans to do things well. They were things that seemed to dominate the boy's mind, ideas that produced a fierce sense of loyalty to his heritage, and Matt wondered if it would diminish in the years ahead, and if so, to what degree.

"I wish the fields around here weren't so full of all those sandburs," Peter said. "Then we could use a dog like Max to hunt with. He used to point birds all the time back *home.*"

Matt winced slightly. It was almost as though the boy had been reading his mind. "Yeah, it would make things a lot easier." Matt kept his eyes on the machine. "You still miss Laos and your grandfather, don't you?"

"Yeah, I guess so," Peter said. He looked sheepishly at Matt. "I don't mean that I haven't been happy here with you and Mother. School's been good, everything, really. I guess I just always think about Laos as being my home. And I miss Grandpère. I really wish he'd come and visit instead of sending Uncle Auguste over every year or two. We write to each other, but it's not the same."

"It's hard for him. It's a long trip and he's getting up in years. And he has a lot of complex business interests to take care of, you know. Things over there are pretty wild and woolly. From a business standpoint it's like a damned frontier. And in business there you have to stay close to the people running the government. When I left, your grandfather owned hotels and restaurants, a pretty good-sized rubber plantation was just getting started, and he did a lot of business in the export market. Everything from currency to ivory." He looked at Peter, watching him drink in the information. "And I wouldn't be too upset about his not coming over here. Business there is very cutthroat. If he left for any extended period of time, he might find he had nothing left when he got back."

"But Uncle Auguste could run things for him," Peter said.

"Auguste's good, Peter. But believe me, there's only one Buonaparte Sartene when it comes to making something work."

"Then I guess I just won't see him until I go back," Peter said.

Matt stopped and looked up at Peter. "Listen, do me a favor.

Don't talk about going back there when your mother's around," he said. "It would upset her."

Peter nodded his head, causing a shock of blond hair to drop onto his forehead. "Yeah, I know. But I don't understand why she gets so nervous whenever Uncle Benito and I talk about Southeast Asia."

"It wasn't a happy place for her, Peter. Not at the end, anyway. Your father's being killed. Benito's being shot by that communist guerrilla. She's afraid of the danger over there. Afraid for you. I'd rather see you stay here myself."

"But Matt, that plane crash that killed my father could have happened anywhere. You were in the same crash. You were just lucky. And people get shot here too."

"I know all that, Peter. But we don't have bandits roaming the outcountry, and there is a bit of a guerrilla war going on there too. And it's going to get worse before it gets any better. Look, tiger, you'll make your own decisions about where you want to go and what you want to do. All I ask is that you not upset your mother until it's necessary, if it ever is necessary." He watched Peter nod his agreement, knowing he would keep his word. It was the one thing about his Corsican training that Matt liked at the moment.

He finished the final adjustment on the trap machine, then stood. "There, that should do it. Now, remember, you don't aim a shotgun, you point it. Let your eye follow the target over the barrel. Your body will move with your eye. And keep following it even after you squeeze off the round. All you have to do is step on the plate to activate the machine."

Matt turned to a sound behind him, and saw Benito rolling toward them in his wheelchair. Behind Benito, Madeleine stood on the rear porch, watching them. Even from a distance he could see the tight look on her face. She had not been well lately. She seemed to draw within herself each day, as Peter came closer to manhood. He turned back to Peter. "Look, you show off for your uncle. I just remembered something I have to tell your mother."

Benito smiled at Matt as he moved past him, then continued on to Peter, the smile broadening as he rolled to a halt next to the boy.

"So, are you going to show me what you can do with this fine new weapon?" Benito roared.

"I'm going to try," Peter said.

"You know your adopted great-grandfather was famous with a shotgun," Benito said.

Peter turned back to him, his eyes bright. "Really? You never told me that."

"Oh, yes," Benito said. "Of course it was different from your shotgun. It was called a *lupara,* and it had a much shorter barrel. It was used in the mountains for protection against wolves. But your great-grandfather was a Corsican freedom fighter, and he used it against a different kind of wolf. French wolves. It is said that when he died, they put him in his coffin with his *lupara* in his arms. Someday you must get your grandfather to tell you about the man you are named for, Papa Guerini."

When he reached the porch, Matt stroked Madeleine's cheek. "You look troubled," he said.

"It's just seeing Pierre with a gun," she said.

"It's only a sport, Madeleine. It's good for him to learn it," Matt said.

Madeleine nodded, then attempted to smile. "I know," she said. "You will teach him a sport. But I'm not sure what Benito will teach him."

He watched her turn and move back into the house, then looked back to the field. Two clay targets exploded from the ground, and he watched Peter's body move with them. The shotgun erupted in rapid bursts and the two clay targets exploded into dust. Damn, he thought. The kid has the reflexes of a cat.

September 5, 1957

Dear Pierre,

   Now, as you are about to begin your final year of secondary school, I know you must be looking forward to all the decisions that are before you. You must treat these decisions with the importance they deserve, for your future life will be greatly affected by them. Because of this, it is my wish that you study history with great care. While a man can never change the way things are in the world, a knowledge of how they came to be so gives him the ability to understand and deal with the problems he must face.

   As I have told you in other letters, it is also my wish that after your years at university, you receive military training. I understand your belief that much of what you have seen of the military in school is foolishness. It has always been so, and always will be. But there are things to be learned that will be of benefit to you. This does not mean that you should become the servant of the people who can teach you these things. Years ago, when you were still a boy, I told you of my wish that you have this training one day. I also told you that you must never allow these people to become your masters, but that you only take what they could give you. I tell you now, as I did then, that a Corsican is no man's servant. He serves only his own family, and those who give him their loyalty. But he is also wise enough to accept the knowledge others can give him. This is what I ask you to do. This training will teach you to survive in this world. It will prepare you for times in the future when others may not want you to survive.

Next month your Uncle Auguste will visit you, and I will be sending some books with him that will help you in your studies. I understand your wish that I also come and visit with you. Right now that is not possible, but know that I wish it as much as you. Each time Auguste returns and tells me what a fine young man you are becoming, I wish for it even more. But one day soon we shall be together here in Laos. And I know when the day comes I will meet the fine man that we who love you have always wanted you to become.

> With much love and affection,
> Your Grandfather

> March 8, 1958

Dear Luc,

I was accepted to Columbia University today, so now I have a choice to make. Right now I'm reasonably sure it will be Stanford. I've decided to major in history, with an emphasis on Far Eastern Studies, and the program there seems slightly better. But perhaps it's just that it's one step closer to Laos. I'm not really sure, Brother Two. I know I still miss it, along with you and Grandpère and everyone else. It's not that I don't like it here. This is an amazing country, a place where people have so many opportunities it's staggering to think about them. And they really don't seem to understand how good it is.

I've watched the farmers here, and thought about the people back in Laos, the way they struggle to raise enough food. Here the farms seem to go on forever, and the men in the fields have machines to do just about everything. Sometimes I hear them complaining about government price supports and operating costs, and I have to laugh to myself, and wonder how they'd like to spend the day walking behind a water buffalo.

You should come here and see it for yourself. I asked Uncle Auguste about that when he was here last month, but he said you're busy working with him. He's very proud of you, but I'm sure he never says so. Write and tell me about it. He's still talking about the time we put the lizard in his room, and laughing about how he and Grandpère scared the devil out of us. When I come back, we'll do it again, just to teach him a lesson. Right now I don't know when that will be. I've talked to Matt about visiting Laos in the summer, but he still feels it would be too upsetting to Mother. She seems to get upset if I even talk about Grandpère and you, or Vientiane. Talk to Grandpère about both of you coming here. If I'm at school in California it won't be quite as long a trip. Do what you can to persuade him, Brother Two, and I'll work on it from this end. I'll write again soon.

Your brother,
Pierre

SOUTH DAKOTA, DECEMBER 1960

He had not learned of Benito's illness until he returned home for the Christmas holidays. The old man had refused to allow Matt to write him, insisting that he would live until Christmas, if necessary, so Pierre's studies would not be interrupted.

When he saw Benito, he was staggered by the physical change that had taken place in only a few months. The stroke had extended Benito's paralysis to the upper left portion of his body, and the left side of his face was slack and misshapen. For the past month he had been fed through tubes, and the robust barrel of a man Peter had known most of his life was now emaciated. When he entered the darkened bedroom, Benito's right eye gleamed out at him, and the right side of his mouth curved up in a grotesque half-smile.

"So, you came home." Benito's voice was little more than a harsh whisper, but his manner of delivery was still forceful. He gestured weakly with his right hand. "Come over here and kiss your uncle."

Peter kissed Benito's forehead and began to speak, but found he did not know what to say.

"How do you feel?" he asked, immediately recognizing the absurdity of the question.

"I feel like I look," Benito said. "Like a dying piece of old shit."

Tears formed in Peter's eyes, and he fought them off, knowing it would displease his uncle. "You should be in a hospital," he said.

Benito snorted. "You sound like your stepfather. I tell you what I told him. That a man should not die surrounded by sick people. It's too depressing."

Peter laughed softly, then reached out and took his uncle's right hand and pressed it between both of his. For the past eight years the man had refused to allow a wheelchair to dictate life to him. Now he insisted on setting the terms of his own death.

"What does the doctor say?"

Benito snorted again. "The donkey told me I'd be dead a month ago. I told him I would die when I was ready. After I spoke to my nephew."

"I'm here now, Uncle. And I'll stay with you until you're well again." Peter squeezed his hand, hoping it would give his uncle some sense of reassurance.

"I always thought that I would go back to Laos with you one day. But God always has one last joke for everyone."

"Has anyone written to Grandpère and Uncle Auguste?"

"I don't want them to know until after I'm dead. It would do no good, and if they knew they would come, and that would not be a good thing." Benito stopped, taking in several deep breaths as though gathering the strength to continue.

"I should let you rest," Peter said.

"No. I'll get all the rest I need soon enough. Now I must tell you something. And I must ask you to promise me two things." He breathed deeply again, staring up with his one good eye as Peter nodded his agreement.

"First, Pierre, you must do as your grandfather has asked.

You must complete your studies, and then get training in the military. Then you must go back to him.''

"It's what I've always planned," Peter said.

"There is also something you haven't planned, Pierre. I always thought I would be with you when you learned of it. I thought I would be there to help you." He stopped again, gathering strength. "When you return to Laos you will learn many things about our family. You will also learn about a man there. And after you learn about him, you will have to kill him. You will have to do this because when this man learns you have returned, he will try to kill you.''

Peter stared blankly at his uncle. The words had come at him like blows, and his first thought was that his uncle had become delirious. "What do you mean? Who are you talking about?''

Benito's right eye fluttered. "I cannot tell you, Pierre. You were to learn none of this until you returned. I have never failed to do anything your grandfather asked of me. But I thought I would be here to help you prepare for the time when you returned to him. Now you must know so you can prepare yourself. If you knew his name, you might go before you were ready. And you will not be ready until you have learned how to kill. If you do not learn this, you must never go back.''

Peter shook his head. "I don't understand. I was twelve when I left Laos. Why would there be a man who wants to kill me?''

"Because he knows he will never be safe while there is still a Sartene alive on this earth.''

"But why?''

Benito drew a deep breath, then squeezed his eyes shut. "Because, Pierre, he is the man who murdered your father.''

The long, hard isolation of winter had finally engulfed them; the snow was already a foot deep, covering any hint of life. Matt and Peter walked slowly across the encrusted field; the harsh wind that moved through the open land cut into their faces.

"I have a right to know more than I've been told," Peter said. He kept his eyes fixed on the blank, snow-white horizon, as if searching for something to break the emptiness that stretched out before him.

"Yes, you do," Matt said. He stopped and turned toward Peter. "I'll tell you what I can," he said. "But I can't answer all your questions.''

"Because you've promised not to?''

Matt shook his head. "I've given no promises. But there are many things about your grandfather, about your family, that I was never told. And there are things I do know that involve work I did for my government that I simply can't tell you."

"Does my mother know?" Peter stared into Matt's eyes. His question had carried a mild threat, and he regretted it at once.

"She knows more than I'm willing to tell you," Matt said. "If you ask her, perhaps she'll tell you." He placed a hand on Peter's shoulder, then let it fall away. "You know she hasn't been well. She never really has been since we came here. Talking about those days won't be good for her. I don't have the right to ask you not to, but I hope you won't."

Peter looked away, taking the full force of the wind in his face. "Tell me what you can," he said.

Matt drew a deep breath and took Peter by the arm. They began walking again. "Throughout the world there is a very loosely knit organization of Corsicans known as the *milieu*. Within that overall organization there are many groups, each headed by a man who is called *un vrai monsieur*. For the most part the business activities of the various groups are legal. In some instances they're not. But then, you know the Corsican attitude about laws made by others." He stopped and looked at Peter. "Your grandfather heads such a group."

As they walked on, Matt told Peter about Sartene's various business interests, those legitimate and those not. The only activity he did not speak about was opium.

They stopped, their path blocked by an uprooted tree; they turned their backs to the wind.

"And my father was killed because someone in the group wanted to control these business interests?" Peter asked.

Matt stared at the ground, wishing the question had not been asked. He cared too much for his adopted son to lie to him. "He wanted to control a particular aspect of those business interests, one your grandfather undertook at the request of my government."

"And you won't tell me what that business was."

Matt shook his head. "I can't."

"Will you tell me who the man was?"

Matt shook his head again. "That's the one thing I could tell you, but won't."

Peter's jaw tightened. "Why not?"

"Because Benito was right. If you knew you might go back before you were ready."

"I could write my grandfather. Telephone him." Peter's voice was harsh, angry.

"That might put him in jeopardy. His moves are watched by various agencies. That's why he's never been able to visit you here."

"And you won't tell me."

Matt shook his head. "No. But I'll give you some advice."

"What?" Peter snapped.

"Don't go back."

December 30, 1960

Dear Uncle Auguste,

We buried Uncle Benito today. It was a simple ceremony, just as he would have wanted.

I know our telegram informing you of his death was a shock. But this too was what he wanted. He knew that you and Grandpère would come if you knew he was so ill. And this, he felt, would not be a good thing.

I cannot tell you how much I share your loss. It was only at the end that I realized how much his life was involved with my own, how much he had devoted himself to my future. Before he died, he told me how he had planned to return to Laos with me, to help me and guide me there, as he had done for so much of my life.

Now I will do the last thing he asked of me. I will finish my studies and my military training, so I will be ready for what awaits me when I return to Laos.

Your nephew,
Pierre

Palo Alto had agreed with him, and when Auguste first saw him, he found it hard to believe how much Pierre had changed in the years since his last visit. He was broader, stronger, and there was an air of quiet confidence about the way he moved. Yet there was something else as well, something he could not identify. Somehow, he did not seem like the same young man.

They met in a small French restaurant in San Francisco, Peter having driven there at Auguste's request. He had told him that he found American cars too large, and difficult to drive. Actually, it had been a precaution insisted upon by Buonaparte. There was still concern that Pierre might be tied to the Sartene family before he gained all he could from his life in the United States. And there was also the lingering problem of Francesco Canterina.

Leaning across the table, Auguste placed his hand on top of Pierre's. The hand was huge, like Jean's, he recalled. "So, this year you graduate from university," Auguste said.

"Yes, sir," Peter said. "It's been a battle, but they're finally going to let me out."

Auguste snorted. "You're too modest, Pierre. I've seen the copies of your grades you sent to your grandfather. You've done this thing very well, and Buonaparte is very proud of you."

Peter only nodded. "How is he? His health, I mean."

Auguste moved his head from side to side. "He is good. He's not as young as he used to be, but his health is good. He's still a pain in the ass, but he takes good care of himself. There's no need to worry."

"And you?"

Auguste sat straight in his chair. "Look for yourself. I'm wonderful." He wagged a finger at Peter. "And still strong enough to teach you a thing or two."

"I'm sure," Peter said. He smiled at the slender little man, who suddenly seemed so strange to him, so much more foreign than he had ever noticed before. The smile faded. "I want to talk to you about Uncle Benito."

Auguste's face seemed to soften, and he began to stroke his chin, remembering his brother. "Benito was a good man, a good Corsican. He never said much, but he understood many things. In some ways he was very much like your father, God have mercy on them. Both of them were strong as bulls, but gentle also. Strong men, as you will be one day."

"Uncle Benito was very good to me. He taught me a great deal."

There was a coolness in Pierre's voice, Auguste thought. "He loved you, Pierre, just as we all do. We are family, and as long as we remain together, we are strong. But I don't have to tell you this." Auguste slapped his palms on the table. "So tell me, what will you do when you graduate?"

"I've been thinking about doing a year of graduate work at Columbia, in New York. I've applied and they've accepted me. Then the army. Uncle Benito explained the necessity of it."

"You don't sound very enthusiastic about it." Auguste watched

Pierre's eyes. They seemed more distant than they had when he last saw him.

Peter looked at him coolly. "If anything, I'm more enthusiastic than ever, Uncle. You see, Uncle Benito told me why I would need the training when I returned."

Auguste stared across the table, his face a mask. "What did Benito tell you?"

"That when I returned I would learn about the man who killed my father. And when I learned about him, I would either have to kill him or he would kill me."

Auguste became rigid in his chair. His nephew's words had come like a wave of cold air, and the chill had also carried to his eyes. "What else did my brother tell you?"

"Nothing. Not even the man's name. He said he had promised Grandpère; that he was only partially violating that promise because he knew he wouldn't be there to help me prepare for that day." Peter looked down at the table, then back at Auguste. "I asked Matt, and he also would not tell me. His advice was that I not go back. Later, I thought of writing Grandpère, but I realized it wasn't something he'd want on paper." Peter folded his hands on the table. "Why don't *you* tell me?"

Auguste leaned back in his chair and studied his nephew. The cold look in his eyes—he had not recognized it before. It was Buonaparte's look. Whatever wrong Benito had done, at least he had not failed with the boy.

Auguste leaned forward, his voice soft, almost soothing. "What my brother told you he had no right to speak of. I am not saying what he told you was not true. I am saying only Buonaparte has the right to tell you the whole story."

"Which means that you will not."

The coolness in his nephew's voice brought a small smile to Auguste's lips. "Do not be angry with me, Pierre, for standing by my word." He allowed the smile to fade. "I will tell you this. The man who killed your father was a trusted member of our group. He did what he did because he wanted to seize the business your father and grandfather controlled."

"A legal business?" Peter interrupted.

Auguste smiled. "I see your mind has been busy this last year and a half."

"It has," Peter said. "You haven't answered me."

Auguste shrugged. "What is legal in some countries is illegal in others. In Laos, what we did was legal." Peter began to speak, but Auguste raised his hand stopping him. "I'll tell you no more, Pierre. If you return to Laos, your grandfather will tell you everything you must know. If you do not return, then there will be no need for you to know any more than you do now."

Peter's jaw tightened. He looked down at the table, then back at his uncle. His face softened. "I do have a need to know, Uncle. For the past year and a half I've been struggling with the fact that a great deal of my life has been a charade, without me ever knowing why. I think it's time I found out who I am, and what that requires of me."

Auguste reached across the table and placed his hand atop Peter's.

"You know who you are, Pierre. You're a Corsican, a Sartene."

Peter leaned forward, his eyes intense again. "That's *what* I am, Uncle. What I've been raised to be. Now I want to know *who*."

Auguste nodded. "For that, Pierre, you must return. But not until you are ready."

Buonaparte Sartene stared down at the table of toy soldiers, set out to depict the 1815 Battle of Quatre-Bras. He picked up one of the soldiers in Ney's army, then replaced it in the position of a fallen warrior, before turning back to Auguste.

"We cannot blame Benito," he said. "He was a man on his deathbed, and he thought he was doing what was right for Pierre."

Auguste watched in silence as Sartene crossed the room and sat heavily behind his desk. The past ten years had been difficult for him. Not only the absence of Pierre, but also his inability to seek vengeance against Francesco.

"It was a cruel way for him to learn about his father," Auguste said.

Sartene nodded. "Sometimes it's the cruelties of life that make a man strong. But in Pierre's case I'm afraid this particular blow has made him feel deceived."

"You must tell him the reasons for it," Auguste said.

Sartene stared at the desk top for a moment, then slowly shook his head. "If I tell him now, then he will know that Francesco will remain safe until he returns. And what would Pierre do if he knew we were forced to let the murderer of his father live in order to keep him safe? Such knowledge might force Pierre to come before he is ready, and that would only mean his death."

Sartene looked across at Auguste, inclining his head to one side to acknowledge the futility of his position. "I must gamble on his love, my friend. I will write him and ask for his trust. I will ask him to believe that what was done, even though it hurt him, was necessary for his protection."

Auguste fumbled with his hands. "I wonder if he will accept it. He will have years yet—maybe too many years—to brood about it."

Sartene's eyes became distant. "It is a problem, isn't it, my friend? I must gamble on his trust, or on his life."

"But when he returns his life will still be in danger."

Sartene nodded his head slowly. "Yes," he said, drawing out the word. "But then he will no longer be a boy. He will be a man who has learned how to kill." He looked up at Auguste with a bitter smile. "A nice inheritance, is it not, that I give my grandson?"

Chapter 18

The Continental Stretch 707 was still twenty miles off the coast of Viet Nam when the war first made itself felt. The pilot's voice drawled through the intercom, announcing the approach of two F-105 fighters, which would soon be visible to passengers, one off each wing tip.

They were U.S. military escorts, he explained, and would accompany the commercial airliner through its final approach to Tan Son Nhut International Airport. That approach, he added, would also not be normal. It would be abrupt, a rapid, spiral descent, to thwart any sniper fire from the jungle surrounding the city. The announcement produced a ripple of nervous laughter in the cabin.

Peter Bently leaned forward and looked out the cabin window, hoping to catch sight of the sleek F-105s. The light reflected off the plastic, revealing his own blurred image, and he realized he too was smiling. It was the captain's voice, the bored reassuring drawl; it had reminded him of a waitress the evening before he left, stoically announcing that all the roast beef was well done. Ask me if I give a damn, her tone implied, just as the captain's did now.

Below, the deep blue of the South China Sea could be seen through breaks in the cloud cover. He twisted his head, again trying to see the fighters, which he knew would be above or below the wing tip. His neck cramped and he sat back, his broad shoulder overlapping into the empty seat next to him. They had been in the air seventeen hours, and had made two one-hour ground stops in Anchorage and Tachikawa, Japan, and the travel time was beginning to wear. He ran a hand through his closely

225

cropped blond hair. Fatigue showed on his face, a face that had grown harder after three years of intensive training. Now the sharp features, handsome by American standards, seemed to sag, the normally square jaw appeared a bit pulpy. Only his eyes seemed unaffected. Fatigue had failed to dim the piercing blue.

Peter stretched his shoulders and grunted softly. He could feel the nervous excitement building in his belly. It had begun at Travis Air Force Base when he had boarded the aircraft, then had dissipated over the long hours of the flight. Now it was back, a tight, tingling sensation, an anticipation of finally returning to a part of the world which he had always considered his home. For weeks now, since learning his request for duty in an intelligence unit in Viet Nam had finally been approved, he had wondered if his boyhood memories would be reaffirmed. It was Viet Nam, not Laos. He smiled, and recalled the contempt Laotians had for the Vietnamese.

But he would go to Laos soon. And he would see his grandfather again, and learn about himself, and about a man who wanted him dead. He leaned his head against the seat and smiled slightly. The idea did not frighten him. According to those who had spent the last three years teaching him how to stay alive, there were also a few thousand others here with the same intention.

But still this would be different. This would have nothing to do with war. This was simply a legacy of the past, a past he was yet to fully understand. Ever since he had learned that the man was once a member of their business group, he had struggled to recall those faces from the past. It had been useless, but it had passed the time. Now he would soon have the answer, and he would do what had to be done. And he would use the army's intelligence apparatus to do it. He smiled to himself, wondering what the military hierarchy would think if they knew they were being used, not served. It was the only reason he still wore the uniform. That and the anonymity it gave him, returning under the cover of a war.

At least his grandfather would appreciate that he had learned one lesson well: Use them, but never serve them. Buonaparte had explained that lesson many times. Now he would have to explain other things, a lifetime of things. His grandfather had asked for his trust, and he had given it blindly. Now he had a right to the truth.

He closed his eyes, recalling his grandfather's face, the soft, rasping sound of his voice. The image was as clear as the day he

left, like an icon burned into his mind. The images of the others
he had not seen had faded slightly, had become vague memories,
like old sepia portraits that were no longer real. But not his
grandfather.

Feeling the aircraft drop into a sharp descent, he looked out
the window again. The South China Sea was still below. Closer
to shore now, it was a white-capped pale green, dotted with the
tiny dark forms of fishing boats, and beyond, the darker gray-
green mass of dense tropical forest hazed over by the heat, so at
a distance it almost seemed to pulsate. He reached for the small
leather bag under the forward seat and removed the playing-sized
deck of survival cards the army had issued him. On the face of
the laminated cards were color photographs of reptiles and plants
of the region. On the reverse were instructions about their dangers or suitability as food. They were intended for those lost in
the bush, but for Peter they provided a small opening to his past,
a return of boyhood memories.

The screech of the wheels touching down brought him back.
Outside, the flat expanse of the airport sped by as the plane
moved down the runway, and in the distance he could see
clusters of military aircraft and vehicles. Near one C-141 transport a mass of silver reflected the sunlight, and he twisted his
body to try to make it out. Military coffins in double rows of
fifteen to twenty, stacked at least ten high. But no way to tell if
they were incoming or awaiting an unhappy journey home.
Either way, he thought, not a good first impression. And knowing the military, they'd expect to use every one of them. *Air
KIA*. He leaned his head back and concentrated on the seat in
front of him, allowing his mind to recall some of the slang used
by men who had returned from their one-year tour in Viet Nam.
Those who hadn't made it back, those who had been killed in
action, were said to have bought the farm and booked a flight on
Air KIA. This same plane, on its return flight, would be known
to the men as the Freedom Bird, and those lucky enough to be
boarding would be "going back to the world." He drew a deep
breath, and thought about his past three years of training. All the
brutality he'd learned to inflict. All of it giving him a better
chance of survival than so many others who were being sent. But
even without that training he knew he would have had a better
chance than most. Since childhood he had been taught to view
the world as a dangerous place, one in which only those with an

inner hardness survive. That knowledge was now a part of his being, and always would be.

The brakes of the Continental 707 groaned as the aircraft eased itself off the runway, and in the distance he could see the old colonial terminal, a dull gray-white mass, blurred by the heat, that seemed besieged by shimmering bodies moving in and out. The plane turned, cutting off the view, and across the airstrip now he could see the dense forest that lay beyond, the place where snipers were known to sit in trees and fire rounds at incoming and outgoing aircraft, even though they knew they would never bring one down. A simple act of terror. Or perhaps just a message of welcome or farewell, telling those arriving or leaving that they were still there.

He had asked a sergeant once why he thought the military had shortened the radio code name for the Viet Cong—VC, Victor Charlie—to just Charlie, but the sergeant had shrugged his shoulders and insisted that they had to call the little bastards something short. The answer had seemed typical of the derogatory attitude toward that invisible peasant army, and it had always made him think of Luc and the other Mua warriors he had known as a boy. Luc, who had been like a brother to him, with whom he had taken karate lessons, and who had always been faster and better at it than he. He doubted the Viet Cong were any different, and if history meant anything they had proved that sense of tenacity with the French, and the Chinese before them.

The plane lumbered slowly toward its place at the terminal, and he could make out the insignia on the various aircraft, the diverse species of Freedom Birds clustered together in their own nesting areas—TWA, Braniff, Pan Am, Delta, each gathering guarded by U.S. Air Force Security Police. Away from the commercial aircraft, the military contingent seemed overpowering, a sprawling expanse of war technology—fighters, sleek and needlelike; massive cargo planes; bombers; gunships and spotter planes; and around and above each, helicopters flitting like insects from place to place—bearing the insignias of the U.S., Korea, Viet Nam and others he could not recognize.

The 707 finally came to a halt, and the aisle immediately filled. Most standing now were young. Eighteen- and nineteen-year-olds. When the line had dispersed, Peter made his way to the front of the cabin, then stepped out on the deplaning ramp. The heat struck him like the first step into a sauna, and he instinctively glanced at his Rolex. It was nine in the morning, yet even now in late summer it seemed hotter than anything he remembered as a child. More intense even than the Everglades, where he had trained, and certainly worse than the dry, dusty heat of the Dakotas.

He knew it had always been hot, and recalled the need to take to the shade on the veranda of his grandfather's house. But this heat was worse. When Peter reached the bottom of the ramp he could already feel the perspiration running beneath his khaki blouse, and each breath felt as though it were being filtered through a hot, damp cloth. Perhaps it was a combination of the air conditioning on the plane and the nineteen hours of travel, he told himself. He started toward the terminal feeling the heat rising from the hot tarmac. No. It was just hot.

Suddenly he felt weak and tired. All around him the noise of aircraft engines mingled with the jabbering of incoming military and civilians, each punctuated by the sound of loudspeakers offering instruction in English and Vietnamese. Ahead, two Vietnamese women, one older and one in her early twenties, hurried past a sauntering, sweating line of GIs. The women were wearing brightly colored *ao dais,* their beautiful national dress which formed a sheath from neck to ankle, slit up to the knee to allow black-trousered legs to move without restriction. Peter watched the younger woman, her head erect, eyes fixed on the approaching entrance to the terminal, ignoring the suggestive remarks of a group of young enlisted men.

"Hey, baby. You in the blue pajamas," one called after her.

"*Ao dai,* asshole," a second GI corrected.

Peter laughed inwardly. The knowledgeable soldier had misspoken the name, which was pronounced *ow-zigh,* something that would mark his ignorance and unworthiness in the oriental mind. These young men would have difficulty meeting anyone but bar girls, he decided.

The interior of the terminal was like a large ballroom, and much to his displeasure Peter found himself very much a part of the herd, struggling to find his duffel bag, which was among hundreds of others in the incoming-personnel area. Here the noise outside seemed meaningless and calm, as hundreds of voices swirled through the vast room. Noncoms wearing green armbands moved through the crowd, directing enlisted men to one holding area, officers to another, and civilians to a third. When he reached his designated area, Peter found a sergeant standing on a box, shouting instructions over the din, while an overweight spec-5 sat at a small table next to him checking documents.

"Records, orders and customs slips, captain," the spec-5 snapped, when Peter's turn at the desk came. He handed them over.

The spec-5 glanced at the papers, then whacked each with a rubber stamp.

"Camp Alpha, captain," he snapped as an afterthought.

"Right."

"Green bus, out front. First one in line. That's for officers. Don't have no other markings. Don't wanna encourage Charlie's fragging instincts." He handed back the papers and reached quickly for the next man's.

Walking away, Peter could hear the same routine being repeated. "Don't wanna encourage Charlie's fragging instincts." The phrase followed like an echo, and he wondered if the man repeated it in his sleep at night.

When he reached the bus, Peter added his bag to a pile next to the baggage compartment. Looking up, he noticed the windows were covered with wire mesh, a grenade-prevention device to thwart Charlie's fragging instincts. The bus was a Japanese Isuzu, and as he stepped inside a smile formed on his lips as the air conditioning hit.

Peter stored his leather carrying case in an overhead rack, then fell into a hard plastic seat next to a Marine major about ten years his senior.

"You have any idea who it was who invented air conditioning, sir?" he said, closing his eyes and drawing a deep, cool breath.

"No idea at all, captain," the major said. "But I know what you mean. Somebody ought to put up a monument to the sonofabitch."

"At the very least. I hope it's not always this hot," he said, again surprised it was not part of his childhood memory. But then, children were always playing, and weather never seemed to bother them.

"Normally, it gets a little worse in midafternoon, but not much," the major said. "Outcountry's a lot worse, but everything there's bad. The whole godforsaken region's like that. When it's hot you pray for the rainy season and when it comes, you curse the mud. This your first tour?"

Peter nodded. "Very first."

"Where you assigned?"

"Unassigned. But I'm hoping for Saigon."

Peter smiled inwardly. He had been told not to reveal his intelligence assignment to anyone, even fellow officers. It was something he knew his grandfather and Auguste would appreciate. Perhaps the only thing.

The major nodded, knowingly. He looked like something out of an enlistment poster, square jaw, hard eyes; only the gray hair at the temples altered the image. "Saigon's not a bad duty, if you can swing it," he said. "But then, you just might. You're young for a captain, even."

"Part of the inducement to go indefinite after my mandatory three. Where are you stationed, sir?"

"I Corps, up at Danang, and let's drop the sir shit. I'm Jack Logan."

They shook hands.

"Peter Bently."

"This is a return trip for me. I got passed over for colonel, and they tell me this is the only way to redeem myself," Logan said. "You'll like Saigon, if you end up here. Just watch your ass. Charlie moves around at will, and we lose almost as many drunken officers on Tu Do Street after curfew as we do in combat. VC pay a bounty on officers."

The bus lurched forward, and Peter glanced back at the terminal. Despite the number of uniforms, it was hard to imagine any war was taking place. The mass of civilians milling outside the terminal far outnumbered the military, and even though some of them might indeed be VC as Logan indicated, the atmosphere was almost festive.

Beyond the wire that encircled the base there was a frantic movement of cars, trucks and motorized rickshaws called cyclos. He turned in his seat, watching it with amused wonder.

Logan noticed his interest. "Real-life bumper cars," he said. "I think these zipperheads play with themselves while they drive. And you get in a bang-up with one of them, you'd better pay him off quick, or forty of the little fucks'll jump your ass."

Peter was too weary to respond, but Logan seemed caught up in the role of tour guide. Just past the terminal, he pointed to a sprawling complex of buildings. "That's HQ, part of it anyway, where Westmoreland sits and dreams up new strategies that don't work, or how to win a war without really trying." Logan grunted at himself. "Look. Don't let me spoil it for you. Just write me off as a disgruntled lifer. That's the truth, anyway." He pointed again, this time across the bus, to the opposite side of the wire, where a group of young women, dressed in garish American clothing, stood along the sidewalk. "That's one of the BOQs over there, and the ladies are working the sidewalk to catch the hornies comin' in from night duty. That's the one good thing about this war. At least you can get laid while the politicians and generals are busy fucking the country. Anyway, enough bitching about my betters. When we get to Camp Alpha, just stick close. It'll be sheer tedium, but I've been through it once before, so I know how to cut out some of the crap. They'll assign you a bunk for the night, then give you your regular quarters tomorrow. If I were you I'd find an apartment or a house if you can get approval from your CO. It's worth the dough, even if it's more than your COLA, and if you're lucky enough to be stationed here in the Pearl of the Orient, you might as well get away from as much of the military crap as possible. Besides, only colonels on up get really good quarters. And I mean good. BOQs with swimming pools, first-class restaurants and hot and cold running nurses." He gave a snorting laugh at himself. "See, that's the real reason I'm pissed off about being passed over for promotion." Logan smiled for the first time.

Despite Logan's promises of cutting through the red tape, Peter's processing went on until well after 1430, and it was 1500 before he found his way to his temporary quarters and collapsed on the spartan military bed.

His quarters were little more than an oversized military tent, jammed with six beds and lockers for the number of men it was intended to house. But he had the tent to himself, something he preferred. It was a slack rotation period, and the sprawling complex of tents that made up Camp Alpha was well below capacity.

Reaching down, he plucked up a bottle of RVN 33 beer that sat on the floor next to his bed. He had bought several bottles when his processing had ended, choosing the local variety over available American imports. The clerk had looked at him as though he were mad, but Peter had wanted something local. He took a long drink of the semicold liquid and realized the clerk had been right.

There was a gentle, hesitant knock on the wooden door of the tent. Peter groaned, then swung himself up and moved wearily across the tent. He opened the door and found himself looking down at a frightened Vietnamese woman.

The woman made several quick bows. "You Captain Bently?" she asked, her voice timid.

Peter studied the woman. She wore an identification tag that indicated she was one of the many Vietnamese who performed servile duties within the camp. He had also learned in his training that many had proved to be VC as well. "He's not here now. But I can give him a message when he gets back."

The woman bowed again and quickly handed him a sealed nonmilitary envelope.

"Who gave you this?" Peter asked.

"Man in taxi, outside gate," she said. "He say Captain Bently please come quick, quick."

"Did he say what his name was?"

"He say tell Captain Bently him Max."

The message delivered, the woman turned and hurried off. Peter watched her go, her small legs moving rapidly as if some devil were behind her. He stepped back inside the tent and stared at the unmarked envelope in his hand. "What the hell," he said aloud. "The mystery of the Orient, already."

He ran his fingers gently over the edges of the envelope, feeling for any explosives, something he had been taught in demolitions training. Feeling nothing unusual, he tore open the seal and withdrew an old black-and-white photograph. It was of him at age seven or eight, dressed in short pants and standing next to the hulking frame of his dog, Max. The thought of his grandfather flashed into his mind, then vanished. His grandfather had always been cautious about contacting him. Excessively so, he had often thought. A taxi outside the gate was blatant. Perhaps he felt more secure on his own ground, but he doubted it. And there was still someone who wanted him dead, someone who had been close to his family. He would find out, he decided. There was little choice. If the taxi held his grandfather, or Auguste, it would be different. If not, then it would be different in another way.

Quickly he stripped off his uniform, replacing it with civilian clothes. He did not want to be any more noticeable than necessary. He went to his leather carrying case and withdrew a carton of cigarettes. He did not smoke. Buried within the sealed carton was a small automatic pistol, an untraceable weapon he had been advised by old intelligence hands to smuggle in-country. He loaded the weapon, then slid it inside his belt, leaving his shirt out to conceal it.

Outside the main gate, a small Renault "Bluebird" taxi was parked ten yards up the street facing him. It held the driver and another man in the back seat. Peter walked casually toward the car, displaying no interest. He stopped abruptly and turned, as if he had dropped something, and quickly withdrew the automatic from his belt. He turned back and continued toward the taxi, the weapon held casually at his side, his large hand covering it completely.

When he reached the taxi he appeared to continue on, until he reached the blind spot just past the rear side window. Then he spun, still keeping the weapon along his leg, opened the rear door, and entered the back with surprising speed, pushing well into the car and crowding the small oriental passenger, limiting his ability to move well.

"You looking for me?" Peter asked. He noted the surprise on the man's face; he saw that his hands were empty. Peter had never seen the man before.

"Are you Captain Bently?" the oriental asked.

Peter was leaning toward him and slightly forward, both crowding him and concealing the pistol he held along his right leg. "That's right," he said. He smiled at the man.

"There's a gentleman who would like to see you," the oriental said in perfect English.

"Who?"

"I was told only to say it was your grandfather."

"What is his name?" Peter asked the question in Lao.

The man's eyes clouded. He had not understood the language.

Peter jammed his forearm against the man, pinning him against the far door, then brought the automatic up under his chin. "Tell the driver to move, and tell him to keep both hands on the steering wheel where I can see them. I speak Vietnamese, so I suggest you do it right. There won't be a second chance."

The taxi pulled out into traffic as Peter searched his fellow passenger for weapons. He removed a large .38 caliber revolver from a shoulder holster, then slid across to the opposite door, where he could watch both men more easily.

"I didn't understand what you said." The oriental messenger was shaking now.

"If you worked for my grandfather, you should have. The people who work for him are Lao. Do you know his name, or what he looks like?" Peter asked.

The man's lips began to tremble. "I never met your grandfather.

The man I work for just asked me to deliver the message and the letter. He is a friend of your grandfather's.''

"Who is this friend, and where did he tell you to take me?''

"His name is Tran Loy, and I am to take you to his restaurant on Cach Mang.''

Peter smiled at him without warmth, then reached across the front seat and patted down the driver, noting that he too was shaking. The driver was unarmed. "Tell him to stop a block before the restaurant," Peter said.

When they exited the taxi, Peter took the oriental by the back of his belt and pulled upward, forcing the crotch of his trousers against his genitals until he could only walk on his toes.

"Is there a rear entrance?" Peter asked.

The man nodded, grimacing in discomfort.

"Show me," Peter said.

They moved slowly up a side street, the oriental toe-dancing along the sidewalk. Peter kept the revolver hidden from view until they reached a rear alley that paralleled Cach Mang. He stopped the oriental short of the entrance.

"Tell me something, my friend. Do all people who work for restaurant owners carry guns?" He allowed the man to see the pistol again, for effect.

"There is a gambling house upstairs. It is my job to guard the door."

The man's explanation rang true. Peter knew of the oriental love of gambling. What he didn't know was how good this man was at making up logical lies.

"If there are any other guards in the alley, you'd better tell them not to move. Because if they do, I'm going to shoot you first." His voice was soft, almost a whisper, and it made the man tremble again.

"There are no other guards," he said. "The only entrance to the gambling house is in the front."

Peter walked him into the alley, remaining behind him for cover. The alley appeared empty.

Halfway down, the oriental motioned to a metal door with his chin. "Here," he said.

"Open it."

The oriental reached out for the door with a trembling hand, then pulled it open. Remaining behind him, slightly crouched, Peter pushed him inside a large noisy kitchen. To his right, seated at a small table, he could see a white-haired European visible only in partial profile. On either side of the man were two orientals, and with the sound of the door each turned defensively. Peter raised the pistol, stopping their movement. The white-haired man turned slowly to face him, and Peter recognized him at once.

A smile spread across Buonaparte Sartene's face. It was older, and the man seemed smaller than Peter remembered. "When you were a little boy, you always liked to play with guns, Pierre. You used to say you were going to shoot tigers. Did you think there was a tiger here?"

Peter lowered the pistol to his side and released the messenger. His mind flooded with memories of his childhood with a force that was overwhelming. The walks taken together. The patient conversations. The endless bedtime stories. His grandfather's need to help him become both physically and intellectually strong. All of it coming from that deep, almost demanding love that was so much a part of the man. All of it rushed back, and he suddenly wanted to tell him how much the moment meant. How much he had wanted it for so many years. But the emotion was too strong for words.

Peter smiled. "Grandpère," he whispered, then moved quickly to his grandfather, instinctively handing the pistol to one of the Mua who flanked him.

They embraced, and he felt the surprising frailty of the man he had waited so long to see. His grandfather stepped back, looked at him for a moment, then hugged him again. There were tears in his eyes.

Buonaparte Sartene could feel his heart beating in his chest, and his mind told him it could not be true. It could not be Pierre who had returned. This large young man, almost as big as Jean had been. Sartene had seen photographs of his grandson, of course. They had been sent regularly. But the image in his mind, the one that had remained with him for fourteen years, had been of the small, hurt child, sitting on his bed, begging not to be sent away.

He embraced his grandson more tightly. "You see, Pierre," he whispered. "I told you I would wait for you."

Peter kissed his grandfather's cheek. "I know, Grandpère. And you told me Corsicans always keep their promises. I always knew you would keep yours."

When they separated, Peter's eyes locked on his grandfather's. "I'm sorry about the gun, Grandpère. It's not the way I wanted to come to you. I've just been trained to be careful. The Viet Cong have bounties on American officers." Their eyes remained locked, each silently acknowledging there was another reason as well, one that would not be spoken about in front of others.

Buonaparte reached up and slapped his cheek gently. His eyes were bright with pride. "I am not offended by the gun, Pierre. I'm only sorry I caused you concern. I should have waited and contacted you in a more normal way. But I couldn't wait. It has been too many years." He hugged him again, then stepped back, taking his arm and guiding him to a chair. "Sit. We must talk. There is so much to say after all these years. Are you hungry?"

Peter shook his head and took a chair across from his grandfather, then leaned forward. "But tell me how you knew I was here. I just found out I was coming a few days ago. Did Matt call you?"

Buonaparte tapped his fingers together, then held them apart. "It is not hard to find things out here, if you know what you're looking for." He smiled at his grandson, indicating nothing more need be said.

Peter returned the smile. Corsicans and their secrets, he thought. They never change. But he was like that himself, had been taught to be. He studied his grandfather more closely. Older, so much older. But the strength he remembered was still there. Especially in the eyes.

"How long will you be here, Grandpère? In Saigon, I mean."

"I must leave in the morning. There is some business that must be attended to in Vientiane." He tapped his nose with his finger. "This was just the whim of an old man, the need to see his grandson after so many years. So now you must indulge my foolishness, and in the little time we have tonight you must tell me all you can about the last fourteen years. I know you have written to me about the important things. Now I want to hear about the friends you made at university, and during your training in the military."

They sat across from each other, sharing a bottle of wine, reliving Peter's life in the United States, his years of schooling, all the things Buonaparte now wanted to hear from Pierre's lips. Hours passed, and throughout the conversation, Buonaparte drank in his grandson's words, along with the wine, savoring each bit of information, stopping him only to ask more detail. When their talk finally turned to Peter's military training, Buonaparte's interest seemed even more intense. He questioned him about the details of Ranger training, demolitions, special weapons, shaking his head at it all.

Peter smiled across at him. "It's not as amazing as it sounds, Grandpère. The training is just very refined."

"I know," Buonaparte said. "I was just thinking of poor Napoleon. All that he missed by being born too soon. He was such an innovator in using the technologies of his time."

Hearing his grandfather speak of Napoleon hurled Peter back into his childhood, the dark paneled study, the books, the toy soldiers, the military portraits. Days that had seemed to be one thing, but had actually been another. He leaned forward again. "Grandpère," he said, "we've talked about me for hours. Now I would like to go somewhere where we can talk of *other* things."

Buonaparte made a circular motion with his hand. "Saigon is not a good place for that, Pierre." He smiled at his grandson. "I know you have need to hear many things. But I must ask you to be patient for a few more days. Then it will be arranged for us to be together, and we will talk about everything you must know." The smile faded from Buonaparte's face. "Until then you must appear to be nothing more than another American soldier. Your safety depends on that."

Peter exhaled deeply, bringing the smile back to Buonaparte's face.

"Indulge an old man," he said. "Just for tonight, let me enjoy my grandson who has come home to me."

There seemed to be a hint of something more in his grandfather's words, something Peter could not quite grasp. "Of course, Grandpère," he said. "But tell me one thing. Why did you choose this place?"

Buonaparte raised his hands and let them fall back to the table. "I thought it would look more natural for a newly arrived officer to go out to a restaurant. I didn't expect you to come in the back door with hard eyes and a gun in your hand."

It was nearly dawn before Peter left the restaurant, and a tired Buonaparte Sartene made his way into the now empty front room, where an overweight Vietnamese awaited him. Wearily, he sat down across from the moon-faced man known as Tran Loy, who for years had run this restaurant and gambling house for the Sartene family.

"Your meeting was satisfactory?" Tran Loy asked.

Sartene nodded. "As always, my friend, you provided well

for my needs. But now I must ask you to do one more thing."
He paused to emphasize the importance of what he was about to
say. "Notify our other people here in Saigon that my grandson
has arrived. He must be watched with great care."

Tran Loy looked at Sartene with open curiosity. "This is a
very unusual request from you," he said.

Sartene's face remained blank. "There is a very unusual need,
my friend," he said.

Chapter 19

SEACON—Statistical Evaluation and Counterintelligence—the unit to which Peter had been assigned, was located in a small cinder-block building adjacent to the command complex inside Tan Son Nhut. The interior of the building was air-conditioned and soundproofed, to keep out the suffocating heat and the noise generated by the constant flow of aircraft only a few hundred yards away.

It was 1700 hours when Peter entered the squat, bunkerlike building—a full fifteen hours before he was due to report for duty—and he was still suffering from the combination of jet lag and the previous night's reunion with his grandfather.

He had been asleep when the sergeant had hammered an insistent fist against the wooden door of his tent. His new commanding officer wanted him to report *immediately*, the sergeant's curt voice had announced, leaving Peter with the distinct need to place his foot squarely in the man's face. He had not been sure whether it was the tone of the sergeant's voice or the fact that he did not want to leave his bed. He had settled for a few angry words.

Inside the unit office, he was directed down a long hallway which ended at a plain wooden door, bearing the name COL. BENJAMIN H. Q. WALLACE, COMMANDING.

Peter knocked twice, opened the door on command, stepped inside and came to attention.

"Captain Peter S. Bently, reporting as ordered, sir."

Wallace sat hunched over his desk and returned the salute with a casual flick of his hand.

"Come in and sit down, Bently," he said. "Sorry to drag you

in a day early, but we work odd hours here, and I won't be around during the day tomorrow. He eyed Bently carefully as he crossed the room. "I wanted to make sure you were squared away and briefed before you started."

Peter seated himself in a straight-backed wooden chair and watched Wallace open a military personnel folder—his own, he presumed.

Wallace went through the folder quickly, occasionally nodding his head, or glancing up at Peter over the wire-rimmed gold glasses that were perched on the end of his flat, fleshy nose. He was in his early fifties, reasonably trim, with the enormous hands of a heavyweight prizefighter, which were conspicuously hairless. He cupped his chin in one hand and massaged his cheeks with his thumb and fingers, then ran the hand over his wiry black hair, which showed no sign of gray. Rubbing his cheeks that way made his face appear highly pliable, almost as if composed of putty. He removed his glasses, revealing slightly bloodshot brown eyes, then eased back in his chair and stared at Peter for a full minute.

"Tell me why you went indefinite and volunteered for duty here," he finally said. "You looking for a career in the army?"

"No, sir. It seemed the logical step, given the training I'd received, plus the opportunity to see a part of the world that interests me."

"This shithole interests you? Judas Priest, why?"

"It has an interesting history. . . ." Peter hesitated. "And my father served here, during and after World War II, so I grew up hearing a great deal about it."

"I noted that in the intelligence investigation report on you. Light colonel, OSS. I have no doubt that's one reason you were accepted for this duty. That, and your ability to speak the language. The army believes in these things. But as far as this place being interesting goes, you'd have to find two hundred years of insanity interesting."

"I was raised with a great deal of military history, sir," Peter said, already growing weary of explaining himself. Suddenly he wished he could tell this man how his war would be lost because he didn't understand his enemy, and never would.

Wallace grunted. "Military history, shit. This is a two-hundred-year-old race riot. There's not even a damned front." He looked back at the folder and flipped several pages. "Says you speak Vietnamese and Lao. Where'd you pick those up?"

"My father employed a man who spoke Lao, and decided I should learn. Vietnamese I studied in college."

The colonel nodded to himself. "Also French, Italian and Corsican. Isn't Corsican just pidgin French?"

"No, sir. Actually it's closer to Italian."

Wallace nodded again, then turned another page. "Interesting training. You seem to have managed to keep it going without ever getting a permanent assignment. That's a pretty good trick. If you hadn't gone indefinite, I would have said you beat the army pretty good." He looked back at the papers in his hand and began to read from them. "Military Intelligence Course; Kennedy Special Warfare Center; Airborne Operations School; Ranger School; Jungle Warfare School; Pathfinder School; Demolitions; Counter-Insurgency Operations; Communications." He nodded again, without looking up. "Special qualifications. Demolitions; Firearms and Special Weapons; Chemical and Biological Warfare; survival techniques; martial arts: karate, aikido, judo and tae kwon do." He sat back in his chair and stared at Peter again. "You sound like a fucking one-man army. On paper, anyway."

Peter allowed the words to fall away, not willing to be goaded.

Wallace waited for a response, then leaned forward, resting his forearms on the desk. "Well, Bently, we don't have time here for much else but chasing down Charlie. You look good on paper for that. But, then again, this isn't school, is it?"

"No, sir." Peter kept his voice flat, unmoved.

Wallace smiled at his failure to provoke, picked up a pack of cigarettes from his desk, offered them to Peter, then lit one for himself. His voice became softer. "Your job will be a simple assignment on paper. It's just not simple to get it done. Maybe speaking the language will make it easier for you. Basically, as part of this unit, you'll be looking for VC operatives here in Saigon. You'll try to learn what the VC here are up to; any information you can develop on upcoming military operations, troop movements, weapon movements, terrorist raids. Also you'll keep track of all new incidents as they occur and try to uncover any new information about overall VC strength in the south." Wallace paused, as if shifting gears from his staccato military prattle. "We keep very precise statistics and records on all this to feed the computer for future use. In addition to that we keep a close eye on any civilian black-market activity that may either co-opt our own people or be of aid to Charlie. When we do find something big, like a VC weapons depot or a command center, we raid it and destroy it. Any questions?"

Peter's voice remained flat. "Only one, sir. How closely do we work with our counterparts on the ARVN side?"

"When we have to, as closely as necessary. Otherwise, be friendly and social, but in your work avoid them like the plague. We have to clear any raid, or anything that involves their people with them. But that's done at my level, so you don't have to worry about it."

Wallace stood and walked out from behind his desk. Peter was surprised at how tall he was. At least six-three.

"Normally we give all new men arriving here a week to get acclimated to the weather, the food, the water, and everything else. Mainly it's to give you time to get your bowels in order. That's policy for all new men in-country. But here, we don't have a week. We're understaffed and we're going to stay that way until the war widens a bit. So I'm afraid you'll have to live with a little bending of policy." Wallace looked at him hard, defying him to object.

Again, Peter said nothing.

After a few moments Wallace smiled. "You don't let things get to you, do you, Bently?"

Peter allowed the trace of a smile to play across his lips. "I try not to, sir."

"That's good." Wallace extended his hand. "Welcome aboard. You just follow the drill, don't go off half-cocked on your own, and we'll do some good work together." Wallace walked back behind his desk, but remained standing. "Tomorrow, you get squared away here in the morning. In the afternoon you're going to take a run up to a village outside our Bien Hoa base. There's an interrogation center there I'd like you to see firsthand. It will give you a quick fix on what we're up against. I'll make sure everything is cleared for you."

"Fine, sir. It should be interesting," Peter said.

"It'll be that," Wallace said. "One more thing. There's a club, of sorts, that most of our command people and just about all the ranking ARVN officers belong to. Called the Room of a Thousand Mirrors. Be a good idea if you joined it. A little personal contact goes a long way in our type of work. It's expensive, but we can cover the membership cost."

Wallace returned to his chair, then looked up at Peter. "Any questions, Bently?"

Peter hesitated. "Just one, sir. The name of that club sounds rather exotic."

Wallace snorted laughter. "Right on the mark. It's a very fancy whorehouse. But they have a good bar, an excellent dining room, and the atmosphere of a gentlemen's club. And it does serve our purposes. The only difference is, you can also go upstairs and get laid in an unusual setting. But I'll let you judge that yourself." Wallace massaged his puttylike cheeks and smiled to himself. "All that, and it's run by a beautiful Korean woman whom we've investigated half a dozen times."

"Investigated?" Peter asked.

Wallace nodded. "A little paranoia among the CIA types over at our embassy. They decided she had to be KCIA. Didn't figure the Koreans would let anybody run an operation like that unless it was one of their intelligence people. After that didn't prove out, they decided she might be VC, sent over by the North Koreans. More nonsense. Frankly, most of the brass wouldn't care if she was Ho Chi Minh's sister, if she'd only work at the trade. Unfortunately, she doesn't. She just runs the place." Wallace allowed his eyes to harden again. "But why don't you eat there tonight and see for yourself? I can call and arrange it."

When he left Wallace's office, Peter found his weariness had been replaced by overwhelming hunger. His last meal had been aboard the aircraft, almost thirty-six hours earlier, and he had no regrets about following Wallace's "suggestion" about where to eat. He only hoped the food was as good as the man had claimed.

Address in hand, Peter walked out through the base, past the ARVN sentries guarding the gate, and began looking for a taxi. As he waited, a jeep pulled up, and Peter watched one of the ARVN guards walk around it, probing the undercarriage with a mirror attached to a long pole. He smiled to himself, wondering what action the guards would take if they found the bomb they were searching out. Then he noticed the sandbag bunker just beyond the gate, and his smile broadened. The only warning a driver would receive would be the sight of the ARVN guards racing for safety, he decided.

But that, he had found, *was* the military. Everyone followed orders, no matter how absurd. The officers did so in the hope of promotion, the enlisted men to avoid problems. And when danger reared its head, everyone covered his tail and prayed for salvation. All else involved the pure pleasure of exerting power over someone else.

Peter thought of his new commanding officer, and the power game that had just been played. You're pulled out of bed and belittled, just to make certain you realize who's in control.

When Peter had first been exposed to the military, he had wondered about his grandfather's intense interest in its history. Then he had realized that what intrigued the old man was not the military, but the tactics of war. For those who lived among the anonymous uniformed ranks, the game was all-important, and war and its tactics were only an extension of the game, one that provided greater opportunities.

When a Bluebird taxi finally pulled to a jolting halt beside him, Peter entered the rear of the filthy, scarred, threadbare blue Renault and immediately began haggling with the driver over the fare to the Room of a Thousand Mirrors. Initially, the driver insisted on a hundred piasters, and only after several minutes of debate did he lower the price to fifty. A pre-departure orientation briefing had warned that cab drivers routinely demanded four or five times the civilian fare from Americans, but would usually settle for double the price under pressure.

Peter had undertaken the debate in English, wanting the full force of the driver's argument, along with the muttered curses he would utter in his own tongue. It was not a question of money— one hundred piasters amounted to roughly eighty-five cents, American—but a chance to recapture childhood memories of shopping with his mother, of reliving the oriental need to haggle over every sale, amid claims that their children would face starvation if merchandise was sold at the price demanded, was irresistible. The driver had not disappointed, and Peter sat back satisfied, determined to give the man an outlandish tip, thereby reaffirming his belief that all white men were truly mad.

The taxi barreled along Truong Minh Giang, across Cach Mang and into Le Loi Boulevard, past the Senate Building and the Vietnamese Marine Memorial. The driver, like the other Vietnamese who raced beside him, seemed oblivious to any notion of safety, and for his own peace of mind, Peter found himself concentrating on the sidewalks, where a mass of humanity hurried past the singsong shouts of street vendors, who sold everything from food to clothing to household utensils. It too was as he remembered. The sights, the sounds, and especially the smells all provoked memories of the past. He had been a child when they left Vientiane and moved to the house on the Mekong. But even now he remembered the smells of that city, the underlying odor of mass rot, mingling with the pungent aromas of the food merchants who lined the streets.

The taxi screeched to a halt outside a walled building, and Peter pried himself out of the cramped passenger seat, then handed the driver fifty piasters, plus a fifty-piaster tip. The driver stared at the money, then back at Peter again, as if trying to decide whether he was dealing with insanity or the simple inability to understand Vietnamese currency. The driver resolved the question with a simple grin, bobbed his head up and down, and repeated, "Thank you, *du ma*," several times before lurching back into traffic.

Peter watched him race away, barely able to restrain laughter. It was the perfect ending to the entire debate, both for himself and the driver. *Du ma* was the Vietnamese equivalent of "motherfucker."

The Room of a Thousand Mirrors was located just close enough to the center of the city to escape the battered slums that dominated most of the outer reaches of Plantation Road. It was a sprawling old colonial mansion, with screened terraces that overlooked a rear garden. It was French opulence at its best, with tasteful sandstone carvings set above the doors and windows.

Inside the carved teak door, Peter found himself facing a floating garden of water hyacinth, the delicate blue blossoms reflecting against the shallow water of the pool in which they floated. An elderly woman of indeterminate age, dressed in a white-and-gold *ao dai*, came from a side room, stopped a few feet away and bowed.

"I am Ba Hai, the official greeter," she explained.

Peter introduced himself and bowed. The bow was lower than necessary, and Ba Hai raised one hand to her mouth, in the accepted manner for a Vietnamese woman about to laugh.

"*Choc vay, Anh Hai,*" she said, using the term "Brother Two," to honor him. "We were told of your coming."

Peter bowed again, properly this time. "You honor me with your kindness, Ba Hai," he said.

Ba Hai extended one hand toward the stone staircase to their left. "You would like interview now?" she asked.

"*Toi kheong biet,*" Peter said—I don't understand.

"This a club," she explained, seeming to prefer English. "You first have interview for membership."

Peter nodded to the elderly woman, who immediately started for the stairs. Watching her, he marveled at the youthfulness of her movements. Certainly she was well past seventy, but, as with many oriental women, her true age was impossible to ascertain. Yet she moved with the ease and grace of someone far younger.

He was led to a large, sparsely furnished office. There, seated behind a delicately carved teak desk, a small, silken-haired woman in her mid-twenties stared at him with jade-green eyes. Peter was instantly in awe of her beauty, her finely chiseled features and round, full lips.

Slowly she stood, revealing the added beauty of her scarlet *ao dai*, and smiled at him. It was a wry, knowing smile, but not unfriendly.

"Welcome," she said, bowing to Peter.

Peter repeated the introduction he had given Ba Hai downstairs.

The woman gestured for him to be seated, then returned to her own chair behind the desk. Behind her, an unusual long, low Japanese ceramic vase, filled with water, held another collection of water hyacinths, the blue blossoms seeming to add a subtle contrast to her scarlet *ao dai*. It made Peter wonder if it was planned to do so.

"You have come to this beautiful country at a very dangerous time," she said. "I hope your visit here is both safe and interesting." She paused to smile. "My name is Molly Bloom, and our club here is available to that end if it pleases you, and if you agree to certain minor rules of membership."

She watched him closely, then laughed softly. "I take it Colonel Wallace did not tell you my name earlier. Like most members, he too enjoys the reaction people have when they first hear it."

"I didn't mean to be rude," Peter said. "I just anticipated a Korean name."

"Most people do. The Vietnamese who work for me here call me Luc-binh. You may also if it makes you more comfortable."

"That's even more intriguing," Peter said. "Do they name you after the water hyacinth because of your obvious affection for it, or because you rival it in your beauty?"

"You speak Vietnamese, I see. That's very unusual and pleasing." She ignored his compliment, not out of annoyance, but almost as if it was expected, and therefore of no importance. She traced the line of her jaw with the index finger of her right hand, almost as if drawing attention to her fine bone structure, then allowed the finger to remain under her chin for what seemed a long time, but was only a matter of seconds. Her striking green eyes never left Peter. It was as if she was memorizing his face. "Tell me about yourself, captain," she said after a long pause.

"Peter, please." He smiled at her. He had met few people in his life who he felt were a match for his own sense of cool detachment. This woman obviously was. He liked the idea. There was something challenging about her.

She nodded at his request that she use his first name, almost as though that too was to be expected. "Please call me Molly, or Luc-binh, whichever you prefer."

"Which do you prefer?"

"Molly. Luc-binh is beautiful, but too ostentatious. The people who work here intend it as an expression of respect, so I allow it. Now, please, Peter. Tell about yourself."

Peter's eyes narrowed almost imperceptibly, then he smiled at the woman. "Nothing much to tell," he said. "Just another American far away from home."

Molly smiled. "Obviously, if Colonel Wallace sent you here, you too must work for SEACON."

He smiled at the woman. "Perhaps we're just friends." There was no harshness in his voice, but his eyes had grown hard.

"Ah, you think it presumptuous of me to ask," Molly said. "But you see, I make it my business to always know enough, Peter. But it's not very difficult. The military men who come here enjoy gossiping about each other." She paused, took a cigarette from a jade cigarette case on her desk, fitted it into a four-inch ivory holder, then allowed Peter to light it.

After exhaling the smoke she looked at him with a touch of sternness. "The rules here, Peter, are few and simple. We allow no abusiveness to any guests or employees, and we expect people to act in a civilized manner. The club has its own restaurant, bar, baths, steam room and billiard room. In addition, there are rooms where one can simply read or be alone. There is also the Room of a Thousand Mirrors, where very beautiful and knowledgeable women can attend to more carnal pleasures. This is not a bordello, however, and guests are not permitted to treat it as one. It is also not a bar where loud, abusive evenings can be spent. There are many of those in Saigon, if one has need." She paused again, then smiled. "I don't mean to mislead you. This is by no means a convent. I simply prefer to run it as a place where *gentlemen* can come, relax, and be entertained if they wish.''

"Have you been forced to . . ." Peter hesitated, searching for the right word. "To cancel the membership of many?''

"No, not at all. Most have found it so pleasurable here, they avoid that possibility.'' She drew on her cigarette again, then exhaled the smoke in a long, sensuous stream. "I don't believe you will cause us difficulty, Peter. Now, do you have any questions I may answer?''

"Just one, Molly. I dislike being predictable. But is there really a Room of a Thousand Mirrors?''

"That's not at all predictable. Those who come here have usually heard of it.''

She reached for the ornate French telephone on her desk and spoke softly in Korean, a language Peter did not understand.

"I'm told the room is not in use now, so if you like, I'll show it to you.'' She stood and smiled at him. "It's only a tour, however," she said. "The Room of a Thousand Mirrors is where our more carnal pleasures are enjoyed, and it is well known that I do not work there.''

They walked down a long hallway that overlooked the entrance courtyard below. The lone wall along the hall held what Peter recognized as excellent copies of French impressionist paintings, intermingled with occasional tables holding fine Japanese ceramics of the Momoyama period.

Walking beside her now, Peter realized Molly was taller than he had first thought—at least five-five, unusually tall for an oriental woman. It was the delicateness of her bone structure that made her appear smaller. Yet her figure, beneath the smooth sheath of her *ao dai*, held both a sense of the delicate and the full. The woman seemed to be composed of one imposing contradiction about another.

"Your art collection, the paintings and the Japanese ceramics—were they part of the house when you purchased it?''

"The paintings were," she said. "But they're only well-executed copies. Some of the ceramics were here, and some were my own. Most of them are the work of Korean masters, however, not Japanese. But technically all Japanese ceramics should be considered Korean, at least in origin.''

"You're speaking of the ceramic war," Peter said.

Molly stopped and stared up at him. "You're aware of the war lords who sent armies to Korea to kidnap artisans?''

"The Japenese tea ceremony developed out of that, if I'm not mistaken," Peter said.

"You're an interesting man, Peter. One of the few American men I've met who doesn't pride himself on being a barbarian."

"You seem to know a great deal about us. And you speak the language so well. It makes me curious, to the point of being rude enough to ask."

Molly smiled. "Rudeness with diplomacy. Very interesting, Peter. Not quite subtle, but interesting. But to answer your indirect question, as they say in the old war movies, I was educated in your country."

"On the West Coast?" Peter asked.

Molly repressed a smile. "Actually, it was Vassar," she said, turned and continued down the hall. Peter thought he had noted a flicker of pleasure in her eyes, but couldn't be certain.

"The room, I think, will interest you," Molly said, as they stopped before a set of double doors of carved teak. "It was here, almost exactly as you will see it, when I bought the house several years ago."

She opened both doors and allowed them to swing apart, then led Peter inside. They stood in a medium-sized sitting room, decorated sparsely with French Provincial furnishings. All about them, the walls, the ceiling, the room's center, were mirrors set at varying angles, and with each step, each movement, the mirrors seemed to offer a glimpse of another portion of some unseen room—a part of a Vietnamese sleeping mat, the leg of a chair or table. He moved slightly again and parts of other invisible rooms came into view, each fragmented, each appearing and disappearing with the slightest movement.

Peter turned to her, his eyes questioning.

"It's a labyrinth of mirrors," she explained. "There are ten rooms within this larger room, and the mirrors are arranged so one sees a small portion of each with the slightest movement. Yet there is privacy of the whole. One might see the leg or arm of what one thinks to be someone else, only to find it is one's own reflected back a thousand times. Or you could be standing a few feet away from someone else and never truly know. When all the rooms are occupied, there is total privacy and, at the same time, the eroticism of the secret voyeur. I am told it is most sensual."

"But how do you find your way through to reach the rooms?" Peter asked.

"It can be done if one knows how," Molly said. "But it is not allowed. There is an entrance chamber, like the one we're standing in, for each of the rooms. Guests are not permitted to wander through the labyrinth. There are also screens that can be lowered electrically from the ceiling, for those who feel inhibited."

"The room was designed for this purpose, then."

"Not at all. It was owned by a strange French gentleman, of a somewhat questionable background. No one seems to know why he built it. But it intrigued me, and I modified it for my own purposes."

"It is intriguing. For any purpose," Peter said, looking about the room again.

"You must try it sometime," Molly said.

He turned back to her. The small smile of something known but unspoken was back on his lips. "Perhaps I shall, one day," he said.

"Good," Molly said. "We have many interesting women, who would be pleased to entertain someone young and handsome."

Peter smiled openly at the rebuff, which he had expected. "I have . . ." He paused. "I have a busy schedule the next few days. But when I return I'd like very much to invite you to have dinner with me."

Molly led him into the hall and closed the double doors. "I seldom dine out," she said. "But I'd be pleased to have you join me here." She looked up at him, her green eyes cool, holding the same knowing expression his smile had offered earlier. "You'll find Viet Nam interesting, Peter. But be careful. It can be a dangerous place."

She started down the hall, her voice businesslike again. "You'll find the bar is the second door to the right, off the courtyard. The restaurant is just beyond. If you're interested in membership, you may give Ba Hai the annual fee of five hundred dollars on your next visit. It, of course, may be paid in military payment certificates, piasters, or gold."

"I don't believe I'm allowed to deal in gold," Peter said. The smile that spoke of some secret was back.

"You'll find here in Saigon that people deal in many things that are not allowed, Peter. Here, in this house, we find it inappropriate to question anyone else's morality."

She returned to her office, and watched Peter descend the stairs before closing the door. She hesitated a moment, running her index finger along the line of her cheek. There was a faint smile on her lips. Slowly, she walked to her desk, seated herself in the carved teak desk chair, then reached beneath the desk's center drawer and pressed a concealed button.

A side door to the office opened almost immediately, and a short, stocky man dressed in a black silk suit entered. He had a square head, accented by a military crew cut and a flat, expressionless face.

Molly took a strand of her straight, silky black hair and toyed with it. Her face also was expressionless now, almost hard. There was a sense of command in her eyes when she looked up at the man.

"Po, the gentleman who just left, Captain Bently. I want you to find out everything you can about him. And I want him watched. But do it very quietly."

The stocky man's eyes narrowed into slits, and he gave one curt nod of his head. He turned, almost as though pivoted by an unseen rod set in the floor, then left as he had entered.

Molly leaned back in the chair, still toying with the strand of shiny black hair. The smile slowly returned to her lips.

Chapter 20

Peter was still amused by Molly's parting words as he bounced uncomfortably in the jeep as it raced toward Bien Hoa Airbase, northeast of Saigon. Insulting Vassar woman, running an exotic bordello in Saigon. It was a bit more than he had been prepared to deal with. He smiled to himself. You just found a woman you don't know *how* to deal with, he told himself. At least not initially. He glanced across the jeep. The driver Wallace had assigned him, an aging, fat sergeant named Walsh, sat behind the wheel, his mirrored sunglasses reflecting the road and surrounding forest. War American-style, he told himself. Naiveté with a touch of Hollywood. The ultimate in conflicts.

Peter stared at the passing vegetation, all of it so familiar, yet not familiar at all. Like the woman, Molly Bloom. A mixture of the American and the oriental. Someone who knew more than she should, and yet made no attempt to hide it. Perhaps that was why he had found her so difficult to deal with. He shook the thoughts from his mind and settled back for what he felt would be a long trip, longer than the sixty-kilometer jaunt to Bien Hoa.

The jeep arced its way around a sharp curve and suddenly came upon a row of shacks, the exteriors of which seemed to be constructed solely of flattened beer cans.

"Interesting architecture, eh, captain?" the sergeant said. "Just some ol' bam-de-bam stands, selling 33 beer and food that tastes even worse than that horse piss."

Peter glanced at his Rolex. It was only 0830 and the stands were already open for business. Several had GIs sitting at overturned wooden cable spools that were set out as tables, like ramshackle outdoor cafés. A half mile later they passed another tin shack, this one with two young women and a young boy seated outside on folding chairs.

"Car wash," the sergeant said. He turned to Peter with a leering grin. "Actually a whorehouse, Viet Nam style. See, prostitution's illegal here. So you pay the boy to wash your car, or truck, or tank, and then his sister, being a polite young lady, offers you tea. Well, bein' a poor country girl, she just gets seduced a lot by us bad-assed soldier types. That way, the only thing that's been paid for is gettin' a vehicle washed. I'll tell you one thing, though. They got them car washes on every damned highway in this country. An' this here army's got the cleanest goddam vehicles that anybody ever saw."

"Also the highest rate of clap," Peter added, bored with the banality of the man.

"Can't expect *everything* to be clean, sir," the sergeant said.

Peter stared off into the forest. A row of thirty-foot rose-apple trees slid past, the bright-crimson pear-shaped fruit adding a splash of color to the surrounding hues of green. The natives called the fruit *bo-dao*, and he remembered eating it as a child, the crisp, juicy, sweet taste, with a slight hint of rose flavor.

Farther along the road they passed a stand of breadfruit trees, the branches tipped with huge spiraled clusters of ribbonlike leaves. *Dua lop*, he recalled, was the Vietnamese name. Then came nipa palms—*dua nuoc*—a form of vegetation, he knew, that usually grew wild in brackish water, or at the mouths of rivers. Odd to see it here, inland, although it was often planted out of its element. But here, he thought, along a highway threatened by guerrillas, it didn't make sense. The reclining trunk and large feathery leaves rising fifteen to thirty feet would provide too much cover. He shook his head. The man returning home after so long a time, tainted by military training, he thought. He wondered if he would ever again look at things without thinking of ways they could be used to kill.

The sergeant was concentrating on the road, whistling softly through his teeth. Peter leaned toward him.

"Walsh. If prostitution's illegal here, how does the Room of a Thousand Mirrors operate in such an elaborate manner?" he asked.

"Right clientele," Walsh said. "But even there, members don't pay the ladies, or so I'm told. It's a club with a membership fee. Members pay for drinks, dinner. And it's limited to officers, Americans, allies and high-ranking RVN. An' nobody wants to bother them." Walsh gave him a knowing look. "The white mice—that's the local police—they satisfy the law by locking up the occasional streetwalker or bar girl. But they don't even do that too much. Not since Diem got knocked off."

When the jungle finally gave way to the gouged-out section of earth that was Bien Hoa, the jeep veered to the right and headed toward the small interrogation center five miles to the east. As they moved away from Bien Hoa, the mixture of tile-roofed houses and military tents seemed to evaporate into the bush, the drab olive green, the white walls and red roofs changing into the dark chocolate color of rice paddies with the bright green of the rice pushing through. Not far from each chain of paddies, mud huts seemed to grow out of the earth like mushrooms, and near each there were water buffalo tended by farmers, who stared skyward at the sound of planes landing and taking off from Bien Hoa airfield. Along the dikes that rimmed the paddies, small boys tended ducks with long cane poles, each stopping to wave the poles as a plane roared past. They reminded Peter of a boy he had seen in Saigon, walking along the street, a large dragonfly flying above him, tethered to a string tied to his wrist. When he tired of the game, Peter knew, the boy would eat the insect as a snack.

"What's our agenda, Walsh?" Peter asked.

The aging sergeant shrugged. "Usual stuff. We gotta check in with the CO and go through all the formal crap. Then if they've got any new VC prisoners, you get a shot at interrogating them. They'll like it that you speak the lingo so good—the local intelligence boys will, I mean. Most of them have to use interpreters who can't really be trusted. Our guys mostly only talk pidgin slope. You know what I mean. 'You VC. You talk, or you go Yellow Springs, quick, quick.' "

Peter smiled. Yellow Springs, the land of death. He hadn't heard the term since he was a boy. He would mention it then every time he wanted to play on the unnatural fear it produced in Luc. The supernatural land of the dead. The older men revered it; the young were frightened by the very words.

"They usually have prisoners?"

"They always got what they call prisoners. Most of 'em's a bunch of farmers tryin' to keep both sides from shootin' their fuckin' buffalo. They do what we tell 'em and they do what the VC tell 'em. But you never know. I've seen bodies of twelve-year-olds with grenades stuffed in their pajamas. Out here everybody's so scared shitless they think everybody's VC. But when you come across a real one, one of those hardcore cadre types, there ain't no doubt. They are hard little motherfuckers.''

"What do they do with them?" Peter asked.

"They interrogate the shit out of them, then turn 'em over to ARVN," Walsh said.

"And ARVN?"

"They claim they rehabilitate them. But I've seen the bodies. They squeeze 'em a little drier, then they pork 'em. One shot behind the ear."

Peter shrugged.

"That's the way I feel about it, sir. Charlie doesn't exactly take prisoners of war himself. Besides, according to Westmoreland, we're fightin' a war of attrition here. So the way I see it, we attrite as many of them as we can. Funny thing is we never seem to run out of them."

"They all have brothers and sisters, Walsh. And the sense of vendetta, especially among tribal people, can last for centuries."

"You make them sound like the Mafia, sir."

"The Mafia didn't invent vendetta, any more than they invented spaghetti." Peter hesitated, watching Walsh for a moment. "My mother was Corsican," he said finally, altering his family history to fit the one created for him years ago. "She talked about vendettas that went on through generations."

"You Corsican? How about that?" Walsh seemed suddenly impressed. "They got a lot of Corsicans around here, sir. Strange dudes. Don't see them much. You just hear about them from time to time. Some of them are supposed to be so bad they're supposed to make the wiseguys back home look like pussy cats."

Peter laughed quietly, thinking of his own family. His grandfather, Auguste, Benito. And now a new generation, just arrived.

Chapter 21

The mud-walled hut was an old schoolhouse that sat on the outskirts of First Cav Headquarters at Bien Hoa. Like everything else in the camp, it had been painted an olive drab and had a camouflage net stretched above it. Inside, it was one large room, electrified by a generator that groaned outside. At one end of the room was a table with several chairs, with large floodlights set on metal stands to either side. The only other furniture was a single chair placed in the center of the room. In it a small, slender VC suspect, slightly younger than Peter, sat stripped to the waist.

"Says his name's Loc Binh, captain," the lieutenant in charge said. "But his papers are as phony as shit. Claims he doesn't speak English, or French. Just sits there repeating *Toi kheong biet*, over and over."

"Maybe he *doesn't* understand," Peter said. "Maybe he doesn't want to. But he sure as hell understands Vietnamese."

Peter walked out in front of the lights, feeling the intense heat they produced against the back of the jungle fatigues he was wearing. He squatted before the man and pushed his helmet back on his head.

"Loc Binh," he said.

"Toi kheong biet," Binh said, stopping him.

Peter smiled. "You don't understand your name?" he said in English. His eyes hardened. *"Xin ong nghe toi"*—Please listen to me.

The prisoner kept his eyes on the floor, trying to appear like a frightened peasant. Peter studied him in the light. The teeth were too even, too well cared for; the body absent of any of the

257

abnormalities caused by poor diet. Peter knew the man was not from a poor outcountry village struggling to raise enough rice to live. He had seen too many of these people as a child. Again he asked his name in Vietnamese.

"Toi kheong biet," Binh repeated.

Peter shook his head slowly. "Your sister sleeps with snakes," he whispered in English, using a peasant curse considered vile to Vietnamese.

Binh's jaw tightened; his nostrils flared almost imperceptibly.

Peter grinned at him. "You understood that, didn't you, my friend? Even in English?"

The man's eyes clouded, then hardened. "Go fuck self, GI," he snapped.

Peter laughed softly. "Goodness, Binh. You certainly do pick up a language quickly."

"Toi kheong biet," Binh said.

Peter shook his head. "Now you don't understand again. *Bat ca hai toy*," he said, using the old Vietnamese proverb, "Catch fish with both hands." "I'm afraid you have to decide which way you want to have it, Binh."

The prisoner looked into Peter's eyes, but said nothing.

"Would you rather talk to the lieutenant?" Peter asked.

"Thong?" the prisoner asked, motioning to the back of the room with his head. He had used a term of contempt that replaced the pronoun "him" or "he."

"Perhaps you'd rather speak to some ARVN people?" Peter suggested.

Binh remained silent, but the mention of the ARVN investigators had produced a slight twitch in one eye.

He was a tough little guy, Peter decided. Not unlike his brother Luc had been as a child.

Peter was still squatting, and turned slightly to face the lieutenant and Walsh. He raised his hand against the interrogation lights, but they still blinded him. "There's no question he's not what he says he is," Peter said. "But this is going to take a little time."

"That'll be ARVN's problem, then." The lieutenant's voice came from behind the lights, bored and hidden.

Peter eased himself up and walked to the rear of the room. Once behind the lights he faced the lieutenant and struggled to focus on him. The lights were still abusing his eyes, even though he was behind them now. Small red and purple circles seemed to float between him and the lieutenant's face. He rubbed his eyes, but the circles remained. It was like looking at someone through a transparent surrealistic painting.

"I didn't mean we couldn't get the information," Peter said. "The man's ID is obviously phony. It'll just take time to get the truth from him."

"We don't have time, captain. Our job is just to determine if they're what they say they are or not. If the ID's phony, that makes them either VC or a deserter. Either way it goes to ARVN's people, and they get the information their way."

The lieutenant spoke as if he was humoring a stupid child. It grated on Peter.

"What's their way, lieutenant?" Peter's voice was cutting and cold.

"They determine that," the lieutenant said.

"Are you talking about just beating the hell out of him, or torture?"

"They decide that, captain. Not us."

"What he means, captain, is they do what we're not allowed to do. At least when there's witnesses around." Walsh's voice was light and sarcastic, but there was no anger in it.

"I can answer my own questions, mister," the lieutenant snapped.

"Shut up, lieutenant. I want to hear what he has to say." Peter stared at the man. His name was Walker and he was no more than twenty-one, and looked as though he had not yet begun to shave. His jaw tightened under the rebuke, but he said nothing.

"Talk to me, Walsh," Peter said.

Walsh shrugged. "ARVN's newest gig is to play telephone company. They take one of those field-telephone batteries. You know, the kind you crank to get juice from. Then they clip wires onto the battery, and clip the other ends to the guy they're questioning. One wire usually goes to the scrotum, one on the penis, and one on each of the nipples. If it's a woman, one of the wires will have a copper rod on the end, and they push that up inside her and tape the wire to her leg. Then one guy asks questions, and if no answer comes, another cranks the battery. If he cranks slow, it's just a little juice. Hard, and they bounce around like they were on fire. They pass out a lot, puke a lot, and sooner or later, if they're really tough, it wastes 'em. Sometimes they talk. But usually by that time all that's left is gibberish anyhow. What it boils down to is the ARVN boys have some fun, and we get shit for intelligence."

Peter stared at the floor. "That's what you want to do now, lieutenant?" he asked.

"I don't decide these things, captain. Those are the orders. Our job is just to make sure nobody who's innocent gets questioned. That's the most we can do. And sometimes we can't even do that." Walker's lower lip began to tremble. "I don't make the rules, captain."

Walker was angry, and his voice came out broken. Peter felt sorry for him, the person, but contempt for his rationalizations. "You know anything about Buddhism, lieutenant?" he asked.

Walker drew a long suffering breath. "No, sir. I'm Episcopalian."

"That's too bad, lieutenant. Obviously these people also know they're going to die later, no matter what they do. If they thought differently maybe some of them would talk. But by enduring the suffering and then dying, they'll reach the higher plane they've been taught to believe in. So the choice of torture and death or talking and death really doesn't give them an option. You give them a hope of survival and they just might tell you something."

"I suppose ARVN's people don't know that." Walker was being defensively snide.

"Maybe they just don't give a damn, lieutenant. Maybe vengeance is more important than winning."

Peter and Walsh left the hut and moved across the compound, toward their jeep. A few hundred yards south, artillery roared to life, spitting shells at the forest, where fire teams had called in strikes. The earth trembled beneath them from the blasts.

"It ain't gonna do any good, you know," Walsh said, between firings.

"What isn't?" Peter asked.

"Trying to explain to that kid. The book says he does it that way, so he does. It's the way the brass wants it."

Peter was silent as another round of artillery fire erupted. He reached the jeep at the next lull, then hesitated. "It's their war," he said, sliding into his seat. I have my own to fight, he thought. And I haven't been told who the enemy is yet. I don't have time for a war no one is trying to win.

Driving back, Peter thought of a conversation he had had with his grandfather as a young boy. He had thought of it often over the years that followed.

War is a science, Pierre, and like all sciences it has theories that work perfectly until someone tries to apply them. . . . Life, in that sense, is not unlike war. Corsicans have always understood that to win in life, you have to build for your family, and for the people who are loyal to you. Build, Pierre. No matter how. How is always dictated by life. Perhaps as Corsicans we understand this because we have no politics, no government to tell us what is good. The Americans and the Russians have big governments, and each of them believes in destroying in order to build. Because of this both will lose. And when history looks back at them it will marvel at their wasted greatness. It will see that every opportunity they had to build, they also twisted into a new way to destroy. Look about you, Pierre. Look at the governments of the world and tell me how much good you see. One group starves, while another eats. One that is stronger crushes the weaker underfoot. Should I choose among them for myself? Centuries ago there was a band of heretics called the Manicheans, who believed in the conflict of light and darkness. They believed that God and the devil were waging a constant battle—a battle which God did not necessarily win. They looked around them and they saw life as it was. For this they became hated, and they were all put to death. I have seen this too, Pierre. And I want no part of another man's world. I will treat it with honor and respect, and I won't take from any man anything that my world does not need in order to survive. And if he tries to take from me, I will stop him.

Chapter 22

The colonel sat behind his desk, big and burly, rolling an unlit cigar between the thumb and index finger of his right hand.

"I understand you got to see an interrogation. That's good. Good for a new man to see what's happening outcountry." Wallace suddenly yanked his wire-rimmed glasses off and stared angrily at the dirty lenses. He pulled a handkerchief from his pocket and began cleaning them. His brown eyes were heavily bloodshot, as they had been the first time Peter had met him. Peter said nothing. He had not gotten back to his billet until 2200 hours the previous night, and had collapsed into bed. Now, tired and irritable at 0830, he decided to say as little as possible. He hoped the colonel would not ask for his views. He was not sure how well he could conceal them.

Wallace finished with his glasses, held them up to the light for inspection, then carefully fitted them back on his flat, fleshy nose. He rearranged himself in his chair, then hunched forward, making himself seem smaller than he was.

"The important thing you have to remember," Wallace said, "is that we don't get adequate intelligence from the field. But we don't need it, if we do our job, because VC orders originate right here in Saigon. Information goes out from here to the VC cadres. The placement of supply dumps, decisions on troop movements. And that's because their goddam intelligence network is centered right here." Wallace jabbed his finger against the desk for emphasis, and Peter noticed there was a slight twitch at the corner of his left eye.

"The main agent they have here is a VC operative we know only as Cao. It's a code name to be sure, but there's no question he's our main problem. All the documents we've seized are routed through him or come from him. And the sonofabitch operates right out of the city, right under our goddam noses."

"Any chance he could work for ARVN or the government?" Peter asked.

"To be completely candid," Wallace said, "the sonofabitch could be anyone. For all I know you could be Cao. I've been after that bastard for three years, and I don't even know if it's a man or a woman." He heaved his body forward and placed his forearms on the desk. "But now we've got something new. It's what I was working on last night. New information that was picked up, indicating Cao is operating a command post across the river in Cholon." He yanked the cigar from his mouth and jabbed it toward Peter. "And you're going to find him for me. That's your main priority from now on. You'll have to handle other jobs as they come along. But your major effort, all your free time, has to be on getting that bastard."

"I'd like to review the material we have on him," Peter said, then adding, "or her," as an afterthought.

"Well, that should take you the rest of the day, but it'll be time well spent." Wallace sucked on his teeth for a moment as if trying to dislodge something, then returned his concentration to Peter.

"You free tonight?" he asked.

Peter groaned inwardly. "Yes, I am."

"Good. Thought I'd like to take you to a little party my counterpart in ARVN is holding this evening. Give you a chance to get to know the slope side of the operation a little better. You're going to run across them off and on, and a little social contact always helps. Name's Colonel Duc. Tran Van Duc. Has a beautiful daughter-in-law named Lin, if that's any inducement." Wallace grinned suddenly. "Speaking of social contact, what did you think of Molly Bloom?"

"Interesting name," Peter said, returning the smile.

Wallace cackled. "Bet you shit your pants when she told you." He scratched an address on a piece of notepaper. "This is the place. Around eight would be good. Don't eat. There'll be a nice buffet and lots of booze. You'll enjoy it. And wear a dress uniform."

Chapter 23

The taxi stopped in front of the Continental Palace Hotel. Peter paid the driver and pried himself out of the tiny rear seat, barely clearing the door before the cab jumped back into the maelstrom of traffic. He remained on the sidewalk, taking in the tall, white, unimpressive building with little interest.

When he had left Wallace that morning and returned to his own cramped office, two hand-delivered letters had awaited him. One was a dinner invitation for the following evening, intriguingly sent by Molly Bloom. The second was less pleasant, a rather circumspect message from a man named Francisci, who identified himself as manager of the Continental Palace Hotel. It had simply requested a noon meeting, on a matter of "mutual interest."

Peter's first thought had been of the contact his grandfather had promised. Then his mind instinctively turned on the warning the old man had issued. *Appear to be nothing more than another American soldier. Your safety depends on that.*

Standing before the hotel now, Peter glanced at his Rolex. It was 1215 hours, appropriately late for a casual military type. He shifted the soft leather briefcase in his left hand. It was standard-issue for members of the unit. Fixed inside was a sawed-off over-and-under 12-gauge shotgun. Each end of the briefcase was made of heavy cloth with slits down the middle, one to allow a hand to enter and reach the trigger and pistol-grip handle, the other to permit the barrel to be pushed through. The shotgun itself was bracketed to a steel bar that ran along the bottom so it could be held steady for accurate firing. Bringing it was his own safety measure.

He climbed the tall staircase that led to a wide terrace and the lobby beyond. At the reception desk a well-tailored and self-important young Vietnamese made himself available. He looked Peter up and down, and it seemed, at least to Peter, that he was quietly sneering at the uniform.

"Mr. Francisci," Peter said.

"I'm afraid he is very busy at the moment. May *I* help?" There was a smirk on the clerk's face.

Peter smiled at him, cold and hard, pausing before going on. "If I knew why he had sent for me, I'm sure you could," he said.

"Perhaps it involved an unpaid bill, sir?" The smirk had intensified now.

Peter smiled again. His eyes had turned to ice and it caused the clerk to nervously shift his weight. "You just tell him I came for the appointment he requested, and that *you* would not allow me to see him." He turned abruptly and started to walk away.

"Wait. Please wait, sir." The clerk came quickly around the desk and caught up with him just as Peter was about to descend the stairs.

Peter stopped and looked down at the smaller man. The smirk was gone now. Soft jobs in nice suits were undoubtedly hard to come by, he decided.

"I will be pleased to get Mr. Francisci, sir," the clerk said. "I did not understand. May I give him your name?"

"Tell him Bently. And tell him I'll be in the bar, but only for ten minutes."

The Glenlivet felt soothing, and he sipped it slowly, alert to any unexpected movement.

"Captain Bently?"

He turned to the sound of the voice and found a man in his late fifties, whose appearance seemed to match the soft silky tone. He was tall, thin, and immaculately dressed in a white suit, with dark eyes that seemed never to blink. There was a pencil-thin mustache, which, like his hair, was gray-black with a hint of oiliness.

"And you are Mr. Francisci?" Peter asked.

"Philippe, please. I am so pleased you could find time to come. May I join you?"

He slid onto a stool next to Peter. The bar was still quite empty, the lunch hour in Saigon being traditionally set at one. He ordered a Perrier on ice, then smiled warmly at Peter.

"You're curious, no doubt," Philippe said. "But my request to meet you is really very simple. There is a gentleman here who wishes to see you privately. I have just such a place here. A lovely suite of rooms on the top floor. Very private."

Peter exhaled and shook his head. "You're a very interesting man. You deliver messages but tell me nothing."

Philippe tapped the side of his nose. "Just good business, my friend. It is the only way to survive here in Saigon."

"Let's meet this man," Peter said.

He reached for his bar check, but found Philippe's hand there first.

"Please," he said. "For the inconvenience of bringing you here at midday."

Peter nodded and stood, then picked up his briefcase from the bar. The sawed-off shotgun within seemed less foolish now than when he had first decided to bring it with him. He held it in his left hand, the false side that led to the pistol grip and trigger facing out, easily available to the quick movement of his right hand. "You lead the way," he said. He was smiling warmly.

The ornate old elevator carried them to the top floor and opened into a small hall, onto which only three doors faced.

"This is the uppermost floor," Philippe said. "And the suite occupies it entirely." He gestured to one of the doors. "That leads to a small kitchen. The door opposite it, to a staircase. This other door is the main entrance to the suite."

Philippe reached into his suitcoat pocket and withdrew a single key, not seeming to notice that Peter had shifted the briefcase slightly with his movement. He opened the door and entered, with Peter close behind.

There was a small foyer, with rooms to the left and right, closed off by doors that were now open, showing the unoccupied rooms beyond. Ahead lay a large sitting room, which appeared gracefully furnished at first glance. Philippe stepped into the room, Peter just behind him.

To the left side of the room a man stood at a window, his back turned. Peter slammed the forearm that held the briefcase into Philippe's back, knocking him forward and to one side, then twisted the briefcase and slid his hand into the false side, taking the pistol grip of the shotgun firmly in his hand.

"Don't move," he snapped, backing away from the entrance to the room, so he had a clear view of the front door and the foyer. "Now, who is *that?*"

The man at the window turned slowly and smiled at him.

"Are you going to shoot me, Pierre?" he said in the Corsican dialect of Peter's youth. "Your grandfather tells me you are very quick with a gun now."

Peter let the briefcase fall away. "Uncle Auguste," he said, shaking his head. "Are the members of my family ever going to meet in a conventional way?"

Auguste smiled. "In time, Pierre." He extended his arms. "What the hell's the matter with you? You too big to kiss your uncle? You haven't seen me in four years."

Peter walked to him. The longing he had felt with his grandfather returned to him now. He hugged Auguste with one arm, then kissed his cheek. Like his grandfather, Auguste felt small and frail to him. He stepped back. "Is Grandpère here?" he asked.

Auguste shook his head. "He's like some wines. He doesn't travel well anymore. This last trip tired him badly." Auguste tapped his finger to his heart. "The doctor tells him not to." Peter began to voice concern, but Auguste waved it away with his hand. "He could still give you a good spanking if you needed one, but still, it's better if he doesn't travel in this heat, and the altitude of airplanes is no good for him." He grinned. "So, he sends me." He wagged a finger in Peter's face. "And I too can still spank."

Peter couldn't help himself. He began to laugh. The tension, the concern, seemed to slip back for the moment, then reemerge.

"Uncle Auguste, there are things I must discuss with you."

Auguste nodded, raised his hand. He looked toward Philippe. "My friend, please excuse us for a moment, so we can discuss family matters."

"Of course, Don Auguste," Philippe said. He looked toward Peter and smiled again. "It has been a pleasure to meet you," he said.

"I'm sorry for the rough treatment," Peter said.

"You just outwitted him," Auguste said. "Didn't he, my friend?" He gestured with his hand to Philippe, a circular movement, conveying the humor of the situation.

"It is not unusual to be outwitted by a Sartene," Philippe said.

After Philippe had left, Peter took Auguste's arm and led him to a large overstuffed contemporary sofa. When they were seated, he turned to face him. "Our family seems to meet in odd places," he said. "First the kitchen of a restaurant." He paused, looked around the casual, yet well-appointed sitting room. "And now this."

"Buonaparte owns this hotel. This"—he gestured to the room—"was the place he stayed whenever he came to Saigon. But it's been years since he's used it. Now it is yours if you want it."

Peter rubbed his face with his hands, then lifted his eyes to Auguste. "I just might," he said. "The military life is becoming a bit trying."

"Why did you choose to remain in it?" Auguste asked. "It was not necessary. And this so-called war isn't worth fighting."

"It will help me in what I must do," Peter said. "Find the man who killed my father."

Auguste nodded. "My brother, rest his soul, had a big mouth."

Peter did not speak for several seconds. His uncle's digression annoyed him, but his affection for the man was too deep for the feeling to remain.

"You told me that four years ago, Uncle. You also told me that when I returned, I would learn the truth."

Auguste smiled at him. "Your memory is good, Pierre. But I also said you would learn it from Buonaparte." Peter began to speak, but Auguste stopped him. "For now, I will tell you what Buonaparte feels you must know." He leaned back, his mouth and eyes becoming hard, as though anticipating the pain he would feel from his own words. "Do you remember, when you were a boy, a man named Francesco Canterina?"

Peter felt his own facial muscles tighten. "Of course," he said, trying to recall the long-forgotten face of the man. "He was the one?"

Auguste lowered his eyes; his face filled with a seething hatred. He nodded his head. "He is the friend who became a pig. The man who killed your father, and nearly killed Matt as well. The man who on that same day sent men to kill your grandfather, and instead turned my brother into a cripple."

Peter found difficulty forming the words. "But why? He was like a member of our family."

"He wanted what we had. But that you will learn from Buonaparte. What you must know now is that this man is still dangerous. He knows he will never be safe while there is still a Sartene on this earth. He still seeks your grandfather's death, but he knows Buonaparte is too well protected. So now he waits for him to die to be safe again. When he learns you are here, he will know that waiting will do no good.''

Peter stared at his uncle. He felt the muscles in his stomach tighten. ''Why is he still alive? Everything Benito ever taught me tells me he shouldn't be. But he is, and I'd like to know the reason.''

Auguste let out a long breath. ''He too is protected,'' Auguste said. ''But now he will know that protection is ended.''

''The protection involved me, then,'' Peter said.

''I can tell you no more, Pierre. It is Buonaparte's right to speak of these other things. For now you must only know he is a danger to you. He is in the north now. We know that, so for now you are safe. But soon his business will bring him to the south. Then, when he learns you are here, he will try to kill you.''

Peter's hard eyes stared at his uncle. ''What business will bring him here?''

''Opium, Pierre. Opium and heroin. It is his business.'' Auguste's eyes softened with the words, as he watched confusion spread across his nephew's face.

''Is that the business he killed for, Uncle?'' Peter's eyes had become hard again, but there was no recrimination in his voice.

''From me you will hear nothing more, Pierre.'' He raised his hand again, stopping Peter's objection. ''It's not for me to tell. In a few days you will be going to see your grandfather. Then Buonaparte will tell you everything. Everything you have to know and, perhaps, more than you want to know.'' Auguste shrugged his shoulders. ''Then you will either understand what you hear, and why it could not be any other way, or you won't. Buonaparte always knew it would be this way. He is a man who believes in the truth of things. But you'll see that in three days.''

''Uncle Auguste, I don't know if I can go to Laos in three days. I have superiors who decide those things.''

Auguste smiled at him, as though he were looking at the small boy he had known fourteen years earlier. ''Your commanding officer will order you to go there. A certain Vietnamese official, whom he can't refuse, will ask for an American officer to help in an inquiry. The man will have to speak Lao, and since you're the only officer who does, you'll be sent. It will involve a matter that will require you to go to Laos often during your time here, and so it will give you easy access to Buonaparte.''

''He has that degree of power here?'' Peter asked.

''It's not power,'' Auguste corrected. ''Power always involves force in one way or another, and your grandfather always tries to avoid that. It's simply a business favor his friend is happy to offer him. One that's owed many times over. Don't concern yourself about it.''

Auguste reached in his inner suitcoat pocket and came out with the business card of an airline. ''This little airline is the one you should use. It is also one of Buonaparte's businesses. Philippe operates it along with the hotel, and he will make certain it is always available to you. If you need anything while you are here in Saigon, Philippe will serve you, just as he does your grandfather. Don't hesitate to ask him for anything.''

Peter felt as though he were suffocating under the weight of everything that now assaulted him, everything he had to know. He tried to speak, hesitated, then tried again.

''Auguste. You *must* answer some of my questions,'' Peter insisted.

Auguste patted his arm. ''You want to know about good restaurants, things of that type, I'll be happy to help you. If you want to know about these things, you must ask Buonaparte.'' He smiled. ''But you. You can tell me much. You can tell me all the things you have done since I last saw you.''

Chapter 24

Peter had spent the remainder of the day reading and rereading the dossier on Cao, struggling to keep Francesco Canterina from his mind. But he had failed. The vision had constantly reappeared. A face that was no longer clear, an out-of-focus image too long in the past. He had wondered if he would even recognize him if they passed on the street, this man who would have him dead, have his grandfather dead. He thought about his father, Matt, Benito. His life for the past fourteen years, the charade he had lived. All of it had now been linked to this one man, Francesco Canterina. Out of frustration, Peter had fed into the intelligence computer the few things he knew: name, opium, North Viet Nam. The effort had produced nothing.

Sitting in the back of a Bluebird taxi now, he decided to put it out of his mind. He twisted his body, searching for some comfort in the cramped back seat of the tiny Renault.

It was 0800, and still the traffic along Cach Mang was at the volume of an American rush hour. The taxi hurtled through the traffic oblivious to everything, weaving crazily between buses and trucks. The driver barreled into Truong Minh Giang, pressed the accelerator to the floor and shot forward amid the sound of blaring horns and shouted curses. The traffic eased as they sped past the crowded outdoor market, the smell of rotting food vying with the Rach Thi Nghe River beyond, its dark chocolate water little more than an open sewer.

All along the riverbanks there were shacks covered with flattened beer cans, converted packing crates, and any other salvageable material turned into little tin ovens in which the poor of

271

Saigon lived out their lives with the rancid smell of the river as an added blessing.

The taxi crossed the river, passing by the Chantareansay Pagoda, where saffron-robed monks plotted their own domination of an endlessly dominated country. He had seen a group of monks that morning, walking the streets with their wooden bowls, begging rice for their morning meal, their shaved heads bowed in supplication. Seeing them it was hard to conceive of the terror their displeasure could produce among those who ran the government.

He glanced back through the rear window at the receding filth and poverty. Here, on this side of the river, there was no hint of the squalor left behind. The tree-lined streets and shaded side-walks held a sense of quiet harmony that reminded Peter of Vientiane years before, the walled houses recalling the days when the colonial French, longing for their homeland, hid them-selves away from the people they exploited. Now it was the Americans, together with the wealthy Vietnamese.

The taxi pulled into a sudden sharp left, then screeched to a halt, almost throwing Peter against the front seat. When Peter pried himself out of the rear seat, he found himself standing in front of a high stone wall with broken glass embedded in its top. In the center of the wall there was a huge wooden gate, covered with a quarter inch of steel plate that would require nothing less than a recoilless rifle to penetrate. He hammered the massive, ornate knocker four times and a small spyhole door opened, revealing the head of a helmeted ARVN soldier. He looked Peter up and down, as if assuring himself the dress uniform was real, then swung the heavy door back.

Inside the gate there was a small courtyard, guarded by three more armed ARVN privates. To each side of the courtyard tropical gardens, tended with obvious care, offered a vision of serenity that defied the existence of the military guards. At the end of the courtyard, the house too offered the look of a time long past, its graceful arrangement of connected rectangles sug-gesting a sense of inner harmony.

The door to the house was opened by an old man dressed in the white jacket and black pajama pants uniform of the Vietnamese servant.

"*Chao, dai uy,*" he said, bowing almost to the waist.

"I am Captain Bently," Peter said in Vietnamese. "I have the honor of an invitation from Colonel Duc."

The surprise of hearing an American speak perfect Vietnamese registered on the old man's face, but he masked it quickly so as not to offend. He offered a small bow that bade Peter to follow, then led him through the small, stone-floored foyer into a large, rectangular room, already filled with a mixture of Vietnamese, Americans and Europeans.

The room was sparsely but elegantly furnished with modern teak and rosewood furniture, each piece placed far enough away from the next to accent the spaciousness of the room. On small occasional tables pieces of fine porcelain and jade were displayed, each appearing to be of museum quality. On one wall there was a large abstract by Manet; on another a small Corot. Although he was no expert, they appeared to be originals.

Wallace spotted him from across the room and started toward him, his tall, burly frame dwarfing the Vietnamese he passed. Large, hairy creatures. The description used by Southeast Asians for Europeans and Americans. It seemed apt at that moment.

Wallace took his arm in his bear's hand, squeezed the biceps, then looked at it approvingly.

"You're harder than you look, Bently," he said. "Glad you could make it. Come, let me introduce you to our host."

The colonel led Peter across the room to an aristocratic-looking Vietnamese dressed in the uniform of an ARVN colonel, the left side of the blouse overladen with decorations. He was at least five feet eight, unusual for a Vietnamese, and Peter made a mental note to check later whether he was wearing lifts in his shoes.

As they approached, Duc turned to watch them. He was easily fifty, but seemed younger, with jet-black hair that seemed slightly oiled, hooded eyes, and a tight, thin-lipped mouth. The way he held himself spoke both of a life of long-standing privilege and of an open contempt for non-orientals.

"Colonel Duc, I'd like you to meet the newest addition to my staff, Captain Peter Bently."

Duc offered a modest bow, little more than an inclination of his head, a near-insulting demonstration of his own feeling of superiority.

Peter made sure his bow was lower, acknowledging Duc's superior rank. *"Chao, dai ta,"* he said, using the Vietnamese for "colonel."

"Ah, you speak Vietnamese?" Duc inquired in English.

"It has been my pleasure to learn your beautiful language, *dai ta*," Peter said.

Duc turned to Wallace with a wry smile. Peter noticed his eyes became even more hooded when he smiled. "So, the Americans are finally sending us young men who can speak more languages than their own," he said. "That's most refreshing."

"Bently here speaks quite a few," Wallace said, missing the subtlety of the insult. "What is it now?" he said, turning to Peter. "Laotian, French, Italian, and some others, I think."

Peter nodded. "Corsican," he said.

Duc raised his eyebrows slightly. "We have many Corsicans living in Viet Nam—perhaps you will find use for that obscure tongue. I doubt you get much chance to use it."

"I am fortunate, *dai ta*," Peter said. "My mother is Corsican, so it is a language I can use frequently."

"Ah, she was born there?" Duc asked.

"In France, in Marseille."

"Then your father must have met her . . ." He paused, gauging Peter's age, then added, ". . . during the war."

"Before it, sir. She had emigrated to the United States. He actually served in the Pacific theater, and then was based here in Saigon after the war."

"So that accounts for your linguistic skill," Duc said. "For a moment I had hoped the Americans were broadening their educational system." Duc smiled, enjoying his own cutting remark, then hurried on. "Unfortunately, I was not here after the war. I was in France for my education."

"It is sad," Peter said, "that in such a beautiful country one must go elsewhere to learn."

Duc's eyes flashed momentary anger, quickly covered by a smile. "Yes, it is unfortunate that beautiful countries must often be poor."

Peter glanced about the room. "All men must be prepared to struggle against poverty," he said. "Otherwise it will come upon us from behind and impose its will. I am told wars have been fought for that purpose."

Duc's eyes flickered, then he turned to Wallace. "I like your new officer," he said. "He seems to have studied our philosophy as well as our language. Perhaps when he is here for a time, he will learn to understand the people as well." Duc's attention was drawn to his right. "Ah, my daughter-in-law is about to join us. Please allow me to introduce her."

Peter turned in the direction of Duc's gaze and found a small, exquisitely beautiful young woman approaching. She was wearing a daffodil *ao dai* that seemed to accent the soft, creamy hue of her skin. Her black hair fell to her shoulders, framing her oval face and high cheekbones. Her eyes, a soft brown, seemed proud, yet shy at the same time, and her small, full-lipped mouth looked as though it had been stolen from some fine porcelain figurine.

Duc stepped forward. "This is my daughter-in-law, Ba Lin," he said, placing heavy emphasis on the "Ba," which indicated she was married. "And this is Captain Bently, a new arrival to our troubled country," Duc added.

Peter bowed. "It is a great pleasure, Ba Lin," he said, rising and looking into the depth of her eyes.

"I too am honored, captain," she said. She held his gaze, longer than appropriate, then her cheeks took on a hint of color and she turned to Wallace. "And to see you again as well, colonel. You honor my father-in-law's house."

"The honor's mine, Ba Lin. All mine. Your father-in-law puts on the best party in all Saigon."

"Perhaps you can introduce the captain to our other guests," Duc said to his daughter-in-law. "The colonel and I have much to discuss."

Lin bowed to her father-in-law, then turned back to Peter. "Would that please you, captain?"

"Very much. It is always difficult for a stranger in a new country. Your father-in-law is most kind."

He had answered in Vietnamese, and her reaction was a mixture of surprise and pleasure, but she said nothing. They excused themselves and began circulating among the guests. The variety was impressive. Each embassy and consulate was represented, along with the ranking military of the various nations involved in the conflict. Peter found himself wondering who among the Vietnamese officials also represented the Viet Cong. Perhaps even Cao himself, if such a person actually existed.

Walking toward the final group, Lin allowed the conversation to become personal. "Tell me how you came to speak our language so well," she said.

Peter offered a shortened version of his father's service in

Saigon, his love of the culture and the life here, and his employ-
ment of a Lao servant who had returned home with him, and his
own subsequent university studies. "He wanted me to know and
appreciate the people and culture as well," he concluded. "So I
had the good fortune to be taught from an early age."

"It is pleasant to hear we have been able to export more than
our difficulties," she said. "I only pray one day we will be able
to again enjoy the pleasure others find here."

"Tell me, Ba Lin," Peter said, taking advantage of the personal turn she had allowed the conversation to assume, "will I
be able to meet your fortunate husband?"

She stopped and looked up at him. She was no more than five
feet two, a full foot shorter than he, and she seemed almost
childlike standing before him. "I thought you knew," she said.
"My husband was killed three years ago by the Viet Cong. He
was captured by them and never found. But there is little doubt
of his fate."

"I am very sorry," Peter said. "My clumsiness embarrasses
me."

She smiled at him. "You had no way of knowing. Colonel
Wallace should have informed you. But the social graces do not
appear to be his strong point. We all pray he is a better soldier."
She began moving toward the group again, then bypassed them
and stopped in a doorway that looked out into the tropical
garden.

"Your garden is very beautiful," Peter said. "I was admiring
what little I could see of it when I arrived."

"Yes, it is very old. I am told in another generation it will
reach perfection. I only hope there will be another generation in
this house to enjoy it." She turned to him and smiled. "Let us
not speak Vietnamese anymore. I seldom get a chance to practice
my English."

"You speak it beautifully," Peter said. "Did you study abroad?"

She nodded. "In Paris. The *lycées* are poor here, and to attend
university in France has become almost a custom for my family.
We are a people who have had many masters," she said. "And
with each we have assumed some of their culture."

"But never surrendered to any," Peter added.

"Surrender is not in the nature of the oriental. We have
always known that we will overcome all eventually. If by no
other means than assimilation. We are like the amoeba, con-

stantly changing shape and form, but engulfing that with which we come in contact.''

"You are a particularly beautiful amoeba," Peter said. "Had I known they could be so lovely, I would have spent many more hours studying my biology."

She laughed, then covered her mouth to hide it. "There must be some French in your ancestry," she said. "The French always waste little time reaching the point of romantic compliments."

"My mother was born in France," Peter said.

"Ah, I thought so." She was still smiling at him.

"I hope I didn't offend you," he said, knowing he had not.

"As I explained, I spent many years in the west—too many, according to my father-in-law. And I have learned to accept western ways."

Instantly Peter wanted to ask to see her again. But he knew it was much too soon, and the situation was dangerous for her. To accept would mean being ostracized by all, even her family.

"Do you miss Europe, and the less restrictive life-style there?" Peter asked.

She smiled at him, seeing through the clumsiness of his question. "Europe is very beautiful, very exciting, but it is always good to return to one's home." She hesitated, toying with the real part of his question. "Restrictions are something, I have found, that one chooses to allow, or chooses not to allow."

"And the penalties for rejecting them?"

"Penalties often produce a greater burden on the person who imposes them. The Viet Cong imposed the penalty of death on my husband, and in doing so, earned the lifelong enmity of those who cared for him."

Peter was forced to admire her deftness at switching the conversation from the personal to the political. "Many of your countrymen, even those who support the government in the south, seem to have great sympathy for the Viet Cong."

"Yes, that is true. There is a great admiration and respect for Ho Chi Minh, and I think it carries over even to those who fight against him. It is a strange conflict in our minds. To us he is, and always will be, a great national hero, a great patriot. Unfortunately he seeks to change a way of life that has been good to us, so we must resist him. But you must remember, captain, we are a country that has fought for hundreds of years to escape the domination of other, larger, stronger nations. That need to be free of others is still at the very soul of our being. It is only a different choice of means to the same end.''

"And that is why your people feel a prejudice toward mine?" He was trying to bring the conversation back to a personal level, knew he was being clumsy in the attempt, but could find no other way. The clumsiness made him feel awkward, a feeling he was not accustomed to, one that annoyed him.

"I'm afraid my people always considered the Europeans to be uncultured. The Americans even more so."

"They also find our odor offensive, I'm told," Peter said, trying to lighten the conversation.

She laughed, covering her mouth again, as required by Vietnamese custom. "Yes, I have heard that. But every race has its own scent, I think. When one becomes accustomed to it, it is no longer either strange or offensive."

"To me you smell like a beautiful flower," Peter said.

The laughter flickered in her eyes now. "You are being French again," she said. "Or you are confusing me with the scent that comes from our garden."

Peter bowed in submission. "Still, I wish the prejudice did not exist. I would very much like to meet with you again. To speak with you at greater length."

She looked away toward the garden. "Each Friday, at four, it is my custom to go to the cathedral, to light candles in my husband's memory. Later, I visit the Street of Flowers to select floral arrangements for the weekend. It would not be improper for two who have been introduced to meet, and for the gentleman to help bring the flowers to my home."

She looked back at him. He felt a nervous tide swell in his stomach, the muscles in his back tighten. Her delicate beauty was almost overpowering.

"I have always had a great interest in flowers," he said. "And a great curiosity about those of this region."

She lowered her eyes and smiled again. "I must see to my other guests," she said.

Peter stood in the doorway to the garden, watching her walk away. Her movements, accented by the *ao dai*, seemed to carry her away in an effortless gliding motion. He found himself watching her long after she had gone.

"Beautiful woman, isn't she?"

He turned to the sound of the gravelly voice that had come from his left. The man was in his early thirties, overweight and sweating. He had unruly brown hair that stuck out in tufts over his ears and a face that showed a love of alcohol. His tropical cord suit, though clean and pressed, looked as though it belonged to someone else, someone thinner.

"Yes, she is," Peter said.

The man squinted at Peter, as though he needed glasses to see properly. "You new here, captain?" he asked.

"Yes. The name's Bently, Peter if you like."

"Joe Morris, UPI," he said, raising a glass of amber liquid in place of a handshake. "Where you from, Pete?"

"South Dakota," Peter said. "And make it Peter, please."

Morris made a face, quietly critical of the formality. His eyes squinted again. "Saw you with Wallace before. You one of his new spooks?"

Peter was forced to smile at the crassness of this sloppy, overweight man. "I'm assigned to Saigon."

Morris snorted. "Bet he's got you working on the great Cao caper, hasn't he?"

Peter raised his own glass to his lips. "Am I supposed to know what that means, Mr. Morris?"

"Aw, come on, *Peter*. You call me Joe. And Cao is no big secret. He's the bogey man, the local make-work project. If your boss ever catches him, he'll have to start investigating some of the real stuff around here. And nobody wants him to do that."

"The *real* stuff, Joe?"

Morris squinted out across the room. "Oh, little things, like narcotics, and how easy they are to get here." He turned back to Peter, trying to gauge his reaction.

Peter's face remained impassive. But the mention of narcotics had made his blood surge. Francesco's business was heroin, and this man wanted to investigate it, write about it. Perhaps he could use Morris to draw Francesco into the open. "If you think there's a drug problem, why don't you write about it?" he asked.

Morris snorted again. It appeared to be his method of laughter. "Tried to, Peter. Tried to many a time. The editors back home don't want to hear about it. They want a nice comic-strip war. Nice happy copy about the clean-cut American kids, fighting the sneering yellow horde."

Peter turned to face the garden. "Your idea sounds interesting to me," he said. "But then, what do I know about journalism?" He turned back and smiled at Morris. "Or narcotics," he added.

Morris looked him up and down. "You never know. Maybe someday you'll come across something."

"If I do I'll let you know," Peter said, smiling again. "Then we might be able to help each other."

Chapter 25

Molly Bloom sat behind her large teak desk, idly playing with a carved jade letter knife. She was listening far more closely than it appeared, as her man, Po, rattled on with his report in a flat North Korean dialect.

Suddenly she looked up, stopping him in midsentence. "The party at Colonel Duc's home," she said in the inflection of someone raised in the south of Korea. "You had someone there?"

Po nodded, then watched as a smile made its way across Molly's soft delicate mouth. "It is so amusing," she said, more to herself than Po. "They all gather together, eating and drinking and telling wonderful stories of war. And all the time, we are standing right beside them. Sometimes I wish I could tell them, Po. Just to see the looks on their faces."

She held the letter knife between her two index fingers, still smiling, then lowered it to the desk.

Po stood silently, his short stocky body like some block of granite that came to life only on command.

"And our friend Captain Bently met this fool Morris there."

"Yes, Luc-binh," Po said, using the name Water Hyacinth, preferred by Molly's employees.

"And what did they talk about, Po?"

"Narcotics, Luc-binh."

The smile on Molly's lips faded quickly. "That is very bad, Po. That news will not be happily received when I pass it on. And what did our young captain do earlier today?"

"He went to the Continental Palace Hotel, and met with Philippe Francisci and later with the man Auguste Pavlovi.

I do not know what they talked about. But I will try to find out.''

Molly waved her hand. "No, that won't be necessary, Po. But I want you to have someone close to our young captain at all times. When possible, I want *you* to be close to him. Observe what he does, who he sees, especially anything involving this narcotics business. But don't interfere. Just let me know what is happening, so if it becomes necessary we can intercede.''

Po bowed his head. "Will the captain be here for dinner tonight?" he asked.

She nodded her head, her thoughts distant from her actions. She looked back at him, her mind in the present again. "Yes. I received a note this morning accepting my invitation. He will be here at eight. Please tell everyone that we will use the private dining room on the third floor." She smiled to herself, her mind appearing to drift off again.

Po bowed and started to leave, but her voice stopped him. "And please send a messenger to me. I must send this information on to our friends.''

The private dining room was beyond even Peter's expectations. The long, narrow trestle table and heavy carved chairs were set before a floor-to-ceiling window that looked down on a lovely tropical garden. Along the walls fine Japanese and Korean ceramics were displayed on pedestals, interspersed with priceless figurines that Peter recognized as from the Jomon period, ranging between 750 and 1000 B.C. The art in this room alone could ensure the comfort of Molly Bloom for the remainder of her life, he decided.

Across the long table, she smiled at him. He looked at her now, needing the diversion of her beauty, yet realizing he was wary of everything else about her.

"This is an evening I'll find difficult to forget," he said. He paused and looked around the room, then down into the garden. "An American guest, wonderful European food, and all in a surrounding of beautiful oriental art." He smiled at her. "It's really what this country is at this time. A blending of three cultures, each different yet, for the time, inseparable.''

"That's very good, Peter," she said. "It's nice to meet an American who doesn't miss the subtleties of things. Unusual, as well.''

Peter leaned back in his chair, steepling his fingers before his face. "That's the second time you've done that. Offer surprise when you find an American who can observe the obvious."

"Perhaps that's because it does surprise me." She stood and walked to the window, slid back a panel of glass and stepped outside onto the narrow balcony.

Peter rose and followed her.

She was dressed in a dark-green dress, forsaking her favored *ao dai*, and the color seemed to match her eyes perfectly, making them seem like the deepest of jade. He stood next to her, looking down at the finely etched profile. "Have you met so few Americans who are capable of appreciating subtlety?' he asked.

The wind rose slightly, blowing her long black hair back, and she lifted her chin slightly to capture more of it against her face. "There have been a few," she said. "But most others have been young boys, or old bores. And subtlety is always wasted on either."

She turned to him, keeping her eyes on the garden, then allowing them to rise slowly until they met his. "You, for example, have been subtle enough not to ask about my rather unusual name. With most others that question would arise within the first few minutes."

"But I have been tempted," Peter said.

She turned back to the garden below. "Yes, but that is the ultimate in subtlety. Understanding when not to speak about something."

"In that case, I shall ask you to tell me about it immediately," he said.

She laughed. It was a beautiful laugh, he decided. Not the normal giggle orientals seemed to misuse as laughter. "Very well. Since you're determined to prove me wrong, I will tell you." She turned and walked the length of the narrow terrace, then turned back to face him.

He was able to see all of her now, and thought that was what she preferred for the moment, allowing the full effect of her beauty to dominate his thoughts.

"My name, Molly Bloom, is something people often find strange, since I am a Eurasian woman who spent most of her youth in Korea. The few well-read people I meet—a number that seems to grow smaller with each passing year—assume my father was a great admirer of James Joyce. Actually I doubt he ever thought much about Joyce, and I'm reasonably certain he never read him. My father was an Englishman of mixed ancestry.

His father was Jewish, his mother an Irish Catholic, and both of those paternal grandparents were long dead when I was born. My mother was Korean, and she too died at the instant of my birth. It seems death has always played a very large part in my life. Perhaps that's why I've always been fascinated by it.

"My name, in fact, came from this combination of deaths. My father was badly stricken by the death of my mother, and decided he could not bear a Korean name in the house because it would remind him of her. I was, therefore, given the name Molly after my paternal grandmother, who, of course, was also dead. Actually, I always thought the name was appropriate for an Irish Catholic Korean Jew, whose father was a British citizen." She stopped and laughed softly, as if enjoying the ridiculous complexity of her own heritage.

"I've always thought my ancestry was confsing," Peter said. "Yours makes it seem mundane. But it must have been difficult for you. Orientals aren't known for their tolerance of religious or racial mix."

"Religion presented something of a problem, at least for my maternal grandparents. My mother had been raised as a Buddhist, and combined with the Jewish and the Catholic, that gave me ancestral roots in three of the world's five major religions. Since that was the case, my father decided I should be raised in none of them, but rather be allowed to choose my own when I matured. Being thus spared religious training as a child, along with all the attendant fears, taboos, prejudice and intimidation, I found, upon becoming an adult, that I needed no religion at all. That was greatly frowned upon by all concerned, and to a large extent still is. But I've been frowned upon for one thing or another for most of my twenty-five years. This one additional frown has had little effect on me."

Peter moved closer, closing the distance between them. "How did an Irish Catholic Korean Jew happen to spend most of her youth in Korea? I would think life would have been much easier for you elsewhere."

"It's quite simple, really. My father was in the British foreign service. He met my mother in England, where I was born. Then, after the end of World War II, he was assigned to Korea, where—as he often said—he helped maintain British influence among the world's lesser beings."

"A fairly common British attitude," Peter said.

"I don't think he really meant it. Just felt he had to say it. He was a nice man who drank too much, and on the day before my sixteenth birthday he died from a touch of liver, as his British physician put it. Actually he committed suicide. He just chose to do it slowly with Scotch, rather than in one of the more traditional and less dignified ways." Molly looked back into the garden. "I didn't mind really. I knew he was much happier dead, even if there was nothing beyond the grave. Life had been an endless torment for him, a series of failures, disappointments, losses, all of which he was much better off without." She turned back and smiled coyly. "It did present a problem for me, however, since it placed me in the hands of my Korean grandparents, who were forced to deal with a maturing young woman who had been raised without any concept of custom or tradition, be it British or Korean." She laughed, as if remembering her grandparents' despair.

"They struggled with that problem for two years without any success whatsoever, then settled it rather abruptly by packing me off to university in your country." The coy smile returned; the voice took on a note of solemnity. "And there I fell into a life of sin and became the woman you see before you now." She tossed her hair and laughed, then looked back, her deep-green eyes flashing with her own enjoyment.

"And, of course, you won't tell me how you happened to buy the Room of a Thousand Mirrors," Peter said.

"Why, I happened to buy it with money, Peter." She laughed again. "Another story for another time. Perhaps when I know you better. Perhaps not."

He closed the distance between them, allowing his size to dwarf her. Her eyes showed no intimidation. "There are some who say you work for the Korean CIA, did you know that?" His voice was soft, amused.

"The KCIA, how intriguing," she said, smiling up at him.

"Others insist it's the VC."

"Oh, the Viet Cong, even better."

"Then, of course, there are those who insist you simply have your own little criminal enterprise."

"And which do you think, Peter? All of the above, none of the above, or am I simply a poor orphan child struggling to make her way in a cruel and devious world?"

"The last one sounds very good, but the least likely," he said.

She lowered her eyes and shook her head. "The military has destroyed your sense of romance, Peter. I rather like the last explanation. It casts me in the role of the beautiful but wayward waif, who can now be redeemed by the good and true American officer.'' She laughed again. ''Tell me, Peter. Are there any secrets in your life, anything you're hiding away from the world? If I searched would I find out what it was?''

He ran a hand along her delicately formed cheek. ''It's much too well hidden,'' he said. ''Even someone with all your resources wouldn't be able to find it.''

''Ah, a challenge.'' She moved away from him. ''Then I'll have to use feminine wiles. Reduce you to your baser instincts and discover all your secrets.''

He stepped forward and leaned down to kiss her, but again she moved away.

''Men are always weaker in bed. They tell themselves it's where they are strongest, but it's not. The bed is woman's domain.'' She looked at him pleasantly. ''But now you've disappointed me. You told me you understood oriental subtlety, and now you show me that you don't.''

Chapter 26

He was still fascinated by Molly Bloom's ability to outmaneuver him the previous evening. They had played a delicately balanced game, each seeking information about the other, each receiving no more than the other was willing to give. In the end she had offered him a sexual challenge he had foolishly accepted. And again, she had walked away the winner in their little war of wits. He was forced to laugh at his own foolishness.

Peter was still thinking of that difficult woman when he was called into Colonel Wallace's office at 0900. Colonel Duc was there when he entered, sitting primly on a small sofa, as if struggling to avoid any wrinkle in his uniform.

Duc and Bently greeted each other formally, then Peter was offered a straight-backed chair opposite Wallace's desk. There was an air of unpleasantness in the room, and Peter had the feeling that the two had been arguing.

"Something new's developed, Bently," Wallace began. "And our friends at ARVN have need of some help." He looked across the office at Duc. "Perhaps it would be better if you explained," he said to the Vietnamese.

Duc looked Peter up and down. "I understand you speak Lao as well as the language of my country. How fluently do you speak it? I know your Vietnamese is good."

"I speak them equally, *dai ta*."

Duc nodded. "Then you may prove of value to us." He paused to check the crease in his trousers, then continued without looking up. "A high-ranking official in our government has received reports of Viet Cong command activity in the area around Vientiane. This, of course, is something we cannot tolerate.

287

The people involved are said to be establishing new routes of supply, which is even less tolerable. If they are allowed to escape punishment, it might produce additional support in Laos, and, of course, this affects our efforts against the communists.''

Duc stood, straightened his uniform, then slowly began to pace the office. "It is felt that a Vietnamese agent would have difficulty getting close to this operation, that the communists would recognize such a person for what he was and quickly eliminate him, or simply disappear. An occidental, however, would not be suspected, and since few speak any of the local tongues with anything more than barroom proficiency, conversations among sympathizers would not be feared in his presence.'' Duc stopped and looked down at Peter, his face giving off a hint of displeasure.

"What we would like is for you to make occasional trips to Vientiane to see if you can determine the location of this new command activity. If you can, you are to bring the information to us, along with any prisoner you might capture. If not, you are to eliminate them there, disrupt their activity and bring back a photograph of their remains.'' He stopped again, this time smiling at Peter.

"Beheading would be a nice touch," he said. "It has a very strong effect among my people, especially the Buddhists. They believe the spirit will be forced to wander endlessly if one dies in that manner.''

Wallace picked up a manila folder from his desk and tossed it across to Peter. "In there you've got information on NVA cadre suspected of operating in Laos. We're not supposed to be in Laos, so you take as much care as you feel you need to protect your own ass.''

"But not too much care," Duc interjected. His look was contemptuous. "We do not want those communists to escape because of excess caution, do we, captain? Do you object to eliminating these people?''

Peter offered Duc a thin smile. "Not at all, *dai ta*.'' He turned back to Wallace. "When do I leave, sir?''

"Tomorrow. Take two days this first trip. No longer unless you came across something exceptional. After that your trips will be determined by reports of observations that come back into ARVN.''

Peter nodded again.

"Use civilian aircraft and wear civilian clothes. Officially our military personnel do not go into Laos. But you'll have the full cooperation of friendly people in their government there, if you need it. Those names are in the folder too. And no one but us is to know about this. Understood?''

"One more thing," Duc interjected. "To ensure against any future disclosure about this operation, by someone who might wish to raise questions about its legality, I think a code name would be helpful. All reports would then be signed just with that designation.''

"Yeah, I like that," Wallace said. "Wouldn't want these fucking newshounds to get wind of any operation going on in Laos. If they ever did come across any documents, we could say it came from friendly forces inside that country.''

Duc gave Peter another contemptuous smile. "Do you have any preference for a code name, captain?'' he asked.

"No, *dai ta*," Peter said. "I will be happy to leave that to you.''

Duc looked up at the ceiling for a moment, then back at Peter. "What year were you born, captain?''

"In 1940, *dai ta*.''

"Ah, the same year as my son, the Year of the Dragon. A very favorable sign.'' He glanced down at Wallace. "Shall we make it Dragon, then?''

"Fine with me," Wallace said. "You got any problem with that, Bently?''

"No, sir. Dragon will do just fine.''

Duc laughed softly to himself. "Very well, Dragon. I hope your hunt goes well.''

He stood in JFK Square, watching her leave the front of the cathedral. She was dressed in a pale-blue *ao dai*, and as she had at her father-in-law's house, she seemed to glide rather than walk.

He moved quickly across the square to intercept her. "What a pleasant surprise, Ba Lin," he said in Vietnamese.

She bowed her head slightly, then smiled at him. "And what good fortune for me. I was wondering who I could find to help me carry flowers to my home.''

"Look no more," Peter said. "Not to do so would certainly violate the treaties between our two countries. And we must never allow that.''

They moved away from the cathedral, then stopped at the next corner to wait for a white-uniformed Saigon police officer to halt the rush of midday traffic. Peter watched the small man standing in the midst of the vehicular madness, and he recalled how Americans referred to Saigon police as white mice, because they always seemed to scurry off and hide whenever trouble developed.

He glanced at Lin, wondering if she had ever heard the term. As they started across the street, he looked back over his shoulder. Two men he had noticed earlier in front of the cathedral had stopped ten feet behind them. Now, as Lin and he crossed the street, they too had begun walking again.

He inclined his head toward Lin and spoke softly. "There are two men behind us, and they seem to be following you."

"Yes, I know. They are my bodyguards. I'm afraid Saigon is not safe for Vietnamese either."

Peter's face clouded with concern. "I hope our meeting will not cause difficulty for you with your father-in-law," he said.

"Because of my bodyguards? No, not at all. They have been with me for many years, and were selected by me. Their loyalty is to me, not to the colonel."

They continued along the sidewalk, keeping a respectful distance between them. Several blocks down, as they turned into Nguyen Hue Street, the crowds along the sidewalk intensified, pushing them closer together; forcing their bodies to touch as they stopped before a flower stall.

"You told me you were very fond of flowers," Lin said. "Was that true, or simply an excuse?"

"Very true," Peter said. He reached out and picked up a lotus blossom from a water-filled tank. It was ten inches in diameter, and its yellow petals, tinged with red, seemed to capture the afternoon light.

"Do you know the Vietnamese name for the flower?" Lin asked.

He nodded. *"Sen."* He pointed to the pale, bell-like blossom in the next container. "This I do not know."

"It is from the portia tree, and next to it, the mahoe." She reached out and touched the small, delicate flowers, some red, others a solid yellow.

"That one I know," Peter said. "A member of the hibiscus family, and as delicate as a beautiful woman."

"We are not so delicate, captain. This country forbids anyone to be delicate. Especially now." She turned and began walking among the stalls, with Peter following close behind. He stopped beside her at another stall, and she looked up at him and smiled. "Are you learning to enjoy Saigon?" she asked.

"I hope to begin very soon," he said. She turned her head away, but he could tell she was still smiling. "I took an unofficial residence off base today, so life should soon be more pleasant," he added.

"And where did you find quarters?"

"The Continental Palace Hotel."

She inclined her head. "That should prove very convenient. But then, I imagine anything would be a great improvement over a military base."

"I'm hoping it will be," Peter said. "It's a suite of rooms, with a small kitchen, which, I hope, will allow me to entertain some friends."

She looked up at him, and he saw the trace of a smile on her lips.

"I would be pleased if you would be my first guest," he said.

"Perhaps when you return."

The look of surprise on his face made her laugh, and she covered her mouth with her hand.

"My father-in-law mentioned at breakfast that you would be performing a service for him. He did not say what, or where. Just that you would be leaving Saigon."

"Only for two days," he said. "It's more of an errand than a service."

"I'm sure you're too modest," Lin said. "If it was only an errand, my father-in-law would not have been so displeased."

"Was he displeased?"

"He's always displeased when he is forced to ask the Americans for help. It injures his sense of national pride."

Peter stopped himself from smiling, from revealing his own pleasure at anything that would offend Duc's immense sense of pride. He caught her watching him, observing his reaction.

"When I return, will you have dinner with me?"

"In your *rooms*?" She forced her eyes to widen slightly.

"I thought it would be more . . ." He struggled to find the correct word.

"Discreet?" she offered.

"For lack of a better word, yes."

"I'm afraid I shall be out of the city then," she said.

"Oh, I see." There was obvious disappointment in Peter's voice. "May I ask where you're going?"

She smiled at him. "Of course. I am going to Vung Tau, what the French used to call Cap St. Jacques. It was once my home, and my mother is still there. She is very old now, and I wish to visit her."

"I've heard about the city," Peter said. "I'm told it rivals the Riviera as an ocean resort."

"Yes, it is most beautiful," Lin said, her eyes distant, almost as if recalling more pleasant days. "And it is the one place in my country where the war does not exist. Both sides use it as a rest area." She smiled. "Odd, isn't it? Enemies each using its beauty to refresh themselves, then returning to continue killing each other."

"I would like very much to see it," Peter said. He hesitated, then continued. "Perhaps when I return in two days. If that is possible, how would I find you there?"

Lin looked down, then back at him. When she did she was smiling. "My mother's name is Ba Trang Do, and her home is well known in the city."

"If it is possible, would you be offended if I called on you there?"

Her eyes remained on Peter's face. "We shall see when you return, captain. But now you must help me carry flowers."

Chapter 27

Peter drove the rented car west, along the road that led to his grandfather's plantation. The trip evoked memories, even though everything seemed different. No, not just different. Smaller, out of scale. The road seemed narrower, and closer to the Mekong River than he remembered. The river too appeared duller, dirtier, far less exciting than it had been to a twelve-year-old.

He glanced into the bush, at places where he thought the sentries might be. He saw none, but was sure they were still there. He had been told as a child they were protection against the Pathet Lao, and the bandit tribes who occasionally raided outlying homes. Now he wondered if that too had been a part of the charade, something needed to keep the truth from a child, to obscure the dangers that had always surrounded his family.

When the road ended at the two narrow paths, Peter took the most southerly, and continued until it opened onto the broad plain. There he stopped the car to pause and remember. To the south was the river, and the dock where he had played as a child. To the north, the house—always a safe harbor—shaded by the mangosteen trees on either side. Everywhere else the forest, dense and immovable.

He drove on to the front of the house, got out and looked back toward the river; a sense of truly returning home seized him for the first time. Days of playing with Luc, of chasing Max, his dog; of playing pranks on Auguste, and always being caught.

When he turned back to the house, his grandfather, dressed in a white suit, stood on the veranda looking down at him. Peter stared back at him, at this man who had kept him safe all these

years. A smile spread across his face, and Peter bounded up the
stairs.

"Grandpère," he said, engulfing the old man in his arms.

Buonaparte Sartene kissed Peter on both cheeks and hugged
him with surprising strength.

"Welcome back to your home, Pierre," he whispered in
Corsican.

He stepped back, holding Peter by his shoulders, and looked
him up and down just as he had in Saigon, as though he still
could not believe he was back. He turned. Auguste had come up
behind him. "Look at him, Auguste. We sent away a skinny
boy, and now this giant of a man has come back to us." He
turned back to his grandson. "You are almost as broad as your
father was. God, how I wish he could see you now. Here. Home
again."

Peter began to speak, but found himself without words for the
moment. "It's very good to be here again, Grandpère," he
finally managed. "I have wanted it for so long."

"Listen to him, Auguste. See how he still speaks his native
tongue. Benito did well with him."

"I would never forget my heritage, or my family, Grandpère,"
Peter said.

Buonaparte kissed him again, then encircled his shoulders
with one arm and led him toward the front door. "Come inside
Pierre. We must drink, we must eat, we must talk."

They entered the foyer, and Peter came to an abrupt halt as he
watched a gray mass of fur and bones amble unsteadily down the
hall.

He pointed a finger at it. "Grandpère, that isn't Max, is it?"

"Of course it is," Buonaparte said. "I think that stupid old
dog has been refusing to die until you came home. He's twenty
if he's a day."

Peter knelt down and scratched the dog under its snout and
along its neck, as he remembered it liked. Max wheezed with
satisfaction and licked his hand. Peter looked back at his
grandfather. "And Luc, is he here?"

Buonaparte smiled. "Yes, Pierre. Unfortunately he's in the
north today. As I told you in my letters, he's my driver now
Although each time I ride with him, I think he's an assassin sent
to kill me."

Auguste laughed. "He's become an old woman, your grand

father," he said. "You'd think he was some old nun, still guarding her virginity."

Buonaparte tossed his head toward Auguste with mock contempt. "Do you remember him being such a bastard? Or has it happened since you left?"

Peter laughed, then stood and looked around the foyer, and into the adjoining rooms. "Nothing's changed at all. Everything is just a little older." A sense of apprehension took hold. It was as though the old house had reinforced how much of his own past—his family's past—was still hidden from him. "There's much I want to talk about. And there's much I have to know." Peter's final sentence was firm and serious.

Buonaparte raised his hand. "I know, Pierre. And you will. But first we will eat, and talk like a family. Then I will tell you what you must know."

Two hours later they were seated in Sartene's study. It too seemed smaller to Peter. But also familiar. The portrait of Napoleon, the toy soldiers, the vast array of books, dealing mostly with military history.

Peter and Buonaparte faced each other from two soft leather club chairs; Auguste sat alone on a small leather sofa a few feet away.

His grandfather seemed so much older, Peter thought. So frail. Even more so than in Saigon. But the eyes and the bearing were still devastating. The way he held his head, still commanding, just as Peter remembered. He had always been forbidding and yet loving at the same time. All of that was still there, and he thought it always would be.

Sartene sipped at the coffee he had brought with him from the dining room, and Peter noticed his hand was still steady, despite his age and obviously weakened state.

He smiled across at his grandson. "Now you are eager to know many things." He smiled again as Peter nodded, then shrugged his shoulders slightly. "That is good, Pierre. I'm only unhappy you had to wait so many years to hear the truth from me. But now I'll correct that." He sipped the coffee again, still looking at Peter, his eyes harder now.

"What you hear may trouble you greatly. I cannot help that. Now it's important that you know. Important even for your own safety. But before I begin, I want you to know two things. First, I've done much in my life that I would have done differently if I could. But still I am not ashamed of anything I have done.

Second, you must never repeat what I will tell you. It's no one's affair but ours. I don't ask your promise in this, because I know the fact that I wish it will be enough." He paused and smiled. "Do you want something to drink? What I have to tell you will take several hours."

Peter shook his head. His mouth was dry in anticipation of what he was about to hear. But he wanted no delay, no interruption once it began.

Sartene nodded and leaned back in his chair. "I will begin when I was a young boy in Corsica. I will tell you about the murder of my sister, about my adoption by a very good man, and my involvement in the *milieu*." He stopped and smiled at Auguste. "How I met this man under unfortunate circumstances, the war in Europe, and how we came to be here." He looked at Peter sternly now. "Then you will hear of our activities in this place, the reasons for them, your adopted father's involvement in the business that ended in the murder of your true father, and the vendetta that followed." He paused again, using his finger for emphasis. "A vendetta that still continues, and which makes life for you here very dangerous." He smiled, allowing his eyes to soften. "Now we begin. First, when I was a young boy, my name was not Buonaparte Sartene."

Three hours later, standing on the veranda, looking out at the quiet beauty of his grandfather's Japanese garden, Peter felt drained. The long story of his grandfather's life, his own heritage, continued to flash into his mind in bits and pieces. The death, the killing, his grandfather's constant struggle to carve a place for himself, his family—this "earning his bread" that he spoke about again and again. And the vendetta that still continued, and made Peter's life now so dangerous. Despite all of Benito's training, much of what Peter had heard was foreign to him. The people larger than life. Yet, somehow, inside himself, Peter felt it, thought he understood it. When his grandfather had finished, they had broken off the conversation to allow Peter to collect his thoughts. Now staring out at the garden, his mind was still awash.

His grandfather came up behind him, and Peter turned and smiled. He loved the man. Always would. And he knew his grandfather was right in not being ashamed of his life. You could not idly judge a man whose life grew from experiences you could never hope to understand

"Dinner will not be ready for an hour, Pierre. It's cooler now. Would you like to walk in the garden?"

"Yes, Grandpère, I would. It's a very beautiful garden."

Sartene laughed softly. "I heard you had a great love of flowers, and that you met a woman who is equally fond of them."

They descended the stairs slowly and walked into the garden.

"How do you hear all these things?" Peter asked.

Sartene laughed softly again. "I know about many things," he said. "I have spent much time, much money, making sure I know things. I found early in my life that a man is only taken advantage of when others know things he does not. Don't you remember your military history? The importance of spies? Napoleon was never a great general. He was a great spy. He knew his opponent, and that made him difficult to defeat."

"But he was defeated," Peter said.

"Everyone is defeated at one time or another. Everyone is, at one time, put in a position where his choices are limited if he is to survive on his own terms." He stopped and took hold of his grandson's arm. "And you have to live life on your own terms as much as possible. Otherwise you become some puppet, dangling on strings pulled by others."

They began to walk again, slowly circling the pond and the lotus and water hyacinth growing out from its edges. Peter thought of the defeat his grandfather had told him about just hours earlier. The agreement Sartene had been forced to make that allowed Francesco to live so Peter would be safe.

"You haven't asked me how I feel about what you told me," Peter said at length.

Buonaparte saw a toughness in his grandson's eyes. "How you feel is something you will decide yourself. I don't ask you for understanding, Pierre. I ask for your love. You will always have mine, and whatever protection that love can give."

"I know that, Grandpère." Peter's eyes had become soft, reflective. "I think I've always known that." He hesitated and looked out across the garden. "When Benito first told me that things were . . ." He paused, searching for a gentler phrasing. ". . . *different* than I'd been told as a child, I was upset, confused. But after Benito died, I thought about it, about my life here with you, about our family. Then your letter came, explaining that what was done was for our good, my good. I accepted it then, and today, after hearing the reasons for it, I know I was right." He turned back to his grandfather. "I don't think you could have told me anything today that would have changed my feelings toward you, or my family. Even if they were things I could not accept for myself. The feelings are just too strong. They're the reason I'm back." A small, thoughtful smile came to his lips. "And to do what has to be done."

Sartene reached out and touched his grandson's arm, then let his hand fall away. "Yes. Now that you are back, that is something you will not be able to avoid." He looked at his grandson with great warmth. "Learning what you did at such a young age, I would not have blamed you if you had chosen a different path."

Peter smiled, recalling days long past. "I was taught by Uncle Benito that you can run from a threat, and allow the fear of it to follow you. Or you can face it, and be rid of it one way or the other."

Sartene nodded. "But Francesco will not face you that way, Pierre. He has no sense of honor, and fear has followed him for many years, and that fear makes him dangerous."

"But he deals in opium, doesn't he?" Pierre asked.

Sartene's eyes narrowed. He could sense the direction of Pierre's thoughts. "More than ever," he said. "At first opium production went through the Opium Board, at least most of it. Now those who deal in it have begun processing it into heroin within the region. Primarily here in Laos and in North Viet Nam. Francesco works in North Viet Nam, under their protection, and that of the Viet Cong when he is in the south." He ran a finger along the length of his nose. "Why do you ask about this?"

"I met a man a few days ago. He works for an American wire service, and he's interested in the narcotics problem in Saigon and among the military units stationed here. The idea struck me that if I found out more about Francesco's operation, and then used this man, I might be able to force him out of hiding. He would have to stop me before I did too much damage."

Sartene shook his head. "It would be a bad thing, Pierre. Bad because it would expose you to great danger from others as well as Francesco, and Francesco will be dangerous enough by himself."

"I could use my own military status for protection," Peter said.

Sartene looked back at the pond and was quiet. "You don't

know who's involved in this thing, Pierre." He spoke the words flatly and without emotion.

"But you do, don't you?" Peter said.

"Yes, I know."

"Will you tell me?"

Sartene shook his head. "It's not your business to know, and it's not mine to tell."

Sartene felt his grandson stiffen. He had told Pierre the basic facts of the agreement he had made to keep him safe. Just speaking about it had left Sartene with an overwhelming sense of humiliation. Now he realized he would have to explain the details of that agreement. Sartene continued to stare across the pond as he spoke.

"Earlier, in my study, I told you how the communists came to me six months after I sent you away, and revealed that they knew where I had hidden you. But in exchange for your safety, they insisted on more from me than my assurance that I would not send people into North Viet Nam after Francesco." Sartene drew a deep breath as if preparing himself for pain. "You see, Francesco was important to them. He could develop their opium market, reach buyers in the south not available to them. He had access to export routes. So as part of the bargain, the communists demanded my word that the people he did business with in the south would also be safe from me, that I would never do anything against them. So, to keep you safe, I was forced to give the pig who murdered my son two things. His safety in the north, and the right to earn his bread under my nose."

Peter could not see his grandfather's eyes, but his voice carried all the pain he knew he would find there. "It must have hurt you very much, Grandpère."

Sartene nodded, then shrugged his shoulders. "I softened it by making them agree to leave the Meo in peace, and that part of the agreement, at least, has done some good."

Peter placed a hand on his grandfather's shoulder. "But the agreement should be over. I'm back, and there's no need to protect me."

"It's over for you, Pierre. But the communists kept their word to me, and I must continue to keep my word to them. That is why I cannot tell you who these others are. The Meo, and everyone who works for me, have a right to expect that I keep my word."

Peter put his hands on his hips and joined his grandfather in staring out into the pond. "If what I'm planning to do is going to hurt you, or your business, I'll find another way."

Sartene looked across at his grandson and nodded his approval. "I'm not involved with these people, Pierre. I was never involved with heroin. Opium, yes. But I haven't been involved in that since a little after your father died. I still have great influence with the people who grow it, and I supply certain accommodations to those who deal in it. This I do so my other business interests are not interfered with. But I'm not directly involved. Your father's death made me understand many things. Opium was one of them." He drew a long breath. "And these people who do it cannot hurt me. But they can hurt you."

"By helping Francesco?"

"Yes. That much I will tell you. But only because you have to know that to protect yourself. If Francesco Canterina learns you are here, he may simply try to hide from you. And then you will have to find him." He raised his finger. "But if he learns who you are, and that you are trying to eliminate the way he earns his bread, then he will seek the help of these others to kill you. And no matter how good your training, don't underestimate these other men. Francesco may want you dead just because you're my grandson, and because he is afraid to come after me. But for these others, a great deal of money is at stake, and because of that they could be even more dangerous to you."

"This may be a way to force Francesco into the open."

"It would. But there are other ways that are less dangerous. And don't ignore what I said about the others."

Sartene's eyes suddenly held all the pain he had carried over the past fourteen years. "In this country, the men who control opium are called kaitongs. It means 'little king.' But they are not kings, and they control nothing. Opium is kaitong here. Opium controls this region. And it corrupts everything it touches, every man who goes near it, every government who deals with it. Those involved with opium pay a price, Pierre, just as I have paid."

Sartene clasped Peter's shoulders in his hands. "You are all I have, Pierre. What I have built here is yours, if you want it. This is your country, Pierre. My people are your people. When you have finished what must be done, if you find you don't want it, then take the money from it and build your own country, your own people. I've talked to Auguste about this, and he agrees.

The others will take what you don't want. And no one will oppose this decision."

He spoke the final words with such force, Peter was left staring at him. Did this man, this old, frail man, still wield that kind of power, or was he simply living in his past?

"There will be time later to decide these things," Peter said. "After I do what must be done."

"You know you don't have to stay in the army. I understand your reason for doing so." He took Peter's shoulders between his hands again. "But your death can be arranged. On paper. And I assure you, even those who know will never question it. Peter Bently would simply be dead. And Pierre Sartene would have returned from Corsica. Then you could do this thing from within the family."

Peter shook his head slowly. "It's for me to do alone, Grandpère. And what about my mother, and Matt? I would like to see them again without always looking over my shoulder."

"You give governments and police who work for them too much credit. They are so busy always moving papers from one desk to another, they lose sight of the people those papers are about. Those papers become everything they believe. And if something is written on a piece of paper, that is all they have to know." He took on a comically sly look. "Papa Guerini taught me something many years ago. He told me that sometimes the best place for the fox to hide is under the nose of the hound. I promise you, if you choose to do this thing, you will give up nothing."

"You make a very convincing argument," Peter said. "But I think I can use the resources of the military now. And that will help in what I have to do."

A look of defeat crept into Sartene's eyes, but he masked it quickly. "And this heroin thing to force Francesco out?" he asked.

"I feel it will be the quickest way to get to Francesco. And I want to get to him before he comes after us. I know your concerns about the others, but believe me when I say I can handle any danger. And I consider it a matter of honor that I try."

"You were taught some things too well, Pierre," Sartene said, turning back to the pond. "If you feel this way, I cannot argue with you. But I'll ask you to do one thing out of respect for me."

Peter felt uneasiness spread through him. Was there more to learn now, or was his grandfather setting him up for some crafty Corsican ploy that would get him what he wanted, while appearing not to? "If you ask from respect, Grandpère, I can't say no."

Sartene nodded his head. "And that makes you suspicious."

When Peter did not respond, Sartene let the moment draw out, playing on the silence. "It is not a devious request," he said at length. "I only ask that if you somehow succeed in finding out who else is involved in this thing, you seek my counsel before you speak about it to anyone else."

"Yes, if I can. But I don't promise to follow your counsel. Only to respect it."

Sartene looked to the heavens and shook his head. "You are so much like your father. Thick and stubborn."

Peter laughed softly. "Isn't there any of my grandfather in me?"

"That, we wait to see," Sartene said. "And part of that will be seen in how cautiously you move." He turned, raising a bony finger like a lecturing parent. "You are smart, and I see you've become a strong-minded man, but I don't know if you are clever. When you deal with some people, it's best to let them think you really don't know everything that is going on. A truly clever man never lets others know how smart he really is. Remember that, Pierre." He slapped his shoulder. "Now, come and we'll have dinner. Then you can enjoy a night in your old room. It is just as you left it."

"I'd like that. But I have to contact people in Vientiane. I'll have to telephone. I'm supposed to be here on a mission for a very unpleasant Vietnamese colonel."

Sartene's face seemed to reflect the pleasure he felt in his own guile. "Yes, I know," he said. "The next time you come here there will be a prisoner for you to bring back to Colonel Duc. It will ensure your future travels. Auguste has some information you can take back this time."

"You mean you're going to do my job for me?"

"It's not a difficult thing to arrange. If you did it yourself you would just waste time we could spend together."

They started up the stairs. Halfway up Sartene stopped. "How do you feel about the men you work with?" he asked.

"I'm not sure." His voice was flat and hard.

Sartene nodded. "Good," he said. "It's good to be cautious with people you must work with."

"You're really asking if I trust them," Peter said.

"Trust no one here," Sartene said. "It's the only way to survive."

At ten o'clock Sartene and Auguste sat alone in the study. Peter had gone to his room, and the two old men sat quietly now over a glass of wine.

Auguste had watched Sartene throughout the day, and had taken pleasure in his friend's joy. Buonaparte's life was almost over, Auguste told himself now. Perhaps there would be some fulfillment for him after all these years of pain.

"What do you think of our grandson?" Auguste finally asked.

"In some ways I wish he weren't here."

"What the hell are you talking about? For fourteen years you've waited for this day, and now you sit there and say you wish he weren't here. You know, I always wondered when your age was going to catch up with you. I think it's finally happened."

Sartene waved a hand at him. "You know what I'm talking about, you old fool."

Auguste looked down into his wineglass. "You can't stop him from being a man, Buonaparte. If you try, you'll only make him weak."

"You know what he wants to do. And you know these people."

"He's been well trained," Auguste said. "You know that. I see great power in him."

Buonaparte nodded. "Yes, the power is there. But training means nothing in dealing with these people." He banged his fist against his chest, showing rare emotion. "You survive from inside yourself. And that you learn when you are very young. Pierre was robbed of that, just as I was robbed of him."

"You don't think he was born with it, Buonaparte? I tell you, I do."

Sartene shrugged. "Perhaps I'm just being a frightened fool. But I lost his father. I don't want to lose him."

"We're not helpless, you know. We could tell him who these people are. We could even do what has to be done for him."

"I lived by my honor all my life, and even though I have no respect for these men, I promised I would never interfere with them. If it weren't for Francesco, I would go to them and make an arrangement. But I could never gamble on what Francesco would do.''

''Then let's kill him. We should never have agreed not to follow him into North Viet Nam.''

''It was necessary. You know that. Besides, he comes to the south. We know he does. We just haven't been clever enough to catch him there.''

A light knocking on the door stopped Sartene from continuing. Auguste rose and opened it, then stepped aside to admit a short, slender Meo tribesman. He was in his mid-twenties, dressed in a cord suit and white shirt, open at the collar, and except for the flat facial features of the Meo, he could easily have passed for a young Lao businessman.

Sartene gestured with his hand and waited for the man to be seated.

''I'm very sorry I had to ask you to hide yourself away today, Luc,'' Sartene said. ''I want you to know that Pierre asked for you, but I told him you were in the north on business. I have reasons for this. There are things I must ask you to do for me, and it would be better if Pierre did not recognize you.''

Luc sat in silence and listened to Sartene's instructions, showing neither happiness nor displeasure.

When he had finished his instructions, Sartene looked at the young Meo warmly. ''I know what I ask you to do is a burden. It will take you away from your family for many months. But it must be done.''

A trace of a smile showed on Luc's face. He bowed his head slightly. ''When my father became old and ill, you cared for him, kaitong. You have always assumed the burdens of your people. For me to do less for you would shame all Meo.'' His smile broadened. ''Besides, kaitong, it will give me a chance to observe the brother of my youth.''

Sartene nodded with satisfaction. The young man had answered as he should. The loyalty he had always demanded had again been delivered. He placed his palms on the arms of the chair and pushed himself up, then reached out and placed one hand on Luc's shoulder. ''You have been like a second grandson in my house,'' he said. ''Your respect is something that will not be forgotten.''

He took Luc's arm and walked him to the door, speaking quietly to him as he did. Auguste watched the scene as he had so many before. Buonaparte was still a master at making people do his will. And they always felt pleasure in doing it. He wondered again what this man would have become if he had not been born to a poor Corsican family. But what difference does that make? he told himself. He could not have more power if he was the head of a country. In fact, he would probably have less.

Sartene walked slowly to his desk and eased himself into his chair. He was tired, exhausted by the emotions of the day. He opened the center drawer and took out the gold medallion he always kept locked away there. He fondled the rectangular emblem of his power within the *milieu*, then raised his eyes to Auguste.

"It's long overdue that I pass this on," he said. His voice was soft and distant. "There must be some continuity of our strength for all those who depend on us for their bread."

"And you worry now that Pierre is not the person. You find him lacking in just one meeting?" There was annoyance in Auguste's voice.

Sartene chuckled softly. "Don't be impatient with me," he said. "Pierre is a good boy, a fine young man. A good grandson. Whether he has the strength to be *un vrai monsieur*, I cannot yet tell. But what is more important is that he may not want to be." Sartene wagged his head from side to side. "And who could blame him? There is wealth, there is power, but the price for it is very large. I've worked all my life for the day he would take my place. What a foolish thing to work for, eh?" He placed the medallion back in the drawer, then closed and locked it. "Who could blame him if he didn't want it now?" He stroked his nose thoughtfully. "I don't doubt his love. But he may see our life here as the life of criminals."

"I don't believe he thinks of us that way," Auguste said.

"It is possible, my friend. Though he would never say it to us. Remember, I sent him off to be raised in a country where everything is viewed as this or that." Sartene used his hands to emphasize the difference. "Even their history ignores the bad in people they choose to make heroes, and puts a mark on the people they decide are evil. And it's a mark that doesn't wash away." He watched Auguste twist uncomfortably in his chair. "You've never read their history, Auguste. I have. The men who built the railroads across their country. How many oriental workers they slaughtered in that no one really knows. How many Indians, how many farmers who were in their way. But these people are great heroes to the Americans. The men who led the revolution were slavekeepers, but no one writes about these Africans who lived in filth and suffered and died at their hands. And the men we dealt with, the men from the embassy who came to us asking us to help build the opium trade. They will go down in American history books as statesmen.'' He jabbed his fingers into his chest. ''And we will be the monsters who helped put heroin into the arms of their children. Not them, Auguste. Never them. And I tell you, my friend, these heroes have committed more crimes with the points of their pens than you and I ever dreamed of. You and I have killed, Auguste. More than any man should ever kill, and I don't excuse us for it. But when we killed it was to preserve our own lives, or those who depended on us. How many men have these heroes killed? How many are they going to kill in this war that they could have won in a year, but choose to go on with so their friends and the people they owe can make money? These are the things that Pierre does not yet see. But he sees us. And to some degree he may see us through their eyes.''

''But you've done good for your people too,'' Auguste said. ''He will see that.''

Sartene shook his head slowly, dismissing the idea. ''I have a good grandson, and I have seen him grow into a man of power within himself. Perhaps the rest was all a dream, and dreams are for children.''

''It can still happen, my friend.''

''Anything can happen, Auguste. But we must also look to others now. If I die before you, it will be you who will have to pass on the medallion.''

''I will give it to Pierre,'' Auguste said.

Sartene laughed, loving his friend for his stubborn loyalty. When he spoke his voice was firm. ''No. A man has to want the medallion. And he has to want the burdens of others that go with it. You will choose for the *milieu*, not for me. But for now, we must just keep our Pierre alive.''

''Have you told him about the woman?'' Auguste asked.

Sartene shook his head. ''She will be no danger to him. And she is being watched by our own people.''

''But if Pierre succeeds with this plan of his, she may act to protect Francesco.''

''I am hoping we will lure Francesco out before that. And if we do, Luc will be waiting. If the woman becomes a danger . . ." Sartene shrugged his shoulders. "Then we will do what must be done."

Peter lay on his back, his head propped on a pillow. The room was like a trip back in time, familiar yet distant. It gave him a sense of warmth to see so much of what he remembered. Yet it all came out of a haze, something that was a part of him that no longer existed. He let his mind wander back. This same room, lying in the bed. His mother coming to say good night to him. His father. Then waiting expectantly. Knowing his grandfather would come. Telling him stories. About Napoleon, the great battles, the earlier life as a poor child in Corsica, the scorn at military school in France that eventually drove him on to become emperor.

He smiled in the darkness. He had been raised with those stories as some children were raised with stories from the Bible. Told with the same degree of love, the same sense that they were necessary, would benefit the person who heard them.

It had been a good life as a child here. He felt that strongly. Playing in the fields and the outskirts of the jungle. Along the riverbank. Luc, his only friend then. Alone much of the time, but enjoying it. Allowing his mind to run, creating the games, his own world existing only in his head. It had strengthened him, he thought. Given him an understanding of competing alone, facing whatever obstacles happened to present themselves.

He looked down from the bed. Max was asleep on the floor. Old and thin and withered now. Too many years had gone by. Too many things that could not be recaptured. Perhaps should not be.

Perhaps his relationship with his grandfather was like that too. A loving memory that could remain only that. The love could remain, the affection. He was certain of that. Understanding, this was something else. And it was really a moot point. Why should he even concern himself with his grandfather's life? It was something beyond his experience, even though he had unknowingly grown up in the midst of it all.

He stared at the ceiling, the faint light from the window filtering through the mangosteen trees, creating strange, twisted shadowgraphs on the plaster. Frightening now, as they had sometimes been as a child? He wondered. Disturbing, anyway.

He must find this man Francesco. And kill him. He had trained for three years, knowing the time would come. He smiled to himself. He had been trained all his life for this, without ever knowing it. Now he would do it. And he would do it in his own way.

Chapter 28

The resort city of Vung Tau sat on a hook of land that curved out into the South China Sea, forming a wide peaceful bay. Within the bay, multicolored fishing boats rode the whitecapped green water. Beyond the broad white-sand beach, a small city of dusty streets and tile-roofed buildings seemed more suitable to a Greek island than a country torn by years of war.

"There is no war here," Lin said, as they walked slowly along the edge of the water.

Peter looked out across the wide bay. "Over there there is."

"Yes, but not here. It is why I like to return here often. It is the one place in my country where I can feel there is sanity."

A wave crashed in, and Lin jumped back against Peter.

"Afraid to get your bare feet wet?" he teased.

"I know. It is silly, isn't it?"

He looked down at her and smiled inwardly. He had called her mother's home before arranging with Philippe for the forty-five-mile flight from Saigon. When he had told her he could come for the day she had seemed pleased, and when she met him at the small, dusty airport, he had realized how much seeing this woman was beginning to mean to him.

"I don't think you could ever do anything silly, Lin," he said. "But I know you could cause others to."

"Have I caused you to be silly, Peter?"

If you only knew, he told himself. He thought of the lie he had told Wallace, about the need to do some apartment hunting, then arranging for the unauthorized trip that could easily put his butt in a very large sling. But Wallace had been so pleased with the information Auguste had provided about new North Vietnamese supply routes that he had happily agreed. If he found out, or even worse, if Colonel Duc found out, life would not be very pleasant for Peter Bently.

"You haven't answered me, Peter," Lin said, her voice holding the hint of inner laughter.

"I was thinking of your father-in-law."

'Oh, I see. Then perhaps I have made you do something silly."

"I hope you continue to," he said.

They stopped, and Lin looked out across the bay.

"When I am here, the concerns and prejudices of my people are like the war—they are hard for me to understand."

"It's a very beautiful place. It must have been wonderful growing up here."

Lin turned and smiled up at him. "Yes, it was. I always loved it here. I always thought that this is what my country would be like if there were no war."

"Sometimes I forget that the people here have never known peace. It's a hard thing to grasp." Peter looked down at the wet sand, drew a line with his toe, then watched it disappear as the next wave inched across it. "All I've ever known is peace. Until now, anyway."

"That was also true for the people here in Vung Tau." Lin looked back across the bay again, as if searching for something that was there. "I never really understood the war when I was a child here. I'm afraid I led a rather sheltered life. It was when I was at school in Paris that I first understood the depth of what was happening here. I felt guilty then. Being there in safety while others were suffering at home."

'Have you ever thought of going back to Europe?"

She turned back and smiled at him, but there was a sadness in her eyes, a melancholy, that for the moment seemed to accentuate her frail beauty.

"No," she said, her voice barely audible. "I would like to visit some day. But I shall never leave Viet Nam. It is my home, it is where I belong." Lin seemed to sense her own mood and shook the melancholy away. She hugged herself, her hands moving along her arms. Doing so, dressed in a simple skirt and short-sleeved blouse, she looked very much like a schoolgirl. "Don't you look forward to returning home, going back to a place you feel you belong?"

Peter stared past her. But I have come home, he thought.

"I guess it's all still too new to me." He looked back at her and noticed she was watching him closely. "I studied the region so extensively, I suppose I developed a certain feeling of closeness to the place and its people. I've wanted to come here for many years now. But the war, my part in it, has made it very different than I had hoped it would be. I would like very much to see it without the war."

They began walking again, back along the beach to where they had left their shoes. Peter was dressed in uniform, the trousers rolled up to his knees, his cap hanging from his rear pocket. It was almost noon, and the sun beat down on them, nullifying the breeze that came off the bay. Ahead there were seafood stands along the beach, with umbrella-covered tables nearby.

"Would you like something to eat?" he asked.

"Yes, that would be nice. And then I shall take you to *cai luong*. There is a performance this afternoon."

"*Cai luong?*" Peter asked.

"Ah, your studies of our country have not been as complete as you have led me to believe." Her eyes glittered mischievously. "*Cai luong* is our opera, folk opera really. It is very stylized, very dramatic, and everyone goes to it, the rich and the poor alike. The actors speak and sing and gesture wildly. It is very stylized and yet sophisticated at the same time. And still it is simple and very colorful. We can lose ourselves in it, and in doing that we can forget the sadness in our own lives."

"It sounds wonderful," Peter said.

Lin began to laugh. "It may be hard for you. Westerners have difficulty appreciating oriental music. Your Colonel Wallace once told me he thought our music sounded like a dozen cats fighting."

"Music is like food," Peter said. "Often it takes time to acquire a new taste."

"Ahh, but the new is often very disturbing. To discover something new, something unexpected, can disturb the harmony surrounding a person's life. Often it can force new directions upon that person that were never anticipated."

"Yes, I know," Peter said.

It was four o'clock before the performance ended, and as they walked together along a crowded, dusty street, Peter realized how much the opera had captivated him. It had brought him back to days early in his childhood, before he had mastered Lao, days when he had struggled to understand the tonal jabbering of the Mua tribesmen who worked for his grandfather. Days after that with Luc, when things oriental were so much a part of his being. He had thought he had lost much of the past, but realized now it had only been driven beneath the surface, waiting to be recaptured.

"You are very quiet, Peter," Lin said, breaking into his thoughts. "Did you find the opera upsetting?"

"In a way. But not in the way you mean. It's hard for me to explain. It was very beautiful, and it made me think of things I have not thought about for many years."

"And you find that disturbing?"

"I find it disturbing that I was able to put them out of my mind so easily."

They entered a small park, walking slowly along pathways bordered with flowers. Ahead, a group of young Vietnamese officers stood talking, their uniforms sharply pressed.

"I've noticed a great many young officers here," Peter said.

"Many have been assigned here," Lin answered. "Like Saigon, Vung Tau is a popular military assignment for the sons of the wealthy. Their parents pay a great deal of money to assure them safe places in which to serve their country. I'm afraid only the poor, and those without influence, are considered worthy of dying in battle."

There had been a hint of bitterness in Lin's words, but it had been almost indiscernible.

"It's been that way in most wars," he said.

She looked away, not answering him. "We should not talk of war," she said finally, turning and smiling at him. "When we return to Saigon it will be with us again all too soon."

"You're right," Peter said. "I wish very much I didn't have to go back tonight. When will you be returning?"

"The day after tomorrow," Lin said.

"I should be settled in at the hotel by then. Would you have dinner with me there when you return?"

"It would be difficult that night. But perhaps the following evening."

As they left the park a group of children rushed forward, calling out in pidgin English for Peter to give them money. He reached into his pocket, but Lin suddenly grabbed his arm. He was surprised by the strength of her grip.

She glared at the children, a ragtag collection of five boys and two girls, all eight or nine years old. "Go from here," she snapped in Vietnamese.

The children stood their ground, glancing from Lin to Peter. Lin took a quick step forward, raising her hand as if preparing to strike out at them. The children turned and ran. She spun on Peter, her eyes flashing with anger.

"You must not encourage their begging," she said.

Peter was momentarily stunned. Lin's lips were trembling, and for a moment he thought she would strike out at him.

"I didn't mean to offend you," he said.

"No. You think it is a kindness to encourage them." She caught hold of herself and looked down. When her eyes went back to his face, the anger was gone. "We have little here, Peter, but our pride. We must not allow our children to lose that as well."

He reached out and touched her arm, then let his hand fall away. "You're right," he said. "I still have a great deal to learn." To remember, he added to himself. "You must tell me when I act foolishly."

She laughed quietly. "Would you believe me if I did?"

"I want to understand, Lin."

"What is it you wish to understand, Peter? My people, or yourself?"

"Both," he said.

Chapter 29

Joe Morris had seemed surprised by Peter's call, but had quickly agreed to meet with him. When Peter had suggested privacy for the meeting, Morris had named a Tu Do Street bar, assuring him that no one there except the hookers would pay any attention to two men sitting alone.

Peter had no trouble finding the Friendly Bar. Its neon sign flashed like a beacon, bathing the seediness of Tu Do Street in gaudy reds and blues. Outside, young Vietnamese men, dressed in the traditional white shirts and black trousers of students, stood on either side of the door, offering looks of contempt to the Americans who passed between them.

The interior of the bar surprised Peter. It was even seedier than its exterior. Behind the bar, which ran the length of the long, narrow room, more neon lighting sent out a sickly blue glow, and it caught the cigarette smoke, giving it an unpleasant, toxic quality. At a table near the door, a large, muscular young man, wearing the shoulder patch of Special Forces, leaned drunkenly toward a strikingly ugly Vietnamese woman. She giggled at his slobbering suggestions and ran her hand up and down his leg.

The tables seemed to have been placed only a foot apart, packing in as many as possible, and Peter squeezed between them, searching through the hazy smoke for Morris. Halfway into the long, narrow room, Peter spotted him waving from a corner table. Approaching the table, Peter decided Morris seemed entirely in his element; the gaudiness and smoke, the heavily made-up bar girls dressed in almost nonexistent miniskirts, seemed to blend perfectly with his disheveled, well-worn look.

"Thought you got lost, or chickened out," Morris said, as Peter shoehorned himself into a chair at the small round table.

Peter rocked back and forth in the chair. It, like the table, was bolted to the floor. "Are they afraid of earthquake or theft?" he asked.

"Breakage," Morris said. "Furniture's tough to get, and this way these wahoos can't use it to dent each other's heads. They lose a lot of bottles, though—empty ones, thank Christ. I do hate waste."

As Morris finished speaking, Peter felt an arm drape around his neck. He looked up and saw a hard but pretty Vietnamese face only inches from his own.

"You buy drink for Sou Yet," the young woman said, leaving out any hint of a question.

Morris snorted. "Not now, Sou Yet. Later, he buy drink, buy blow job, buy everything. Not now."

The young woman grinned at Peter. At the corner of her mouth, he could see some teeth were missing.

"Okay, I come back." She ran her hand up the side of Peter's neck. "You no find other girl," she said. "They number ten. They no same me. Me beaucoup good. Number one. You see."

The woman turned and quickly moved to another table, her slender hips undulating in an exaggerated way. Peter looked back at Morris and exhaled heavily.

Morris laughed. "Don't worry, kid, these girls hand out a penicillin prescription with each trick."

"I'm allergic."

"To which?"

"Both."

He snorted. "Wanna drink? You're not allergic to that, I hope."

"Beer will do fine, thanks."

Peter looked around the room, as Morris caught the attention of a waitress and ordered. The cramped room was filled with at least a hundred GIs and half as many bar girls, each dressed in an outrageous costume, each plying her trade to drunken semi-enthusiastic response. Along the bar there was a girl for every third man, and if one potential customer's response was not eager enough, the girl would simply rotate in place and begin work on the next. When Peter turned his attention back to the table, Morris was grinning at him.

"The Saigon meat auction," Morris said. "You see those kids outside, the ones who looked like they'd like to cut your balls off?"

Peter nodded.

"Boyfriends and brothers," Morris said.

"Pimping?" Peter asked.

"Surviving," Morris answered.

There was a note of compassion in Morris' voice that seemed to contradict the hard-bitten image he tried to project. Peter felt Morris might well be a far better man than he had first assumed.

"How long have you been here, Joe?" he asked.

"Almost two years." Morris snorted at himself. "Believe it or not, I asked for the assignment. For ten years I struggled through a bunch of small daily newspapers in New Jersey. Then finally, after I managed to win a couple of regional awards, I was offered a job with UPI." He laughed, then took a long pull on his drink. "You know what they did? They assigned me to their Newark office. And bingo, I was right back where I started." He shook his head and smiled at the irony of it. "Anyway, I thought some duty here would change my luck. But so far all I've had to report is the bullshit that comes out of the Five O'Clock Follies."

Peter cocked his head, questioning the term.

"The press's name for the briefing reports we get every day from Westmoreland's PR staff," Morris explained.

Peter smiled at the disrespect. "And you want to go beyond that."

"You bet your ass I do."

Peter looked back toward the door. The young Green Beret was gone, his place taken by a middle-aged petty officer, dressed in navy whites. He was talking to the same ugly young woman. His beer arrived, and Peter took a long drink. "Tell me about heroin," Peter said.

"Why?" Morris asked.

Peter remained silent. He just stared at Morris, knowing that would make any man say more than he intended.

"Why you interested?" Morris asked. "You want to look into it?"

Peter waited, holding Morris' eyes until he shifted in his seat. "Let's not play games, Joe. Let's just say I'd like to find out about it if I can. Purely informational. If you can help, fine. If not . . ." He allowed a shrug of his shoulders to finish the sentence.

"I'm not interested in giving out information, kid. Not unless you're a lot smarter and a lot tougher than you look. This scam isn't being run by a group of guys who are looking over their shoulder for the cop on the beat. They own the cop on the beat. All of them." He paused, taking a long drink of Jack Daniel's.

"I'm particularly interested in a Corsican I've heard about," Peter said.

"That's not surprising. The Corsicans here are involved in just about everything," Morris said. "What's so special about this one?"

"He's supposed to be running a heroin operation out of North Viet Nam, and selling it in the south."

"And you think the North Vietnamese get a cut of his action?"

Peter nodded his head, then repeated the information his grandfather had given him. "And use it to help finance the war."

"Jesus. That's a great story, if you can prove it. What's this guy's name?"

"Francesco Canterina. Have you ever heard of him?"

Morris shook his head. "Never. Do you know who his buyers are here?"

"That's where I hoped you might help," Peter said. "It could be local merchants, politicians, or even corrupt ARVN brass."

Morris' face filled with frustration. "Christ, if I knew any of that, I'd have the Pulitzer in my hip pocket."

"Do you know anything about distribution?" Peter asked. "How they get the stuff out of the country? If I could find that out, I could trace it back to the buyers, and then to Canterina."

Morris rubbed his chin, trying to appear thoughtfully calm. But Peter could see the excitement in his eyes.

"All I've heard are rumors, and a few code words." He stared across the table at Peter. "If I tell you what I have heard, what do I get out of it?"

"Everything. All the names, even photos and tape recordings of a deal going down, if I can get them."

Morris' eyes narrowed. "What if it involves some heavy people in the south? People whose names might embarrass the boys at the embassy?"

"You get whatever I get," Peter said.

"Your bosses won't like that," Morris said.

Peter smiled. "No, they won't, Joe. But that's the deal. If you don't want it, I'll find somebody who does."

Morris held up both hands. "Okay. Don't be such a hard-ass. What I have to tell you isn't all that great anyway." He took another long drink. "About six months ago there was a young kid working in G-2 who started poking his nose around. His name was Constantini, and seems he had a kid brother who was hooked on junk back home."

"Why'd he come to you?" Peter asked.

"He claimed he told the officer he worked for, and was told to butt out. Anyway, he said the stuff was being stored right on base at Tan Son Nhut, which would indicate some ARVN involvement, and would also explain why he was told to mind his own fucking business."

"That's all he found?"

Morris shook his head. "No, but the rest of it is crazy shit. He said the junk was going out of the country on something they called the 'long silver train.' And that everything went through somebody they called the 'green vulture.' Had his special stamp of protection on it." Morris shook his head. "He said it was so simple it was sickening. Said he stumbled across it while doing a routine investigation on somebody in his unit who had bought the farm."

"So why didn't he tell you more?" Peter said.

Morris' lips curved up into a sickened smile. "He was going to. But the next day some VC sapper blew his brains out about three blocks from here. And if you believe that, I've got a bridge back home I want to sell you."

"It doesn't make any sense," Peter said. "It all sounds like something out of a comic book."

"No shit, Red Ryder. There are no trains in this goddam country, long silver ones or any other kind. And the green vulture . . ." He raised his hands and let them drop back to the table.

Peter sipped his beer and stared at the grimy, knife-scarred table-top. The words FUCK VIET NAM had been scratched in the wooden surface. He drummed his fingers on the table. "Well, it's a start," he said at length.

"What can I do to help?" Morris asked.

Peter smiled at him. "Start asking around about Mr. Canterina."

Chapter 30

Francesco Canterina ran his fingers through his gray wavy hair and looked around at the cramped dank chamber. His nose and mouth wrinkled with discomfort. The room was nothing more than a carved-out section of tunnel, running beneath the streets of Cholon, the ceilings so low even the smaller Vietnamese had to stoop to walk through them.

Francesco hated cramped spaces, this one even more so because it was dark, illuminated only by the light of two Coleman lanterns stolen from the U.S. military. He took a deep breath and immediately regretted it. The tunnel smelled like a sewer. No place for a fifty-five-year-old man to be doing business, he told himself. This was worse than the days in the resistance. At least the hills of Provence didn't always smell of shit and rotting food.

Cao sat behind the makeshift desk, watching Francesco, amused by his discomfort. "You would not make a good revolutionary. You've learned to enjoy your comfort too much."

"It would be nice to meet somewhere that wasn't a hole in the ground, my friend," Francesco said. He gestured with his hands, trying to dismiss his words even as he said them.

"Oh, perhaps a nice restaurant, or a bar in one of the nicer hotels." A disquieting smile filled Cao's face. "I'm afraid being seen with you in public would harm my reputation."

Francesco laughed. He was older now, but still strikingly handsome and fit. He lit a cigarette and allowed it to dangle from the corner of his mouth. "We all know what an excellent reputation you have," he said. "I wouldn't want to tarnish it. It might upset your father-in-law, Ba Lin."

"I prefer you to use my revolutionary name," Lin said. "And you never will harm my reputation. Not if you wish to continue working under our protection in the north. You see, Francesco, you're a necessary evil. Your expertise provides a way to fund the war against the imperialists, while not using manpower needed in that fight. But we could spare the manpower if you forced us to do so."

Francesco smiled at the warning. "But that would make it difficult for those in authority to earn some small personal profit, would it not?"

"That's an interesting point, Francesco. But don't rely too much on it." Lin fitted a cigarette to a small ivory holder, lit it and exhaled the smoke in a direct line toward Francesco's face. "I do enjoy your company, but I think it's time we turned our attention to business matters. We will need an additional twenty kilos by the end of the month."

Francesco's eyebrows rose at the figure. "I'll have to work my chemist day and night," he said. "Why the sudden need for more?"

"It seems our customers have run into difficulty. There seems to have been some pilferage. They will fall short in the amount that has been ordered. And since the latest silver train has already been arranged, they don't want to send any of it off empty. You can deliver, I assume."

"I'll have to pay my chemist more."

A hand covered Lin's mouth, as laughter filled the small dirt-walled chamber. "You have no grace about you at all," Lin said, eyes hard now. "The additional amount will be a private transaction that will not involve the north. If you can arrange that as well you can expect another ten percent."

"I always think of how much more I could make if I dealt directly with the generals myself," Francesco said.

"Yes, but then you would have to worry about finding a certain old man standing at your door some evening."

"Even Buonaparte Sartene cannot live forever," Francesco said.

"That's true," Lin said. "But I'm told Corsican vendettas can outlive any man."

Francesco felt the hatred build in his belly. Having to rely on someone for protection offended him. Being forced to hide in the boredom of Hanoi cut him even more. Fourteen years and he was still at that bastard's mercy. And every time he came to the south to earn his bread he was forced to watch for Sartene's hand. He forced a smile. "Vendettas, my dear Cao, are the dreams of old men. Today's young people forget the need of them."

Lin laughed again. "You lie to yourself as easily as you lie to me." The cigarette smoke streamed across the chamber again. "There's one other matter we must also discuss. This American newspaperman, Morris. You remember him. He was involved with that young man, Constantini."

Francesco nodded.

"At a dinner party a few days ago, Mr. Morris became very involved with a new young officer in Colonel Wallace's foolish little group of spies. I'm afraid the investigation the generals so cleverly put an end to may start up again."

"The solution, my dear Cao, as I told you before, is to arrange a traffic accident for Mr. Morris."

Lin raised a hand. "We do not want to kill newspeople. They have been useful, and killing one might turn others to the side of our enemies. But we should find out what he is up to, so we can neutralize this new officer if necessary. I am already keeping close watch on him, but it is something I must do carefully."

"Who is this new officer?" Francesco asked.

"His name is Bently. Peter Bently."

Francesco's features hardened.

"The name is familiar to you?" Lin asked.

"I knew a man named Bently once. But his name was Matthew."

"I'm told it is a very common name for an American," Lin said.

Francesco nodded. "Yes, so is Peter. I knew someone by that name also." Francesco forced a smile to his lips. "But I will look into it, my dear Cao. And if it proves dangerous, I will take care of it in a way that will never find its way back to me."

Out on the street, Francesco climbed into the rear seat of a waiting Citroën. He had planned a speedy return to Hanoi, a plan he had now decided to change. Cao believed his only protection came from the north and the Viet Cong. But there were others who ensured his safety here to a limited degree, in exchange for certain services about which Cao would never learn. It would take several days to find out what he now had to know. Probably a waste of time, he told himself. But he had not stayed alive the last fourteen years by failing to give a few days over to waste.

Chapter 31

He had watched her throughout dinner, fascinated by the delicate grace that seemed to mark everything she did. He had kept the room dimly lit, and the very faintness of the light seemed to accent the silver *ao dai* she had worn, further heightening the contrast to her soft, clear, sallow skin, the silky black hair, and the endless warmth that seemed to come from her dark-brown eyes.

She had looked at him and smiled repeatedly throughout the meal, knowing how greatly her beauty was affecting him, confident in her ability to maintain his interest. Gone now was the tension of Vung Tau, replaced by the pleasure of being alone together for the first time.

Peter had always known he was attractive to women. But it had never before been important that he be attractive to one in particular. With Lin it was, and it left him feeling almost adolescent.

They sat on the small terrace just off the sitting room. In the distance the Saigon harbor could just be seen, the lights from the endless flow of cargo ships glimmering far off like yachts dotting some Mediterranean port, a far cry from the reality of war supplies being offloaded in the endless heat. From the terrace even the heat was softened by the breeze that floated above the city. Peter stood, leaned against the terrace railing and stared toward the distant harbor.

"From here, even the harbor looks beautiful. Nothing at all like it is," he said.

"The longer you are here, Peter, the more you will learn that nothing, no one person or thing, is as it appears to be. It is the

324

great truth about Southeast Asia.'' Her voice had been soft, with a slightly tolerant, laughing quality.

Peter thought about her words for several minutes. "The war certainly isn't as it appears to be," he said at length. "The bursts of violence, mixed with the endless lethargy. I've come to believe that the lethargy is more damaging to the men fighting here than the violence. It's the lethargy that produces the fear, the despair. When there's violence there's no time for either."

She stood and walked up beside him. Her voice held a note of laughter again. "You would prefer that the Viet Cong choose a site, bring their army to it, and fight your army to the death. And after a series of such battles a winner be declared."

Peter laughed softly at the idea himself. "It would be nice. Win or lose, there would be some end in sight."

"Then you ask your enemy to give up the only powerful weapon he has," Lin said.

"Which is?"

"Time, Peter. Your enemy knows that someday you will have to leave. That someday your countrymen will tire of sending their children here to suffer and die."

Peter turned to her. Lin was standing in profile, her delicate bone structure picking up hints of light from the city below. "And the people here in the south believe one day we'll abandon them?"

She smiled slightly. " 'Abandon' is such a harsh word," she said. "Lose interest, perhaps. Or become more interested in some other area of the world. The people here in the south only hope it will not happen until there is strength enough to fight the war alone. To do that they will have to have a strong government, and a strong army in support of that government. Now there is neither."

"That could take many years," Peter said.

"Years are only drops of sand, Peter. If I said twenty years, you would think I was exaggerating. Others, who know my country better, would accuse me of being overly optimistic. Do you think your country will send people to die here for the next twenty years, Peter?"

"No, Lin. I don't."

"Neither do the Viet Cong," she said.

Almost as if on cue, flares burst in the distance beyond Cholon, spreading their eerie glow outward like some signal that death was now taking place.

"It seems the Viet Cong are listening to you," Peter said.

She laughed, then turned her head toward him and smiled. "Why do you call the Viet Cong 'Charlie'?" she asked.

"On military radios we spell words out, giving each letter a name. Alfa, Bravo, Charlie; A, B, C. Viet Cong is VC—Victor Charlie. Charlie for short. I think Americans have to have derogatory names for their enemies. It makes them less threatening."

"Ah, so you feel threatened by the Viet Cong," she teased.

Her eyes were warm with laughter, and it made him want to reach out and touch her. He resisted the impulse, afraid it would somehow shatter the beauty he felt for the moment.

"I feel threatened by any person or thing that would try to kill me. The kraits in the grass make me feel threatened, so I learn how to deal with them. I avoid them." He laughed suddenly. "Do you know what our men call the kraits?"

She shook her head slowly, keeping her soft brown eyes on his.

"Two-step Charlie."

"Why is that?"

"They claim that's just about how many steps one can take after being bitten. Before the snake's venom takes effect, that is."

She pursed her lips. "It's such a gentle little snake. It bothers no one unless it's molested. The Viet Cong do not have to be molested to strike." She smiled again. "And they cannot be avoided like the krait."

Peter reached out and took her hand, held it up, studying the long slender fingers, then released it. "Like all Vietnamese, you seem to have a grudging admiration for the VC."

"As I told you before, Peter, they want what all Vietnamese want. Freedom from outside influence. We only differ on the end result, once the goal is achieved, not the goal itself. Not so different from the radical conservatives and radical liberals of your country."

"It would be nice if it could be settled with one nice tacky election, full of baby-kissing and handshaking."

"I fear both sides are too afraid they would lose. Guns are a much more effective way to take control. Once one has control, one can choose one's opposition. And in doing so, one can limit its power and effectiveness."

Peter shook his head slowly. "What did you study in Europe?"

The half-knowing smile was on his lips now, and seeing it, Lin was amused. "Political science, Peter. And philosophy."

"Such a strange interest for such a beautiful woman," he said.

Her eyes widened; her mouth formed a small circle. "Oh, in your country beauty and intellect do not mingle?" she asked.

Peter winced. "That was a bit chauvinistic, wasn't it?"

"No more than if I asked why a big, strong man like Peter Bently had such a deep interest in flowers. Here in my country, a strange phenomenon has developed. In the north the men have always been the dominant force in family life. Here in the south that role has fallen to the women."

He held up both hands in surrender. "I will never speak such words again." He laughed softly. "But my interest in flowers is rather closely linked to you."

She turned away from him as he spoke, allowing her eyes to move over the city below them. Peter joined her gaze. To their left even the neon gaudiness of Tu Do Street appeared gentle in its beauty. Her words returned to him. *No one person, or thing, is as it appears to be.* He looked at her in profile again, allowing himself to be slightly overwhelmed by her beauty. There had been subtle suggestions of availability. Just coming to his hotel was an unheard-of act. And he knew he wanted her, but somehow, at the same time, did not.

He had difficulty understanding it himself. It was as though reaching out for her, as he wanted to, would somehow destroy his image of her. He wondered if perhaps he feared he might shatter the illusion of her in his own mind. It was pure adolescence, all of it. And it was foolish.

"Have you ever wondered why the rich, who live in cities, always choose to live high above those cities?" Her voice was soft and distant, almost as if she was asking the question of herself.

"I suppose one gets a sense of power looking down on everyone else," Peter said.

"I'm sure that's a part of it. But only a small part," Lin said.

He waited for her to continue, to finish the thought. She looked at the city below, taking time before she did. "I think much of it is that from elevation, one only sees the beauty of the city. The poverty, the decadence, even the suffering are all hidden from view. Perhaps that is why politicians, like the rich, never see what is wrong with their society. They view it from too lofty a height."

"Soldiers are like that too," Peter said. "They prefer to concentrate on the effect, rather than consider the cause."

"But that's not the job of the soldier, is it?" She turned back to him, her face serious. "The soldier merely carries out the will of those in power. He is told to kill and he kills. He is not supposed to question the reason for the killing. To do so is to be disloyal."

"Your husband was a soldier, as is your father-in-law. Haven't you heard them question?"

"My father-in-law merely protects me," Lin said. "To him I have become a living memory of his son." She smiled softly. "It is not that his devotion to me is not real. It is merely self-directed. I represent to him something he has lost. Something that meant very much to him. And he loves me because I share that loss with him." She turned back to the city. "But he would never discuss his inner thoughts with me. His work, perhaps. But never his thoughts about that work. To discuss that with me would be to display weakness."

"And your husband?"

"My husband, like you, was young. He was very much in love with being a soldier. He loved the power, the romance, the illusion of danger that it held." She brushed back a strand of hair the wind had blown across her forehead. "Like many Vietnamese women, I knew my husband as a boy. It was very interesting to see the boy become a man. Even more interesting to see how much of the boy remained. But he, like his father, would never display weakness to me. He enjoyed what you call the bravado of his life. I'm sure, in some way, he even enjoyed the death of a soldier, because of the romance the idea held for him."

An involuntary shiver passed through Lin. She hugged her shoulders.

"Are you cold?" Peter asked.

She shook her head. "Too much talk of death and those already dead, I think."

He stepped toward her, placing his hands on her arms. "I'm sorry," he said. "It wasn't very considerate of me. And not very good use of our time together."

Lin moved closer to him and looked up into his face. Her body seemed to soften under his touch; her eyes appeared to grow deeper. "There should be no time together," she said. "It is wrong for me to even want this time together."

"I know," Peter said. "It's something I should not have asked for, but I didn't know how not to."

She rested her head against his chest. "It will cause problems for you if it is discovered."

"I'm more concerned about the effect on you." He ran his hand along her back, allowing his fingers to enjoy the brocade of the silk *ao dai*.

"The reactions would not be equal, Peter," Lin whispered. "If my father-in-law were to find out, I would simply cease to exist in his eyes. You he would have to punish, or he would lose face."

He stepped back and took her face in his hands, allowing her hair to run between his fingers. "I'm not afraid of his punishment. But I'll do everything I can to see he doesn't find out you were here. The manager is a friend, and arrangements were made to ensure privacy."

"There is no difficulty with accidental meetings on the street." She was smiling at him as she spoke.

"I want more than that with you," he said. "Much more."

"I know," she whispered.

She raised herself to him, and he took her gently in his arms. Their mouths met, tongues playing wildly against each other, and her body seemed to explode with its sheer want of his own.

"The Vietnamese are very passionate people," she whispered, kissing his cheek and neck. "And I am very Vietnamese."

He lifted her, carrying her inside and into the bedroom, smiling to himself that he had seen this done before in too many Hollywood romances. But that was exactly what he felt, an amusing but wonderful sense of romance that made no sense at all.

He placed her on the wide, soft bed and bent toward her, kissing her face and neck. The scent of her perfume, a trace of lotus, faint yet strong, seemed to ooze from her pores in the excitement of the moment—a scent favored by wealthy oriental women because it intensified with their excitement, and in turn excited in itself.

"Make love to me for hours, Peter," she whispered.

"There won't be enough hours, Lin. There won't ever be enough." His voice was slightly hoarse, Lin, the scent of lotus, reaching him more each moment.

Slowly, patiently, he undressed her, taking time to embrace each part of her that became exposed. When they were both naked they moved against each other, bodies oiled by the heat, the scent of lotus growing greater with each moment, adding to his internal frenzy, making it difficult for him to forestall what he wanted more than the breath in his lungs at that moment. Her body shuddered with her first orgasm as his mouth moved slowly along it, lingering along her breasts, then moving to her hips and across her belly, pausing greedily along her inner thigh, his tongue picking up the scent of her now, filling his head with it, until he felt a gentle yet pleasant throbbing in his temples.

Her body, long and lithe, yet full with a delicate, graceful ampleness, responded in a series of rapid orgasms, each seeming to reach higher than the one before, each threatening exhaustion, before recapturing her passion and lifting her again.

Finally, she intertwined her hands in his hair, lifting him away from her and urging him up. "Come to me. Now. Please." Her voice was rough and pleading, and when he entered her she seemed to explode in a wild, rhythmic acrobatic dance, delighting in her own movements, joining her pleasure with his.

When his own climax could no longer be withheld, Peter felt his own passion and pleasure flowing through him in a rush longer and more shattering than he had ever known. Even when it was over his body continued to move with a will of its own, thrusting against her, into her, grasping for the warmth that seemed to rise from her, the scent of lotus overpowering.

He lay next to her, stroking her, drained, exhausted, eyes closed, mind continuing to enjoy the pleasure that had just ended.

Minutes passed. He could not be sure how many. She rose up next to him on an elbow; her hair hung down, surrounding her face like a dark, silken veil. He felt a smile come to his lips, matching her own.

"You've had your way with me," she said, her eyes glistening with mischief. "Now it is my turn to have my way with you."

And so it began again.

Chapter 32

"I think he should be told who this woman is." Molly Bloom sat in the dark-paneled study, her eyes intense, her delicate body appearing almost childlike in the oversized leather chair.

Buonaparte Sartene steepled his fingers before his face. He looked at the woman thoughtfully. "We have no reason to believe that she knows Pierre's identity. Or that she has had any recent contact with Francesco. Your people still follow her? And Pierre?"

Molly nodded, but the note of concern remained in her eyes. "My man, Po, remains close to him. I have kept it that way, even though Luc is now also nearby." She shook her head. "But there are times when we cannot be close enough. There are times when they are alone, Buonaparte. The other night, in his hotel room, for example."

Auguste spoke from the corner of the sofa. "Philippe had someone in the kitchen then. There was protection."

Molly twisted in her seat. "There is also the question of Cao's possible contact with Francesco."

"There has been no evidence of that," Buonaparte said.

"No, but I can't be certain." Molly sat forward in her chair. "Cao wields a great deal of authority in Saigon, and Francesco's protection, when he is in the south, comes from her people. We have a servant working in Colonel Duc's home, and we know whenever she leaves the house and are able to follow her. But when she goes to Cholon we have no way of knowing who she meets. There are dozens of entrances to the tunnels there."

Sartene remained silent, then looked across to Auguste.

"Molly may be right, Buonaparte," he said, responding to

331

Sartene's questioning stare. "We know she met with Francesco almost two years ago. It was something we learned by chance, and we have watched her since then without success. But she could be meeting with him even now."

Sartene picked up a letter opener and balanced it between the index fingers of each hand. "This woman is still the closest contact we have to Francesco's movements in the south." He placed the letter opener back on the desk. "We did not anticipate this *friendship* between Pierre and this woman. But perhaps it is a good thing."

"It is also more dangerous for Pierre," Molly said. "There's Colonel Duc. If he knew of their friendship . . ." She let her words fall away.

"And there's the woman herself. She is very clever and very committed. I don't doubt she finds him attractive, but her reasons for being with him go beyond that."

Sartene steepled his fingers again and nodded. "Yes, Duc could present a problem, and we will have to watch for that." He sat up straight and leaned forward. "But we know this woman has had other 'friendships' with both American and Vietnamese intelligence people. It is the way she stays one step ahead of them. And our pompous little colonel always remained ignorant of it all. As far as the woman is concerned, you are right. She is very clever. But that's another reason why Pierre should not know who she is. If his reaction to her suddenly changed, she might be even more dangerous." He drew a deep breath. "But the main threat is still Francesco. And the only way we can protect Pierre is by drawing Francesco out in the open. Pierre understands that. I only hope we can do it before Pierre becomes too involved in this heroin plan of his, and draws in others who are just as dangerous to him as Francesco."

Molly was silent for several moments, as if trying to decide if she should say more. Buonaparte noticed the hesitation and smiled. "Is there something else?"

"Yes. But I'm not sure it's something you want to hear."

Sartene lowered his voice to a soothing near-whisper. "Molly, we have worked together for several years now, and I know you always speak for the good of our group."

"This is more about your own good, Buonaparte. And Pierre's." She hesitated again, then set her jaw firmly and continued. "Have you considered that he might become emotionally involved with this woman, and then learn later that certain facts were kept from him?"

Sartene stared at the top of his desk, then back at Molly. "I understand what you are saying. I can only hope he will understand."

Sartene stood, walked around his desk and took Molly's hand. "You are going back to Saigon this afternoon?"

"Yes." Molly stood and looked into Buonaparte's eyes. She had a great affection for the man, and she knew he was gambling with things that meant more to him than his own life.

"Watch Pierre closely, Molly," Sartene said. "We are entering a very dangerous time."

Auguste walked Molly down the long hallway, noting that she seemed distant, worried. He took her arm, stopping her.

"You are bothered by Buonaparte's decision," he said.

She nodded. "There are too many risks in it," she said.

"Yes. But we always knew they would exist. And so does Pierre."

Molly's green eyes flashed at him. "He doesn't know them all."

"The woman worries you." He paused, then smiled at her. "Perhaps you too find our Pierre attractive?" he teased.

Molly looked at him sharply, then laughed. "I've told you, Auguste, I'm saving myself for you." She looked away. "Besides, I doubt Pierre would be interested in a woman who operates my type of business."

Auguste took her arm again. "We have raised him to be a better man than that."

It was late afternoon when his "chance" meeting with Lin took place amid the flower stalls of Nguyen Hue Street. She was wearing a simple western dress, a pale blue that seemed almost silver in the muted sunlight. She smiled discreetly as he approached, but in her eyes he could see the same desire he felt spreading through his body.

"What a lovely surprise, Ba Lin," he said in Vietnamese. "And such a wonderful afternoon to be among the flowers here."

"It is also good to see you, captain," she said, her voice demure and proper for any who might overhear. "I seem to be getting carried away with my purchases and I was beginning to wonder who I would find to help me."

"Ah, Ba Lin. We Americans are here to assist in any way we can. President Johnson has ordered it."

She stepped closer and whispered in English, "Don't you get carried away, captain. If I ask for the assistance I truly want, we shall be the scandal of Saigon."

"That's a lovely thought," he whispered back. "But I'm afraid all these flowers would wilt if that happened."

She spun quickly, moving like a dancer, and gathered up her flowers, then turned and thrust half of them into his arms. "I must get them home before they do wilt," she said, repressing a smile. "I have left my car on Cach Mang. Will you help me with them until there?" She had begun speaking Vietnamese again, and the high, lilting tonal quality of the words seemed almost songlike.

"Of course I will, Ba Lin."

They walked slowly along the crowded street, turned into still another and continued on until they could see JFK Square in the distance. Peter could not help but notice that no angry eyes met them as they walked. There was no open displeasure at seeing this American with a Vietnamese woman. Not this woman, anyway.

Peter glanced at Lin, and immediately understood. The dignity and self-possession with which she walked defied any accusation, no matter how veiled. Her obvious social stature and presence were such that her chance meeting with an American officer and his willingness to help her simply could not be questioned.

As they approached JFK Square the crowds thinned. Peter shifted the shotgun-weighted briefcase that he now carried at all times. Doing so, his grip loosened on the flowers and several fell to the ground.

"Clumsy occidental oaf," Lin whispered.

"I thought the term was 'big hairy American,' " he whispered back.

"That too," she said. "But such lovely soft blond hair."

He stooped to pick up the fallen flowers. A quick movement caught his eye, a man turning away. Too abruptly, he thought. It was a swarthy man, with graying hair. Innocent enough. But still turning away too quickly. He picked up the flowers and they started again. At the center of JFK Square he paused and looked around, playing the tourist. The man had continued to move behind them, and now had turned away again, this time to light a cigarette.

"Where are your bodyguards?" he asked.

"Only my driver is with me today, and I had him wait at the car."

Concern began to mount in Peter. Not for himself, but for Lin. He did not want trouble with her there. He would make an excuse, get her to her car, then find the man and learn his reason for following them.

She pouted openly when he told her he had to return to the office.

"But this evening, for dinner?" he said.

"It's the dessert I really want," she said. "But I can't. I have a commitment I cannot escape."

"Then tomorrow," he said. "Dinner at the hotel?"

She smiled. "And dessert," she added. "Definitely dessert."

When her car was off, he doubled back quickly, cutting down a nearby alley that ran into a short side street, then led to another alley that would place him behind anyone following. When he emerged back on Cach Mang there were few people, none that were European. He doubled back through the two alleys and returned to where Lin's car had been parked. Again no one. His imagination? Probably. But he doubted it.

The disappearance of the swarthy man, and the prospect of being alone that evening—without Lin—depressed Peter, and he decided he would treat himself to dinner at the Room of a Thousand Mirrors.

When he entered the elaborate old mansion shortly after seven o'clock, Molly Bloom was descending the elegant stairway that led to both her office and the exotic playroom above. She was dressed in a shimmering silk *ao dai* of emerald green, and even from a distance it seemed to accentuate the green in her eyes.

She nodded to Peter as she moved down the stairs, the look knowing and slightly deprecating in an amused way. He watched her descend, again struck by her fragile yet enduring beauty. Immediately he began to compare her with Lin. She was more beautiful, more exotic, he could not deny it. Yet there was something about her, something hard and . . . no, not hard, he corrected himself. It was an inner toughness he found difficult to accept in a beautiful woman. He immediately wondered why. It was something he found agreeable in men.

She approached him with an effortless grace that seemed to contradict everything else about her. She stopped beside him, lifted a cigarette set in a gold holder, and smiled. "Do you have a light, Peter?" she asked.

He reached into his pocket and withdrew a battered Zippo lighter, opened its large, clumsy top and lit her cigarette.

She blew the smoke to one side, then turned back to him. Her eyes were amused again.

"Tell me, Peter. You don't smoke, so why do you carry that decrepit old lighter?"

"To light cigarettes for ladies who ask unnecessary questions," he said, damned if he would allow her to use her extraordinary verbal combativeness on him tonight. He softened his words with a smile that matched her own. "Actually it was my father's. He carried it through his war, and gave it to me as sort of a good-luck charm when I left home. He told me it would come in handy. Now it has, hasn't it?"

She ignored him, glancing instead into the crowded bar to her left. "Did you come for dinner, Peter?" She watched him nod, then looked toward the front door. "It's going to be crowded and noisy tonight. I was going out to the My Canh floating restaurant in Cholon. Would you care to join me?"

"Only if you'll be my guest this time," he said.

Molly allowed her eyes to close slightly, as if recalling their last dinner together. It forced Peter to remember it as well. "Of course," she said, smiling as if reading his mind. "My car is out front."

Molly Bloom's car was a large black Citroën, with a glassed and curtained divider between the driver's compartment and the rear passenger area. The interior was a deep-green velour, soft and sensual, with seats that seemed to engulf and caress the body.

Molly turned toward him, her eyes picking up the color of the seats, as the car moved slowly into the evening traffic. "We have not seen you in several days, Peter. But from what I hear, you have been very busy."

"From what you hear?" Peter questioned.

"Ah, Saigon is such a gossipy place, especially among your military. And intelligence officers seem to gossip more about each other than anyone else."

"I doubt that, Molly. But I don't at all doubt your ability to keep watch on all of us."

"Only those who interest me, Peter," she said. She was still turned toward him, and her eyes glistened with the pleasure of her own word game.

"And I interest you?" he asked. "Even though I lack subtlety?"

She leaned back, then looked out the window at the passing traffic. "There are many levels of subtlety in this region, Peter. And people can live here for years without ever understanding them all." She turned back to him, her face soft, contemplative. "It's part of the culture. People mask their feelings, their beliefs, even what they are. And they expect others to do the same. So they watch carefully, trying to see what is behind the mask of another. It's a necessary practice here, one you should try to cultivate yourself." She looked away again, wishing she could say more, knowing it would be an offense to Buonaparte to do so.

Peter studied her for a moment. It was the first time he had seen her veneer soften. He thought of the man who had seemed to follow him. Perhaps his own mask was now being probed. He wondered if Francesco would be foolish enough to do that himself, or if he would use someone else.

He smiled. "Is that why you keep such a close watch on people? To see behind the masks?" He watched her eyes, looking for some reaction.

"Perhaps," she said. Her voice was flip, her eyes offered nothing. "Or perhaps I'm just an inquisitive woman."

An hour later, seated on the deck of the floating restaurant, Peter felt relaxed for the first time since leaving Lin. He stared across at Molly as she studied the menu, wondering what it was about her that made him uneasy, unsure of himself.

"You look suddenly very thoughtful, Peter," Molly said from across the table.

"I was thinking about masks." He looked about him. The Japanese lanterns hanging along the deck of the restaurant gave it a magical quality, the gently flowing river, its filth hidden by the night, a sense of peace. "A friend told me recently that everything in this country, in this war, is an illusion. That it appears to be one thing, but is actually another. This place seems almost a caricature of that idea." He motioned with his head toward the river. "It looks so beautiful. Dark and peaceful. Moving by very gently. But I've seen it in daylight and it's filthy." He gestured again toward the shore. "From here, with the linen tablecloths and the hanging lanterns, everything seems in perfect harmony. We don't see the filthy docks, or the squalid fishing boats. And certainly not the pitiful tin shacks beyond them, and the thousands of people there. Hungry, frightened, desperate, hopeful. Mostly hopeful, I think, because other people promise them hope where there is none. Not for them, anyway. Perhaps for their children, or their grandchildren, but probably not even for them.''

Molly leaned back and studied the thoughtfulness behind his eyes. ''That's true of most of the world, Peter. The people who control it see to that. It gives them someone to dominate.''

Peter rubbed his chin with his thumb and index finger. ''You sound like a man I knew as a child. He believed that every man, every family, was its own country, and he rejected all others that were imposed on him.''

''He sounds like a very wise man.''

''I learned a great deal from him as a child.''

''Not as an adult?''

''I'm afraid I missed that opportunity.''

The waitress, a young Vietnamese dressed in a black vest and pants, came to their table. She bowed quickly and offered a seemingly shy *''Chao, dai uy''* to Peter, then turned and offered a silent bow to Molly. ''You want order now?'' she asked in English.

Peter smiled, nodded, and spoke to her in Vietnamese, praising her English.

''Toi hic tieng Anh,'' she said, giggling—I am studying English. ''But not so good yet,'' she added in English.

''Much better than most Americans speak your language,'' Peter said.

Molly noted the gentle tone of Peter's voice, the genuineness of his interest. It reminded her of Buonaparte, the way he dealt with those who served him.

For appetizers they ordered a dish of *tom kho*, dried shrimp, and *ca thu*, dried fish, each garnished with *ot*, crimson hot peppers, that required an ample amount of wine. As a main course Peter chose *thit kho nuoc dua*, pork in coconut milk, served on a bed of herb-flavored rice. Molly ordered *cha gio*, paper-thin rice-flour dough wrapped around onions, mushrooms, beaten egg, bean threads and meat, then deep-fried and dipped in a spicy *nuoc nam* sauce before eating.

After a dessert of French cheese and durians, a foul-smelling but delicious fruit, they ordered brandy and a strong Vietnamese tea.

"That was a delicious meal, Molly," Peter said. "Every bit as good as your own kitchen."

"How did you enjoy the durians?" she asked. "The people of the region believe they have the ability to restore sexual vigor."

He laughed softly. "Is that why you recommended them?"

"Purely informational, Peter."

He leaned forward, watching her eyes again. "Every time I see you, I seem to find something different," he said. "How many masks does Molly Bloom wear?"

Her eyes remained steady, serious. "It's as your friend said, Peter. No one here is what he appears to be. You should remember that with whomever you deal."

"I shall," Peter said. "Starting with you."

It was ten o'clock when Francesco made his way along the dank narrow tunnel to the carved-out chamber that Lin used as a command post. He was tired and sweating when he dropped into the canvas folding chair across the table from where Lin sat.

"How long have you been here now? In Southeast Asia," Lin asked.

"Since '46, my dear Cao," Francesco said, mopping his face and neck with a handkerchief.

"Twenty years and still you haven't gotten used to the climate. How sad for you."

Francesco's eyes flashed across the desk with a mixture of amusement and dislike. "It would help if I didn't have to come through a tunnel practically on my hands and knees," he said.

"The tunnels are high enough. You could almost stand, my friend," Lin said.

"Yes, that would amuse you, wouldn't it? It would also amuse the little pets you keep tied in those holes in the ceiling."

"Are you afraid of little snakes?" Lin asked.

"Only when they bite me before I can bite them," he said.

Hand to mouth, Lin began to laugh softly. "You must admit it's a wonderful defense system. Especially against those wonderfully tall Americans."

"Corsicans are tall too," Francesco said.

"Yes, aren't they?" Lin's eyes hardened, but only for a moment. "But you're a valuable Corsican."

"You asked to see me," Francesco said, impatient now with Lin's gamesmanship. "I assume it's about the heroin. It will be here at the end of the month. Delivery direct into Tan Son Nhut.''

"That is good. But it is not why I asked you to meet me." Lin leaned forward, forearms on the table, eyes hard again. "Why are you following Captain Bently? You did follow us after we left the Street of Flowers."

Francesco smiled, but only with his mouth. "Ahh, I should have known you would discover me."

"That's the price one pays for incompetence," Lin said. "Now why?"

"Because Peter Bently is not Peter Bently. His name is Pierre Sartene. He is Buonaparte Sartene's grandson. And that makes him very dangerous to me. I intend to kill him, Cao."

"No, you won't, Francesco. He is being cultivated, and he is going to be very useful to me. If you're right, and this nonsense about his being Sartene's grandson is true, he is going to be even more useful than I hoped. Now tell me how you developed this fairy tale."

"It's no fairy tale, my dear Cao." Francesco sneered. "Like you, I have friends who have access to information. When you told me his name I became concerned. I contacted my friends and saw what they call his personnel file. His supposed father, Matthew Bently, was an OSS officer who served here. I knew the man. He worked with us in Vientiane. He had no wife. No son. But when I saw Pierre, I knew. I have not seen him since he was twelve. But still I knew. Buonaparte sent him away. I always thought to friends in Corsica or France. But now I know he sent him with Bently. There's no question. And there's no question I have to kill him. If I don't, he will kill me."

"Why should he kill you, of all people?"

"Don't be stupid, Cao. You know I killed his father. He's Corsican. He won't rest until he kills me."

Lin placed a cigarette in a carved bone cigarette holder and lit it. "Don't be a fool. Peter Bently is no more Corsican than I am. He's a spoiled American who's more concerned about his sex life than anything else. And what if he does find out? What is he going to do, chase you to Hanoi?"

"He's not bound by the agreement with Buonaparte. And blood is blood. You don't know about these things."

Lin jumped up behind the desk. "Don't presume to tell me what I don't know. What I know is that you won't touch him until I'm finished with him. He's an intelligence officer, one of those fools who are supposed to find me. And I have arranged to know what he is doing. Not only does that protect me, but it also gives me a chance to learn things valuable to us.''

"Like his work with the man Morris, who worked with that other American fool, Constantini?"

"That too," Lin said. "And anything else he may talk about. And believe me, he will talk. So you won't touch him. Not until I'm finished with him."

"That I don't promise," Francesco said.

"Then promise yourself this. Whatever you do to him, I will have done to you."

Francesco glared across the chamber. He was being asked to risk his life, to let the Sartenes satisfy their vendetta. It was something he would never agree to. He forced a smile. "As you wish, Cao," he said.

Chapter 33

The last light of day hung over the city, a mixture of muted, changing colors that seemed to linger in the sky just beyond the old colonial rooftops, as though unwilling to surrender to the night. The side streets were empty now, most people taking time for an evening meal, moments with their families, or in the case of the Americans, another long lonely night in a Saigon bar.

The day had been brutally hot, and now, for the first time, the temperature had dropped below a hundred. The empty, heat-soaked streets appeared to breathe a sigh of relief that was almost audible. Or so it seemed to Peter as he walked them, trying to offer some exercise to legs that had been stuffed behind a desk all day. Even in the lingering heat the effort was worthwhile.

Three weeks had passed—strange weeks for Peter; a mixture of lethargy and excitement in combination such as he had never known. The work side had been dreary, marked by only one success, an NVA major, furnished by his grandfather's Muu tribesmen, and met with an excitement bordering on the ridiculous from Wallace. But the colonel had recovered quickly, and had demanded progress on the Cao investigation. That, in itself also approached the absurd. Reports came in several times a week identifying Cao as everything from a waiter in a Plantation Road restaurant to an outcast monk living near the Saigon docks. Peter had gradually become convinced that Cao was either several VC agents using a common code name, or an imaginary figure created by the Viet Cong to keep his unit running in time-wasting circles.

But it wasn't only Cao. His private search for Francesco'

drug connections had gone nowhere either. The time he had spent in the seedier drug-related bars had produced nothing.

He had been to every corner of the sprawling Tan Son Nhut base; had checked every plane arriving from Vientiane under the guise of watching for infiltrating VC. If heroin was there, and if more was coming in, he simply could not find it. And if it was going out, he had no idea how, or who was arranging the shipments. There simply was no "long silver train," none that he could locate at any rate. And the other comic-book phrase, the "green vulture," was even more elusive.

He had talked to Morris about it and the newsman had simply shaken his head, insisting it sounded like typical GI lingo, hackneyed and trite enough to be real, but nothing he had ever heard. He had sought an outside source, someone who knew Francesco Canterina, but had found the man was a mystery to all his normal contacts. Peter only hoped that the questions would draw Francesco out.

He tried to push it all from his mind, something he had been attempting daily with greater frequency. Each day seemed to blend into one endless flow of khaki-clad bodies moving in and out of the base, offering nothing, proving nothing, just existing within a framework of endless orders and procedures. God, the military was boring, he realized. He had escaped it all these years by his constant training. But once that training was over, once there was no more that was new to learn, it all became one endless banality that would threaten the patience of the retarded. It was no wonder career military people looked forward to war. At least then there was a purpose to it all. Unless you were stationed with the headquarters paper merchants, as he was now.

His mouth had grown dry, either from the heat or the realization of how bored he was. At least the evenings had been good. Increasingly, over the past weeks, he had found himself waiting for his work day to end so life could begin. What a dreary fact it was. It made him understand the bars of Tu Do Street, the sad young prostitutes in their garish costumes, crudely offering minutes of release in comical pidgin English. Suddenly they were desirable, even to men who would find them otherwise repulsive.

But he had escaped that. The one saving grace of the entire experience. His evenings had been filled with Lin. Or on days when she could not excuse herself from Duc's home, evenings at the Room of a Thousand Mirrors, and occasional conversations with Molly. He thought of Molly, walking now. Odd, he told

himself. Without question the most physically beautiful woman
he had ever known. And without question the most disquieting.
She was far too interested in him, and the interest seemed
professional.

His thoughts turned to his grandfather. The man amazed him,
even more so now than as a child. It was as though a network of
wires went out from the massive old house, reaching everywhere,
then reporting back on all that occurred. Even unimportant things.
Yet nothing, no small bit of information, seemed unimportant to
the old man. He was like a senile old pack rat. But instead of old
newspapers and bits of string, he collected old happenings,
scraps of conversation, and Lord knew what else.

This last time their talk had strayed away from anything to do
with his grandfather's business, or his own. Only when he was
about to leave did the old man again caution him to move
carefully, to reconsider the method of his search for Francesco.
Their talk had been just that. Talk. They spoke in more detail of
his life in America. His growing up with a lack of interest in
team sports—anything involving chasing a ball, as he liked to
put it—preferring activities that challenged him alone against an
obstacle or a solitary individual. It had seemed to please his
grandfather, to be something he could understand. He had also
understood the loneliness Peter had felt growing up. Unsure of
his place throughout his teenage years. Remembering past places
he could not return to, nor speak about to others for fear of
discovery.

But it had been like that for his grandfather as well. In that
one way, at least, they were alike. He had questioned him more
intently about his youth in Corsica, the days in Marseille and
later in the resistance. He had not asked about the years in Laos,
knowing somehow he should not. The only exception had been
questions about his father, more details about his death. And he
had regretted those questions almost as soon as they were asked,
seeing the strain and the suffering they caused the old man. He
had wondered if his life made any sense at all without the life of
his grandfather, and the past that it involved. And if that was
true, how then could his life, so different, relate to the life of
that old man sitting on the banks of the Mekong?

Peter ran his tongue over his lips, realizing his mouth was
even drier now. Too much work, all this thinking, he told
himself. Ahead, at the corner joining Nguyen Hue Street, an
old peasant woman was beginning to gather her merchandise

together after another day of street sales. Among the items were small boxes of dried fruit, which he thought might ease his growing thirst.

The old woman looked up at him expectantly as he stopped before her. She was small and thin and had a conical hat pushed back on her head, and as he squatted down to face her, the shape of the hat reminded him of the halos in religious paintings, a golden circle that surrounded her wrinkled, flat-featured head.

"A bag of fruit, Grandmother?" he suggested in Vietnamese. "But just a small bag that I can eat while walking."

His clear use of the language, properly spoken, appeared to amuse her. He could see it behind her eyes. She turned her head to the side and spit red betel nut juice into the gutter beside her.

The old woman extended the small bag of fruit. "Fifty P," she said, her voice high and broken with age.

The price was so outrageous Peter was forced to laugh. He looked at the old woman sternly, noting the small gold cross she wore around her neck.

Peter reached into his pocket and took out the money, pulling it back as she reached for it.

"Will you go to church tonight, Grandmother?" he asked.

The old woman gave him a strange look, then shrugged her shoulders.

"I want you to go to church tonight, Grandmother. And I want you to confess to the priest that you robbed a poor young American."

He held out the bill to her and she took it, raising it to her mouth to hide her giggling. "One cannot steal from the rich," she said. "One can only take back what they have already taken from the poor."

Peter widened his eyes. "Grandmother," he said, feigning shock. "You talk like a communist. Are you VC, Grandmother?"

The old woman tittered again, hiding her mouth from him.

"You must confess that also," Peter said. "The Pope, in Rome, he does not approve of communists."

"The Pope in Rome is rich also," she said, again giggling over her outrageous sacrilege.

Peter walked on, leaving the old woman behind. He shifted his shotgun-filled briefcase up under his left arm, so he could hold the bag of fruit in his left hand and pick into it with his right. He could hear the old woman's laughter fading behind

him. Another name to add to the list of Cao suspects, he told
himself.

He had begun his list of suspects last week, partly to amuse
himself, partly to relieve his own frustration with his search for
Francesco. He had told Molly that he had placed her chief
barman on the list; Lin, that her maid was his primary suspect.
Even Morris' pet hate, a notorious Australian journalist who
reported the war from Hanoi and specialized in fictitious American germ-warfare stories.

Peter walked on, telling himself none of it mattered. Every
army throughout history had believed its side just, its enemies
evil. He thought of his grandfather's words, used to describe, but
not explain, his own life. *I never tried to understand what was
good and what was evil in the world,* he had said. *I only tried to
understand how the world was, and what I had to do to survive
in it.*

Peter smiled to himself. Not a very ethical view. Certainly not
according to Judeo-Christian standards.

He continued along the sidewalk of this street, which had
become his favorite in Saigon. The Street of Flowers. Now
nothing but empty stalls, only the fragrance of the cut flowers
left behind.

Peter popped a piece of fruit into his mouth and sauntered on.
He would not see Lin tonight, and had not yet decided if he
would go to the Room of a Thousand Mirrors. Perhaps a quiet
meal alone and early sack time. It would be a novelty, certainly,
he decided.

Across the street, about twenty-five yards ahead, a casually
dressed Vietnamese stepped from a doorway, looking in his
direction. He continued up the street at a pace slower than
Peter's. Alerted to the man's interest, Peter forced his senses to
sharpen. There was movement behind as well. He paused at a
flower stand, picking up a wilted stem. Directly behind him,
thirty yards away, two more Vietnamese kept pace, eyes on him.
Across the street from them, a fourth, and twenty yards behind
him, a fifth, who might or might not be part of the others.

Peter felt his stomach tighten; his mouth began to turn dry
again. Perhaps his imagination was playing games with him, but
every instinct in his body told him otherwise. Slowly he shifted
the bag of fruit to his right hand and allowed the briefcase to
drop down into his left. The 12-gauge over-and-under shotgun
was loaded with double-O buck magnum shells that would drop

a bear in its tracks at close range. But there were only two shells, and four or five men. He thought of the .25 caliber Colt automatic in his wallet holster, knowing he would have to get to it before they moved. Once they did, if they were good, if they were professionals, there would not be time. He erased all thought of the men's being amateurs. They had moved in on him without his knowing. They had bracketed him. Stupid, stupid, stupid, he told himself. Out walking in a deserted area alone.

He started back up the street, studying the stalls. The man ahead began to cross the street. No time left to pick a place, he told himself. At the next break in the stalls, he ducked and darted between them, circling one and coming up in the narrow opening between the next two. The stalls were close together, with solid facing on the front and sides. Enough for concealment, but certainly not adequate cover against incoming rounds. He came to a crouching stop between the two stands and reached for the Colt in his hip pocket. Footsteps pounded the sidewalk, coming in both directions. Before the automatic was free the first man, the one who had been ahead of him, came to a sliding halt between the stalls. Peter grabbed the briefcase, shoving his right hand into the side opening, hitting the safety and the trigger simultaneously with his thumb and index finger. The briefcase erupted just as the Vietnamese leveled his own automatic pistol. His chest absorbed the full impact of the double-O pellets. The body of the small man lifted into the air and hurtled back, almost like someone pulled up and away by a parachute harness. Then he dropped raglike into the street, the white shirt now red with blood.

Peter spun, moving mechanically now, and circled the stall, heading back toward the point where he had first ducked between the stalls. The sound of running feet passed him on the sidewalk, followed by gunfire into the position he had just left. He stood quietly, leveled the briefcase and fired again, the pellets smashing into the head of another Vietnamese, shredding pieces from it like chunks of melon.

Dropping the briefcase, Peter yanked the Colt from the holster and threw himself forward, rolling as he hit the ground, then scrambling forward when he reached another opening between the stalls. Around his head the stall began to explode as bullets sent chips of wood slicing through the air. Peter darted forward, rose up and fired at one of the two remaining men. The shot missed and the automatic jammed, breech open. Frantically Peter pulled at the slide, trying to clear the pistol. A short, squat Vietnamese wearing a black T-shirt jumped into the opening between the stands and swung his weapon toward Peter, then suddenly flew from view as if pulled by some unseen hand. The fourth man appeared, his eyes darting to Peter, then back along the street. Peter did not wait. He jumped forward and stuck out with his foot, a sharp, crisp blow that caught the man on the side of the head and sent him flying into the street. More footsteps. He spun. The fifth man, pistol in hand, was four feet from him. Peter was off balance and lashed out wildly with his foot, but the man sidestepped the blow easily and a returning kick caught Peter in the ribs, just below the heart, driving the breath from his body and sending him crashing back into a stall, then spinning to the ground. The Colt clattered into the street. Before his eyes could clear, the man straddled him, pressing the silencer-equipped pistol into his throat.

Through a slight haze Peter could see the hard eyes of the oriental, the flat emotionless face. The tip of the silencer pressed harder against his throat. He waited, watching the man's face, anticipating the impact of the bullet. The oriental's face broke into a slow smile.

"You were never very good, Pierre. I always said you were too big and too slow. But you did take three of them, and that's not too bad."

Peter's brain fogged, then quickly cleared. The pistol came away from his throat. "Luc?" he said, his voice still trembling with the expectation of death that continued to course through his body.

Luc stood and held out his hand. "Get up, my brother. You look foolish."

Peter took his hand and allowed Luc to pull him to his feet. "But how . . . why?"

"Your grandfather. But now we must leave here."

A groan came from behind him, and Luc spun with the quickness of an animal, setting himself to fire as he did. The man in the street, the one Peter had kicked, twisted in pain. Luc leveled the pistol.

"No," Peter said, touching his arm. "I want to find out who sent him."

"I'll do it," Luc said. He moved to the man and jammed the gun against his nose. "If you wish to live you will say quickly who sent you," he snapped at the man.

Peter heard the name and felt his stomach tighten.

Luc raised the pistol and stood. "Go tell him that he has offended my kaitong, Buonaparte Sartene. Also tell him further offense will mean his death and the death of all his family."

Luc turned away and grabbed Peter's arm. His eyes were colder than any Peter had ever seen. "Come, we must get out of here before the police arrive. Get your briefcase, while I get your pistol." Peter obeyed without question, stopping only to glance at the dead.

Back at his hotel, Peter held a glass of Scotch in his hand, and noticed a slight tremor. He placed the glass on the table before him, looked at his hand, then at Luc.

"I don't remember it shaking while it all was going on, but it sure as hell hasn't stopped since it ended."

Luc watched as Peter drew a long breath. "Sometimes the hand has more sense than the man. It knows when it should be afraid."

Peter continued to look at his hand. "It also never killed anyone before. I think it's surprised at how easy it was."

"Killing a man who tries to kill you is never difficult, my brother," Luc said.

Peter raised his eyes to Luc. "And harder when the man isn't trying to kill you?"

"That depends on the man," Luc said.

"And you've done both for my grandfather." There was no question in Peter's voice.

"I've done both. The reasons and for whom are unimportant." Luc said.

Peter stood, walked toward the terrace, then turned back to face Luc. "That man," he said. "You told him to tell the one who sent him that a further offense would mean his death and the death of his family. Will he believe the message?"

"He will believe it," Luc said. A slight smile formed on his lips. "Colonel Duc will believe it more than if it came from the president of your adopted country. Sometimes presidents forget offenses."

"But my grandfather doesn't."

"That is why he is seldom offended."

Peter walked back to his chair and sat heavily. He paused a moment. "By the way, Luc. The third man, the one who fell after my weapon jammed. Was that you?"

"It was an easy shot," Luc said.

"Well, thank you for the easy shot. I thought I'd bought the farm right there." Peter laughed. "I was sure of it after you knocked me on my ass and shoved your pistol in my throat."

Luc's face screwed up. "Bought the farm?" he asked.

"A military expression. American," Peter said. "It means dying."

"A strange language," Luc said, shaking his head. "So different from English."

Peter poured more Scotch into his glass, and took a long swallow. "I suppose I owe you an explanation about why those men came for me," he said.

Luc grinned at Peter, reminding him of their days together as boys. "I know why Colonel Duc sent them, Pierre," he said. "I've been close to you for several weeks now."

"Grandpère again," Peter said.

Luc shrugged. "He worries. He is old now, and he worries."

Peter's eyes blinked. "Luc, when you warned about harm coming to his family. That did not include Ba Lin, did it?"

"She is no longer a member of his family," Luc said. "She no longer exists for Duc."

Peter rubbed his face, his jaw tightening. "That's right," he said. "She has a price to pay too. I wish I could do something about that."

"You can do whatever you want," Luc said.

Peter stared across at him, confused. "I don't understand."

"Duc will be visited soon for a . . ." He searched for the correct word. "For a discussion of this matter. I think he will do whatever he is asked."

"Even as far as Lin is concerned?"

"If you want, that could be a condition."

"Well, of course I want it," Peter said.

"Then it will be done," Luc said.

Peter stood and paced again, still not understanding all he was hearing. He turned quickly back to Luc. "Who's going to meet the colonel?" he asked.

Luc's eyes widened. "Why, your grandfather, of course. When we telephoned him about this he told me he would be here in the morning."

His grandfather had not mentioned that when they had subsequently spoken. He had only wanted assurances that Peter had not been hurt. It made Peter wonder why the information had been withheld.

Peter poured another Scotch both for himself and for Luc. They were getting a little drunk, but right now that was exactly what he wanted. He stared across at the smaller Mua tribesman, who had been such a major part of his life as a boy and who now had probably saved his life as a man.

"I'm troubled by something, Brother Two," he said.

Luc stared across at him, waiting for him to elaborate.

"It seems there are many things I'm not being told. You being so close all these weeks. Grandpère meeting with Duc tomorrow. I understand the reasons for them, but I don't understand why I wasn't told. It makes me wonder about the things I was told about." He stared at Luc. "Will you talk to me about these things?"

Luc shifted uncomfortably in his seat. His eyes were slightly glazed now, and he seemed to be having trouble deciding what to say. "It is difficult for me, my brother. I owe your grandfather much. He has trusted me. He has cared for my family and my people. I do not want to be disloyal to him."

Peter raised his hands. "I understand that. But as brothers we have a loyalty to each other as well. Do this for me. Let me ask you things. If you can, answer me. If you feel an answer would be an offense to Grandpère, I will understand your refusal."

Luc took a long drink of Scotch and shrugged his nervous agreement. "I think I'm getting a little drunk." He laughed softly. "But how can I refuse the man I helped put snakes under Auguste's bed?"

Peter joined the laughter, and wondered if they could ever recapture those boyhood days together. Luc was far different from the boy he remembered. Tougher, colder. But so are you, he told himself.

"How long have you worked for Grandpère?" Peter asked, hoping to start slowly, to move around his concerns.

"From the time I was twelve, right after you left. I worked as a houseboy. Then later, at seventeen, I began carrying messages to the Meo at Xieng Prabang, taking merchandise from one place to another. When I was twenty-one, my father died of an illness. He was your grandfather's bodyguard then, and your grandfather honored me by giving me the job of my father."

"I'm sorry about your father," Peter said. "I was never told, or I would have written you."

"Death is only a passing from one place to another," Luc
said. "Your grandfather made it easier for those of us left behind
by caring for my mother, and by allowing me to assume the
honor he had given to my father."

"And you're still his bodyguard?"

Luc nodded, then took another long sip of Scotch.

"Does his business involve that much danger?"

Luc inclined his head to one side. "Southeast Asia is a
dangerous place, as you are finding out."

"That's not what I meant, Luc."

Luc remained silent, then smiled. He waved his hands toward
the windows and French doors that led to the terrace. "You
noticed the windows in this room," he said at length. "The glass
is bulletproof. Let us just say that your grandfather's life still involves difficult people."

"Like those who deal in opium?" Peter asked.

"The Meo who grow it are under his protection. Sometimes
this offends people."

"They grow it for him?" There was a hard edge to Peter's
voice, and he realized he must control it.

"They grow it for themselves, Pierre. It is the only way they
can live."

"You mean he takes none of it for himself, none of the
profit?"

"I don't know, Pierre. I know they do other services for him,
and that he protects them from the government, keeps others from
cheating them, lowering prices. You must understand, Pierre,
nothing happens in Laos that your grandfather does not know
about. Some things he chooses to involve himself in, others he
does not. Very few people know what those things are, and I am
not one of those people. It is part of his strength, Pierre, that few
people know a great deal about him."

"He told me he was involved in the opium trade years ago,
helped establish it as it now exists. He also told me he was no
longer involved."

"It is as I said, Pierre. People think he controls many things,
and he allows them to think so. I don't believe he would lie to
you. I think he might choose not to tell you something, but I do
not think he would lie. Your grandfather is not ashamed of his
life, and he asks forgiveness of no man, not even you."

"You sound like Benito and Auguste," Peter said. "I think
you're more Corsican than I am." He stood and paced the room

for several moments, then turned and spoke softly to Luc. "There are people, in other parts of the world, who think dealing in opium is not an honorable thing."

"I cannot speak for other parts of the world, my brother. Here it is a way of life. The tribesmen grow what people will pay them to grow. If they do not, they do not live. It has been so for centuries. I know it is abused by some people, and so does your grandfather. It is why it is banned among the Meo."

"What do you mean, banned? Tell me about that." Peter returned to his chair and sat on its edge, leaning toward Luc.

"Years ago, an arrangement was made with the headman of the Meo who your grandfather protects. The headmen were angered because some of their people were smoking opium, and the production from their fields had become very low. Your grandfather told them to make it an offense to use opium. Now if a tribesman does so, he is banished from his village and can never return. All his property, even his wives, is taken from him, and he is driven away. If it is found he has given opium to others, the punishment is even greater."

"What happens then?"

"He is beheaded."

Luc had spoken the final words as though referring to the death of some insect. Peter sat stunned by the coldness of it, the unreality it registered in his mind. "On my grandfather's orders?" he finally said.

"There are no orders, Pierre. It is the law among the tribes."

Peter stared off at a far wall. "I don't know, Luc. It's difficult for me to grasp, to understand."

Luc leaned forward in his chair. His eyes were heavily glazed now, and there was a slight slur in his voice. "What is there to understand, Brother Two? Your grandfather protects these people, just as he has protected you."

Peter snorted, the Scotch having its effect on him as well. "I guess I have caused him a bit of a problem, haven't I?"

"I too once caused him embarrassment," Luc said.

Peter perked up. "Really? What did you do?"

Luc shook his head. "It is something I have great difficulty speaking of, my brother."

"Come on, Luc," Peter urged. "Brother to brother."

Luc twisted in his seat, stared at the floor for a moment, then looked across at Peter, a sick expression on his face. "I will tell you as much as I can. The rest gives me too much shame." He paused as if not knowing where to begin.

Peter leaned closer to him. "Well?" he said.

Luc twisted again, then began to blurt out the story. "Several years ago, I was sent here to Saigon to help Philippe handle a business matter for your grandfather. I became distracted and the business matter went badly. Your grandfather was cheated out of much money."

"Grandpère, cheated?" Peter began to laugh. "I didn't think that was supposed to happen to Corsicans. Who cheated him?"

"That I cannot tell you, my brother. It is still too painful for me." Luc's eyes were riveted on the floor again, and he took a long drink of Scotch without looking up.

"So what happened?" Peter asked.

"Your grandfather had to come here and correct matters. I was much dishonored."

"But he obviously forgave you," Peter said. He hesitated, wondering if he should pursue the matter further. "What was the distraction you spoke of?" he finally asked.

Luc looked at him sheepishly. "A woman," he said. "It's a weakness I have."

Peter began to laugh softly. "It's a weakness I obviously share with you, my brother. It seems that Grandpère has had to get us both out of bedroom problems."

"For me it was even worse," Luc said.

"How so?" Peter asked.

"I never even got to a bedroom," Luc said.

Chapter 34

Philippe Francisci's house was small and unassuming, hidden behind a high wall in the same section of the city where Colonel Duc lived. Sitting in the small living room, overburdened with heavy old European funishings, Duc felt fully out of his element. Even his crisply pressed uniform carried none of the weight and power he normally felt when he wore it. He had been summoned and he had come, and much to his chagrin, he knew he had no choice in the decision.

On the table before Duc was a tray of croissants and a silver service of coffee. Across the table sat Buonaparte Sartene, his mood rigid behind a soft voice. They spoke in French, further emphasizing—to Duc—that he was without power within these walls.

"If I had known I would have come to you before acting," Duc said. "There was no way for me to know." Beneath his uniform he could feel the perspiration run along his chest and back.

Buonaparte nodded, his face showing none of the age and weariness it had in recent years—almost as though he had been revitalized by the renewed activity. "I understand that, my friend. I am sorry that your men had to die. It was unfortunate." He paused a moment, as if remembering something. "How was that handled with the authorities?" he asked.

"Like most deaths here," Duc said. "It was blamed on the Viet Cong."

"Good," Sartene said. "I wish it could have been avoided. We all see too much death. But I'm sure you understand, I will not allow my grandson to be harmed."

355

Duc twisted in his seat and offered a rare smile. It reflected both his discomfort and his fear. "It was a matter of face, Don Sartene. I know you understand these things. Like my people, you Corsicans have great pride in your honor."

Buonaparte nodded. "I understand that and accept it, my friend." His voice was so soft that Duc was forced to watch his lips to be sure he caught every word, every nuance. "And I promise you will be compensated by me, for this unfortunate attack on your honor." He gestured widely with his hands. "The boy is young, and foolish, and he lacked understanding in the matter. I assure you of that." He looked Duc straight in the eyes. "I assure you of one other thing. Whatever befalls Pierre while he is here, in your country—large or small—the same will befall you."

"But I can't—" Duc was cut off by Sartene's raised hand.

"You will make it your business to see he is not harmed. If it is something outside your own doing you will warn me of it . . ." He paused, then added, ". . . before it happens."

"I will try," Duc said.

"There are two other matters," Buonaparte said, watching the apprehension in Duc's eyes deepen. "The woman, the wife of your late son. She must not be disgraced."

"But . . ." Duc's objections were stilled again by Sartene's hand.

Buonaparte smiled. "Think about it, my friend. To disgrace her would require a reason in the minds of your peers. If they learned of it, they would ask why the man had not been punished. Then your honor would truly be in jeopardy."

Duc nodded his head, unable to raise his eyes from the table. The humiliation was too great. But resisting the request could bring even greater harm. If not death, then certainly disclosure of past and present business activities that were better left hidden. "You said two things more," Duc finally said, still staring at the table.

"I want to know who told you of this matter between Pierre and Ba Lin."

Duc looked up, mildly confused. "I thought you knew," he said. "It was one of your countrymen. A man who once worked for you."

Sartene's eyes hardened. He knew the name before Duc spoke it.

*   *   *

Francesco smiled across the chamber at Lin. "If I had been involved, my dear Cao, or if I had chosen the men who were, Pierre Sartene would not have had breakfast this morning."

Lin's eyes were cold, unmoved. "I don't believe you. It would be typical of you to find someone else to do your work for you. That old man in Vientiane still makes you tremble in your sleep."

"You push too far, Cao," Francesco said, his voice gravelly and dry.

"No, *you* push too far. I warned you not to interfere. You think because Faydang protects you in the north, he protects you here as well. I assure you no such protection exists. If I find out you were involved, you'll wish Buonaparte Sartene had found you years ago."

Francesco's jaw tightened as he watched Lin extend a cigarette holder and then flick the ash with a long, polished fingernail. "I don't like being threatened," he said.

"Is that what bothers you, Francesco? I don't think so. You just don't like being threatened by a woman." Lin stared coldly across the chamber. Then she smiled.

Chapter 35

"I can understand your sending Luc to back me up. And, given what happened, I certainly can't object. But why didn't you tell me?"

Buonaparte Sartene sat on the hotel terrace, shaded from the late-afternoon heat by a canvas canopy. He allowed his eyes to drift from his grandson, out toward the distant harbor. "Sometimes it's better not to know, Pierre. Sometimes when there is protection a man depends on it and becomes careless. It has happened to me that way."

Peter was forced to recall his own carelessness. His foolish walk into a deserted area; his obviously indiscreet meetings with Lin. He felt a mild rebuke in his grandfather's words, and he knew it was deserved.

Buonaparte smiled at him. "Anyway, we know now Francesco is watching. The hound sniffs for the fox."

"How do we know that?" Peter asked.

"Colonel Duc," Sartene said. "It was Francesco who told him of your friendship with his daughter-in-law. It's a coward's ploy that fits this man. A surrogate assassin."

Peter's thoughts raced back three weeks to the dark, swarthy man behind him in the street. He shook his head. "Three weeks ago I thought there was someone following me. I was with Lin at the time. But I dismissed it when it didn't happen again. And, to be honest, I never thought Francesco would dare get so close."

"Remember Papa Guerini's words about the fox and the hound," Sartene said. He thought about the possibilities. "If it was he," he said at length, "he did it well. Even Luc did not see him. But then, Luc was also a child when Francesco . . ."

358

He allowed his words to fall away. He sat up abruptly. "But there is good in all this too."

Peter laughed softly. "Really," he said. "Please tell me what it is."

Sartene looked at him sternly. "There is no need to pursue this heroin matter now, and expose yourself to others. Now we can lure him out. But still you must be careful. He may try again to use others." Sartene thought of the woman, and for a moment he was tempted to tell his grandson. He decided against it. If Lin knew Francesco had gone to Duc, had betrayed her, then their relationship, if it still existed, had ended. If not, then Francesco might try to use her again. He decided he would watch for a while. He was uncomfortable with the decision. But if Pierre was told and his attitude toward her changed, they could lose this advantage. And it would also place Pierre in danger.

"Have you seen the woman since this happened?" Sartene asked.

Peter shook his head. "I thought it best not to, that it might be dangerous for her."

"That has been taken care of," Sartene said.

"Then I'll see her soon." He reached out and touched his grandfather's hand. "Thank you, Grandpère," he said.

Robert Brody ran a hand through his soft, sandy hair. It was the only thing soft about him. Years of work in the CIA had kept his body tough; the past three in Viet Nam had toughened his mind as well.

He stared again at the letter that had been hand-delivered to the embassy. Francesco Canterina had been the best double agent he had ever worked. Now, he had to admit, the man had again proved his worth, even at the price they paid for that service. He reached for the telephone on his desk, glancing at the mandatory photograph of the president that hung from his office wall. As he dialed the number he wondered how far up the ladder it all went. How much was known about the deals made, the corruption tolerated, even condoned, just to keep the intelligence machinery operating. The voice that came over the receiver was sharp and correct, shaking away the thoughts.

"Colonel Wallace, please. This is Bob Brody at the embassy."

A minute later, Wallace's voice crackled into the phone. "Well, well. How's my favorite civilian spook? How's the old dong hangin'?"

Brody grimaced, his square, craggy face wrinkled with disgust. There were Tu Do Street pimps he liked better than Wallace. "Flaccid," he said. "But I think I have something that will put life in yours."

"What's her name?"

"Not a her, a him," Brody said, enjoying the conversation for the first time. He was well aware of the military's paranoia about homosexuals.

"Don't play that game," Wallace snapped. "Not even for God and country."

"How about for Cao?" Brody listened to the silence that met his words; he was smiling, something unusual for him.

"What do you have on that slippery little fuck?" Wallace asked at length.

"One of my best people just offered to hand him to us. How does that sound?" Brody asked.

Wallace grunted. "We get five offers like that a week. So far we've been offered everybody from Colonel Ky to Uncle Ho himself."

"You haven't been offered anything from my man," Brody said.

"You think he's that good?"

"How good is a white man who lives in Hanoi and works for us?"

"And them too, I suppose," Wallace snorted.

"Of course," Brody snapped. "Listen, if you don't want it, I'll take it myself."

"I didn't say I didn't want it," Wallace said quickly. He paused, thinking over the embarrassing possibility of someone else finding Cao. "He can really ID Cao for us?" he finally asked.

"Nope. But he can do better than that. He can take us to Cao's hole and guarantee he'll be there when we arrive."

Wallace let out a low whistle. "And you think he can deliver?"

"All I can say is that he's never bullshitted me yet," Brody said. "I take it you're interested?"

Wallace began to chuckle. "Indeed," he said.

"Good. Then be at the safehouse at nineteen hundred hours sharp."

"I'll be there, and I'll bring the officer assigned to the hunt," Wallace said.

"No dice," Brody snapped. "My man says it's me, him and the top military man in charge. Anybody else and he walks."

Wallace grunted again. "Okay, you got it. Fussy sonofabitch, isn't he?"

Chapter 36

They lay next to each other. Peter gently stroked Lin's naked back and arms, feeling the tears roll from her cheeks into the hollow of his shoulder.

"There's nothing to weep about," he whispered.

"It's my fault, Peter," she said hoarsely. "And because of it you could be dead."

"But I'm not dead," he said. "And if you'll stop crying I'll show you how alive I am."

She slapped weakly at his chest. "How can you think of sex after all this?" she demanded.

He began to laugh softly. "I don't know," he said. "I guess having a beautiful naked woman lying in my arms might have something to do with it."

She sniffled, then ran her index finger under her nose. "It's perverse," she said.

"Didn't you know? All big hairy Americans are perverse. That's what you Vietnamese ladies love about us."

"Is not," she said. "We're after your money, not your bodies. We are a poor people, exploited by rich American industrialists."

He felt her shoulder shaking, and tilted his head to the side to look at her. "You're laughing," he said, reaching across her body to slap her buttocks. "I almost die and you lie there laughing."

She stretched herself and kissed him, filling his nostrils with the rich smell of lotus, her smell. "Don't talk about it," she said. "Make love to me. Make me forget it all."

He turned toward her, then pulled her closer. He kissed her eyes, her nose, chin and neck. He would kiss every part of her, he told himself. Starting at one end and working slowly to the other, then returning again. Thinking of her, he felt himself grow and harden. The soft skin, the scent of her.

They made love slowly, gently, taking time with each other, for each other, moving individually, then as one. He felt closer to her, more so now than before, almost as though he had earned the closeness, paid a price for something worth having. When he entered her this time, her body seemed to engulf him, pull him down within her and hold him.

He heard her breath coming in gasps, grabbing for air as he was grabbing for her; the smell of her, the sweet pungent scent, overpowering him, arousing him even more than the friction of their bodies rubbing together.

She groaned, her voice out of control, as she reached toward her final climax, and inside her he could feel the spasms of her muscles, pulling on him, pulling him down deeper within her, making him wish he could remain there, never leave, simply lose himself within her and hide there safe, happy, secure in his feelings.

"Oh, Peter," she groaned. "I never want to leave you. Stay close to me, Peter. Stay close, stay close."

"I will," he whispered, his voice hoarse, weak from exertion. Now it was right, he told himself, and it would remain so. Nothing would change it. Nothing.

"This is the big one. I feel it." Wallace paced behind his desk, the morning sunlight streaming past his bulky frame and flooding the office. "Now we catch the bastard, once and for all." He slammed a fist into his hand for emphasis.

"What time are we going in, sir?" Peter asked, though not really caring. It would be one more misadventure, he was sure. There might be VC, probably would be in a tunnel beneath Cholon. But not Cao.

"Seventeen hundred hours, on the dot," Wallace said. "CIA's man says the little fuck has a meet set then. We'll catch 'em right in his fucking nest trying to hatch some eggs."

Peter repressed a smile over Wallace's abundant use of metaphors. "How large a force do you plan on, sir?"

Wallace took a cigar from his desk, bit off the end and spat it out on the floor to his left. He lit the cigar, taking time to be sure it was drawing properly. "Well, that's the sticky part. Our source claims the fewer the better. Actually suggested two or three men. Well, I told him where to fuck off, you can be sure. He claims the tunnel is narrow and long and carries noise too well. Says too many men would give too much warning and botch the whole show.''

Peter eyed him, waiting for the number.

''I figure five or six, no more than a squad, anyway. You'll run it underground, I'll coordinate things above.''

''Not too many troops, colonel,'' Peter finally said.

''We're only after one gook,'' Wallace snapped.

''I just don't want to get down there and find out he invited company today,'' Peter said.

''I'm assured that won't be the case,'' Wallace snapped.

But you won't be there to find out, will you? Peter mused.

''How about escape routes? For Cao, I mean?'' Peter asked.

''There are probably dozens,'' Wallace admitted. ''All those damned tunnels are connected. All we can do aboveground is fan out and watch for anybody running. And back you people up, of course.''

Let's hope, Peter thought.

''What about defenses, colonel?'' Peter asked. ''Any possibility of booby traps?''

''According to CIA's man, the tunnel was not mined when he was down there.''

''He saw Cao?'' Peter asked. ''Actually met him?''

Wallace squinted at Peter, having sensed the incredulity in his voice, then puffed on his cigar again. ''Not exactly. But he's met the person Cao's meeting with. Look.'' He jabbed out with the cigar. ''This isn't my source, but he's supposed to be damned good. SOB's a white man who actually lives in Hanoi. Works for them too, of course. But that's still no easy trick.''

Peter's body stiffened. Francesco, complete with another surrogate. And planned so he could not walk away from the trap. He was beginning to feel a grudging admiration for the bastard.

''I'd like to talk to this guy before we go in, sir,'' Peter said.

''Can't do,'' Wallace said. ''His terms, not mine.''

A thin smile formed on Peter's lips, a sharp contrast to the knot he felt growing in his stomach. There would not even be time to reach out for his grandfather or Luc.

Molly Bloom sat behind her oversized desk, staring into the expressionless face of her man, Po.

''Are you sure? There's no question at all?'' she asked.

Po only nodded, his eyes blank, his face a stolid, square mass.

She sat back in her chair, placed the cigarette holder to her mouth and drew heavily. Exhaling, she tapped her fingernails on the desk. "Young Pierre is moving onto dangerous ground," she said. "But I don't think he's done it by himself. This has a Corsican smell to it, don't you think?"

Po did not answer, knowing it was neither necessary nor required.

Her eyes, gleaming green anger, turned back to him. "You stay especially near to our friend today," she said. "If he gets close, come to me immediately. He may already know, but I doubt it. But if he gets close enough he will. Then, I'm afraid, our friend's life will have lost its value."

Cholon was Saigon's twin city, inhabited primarily by the area's Chinese population and virtually run by both the VC and the Binh Xuyen river pirates. It was the VC who dominated the political side, a fact attested to by the repeated night skirmishes fought on its streets, and the inability of the military to flush them from the labyrinth of tunnels. The Binh Xuyen controlled the economic side, which consisted of the endless number of opium dens that flourished in the area, along with equal amounts of outright banditry, smuggling and extortion. The Binh Xuyen had been given status by the French SDECE, to combat the Viet Cong. But the Americans and their South Vietnamese counterparts had not treated the Binh Xuyen well, often driving them to the sanctuary of the Rung Sat Swamp at the mouth of the Saigon River. Rung Sat, translated as the Forest of the Assassins, had become their sanctuary in times of oppression, while Cholon had remained their economic stronghold. And the Viet Cong had become their friends. The ARVN government and the Americans now had no one they could turn to for help in Cholon. It was, in effect, the capital city of the Viet Cong.

Peter looked up from the map at the four MPs dressed in combat gear. "We're going to have to move to the tunnel entrance and just go," he said. "As soon as we're spotted the word will go out and the whole district will know."

"Like a white cop in Harlem," a black MP agreed.

Peter ignored him. "So we'll hit the hole and go. Wallace and Brody will fan the troops out after we're in." He paused to look at one of the men. "You don't seem worried. Why?"

" 'Cause I've done this number before, and we're not gonna

find anything," he said. "Unless you call some old VC delivery boy something."

You may be surprised this time, Peter thought.

The tunnel entrance was in the rear of a gutted building in a onetime shopping district that had been ravaged by street fighting. Outside, it looked like something that had been plucked from the slum of an American city, battered and beaten, waiting for an excuse to fall down. Inside, it had the smell of an open sewer, and from the crumbling staircase Peter could make out the shining eyes of rats watching him and the four men who trailed behind.

"Reminds me of home," one MP whispered. "Only it smells worse. Some Chinaman's been eating Szechwan and dumping in here."

Peter glanced over his shoulder, silencing him. He could see the tension in the men's eyes, and understood the need for humor to relieve it. But now he needed quiet. He raised his hand. "The tunnel entrance should be in the wall in the next room," he said. He looked at the older MP, who had insisted they would find nothing. "You wanna go first, I guess?"

"Fuck that, sir," the man snapped. "You wear the silver railroad tracks on your collar and get the extra money. I follow you."

"That's what I like. Loyal troops." He looked the other three men over. They too carried M-16 rifles and sidearms, none of which would be very useful in the tunnel. It would be necessary to make their way down and hit the inner chamber in force. Any noise before then and whoever was there would have a deadly field of fire.

"Okay. We move in quietly. *Quietly*. We stay close to the walls, one man to one side, the next to the other, fairly close interval. We have to hit that chamber with force. Watch the ground for wires. We've been told there are no booby traps. But that could be bullshit, so keep your eyes open. The tunnel's supposed to be lit with Coleman lanterns every thirty yards or so, but they don't give off much light down there, so keep watch."

One hundred yards down from the building. Po had watched the assault team enter. It was time for him to move, to reach Molly and warn her that what she feared was about to happen. He would have to move slowly, he knew. Other Americans would be in the area waiting for the raiding party to flush the quarry. But there was time. Molly would be ready to act when necessary, if necessary. He hoped secretly the whole matter would be resolved before then.

Sweating stone stairs led down into the tunnel. It was cooler than aboveground, and the smell of rot and feces was less noticeable, overcome now by the claustrophobic closeness of the narrow, dark tunnel. One hundred feet ahead a Coleman lantern sent out a dim, eerie glow, as most of the light was swallowed by the black earthen walls. At the bottom of the stairs the five men crouched and listened. Far ahead, muted voices could barely be heard. The raiding party formed their intervals and began inching along the walls. Across the narrow tunnel Peter could barely make out silhouettes of his men. He moved slowly, back against the wall, his left foot forward, his boot gently feeling for any wires that lay in his path. They passed the first lantern crouching low to the ground to avoid detection by anyone farther along the tunnel. Peter could feel the sweat rolling down his arms and neck, and beneath his steel helmet. One false sound, one grenade tossed among them . . . he forced the thought from his mind. Damn you, Francesco, he told himself. Past the first light they moved in almost complete darkness again. Above, water dripped from the ceiling, filtering down from somewhere above. He looked toward the water. Something dark seemed to sway just beyond it. A wire, some warning system. Peter reached out for it, then stiffened and pulled back.

"Snake," he whispered, pointing at the twisting body.

Peter's mind clouded with the word, not wanting to realize there would be more. It was a VC trick he had learned of during his training. His body tensed; his eyes scanned the tunnel in front of them.

He pulled one man closer, speaking so softly he could barely hear the words himself. "Snakes tied to wire inside holes. Drop down and strike. Have to stay low. Low. Two-step Charlie. Pass it back."

A cold shiver ran along Peter's neck. He crouched lower, twisting his head to see above. The shadow twisted slowly, then seemed to pull back, then lower itself. It hung two feet down into the tunnel. The tunnel was less than six feet high, and already they had been forced to crouch slightly while moving through. His mind told him he would have walked face first into the venomous mouth of the krait. Francesco had killed his father with a snake, and now had nearly repeated that success.

His body tensed at the idea; the perspiration intensified and again his body loosed an uncontrolled shiver. He looked back at the other men and gestured with his hand for them to drop to all fours. He jabbed a finger toward the tunnel ceiling, then back to the floor, making sure each understood. The krait, he knew, though sluggish and shy, could inject a poison five times the lethal dose for a man. If abused or oppressed it would strike out again and again.

They moved forward again, struggling to stay near the wall, to grab what cover they could if incoming fire erupted. Ahead the voices seemed to rise in intensity, then fall into hushed whispers again, the words, the sound itself, swallowed by the long, dark, oppressive walls.

They passed another lantern, the dull yellow glow itself swallowed within moments, the black again reasserting itself after a few yards. Peter could feel the sweat pouring from his body now, moving in rivulets along his arms, legs, chest and back, dripping from his face onto the hard-packed dirt. He paused to wipe his palms on his combat fatigues, feeling the wet from within already pressing out through the lightweight fabric. The M-16 seemed to slide in his hand as he grasped it again and struggled forward. They were only fifty feet from the chamber now, and the voices had become more steady, but were still indistinguishable. He inched along the ground, the others close behind, each moving so silently he had to glance over his shoulder to be sure they were still there. A figure was silhouetted in the opening to the chamber, someone small, slender, gesturing with one hand. The figure turned, then seemed to jump straight back, and Peter heard the shouted words echo toward him in flat tonal Vietnamese, translating immediately in his mind. "They come, they come."

He jumped up, still crouching, still aware of the danger above, leveled his rifle toward the chamber, and opened fire in a rotating arc that sprayed a steady stream into the chamber entrance ahead.

"Move," Peter snapped to the others, rushing forward, keeping the automatic fire spewing out in short bursts. A shadow moved into the tunnel entrance, then spun away. The chamber was twenty feet ahead now, and he could hear the clatter of movement, the frantic rush to escape. "Move, they're running," he shouted, the report of his rifle devouring his words, the flash from the barrel obscuring his vision.

He hit the chamber entrance and flattened against the tunnel

wall. Bodies darted away, toward another tunnel. He raised the
rifle, then hesitated. A flash of long black hair, and a green *ao
dai* flashed in and out of view. He caught himself and fired
again. Too late. They were in the tunnel.

He jumped forward into the chamber. Two Vietnamese lay on
the ground, one dead, the other badly wounded in the chest,
squirming in pain. The others rushed in behind.

"You three," he snapped at the MPs, "the other tunnel. Get
them."

He stood over the wounded man, his rifle leveled at his head.
One of the MPs knelt beside him and patted him down for
weapons. He looked back at Peter. "Cao?" he asked, not believing the words himself.

Peter shook his head, his voice coming in short, fast gasps. He
continued to stare at the man, the blood bubbling from several
wounds in his chest. He was small, almost like a young boy,
only his face showed the age of a mature man, and now it was
distorted in pain.

"Cao," the MP snapped at the man, repeating it again when it
produced no response. The man lifted his head and tried to spit,
then fell back shuddering, his sallow face turning a pale gray.

"He's just about had it," the MP said.

Peter nodded and turned away. Behind him he saw a field
table and chair. There were papers on the table, and next to
them, in an ashtray, a cigarette burned in a carved bone cigarette
holder. Slowly, he walked to the desk, and looked through the
papers. The odor hit him almost at once, overcoming even the
smell of cordite and powder that filled the chamber. Peter fell
back into the chair behind the table and stared at the burning
cigarette.

"He's dead," the MP said. "Sir? I said, this one's dead."

Peter nodded. "He's not Cao," Peter said.

The MP looked up at him. Peter's eyes were dazed, distant.
"How you know that?" he asked.

Peter stared past him, and shook his head.

It was 2100 when he returned to his hotel room. Lin was not
there. There was a note on the table. *I waited, darling, then went
home. Call me.* He dropped the note on the table, walked to the
bathroom, stripping off his fatigues as he went, and climbed into
the shower. The water beat down on his head, his face turned

away from the force of the flow. Peter's eyes were blank, staring at the wall of the shower.

He dressed slowly, then placed the wallet holster in his pocket. Outside the hotel he caught a Bluebird taxi, handing the driver the excessive fee asked, then settling back, watching the city flash past the window.

The gate was unlocked when he arrived, the guards gone. He opened the front door of the house and entered. She was seated in the large, formal room where they had first met. She saw him and stood abruptly, dressed in a white blouse and western slacks.

"Peter," she said. She stood, staring at him, her expression uncertain.

"Where are the guards?" he asked.

"My father-in-law is out of town," Lin said. "The guards went with him. They no longer protect the house when he is away."

"You left the door open," he said.

"I had hoped you might come," she said. She smiled softly, then turned and sat back on the large sofa. "You look tired," she added.

He stood staring at her. The empty room was cavernous, and her voice seemed to echo off the walls. "Why didn't you tell me?" he asked.

He watched her hand slip down along the side of the sofa cushion, then withdraw, holding a small blue-black automatic. She smiled at him. "That would have been very foolish of me, wouldn't it?"

He shifted his weight, and watched as she raised the gun with his movement. She stood and smiled again.

"How do you know I didn't bring people with me?" he asked.

She laughed, her voice harsh and cold. "You were followed from the tunnel, Peter dear. If you had come in force I would have been warned and you would not have found me here."

"Perhaps I've already told others about you," he said.

She laughed again. "Then they would have made you come in force."

Peter stared at the carpet, then back into her eyes. "It wouldn't have mattered to me if you told me," he said. "Things could have been arranged."

"Oh, I'm sure they could. Your grandfather no doubt would have hidden me away." She walked in a slow semicircle, keep-

that he addressed to a cousin living in Augsburg. Those
that have been published contain many asterisks indicating that deletions have been made. No editor or biogra-
pher would print the whole, feeling that they would distress
the reader and leave a stain on the image of the composer.
These letters to his *Bäsle*—a German and Austrian di-
minutive for a female cousin—are one long chain of
childish indecencies. Not long ago the famous author
Stefan Zweig bought them and printed them, with a pref-
ace, for private distribution among his friends. I have
not seen the brochure, but a musicologist I know, living
in Princeton, gave me a detailed account of them and of
Stefan Zweig's introduction. They are what is called
scatological—having to do with the bodily functions. As
I was told, there is little or no allusion to sexual matters;
it is all 'bathroom humor.' They were written in the composer's middle and late teens. How can one explain that
Mozart who matured so early could descend to such in-
fantile jokes? The beautiful letters to his father, preparing
him for the news of his mother's death in Paris, were
written not long after. Herr Zweig points out that Mozart
never had a normal boyhood. Before he was ten he was
composing and performing music all day and far into the
night. His father was exhibiting him about Europe as a
wonderchild. You remember that he climbed on Queen
Marie Antoinette's lap. I have not only been a teacher at
a boys' school, I have earned my living during the sum-
mers as counselor at camps and have had to sleep in the
same tent with seven to ten urchins. Boys pass through a
phase when all these 'forbidden' matters obsess them—
are excruciatingly funny and exciting and, of course,
alarming. Girls are supposed to be given to giggling, but
I assure you boys between nine and twelve will giggle
for an entire half hour if some little physiological accident takes place. They give vent to the anxiety surrounding
the tabu by sharing it in the herd. But Mozart—if I may
put it figuratively—never played baseball in a corner lot,
never went swimming on a boy scout picnic." I paused.
"Your son Charles was cut off from his contemporaries
and all this perfectly natural childish adjustment to our
bodily nature was driven underground; and has festered."

She addressed me coldly, "My son Charles has never
uttered a vulgar word."

"Mrs. Fenwick, that's the point!"

"How do you know that something is *festering?*" There was a sneer in her voice. She was a very nice woman, but she was being hard pushed.

"By sheer accident. In our conversation he gave me pretty hard treatment. He asked me if I had belonged to certain extremely exclusive clubs at Yale, and when I told him I had not, he tried to humiliate me. But I have had a lot of experience. I was beginning to think very well of him; but I could see that he was living in a capsule of anxiety."

She put her hands over her face. After a moment she regained possession of herself and said in a low voice, "Go on, please!" I told her about the musical club in Baltimore and about Charles's crimson reaction. I told her that I had made an experiment and invented a club for card-players which offered rewards for the best and the worst players called the "Tops and Bottoms Club" and aroused the same response. I explained that for boys —and probably girls—during certain years the English language was a mine-field sown with explosives—words, dynamite; I said that I had remembered Mozart's letters and that Charles had been brought up by tutors, cut off from the life usually led by boys. I said that he was entrapped in a stage of development which he should have outgrown years before and that the trap was *fear* and that what she had called his snobbery was his escape into a world where no shattering word was ever spoken. I had asked him if he would like to work with me in the hope of bringing his French up to Eloise's standard—and that he had agreed to it and that before he left he had shaken my hand and had looked me in the eye.

"Mrs. Fenwick, you may remember Macbeth's question to the doctor concerning Lady Macbeth's sleepwalking: 'Canst thou not . . . Cleanse the stuffed bosom of that perilous stuff Which weighs upon the heart?' "

With no tone of reproach she said, "But you are not a doctor, Mr. North."

"No. What Charles needs is a friend with a certain experience in these matters. You cannot be sure that doctors are also potential friends."

"You believe that Mozart outgrew his 'childishness'?"

"No. No man does. He outgrows most of his anxiety;

the rest he turns into laughter. I doubt that Charles even knows what it is to smile."

"Oh, Mr. North, I've hated every word you've said. But I think I can see that you are probably right. Will you accept Charles as a pupil?"

"I must make a proviso. You must discuss it with Mr. Fenwick and Father Walsh. I could teach French syntax to Tom, Dick, and Harry, but now that I have glimpsed Charles's predicament, I cannot spend all those hours without trying to help. I couldn't teach algebra—as a friend of mine was paid to do—to a girl who was suffering from religious mania; she was secretly wearing hair shirts and sticking nails into her body. I want your permission to do a thing that I would not dream of doing without your permission. I want to introduce into each lesson a 'dynamite word' or two. If I had a student whose mind and heart was absorbed by birds, I would build French lessons about ostriches and starlings. Learning takes wings when it's related to what's passing in the student's inner life. Charles's inner life is related to a despairing effort to grow up into a man's world. His snobbery is related to this knot inside him. He won't realize it, but my lessons would be based on these fantasies of his—of social grandeur and of the frightening world of the tabu."

She had shut her eyes, but opened them again—"Excuse me; what is it you want?"

"A message from you that I may occasionally use low earthy images in the lessons. I want you to trust me not to resort to the prurient and the salacious. I don't know Charles. He may develop an antagonism against me and report to you and to Father Walsh that I have a vulgar mind. You probably know that ailing patients *also* cling to their illnesses."

She rose. "Mr. North, this has been a painful conversation for me. I must think it all over. You will hear from me. . . . Good morning."

She extended her hand tentatively. I bowed saying, "If you agree to my proviso, I can meet Charles in the blue tea room behind us for an hour every Monday, Wednesday, and Friday at eight-thirty."

She looked about confusedly for her children, but Eloise and Charles had been watching us and hurried forward. Eloise said, "Mr. North won't let me come to the classes,

too; but I forgive him." Then she turned and threw her
arms about her brother's stomach and said, "I'm so glad
Charles is going to have them."

Charles, standing very straight above his sister's shining
head, said, "*Au revoir, monsieur le professeur!*"

Mrs. Fenwick stared at her children with a distraught
air and said, "Are you ready to go to the car, dears?"
and led them off.

Two days later Eloise approached me at the close of
the last of my tennis classes and gave me a note from
her mother. I put it in my pocket.

"Aren't you going to read it?"

"I'll wait. Just now I'd rather take you to the La Forge
Tea Rooms for a hot fudge sundae. . . . Do you think this
note engages me or dismisses me?"

Eloise possessed three forms of laughter. I now heard
the long low dove's ripple. "I shan't tell you," she said,
having told me. This morning she had chosen to be all of
twenty years old but she slipped her hand into mine—in
full view of Bellevue Avenue, astonishing the horses,
shocking the old ladies in their electric phaetons, and very
definitely opening the summer season.

"Oh, Mr. North, is this really our last class? Shall I
never see you again?"

We didn't sit on high stools before the soda fountain,
as once before, but at a table in the furthest corner. "I
was hoping that you'd have a hot fudge sundae with me
every Friday morning at exactly this time—just when I
finish my lesson with Charles." We were hungry after all
that exercise and addressed ourselves to our sundaes with
a will.

"You really do know a lot about what's been going on,
don't you, Eloise?"

"Well, no one ever tells a young girl anything so she
has to be a sort of witch. She has to learn to read people's
thoughts, doesn't she? When I was a little girl I used to
listen at doors, but I don't do that any more. . . . You
grown-ups suddenly woke up about Charles. You saw that
he was all caught in . . . a sort of spider's web; he was
afraid of everything. You must have told Mother something that made her frightened, too. Did you tell her to
ask Father Walsh to dinner?" I remained silent. "He came
to dinner last night and after dinner Charles and I were

sent upstairs, and they went into the library and had a council of war. And way upstairs, miles away, we could hear Father Walsh laughing. Mother's voice sounded as though she had been crying, but Father Walsh kept shouting with laughter.—Please read the letter, Mr. North—not to *me*, of course, but to yourself."

I read: *"Dear Mr. North, Reverend Father says to tell you that when he was young he had worked as a counselor at a boys' camp, too. He told me to tell you to go ahead —that he'll do the praying and you do the work. It comforts me to think of the lady in Salzburg for whom things worked out so well. Sincerely, Millicent Fenwick."*

I don't believe in unnecessarily hiding things from young people. "Eloise, read the letter, but don't ask me to explain it to you yet."

She read it. "Thank you," she said and thought a moment. "Wasn't Beethoven born in Salzburg? We went there when I was about ten and visited his house."

"Is it hard to be a witch, Eloise? I mean: does it make living harder?"

"No! It keeps you so busy. You have to be on your toes. . . . It keeps you from growing stale."

"Oh, is that one of your worries?"

"Well, isn't it everybody's?"

"Not when you're around.—Eloise, I always like to ask my young friends what they've been reading lately. And you?"

"Well, I've been reading the *Encyclopaedia Britannica* —I discovered it when I wanted to read about Héloïse and Abelard. Then I read about George Eliot and Jane Austen and Florence Nightingale."

"Some day turn to *B* and read about Bishop Berkeley, who lived in Newport, and go and visit his house. Turn to *M* and read about Mozart, who was born in Salzburg."

She slapped her hand to her mouth. "Oh, how boring it must be for you to talk to young girls who are so ignorant!"

I burst out laughing. "Let me be the judge of that, Eloise. Please go on about the *Encyclopaedia*."

"For another reason I read about Buddhism and glaciers and lots of other things."

"Forgive me asking so many questions, but why do you read about Buddhism and glaciers?"

She blushed a little, glancing at me shyly. "So that I'll have something to talk about at table. When Papa and Mama give luncheons or dinner parties Charles and I eat upstairs. When relatives or old friends are invited we are invited, too; but Charles *never* comes to table if anyone else is there—except Father Walsh, of course. When just the four of us are there he comes to table but he scarcely says a word. . . . Mr. North, I'm going to tell you a secret: Charles thinks he's an orphan; he thinks Papa and Mama adopted him. I don't think he really believes that, but that's what he says." She lowered her voice. "He thinks he is a prince from another country—like Poland or Hungary or even France."

"And you're the only one who knows that?"

She nodded. "So you see how hard it is for Papa and Mama to make conversation—and in front of the servants!—with a person who acts as though he were so far away from them."

"Does he think that you are of royal birth also?"

She answered sharply. "I don't let him."

"So at mealtimes you fill in about Buddhism and glaciers and Florence Nightingale?"

"Yes . . . and I tell them the things you've told me. About the school you went to in China. That filled a whole lunchtime—I embroidered it a little. Do you always tell the truth, Mr. North?"

"I do to you. It's so boring to tell the truth to people who'd rather hear the other thing."

"I told how in Naples the girls thought you had the Evil Eye. I made it funny and Mario had to leave the room he was laughing so."

"Now I'm going to tell you something. Dear Eloise, if you see that Charles is cutting his way out of that spider's web a little, you can tell yourself that it's all due to you." She looked at me in wonder. "Because when you love someone you communicate your love of life; you keep the faith; you scare away dragons."

"Why, Mr. North—there are tears in your eyes!"

"Happy tears."

So I met Charles at eight-thirty on the following Monday. In the intervening time he had relapsed somewhat into his haughty distrust; but he deigned to sit in his do, the need to protect him. No, not protect. To watch over him while he made his own way through the covert labyrinth that surrounded every step he took, and still did.

Perhaps if you had allowed feelings to be known, reached out even slightly, allowed him to reach for you. Perhaps then the involvement with Lin could have been avoided. A slight sense of envy gripped her, and she dismissed it, sensing the unworthiness of it. No, there had been no time for emotions, for personal desire or need. Throughout her life there had never been enough time for those luxuries. There had been time only for struggle. She thought of Peter again, his face, the pain, the hatred. Then earlier, the small knowing smile, the sense of gentleness hidden beneath the strength. Tears came to her eyes, and she brushed them away with one hand. Molly Bloom does not cry, she told herself. Again the tears returned.

Chapter 37

Morris had noticed the change in Peter. He did not know Peter well, hardly at all really, but the flip confidence and the quiet, amused intelligence had dulled, hardened into something else. Morris had seen it before. Young reporters out to save the world, young people who had had their tails kicked severely for the first time, jaded now, realizing nothing would be saved by them or anyone else, could not be, and, perhaps even worse, was not worth saving even if it could be.

Still, he was pleased with the new devotion to the cause, the trail of heroin inside the paper war his country was inexplicably fighting. And Peter's new intensity heightened his own. They just might find out, he told himself, wanting to believe it, needing to, just to make the day-to-day madness tolerable. But still he wondered about the man, the change in the man.

Nine miles west of Vientiane, Buonaparte Sartene wondered as well. The anger his grandson felt preyed on his mind. But he did nothing, knew from experience there was nothing he could do. Pierre had to learn by himself, come to his own understanding of the life that surrounded him. He hoped it would happen. His people would keep watch over Pierre while he waited, and he knew the major danger to his grandson would come now from Pierre himself. That, he knew, was something he could not control.

Another man also worried about control. Hidden away in Cholon, Francesco Canterina mulled over his repeated failures, tried to rationalize them, knowing in his own mind that he was still fighting the protection of the man he had hidden from for fourteen years. The fool Duc had failed him. Even Cao, whom he had used even though it jeopardized his own safety, had failed. Only Buonaparte could be behind it, controlling it all. He knew it, felt it. It left only one alternative, one he had hoped he would not have to use. But now it was a question of his own survival. He would use this man Morris to lead Pierre to the heroin supply route, and to the men who would then have to destroy him. It might also destroy everything he had, everything he had worked to achieve for himself. It would, unless he was clever, more clever than he had been so far. But he had no choice. Eventually Pierre would find him and try to kill him. Only a fool would not strike first. And he was not a fool.

Morris was hung over and irritable. Eight o'clock in the morning was not his time of day, not anywhere near it. As he stood in the Tan Son Nhut terminal the fact was made clearer every moment. The crush of bodies, moving in and out. Fresh, young, expectant faces of new troops arriving. The anxious anticipation of those about to leave. The uncaring faces of the Vietnamese, themselves tolerating the crush they had no hope to control, merely living with it, just as they had lived with the French and all the others who had come before, and would probably come after.

Morris mopped his forehead. Eight o'clock, and already the heat made you sweat. He smiled to himself, thinking that the better part of a bottle of Jack Daniel's the night before might have something to do with it as well. He wondered if he would ever stop pouring booze down his throat that way. He doubted it. At least he didn't drink in the morning, not yet anyway.

He stretched his body, craning his neck to see over the mass of humanity moving through the terminal. It made his head hurt, so he resigned himself to wait patiently. He had met the Frenchman three days ago, a casual conversation in the Caravelle Bar. Somehow they had begun talking about heroin, about the drugs the kids fighting the war were pumping into their bodies. He wasn't sure how the conversation had begun, but he was not surprised that it had. It was part of the war to him, perhaps the worst part, and if it continued the way it was going—children fighting a war no one was trying to win—even those who went home would not survive it. So he talked about it to anyone who would listen.

The Frenchman had said he could help him, show him something that would open the door for him. He had laughed at the time, but the Frenchman had insisted. He had been in Southeast Asia for more than a dozen years, he had explained. He knew things, he had said, things a reporter interested in heroin would like to know. They agreed on a price of two hundred dollars, U.S., if the information was worthwhile. Cash on delivery. He reached in his pocket and fingered the money, hoping he would spend it, not believing he would. He had gone this route too many times before. He looked at his watch. His newfound friend and benefactor, Edouard, was ten minutes late.

"You look worried, my friend. Impatient and worried."

Morris looked to the sound of the voice. The man he knew as Edouard grinned at him, the cigarette dangling from his mouth twitching with the curve of his lips.

"I was beginning to think you were going to stiff me, Edouard," Morris said.

Francesco Canterina laughed, enjoying the aptness of Morris' choice of words. "Never, my friend. I'm going to show you something you've been wondering about for a long time."

"Really?" Morris smirked. "And what would that be?"

Francesco took Morris' arm and began walking him toward the stairs that led to the observation desk. "Oh, nothing very much on the surface. But if you have a friend who can investigate within the military compound here, I can show you where to look to find how heroin leaves Saigon. Something those involved call the long silver train."

When Peter reached the observation desk, Morris was pacing back and forth like a circus cat awaiting his daily ration of meat. He looked terrible, more rumpled than usual, Peter observed, and his attempt at shaving had been only partially successful. But you know the feeling, Peter told himself. Especially over the past weeks.

Seeing him now, Morris raced toward him with a degree of energy that forced Peter to smile. Morris grabbed his shoulders between his hands. "We got it," he said. "By Jesus, I think we really have got it."

Peter eased himself back. The smell of stale booze that poured off Morris was overwhelming.

"What have we got?" he asked. "All you said over the phone was that it was big and to get my ass down here. What's so big?"

"I'm sorry about all the mystery, but I didn't want to risk saying anything on the phone. If it's right, and goddammit, all of it seems to fit like a glove, then we've got the bastards. We can follow the stuff right back to the people behind it."

"Where'd you get this?" Peter asked.

"That's the one thing I can't tell you, buddy. It cost me two hundred bucks and the promise of confidentiality. I'm afraid that still means something in my business."

Peter nodded. Francesco's new game was beginning. He could feel it. Now there would be new surrogates. But this time Peter intended to use them as well. "At least tell me what you've got."

"I'll do better than that." Morris grinned. "I'll show you."

He took Peter by the arm and led him toward the observation window. He scanned the tarmac for a moment, then jabbed a finger toward a hangar to his left. "I couldn't figure out why my source dragged me out here so early. But he said they only moved what he wanted to show me in the morning, before the sun got too strong. Over there coming out of that hangar two hundred yards to our left."

Peter stared at the hangar, watching a small tractor pull out onto the tarmac. Attached to the tractor were a series of flatbed baggage carts, each carrying four aluminum military coffins. Moving along the tarmac, the sun glinting off the aluminum, the tractor and baggage carts resembled a long silver train.

Peter turned back to Morris, his face slack. "In the coffins," he said, his voice suddenly dry. Very Corsican, he thought.

"And if we follow it back to the source, we find out who," Morris said. "My man claims there's supposed to be another shipment of heroin due in a few days. You can watch them pull it off, witness it."

Peter heard his words, the excitement in Morris' voice, but it all came from a distance.

"Those are American dead," he heard himself say. The sound of his own words snapped him back. He stared into Morris' face, watching the excitement grow.

Morris' eyes became cold. "Yeah. It hit me that same way too, at first. It means that it's not just ARVN. It means that some of our people are involved. And they'd have to be pretty high up to pull it off. In small shipments, the heroin goes into the body cavity. In big ones, the coffins with the heroin are empty. That's what my man claims. The only weight is the weight of the heroin and packing. That means that in big shipments, somebody's making up bodies, making up dead who don't exist and never did. Or some of our dead are being listed as missing in action so their bodies can be used under phony names. Whichever it is, it's got to be somebody who can play with records and never be questioned. And that means brass. Big brass." He waited, letting his information register. "Does it surprise you?" he asked.

Morris watched Peter's eyes harden. God, this man could grow cold, he thought.

"Nothing surprises me anymore," Peter said "Not a damned thing. This friend of yours, what nationality is he?"

Morris shrugged. "I guess I can tell you that. He's French."

Peter smiled. Almost French, he thought.

From the small coffee shop at the opposite side of the terminal, Francesco Canterina watched the two men descend the stairs from the observation platform. He smiled to himself. The wheels were turning. Only one more step was needed and then others would take over and do his work for him.

It was unfortunate, he mused. People would be frightened, just as they had been frightened when they had been forced to act against Constantini, and, for a time, that fear would affect business. It might even mean the loss of the shipment coming in, but that was doubtful. The price of doing business, he told himself.

But there would also be the pleasure of Pierre Sartene's death, and the knowledge of the pain that would cause Buonaparte. And others would now do it for him. Buonaparte would suspect, but he would never have proof. There would be no way he could honorably force an end to the agreement with Hanoi.

He smiled again. Now he must just make sure that those at the top were exposed. Give young Pierre time to discover who they were. Then a quiet trip to his friends, a worried conversation about Captain Bently's involvement with a certain newspaperman. They would have no choice at all.

He sipped his coffee, watching the two men start across the terminal, heading for the street. His only regret would be that he had not killed the man himself, he thought. He smiled again. And that he had never fucked his mother.

Chapter 38

Michael Pope was short and slightly overweight. He had a round florid face, accented by bad teeth that he constantly displayed with a mildly silly grin, and the natural bonhomie of a midwestern upbringing which made all else about him tolerable. Peter liked him when they met, and immediately hoped he was not directly involved with the heroin shipments.

Pope worked in Admissions and Dispositions, the refrigerated holding area where those killed in action were identified, autopsied if necessary, then packaged in aluminum coffins and carted off to Graves Registration for the one-way trip home. He referred to himself as the head of the KIA Travel Bureau with all the sad cynicism of one forced to deal closely with death at too early an age. He was eighteen.

They had met in a bar on Tu Do Street, an accidental encounter for Pope, but one that had been well planned. Peter was posing as a fellow enlisted man, and the friendship would give him an excuse to drop in and visit Pope at work. It was not a place people went to without reason, and now he needed to know the area well.

"It ain't a bad place to work, once you get used to it," Pope said, searching Peter's eyes for discomfort. "You just gotta force yourself not to think about it."

They were standing next to a row of stainless-steel carts, each holding a corpse wrapped in a canvas bag. Opposite the carts was a large walk-in refrigeration unit, similar to those found in butcher shops, only bigger and far more ominous. Pope had opened it earlier and an odor of decomposition had flooded the room. It was gone now, but Peter was sure he could still smell it, sure he would for several days.

Pope had apologized. "It's the fuckin' heat," he explained. "They turn ripe so fast, and the smell don't go away until they're frozen stiff. And if we gotta thaw 'em out it can get pretty bad. But that only happens when the vulture's gotta do an autopsy. And he's pretty decent about it. He sends us outta here when he's gonna do a bad one."

"The vulture?" Peter said, trying to hide his excitement with laughter.

Pope hushed him, and gestured to an office at the far end of the holding area. "The colonel," he explained. "The chief pathologist. He's a bird colonel, a real gung-ho motherfucker. Even has green cloth eagles sewn on his medical gowns. We started calling them green vultures, then the name kinda got identified with him. A lotta people use it now, but he sure as hell don't like it."

Peter crinkled up his nose, playing his part. "Is that all he does, all that autopsy shit?"

"Nah. There ain't too much of that," Pope said. "The cause of death ain't usually too hard to tell around here. When a guy's got a hole in his chest the size of a fuckin' baseball, there ain't much question how he bought the fuckin' farm. Sometimes though, when the decomposition is bad, he's gotta check 'em out. Mostly, though, he just marks the coffins ain't supposed to be opened by the family or nobody else. They don't want the folks back home seein' some of the meat we ship outta here."

"But *you* gotta look at it, man." Peter feigned a shiver to emphasize his sympathy for the young man.

Pope flashed a grin, showing off his rotting front teeth. "Naw, not really. We keep 'em in the bags mostly. When he's gonna open 'em up and do that 'Do not open' shit, he usually lets us split. Like I said he's pretty decent about it."

Yeah, pretty damned decent, Peter thought, seated back in his office. No witnesses when the coffins are filled and marked "Do not disturb." A real sweetheart. Peter drummed his fingers on the desk, his mind filtering ideas. Pope had said they were told when they were about to get time off, when the colonel was going to do this little "Do not disturb" act. Always a day's notice so they could plan to use the time off. It also made sure nobody would walk in accidentally or volunteer for extra duty to pick up points.

Peter had made arrangements for Pope to let him know the next time he got unexpected time off. Told him he knew some ladies who were available for some night work, as long as he gave them a day's notice. He'd call, Peter knew. He was young and *very* horny.

Colonel Max Warren entered the cavernous Admissions and Dispositions section at 1900 hours, paced through the entire area, satisfying himself that no one had mistakenly come to work, then entered his small office. Out of habit, he slipped off his uniform and climbed into a pale-green medical gown. He was of average height and build, about fifty years of age, with a balding head that he vainly tried to conceal by combing long strands of hair up and over the top of his head. It made his baldness even more noticeable. His face was soft and fleshy, almost puttylike, and taken together his features would be described as those of a person who would not be noticed in a crowd, no matter how small.

Warren rubbed his chin in thought, then walked to a small window and peered out. There were no stationary sentries to worry about. Admissions and Dispositions had nothing anyone would want to steal, and he had stopped the Military Police jeep that patrolled the area to tell the MPs he would be working late that night. The lights coming from within would not arouse their curiosity.

He closed the blinds on the window, then went directly to the large safe that sat in one corner of the office, opened it and withdrew five rectangular packages, each weighing about nine pounds. Now it was just a matter of waiting for the others and the simple job of packing and labeling the coffins could begin, an hour's work at most. He lit a cigarette and seated himself behind his desk, wishing he could do this work during the day and avoid disrupting his evening.

Peter was stretched out on the top shelf of a deep supply rack, only a few feet from the ceiling. He was surrounded by boxes, well hidden from view, but with a clear field of vision of the entire room. He had two cameras, one with a telephoto lens, one equipped with a wide-angle, and two directional microphones hooked into separate tape recorders. Additional recording devices had been placed in Warren's office and the refrigeration unit. Earlier that afternoon he had followed a large carton that had been delivered to the section. It had been marked "Medica

Books,'' and addressed to Warren. That evening he had found the box opened and discarded. Since he had found no new books in Warren's office, he was sure the shipment had arrived.

Peter stared at the office door, watching the light that shone through the frosted-glass panel. He had seen the safe earlier and had wished he had the skills to open it and confirm his suspicions. No matter, he told himself now. Whether you found anything or not, you'd still be here. The plan would mean nothing without the photographs and the recordings.

Below him the bodies of the dead, those delivered that night, lay in canvas body bags, the interiors lined with heavy rubber. They were laid out on the cement floors like so many wooden logs, waiting to be tossed on carts and wheeled into the refrigeration unit.

The thought of the unit now caused Peter's stomach to tighten. He had placed the recording device there, and when he had opened the door, the odor had nearly forced him to his knees. Even worse was the light. It had gone on automatically when the door opened, a harsh neon that flooded the interior, drenching everything in a blue-white glow.

He had never seen recently autopsied bodies before, splayed open from sternum to pubis, then sewn back together with random, widely spaced stitches. Others, some that had not required examination, were equally grotesque, their gaping wounds seeming to scream out the pain they had known, their flesh pale gray interspersed with deep-purple bruises. And all of them so young. Children, really. Some waiting now to be *used*.

It had angered him then, as it did now, and he forced the thoughts from his mind, maintaining his concentration on what had to be done. He focused the wide-angle lens. On the shelf in front of him the Colt lay ready for use. *Bird hunting. Open season on vultures.*

The knock on the exterior door brought Warren from his office, his heels clicking in rapid succession on the hard concrete floor. At the door he hesitated, glanced at his watch, then opened it a crack and looked outside. He stepped back and admitted two men in U.S. Army uniforms. Peter felt his throat tense as he watched the major general and the brigadier enter.

"We all set, Max?" the major general asked.

Warren's face registered surprise. "I didn't expect to see you gentlemen here. I thought your subordinates would be coming as usual."

"Not this time," the major general snapped. "Word came down from one supplier that the pilferage problem we've been having just might involve that damned little civilian mortician you've got working here. He also said that little dago might be working through some of our subordinates."

Warren's face tightened. "That's crazy, sir. He's tied in with the people at the funeral homes where the bodies go. He'd be stealing from his own people."

"Wouldn't that be unusual," the brigadier snapped.

Warren turned to the brigadier, his face paler than before. "Sir, I hope you don't think I'm involved in this."

"Not at all, Max," the major general said. "It's just that this is a big shipment, and this time we're going to see it packaged and sealed. That way if there's anything missing, we'll know it's being done on the other end. And then, by God, it'll be taken care of over there. Now, are we ready? I don't want to be here any longer than I have to be."

Warren made sure the door was locked. "Ready to roll," he said. "All I need is the names, ranks and serial numbers, and the names and locations of the funeral homes."

"I've got everything right here," the brigadier said, lifting an attaché case he held in one hand. "But there'll only be one funeral home this time, and one coffin. Everything goes to one location this trip."

Warren hesitated, his face showing concern. "That's unusual isn't it? We risk the whole load sending it out that way, don' we?"

"What's to risk?" the major general said. "Once it leaves here nobody's going to open it until it gets to the funeral home Besides, this time it has to go this way. That's how the directive came in from stateside. And I'm not about to question those orders. Are you?"

Warren snorted false laughter. "Not today," he said.

"Or tomorrow, or the day after," added the brigadier. "Where' the merchandise?"

"In my office," Warren said, turning to lead the way for the others.

The conversation replayed in Peter's mind as the trio retreate into the office. Orders were coming in from somewhere, someone who made one- and two-star generals jump. He had been watch ing them through the telephoto lens of the second camera, clos ing in on their faces individually as they talked, catching the venal expressions in their eyes.

He switched cameras, moving slowly, avoiding any possible noise. Even under the cover of the refrigeration generator he did not want to risk exposure.

The three men emerged from the office, the scene comical, even in its venality. The brigadier and the colonel each carried two wrapped packages, held one atop the other; the major general carried only one. Even in a drug deal rank held sway, Peter told himself.

The packages were placed on one of the stainless-steel carts, and as the major general began to unwrap them, Warren and the brigadier moved off to the storage area, hoisted an aluminum coffin between them and carried it back to a second cart.

Peter worked the cameras. He had already reloaded once, and now did so a second time. Using a penknife, the major general had cut through the exterior wrapping on the first package. Carefully he removed the inner covering, then lifted a plastic bag and held it up to the light. Peter focused in on the package. The outer plastic covering was stamped with an emblem depicting a tiger running above a globe.

"Huh, Tiger and Globe brand. I haven't seen this stuff in a while. Is it number four heroin?" he asked.

Warren nodded his head. "Guaranteed. Should be between eighty and ninety percent pure. It usually runs on the high side. Last shipment we got was eighty-seven. Do you want me to get the equipment and test it, general?"

"No. What the hell difference does it make? We don't have time to reject it and get more. With those problems at the Vientiane plant we'll just have to take what we get." He moved the bag up and down in his hand, weighing it. "It seems light, though," he said.

"You're used to the Double U-O Globe brand," Warren said. "They ship in full kilo packages. This stuff is packaged at seven-tenths of a kilo. Our friend in the north claims it's better for smuggling at that weight."

The brigadier chuckled softly. "Shit, he could package it in duffel bags for our purposes. Except for the stuff kept locally."

"That reminds me, sir. What amount do I hold back for our local buyers?" Warren asked.

"Two kilos," the two-star answered. "The rest goes. When are your local people due here?"

Warren checked his watch. "Forty-five minutes."

"Well, we'd better get our asses moving. I want to be out of here long before then." He turned to the brigadier. "Jim, you have the paperwork?"

The brigadier retrieved his attaché case, removed a folder and handed it to Warren. "Everything you need is right there. Can you handle the rest from this point?"

"No problem. I'll have the coffin packaged and sealed in ten minutes," Warren said.

"All right, then, get to it," the major general said.

With the generals watching, Warren began loading the coffin, setting aside the packages that would not be shipped. The heroin was placed in the center of the coffin, with heavy canvas body bags around the sides. On top of the canvas, Warren carefully placed several lead weights, distributing them along the length of the coffin, then covering them with more canvas. Then he replaced the top and began the process of sealing it. As a final step, the colonel prepared the label, detailing the shipping instructions, and affixed it to the side of the aluminum container. Peter focused in on the label, clicking off five frames of film.

Through the lens of the camera he read PVT. WALTER MONTANA, the name followed by U.S. ARMY and a serial number. Below was the name of next of kin, and a final destination. Paglietti Funeral Home, 249 Fifth Avenue, Brooklyn, New York, U.S.A. It was followed by the words: POSSIBLE CONTAGION. NOT TO BE OPENED. NOT TO BE VIEWED BY FAMILY, in large red letters.

Warren showed the generals to the door, opened it, then stopped. "Will somebody be by for the money from the locals tomorrow, sir?" he asked.

"Oh nine hundred, sharp," the major general said.

"It'll be here, sir. In an envelope addressed to you and marked 'Eyes Only,' as usual."

When the generals had left, Warren picked up the remaining heroin and returned to his office. Forty minutes later new visitors arrived, an ARVN major, accompanied by two armed sergeants. Warren led them into his office, closing the door behind them. Peter ground his teeth. There would be no film of the exchange of heroin and money. He could only hope they were vocal about it, and that the bug he had placed in the office was working properly.

When the ARVN trio left, Warren remained in the outer room.

pacing back and forth near the coffin. Fifteen minutes later two men from Graves Registration arrived. One of them glanced at the label and grimaced.

"Another 'Do not open,' huh, Doc?" he said.

"Heavy decomposition," Warren said. "You always have to be careful of contagion in those cases."

The man who had spoken took a small step back.

Warren laughed. "Don't worry. As long as it isn't opened, nothing can get through the container."

"What happens if they open it on the other end?" the second man asked.

"They don't," Warren said. "That seal carries a lot of weight. For all they know, it could mean typhoid."

The men lifted the coffin and carried it outside. Warren followed, locking the door behind him. Peter remained in place for a half hour, in case of an unexpected return. When he was certain, Peter manipulated each tape recorder, listening through earphones, hearing again the conversations he had just witnessed. It seemed even more unreal, Peter thought, but combined with the film, and what he still had planned, it would present quite a conclusive package. Soon Francesco would ask his new surrogates to move against him, but now he would be ready to use them himself.

Chapter 39

"Peter, he feels it's important that he speak to you. I think you owe him that small degree of respect. If you can't go there, a telephone call would do."

Molly Bloom was seated on a small sofa in her office. Her beauty bordered on the luminous; the silver *ao dai* she wore, the brilliant green eyes, sent out waves of attraction. Sitting across from her, Peter tried to ignore it, just as he tried to avoid the image of Lin's body falling to the floor, the crimson stain of blood pushing through the white blouse. Molly and her man. The automatic in his hand. She had looked every bit as beautiful then as she did now.

She had sent him an imploring note, and he had come. Now he wished he had not.

"I have nothing to say to him right now," he said. She began to object, but he cut her off. "I would like to know something from you, though."

"What is that, Pierre?" There was a defensiveness in her voice in response to his antagonism.

"I'd like to know how you happened to join his happy band of Corsicans."

"Why don't you ask your grandfather?" she said.

"I'd rather hear it from you. Or is it another Corsican secret that I have no need to know about?"

Molly leaned back and stared at him. Her look was hard, but only for a moment; she sympathized with the pain he felt, the sense of betrayal, and understood it. "There's no secret, Pierre," she said at length. "I came here several years ago, wanting to start my own business. This business. Your grandfather had thi house up for sale. It was to be sold with the furnishings, some of which were quite valuable, especially the art works. In any event, it was much more than I could afford. Prior to putting the house on the market, your grandfather asked Philippe and Luc to have the house and the furnishings appraised. I managed to pass myself off as an art expert, and I gave them a very low estimate of the value of the paintings and ceramics, low enough so I could afford to buy it all later through a third party."

"So you outwitted the Corsicans," Peter said.

She tapped her fingers together and smiled, remembering her short-lived coup. "For a time. Later, your grandfather found out, but he did nothing until I had finished some rather expensive renovations and had opened for business. Then he had the local police close me down."

"But you opened again," Peter said.

"The day after I was closed down, he came to visit me. He suggested I sell the house back to him at the price I had paid. I agreed, and when I did, he asked me to reopen and run the business for him as an equal partner. In short, he gave me what I had always wanted, what the rest of the world wouldn't give me, a chance to make my own way. He simply refused to allow me to do it at his expense."

"No wonder he trusts you so much. You outwitted his lieutenants. And through them, him. Luc still winces when he talks about the time he let my grandfather down."

"We have learned to be friends since then," she said. "Just as I have learned to be your grandfather's friend. Will you call him now?"

"I told you, I have nothing to say to him." He watched Molly's face fill with exasperation, and then soften again.

"Pierre, Buonaparte knows you've found out about the heroin supply, and he wants you to discuss it with him before you go to anyone else. He said you promised you would do that. He also says it's important that you keep that promise."

Peter smiled and looked off to one side. "Another matter of Corsican honor, Molly. I think I have to finish this my way."

Her eyes, her silence, drew his attention back. "It will be more dangerous that way. Let him help you."

He stood, stared down at her for a moment, then started for the door. "I have to finish what I started. If it doesn't work, then I'll seek his help."

She stopped him as he reached the door. "There's something

else you still have to learn, Pierre.'' She watched the cold smile
form on his lips, wishing she could slap it away. ''Someday
you'll learn, Pierre. Someday you will realize you can trust the
people in this life who love you.'' She allowed a soft smile to
form on her own lips. ''Even though they may disappoint you at
times. Buonaparte is one of those people. He loves you, Pierre.''

Peter shifted his weight. He turned his head and stared out into
the hall. ''I know he does, Molly.'' He turned back to her.
''You tell him this is something I must do by myself.''

What the hell do you mean, I *don't* get the information?''
Morris paced his small, unkempt hotel room, kicking at a pair of
shoes that lay in the middle of the floor.

Peter sat in a corner chair, waiting for Morris' rage to subside.

Morris spun on him, jabbing a finger toward him. ''We had a
fucking deal,'' he snapped. ''You *used* me.''

Peter nodded. ''I'm afraid so. But it was necessary.'' Morris
began to object, but Peter stopped him with a raised hand.
''Someone once told me that nothing here is as it seems to be,
neither the place, nor the people. It's very true, Joe. The man
you dealt with, for example, the one who told you how to find
the long silver train, was Francesco Canterina. The man who
provided them with the heroin.''

Morris began to stutter. ''But why?''

Peter smiled. ''He wants me dead, and he wants the people
whom the information would threaten to kill me for him.''

''That doesn't make sense. He'd be cutting his own throat to
get you.''

Peter stared up at him, wondering if he could ever make him
understand. ''It makes sense, Joe. You'd understand it if you
were Corsican.''

''So what do you do with the information now?'' Morris
asked. His face was still crimson with rage.

''I trade it for what I want, what I've always wanted. Francesco
Canterina.''

''And they're just going to hand him to you, and give up all
the loot? Bullshit,'' Morris snapped. ''They'll blow your brains
out.''

''Perhaps,'' Peter said. ''But if they do, they'll know that the
information will end up in your hands or, if they try to harm
you, some other reporter's. If they try to kill me and fail, then

I'll kill all of them and Francesco, and then use the information to buy my safety.''

Morris glared at him. ''You're a bastard, Bently.''

Peter stood, preparing to leave. ''I expected you to think that,'' he said, smiling. ''But you can always hope that they kill me.''

''I just might,'' Morris snapped.

Peter's smile broadened. ''I hope to disappoint you, Joe.'' He let the smile fade. ''But remember this. If you don't hear from me again, make sure the person who comes to you can be trusted, and isn't from Francesco Canterina and his friends.''

Robert Brody smiled at Peter from across the desk of his modern embassy office. Stretched out before him were copies of the photographs and tape recordings.

''Very impressive, captain,'' he said. ''But why bring it to me?''

Peter stared back at him, his eyes cold and hard. ''Let's not play games. I told you these were only copies, and I was only going to make my request once. Francesco Canterina worked with you. You found out about Cao through him. And that means you're the man who can deliver him.''

Brody grinned at him, but his eyes gave off pure hatred. ''You know you're not dealing with a bunch of dope pushers. I admit some of this stuff gets skimmed off the top, but that always happens. This is used to finance our activities here, *for* the country.''

Peter leaned forward. ''Spare me the rationalizations. I'm aware of how you finance your operations. My family helped you set it up years ago.''

Brody leaned back and raised his eyebrows. ''*Your* family?''

Peter imitated Brody and leaned back as well, steepling his fingers in front of him. ''If you decided to betray me, Francesco would have told you anyway. My grandfather is Buonaparte Sartene. I'm sure you know the part he played, years ago, to help you arrange all this. And it should also tell you why I want Francesco.''

Brody inclined his head to one side and stuck out his lower lip. ''It does, and I'm impressed. You're well hung, captain.''

Peter looked at him with contempt. He found sexual metaphors the greatest of banalities.

"So I give you Francesco, and you give me the evidence. Right?"

Peter smiled and shook his head. "You give me Francesco, where and when I say, and Peter Bently disappears. The evidence disappears too, just to make sure you don't change your mind someday and decide the Sartene family needs to be punished."

"Not much of a deal. Francesco is valuable to us."

"I assume your reputation and the reputation of your government is also valuable."

Brody sucked loudly on his teeth. "I suppose Francesco can be replaced. But I'll have to talk to some people about it. Where can I reach you?"

Peter stood. "You can't. I'll reach you. Please arrange it so Peter Bently is on an indefinite leave of absence. When I contact you, let's say in two days, I'll expect you to be ready to deliver Francesco within forty-eight hours, at a location of your choosing, close to the Lao border. I'll want no more than one guard with him."

They were gathered in a large conference room in the sprawling, modern U.S. embassy. Robert Brody sat at one end of the conference table and looked over the six other men. Two colonels, three generals and a diplomat, he thought. Between them, they were certain to screw the whole thing up.

At the other end of the conference table, Chargé d'Affaires Morton Christopher tapped a pencil against the legal pad laid out before him. "Gentlemen, let's get down to details, please," he said. He had a lean, almost emaciated face, thinning hair, and a long pointed nose. Except for his well-tailored suit, he closely resembled drawings of Ichabod Crane.

He looked down the table, waiting for the others to stop talking. Colonels Wallace and Warren sat next to each other, both uncomfortable, both keeping close watch on the three generals across from them. Major General Walter Mallory and Brigadier James Wainscott were irate. The only calm person among the military was ARVN General Binh Da Lat. He was smiling, inexplicably, his round, moonlike face appearing unperturbed by the matter that had brought them together. Christopher let his eyes come to rest on Brody. Calm and immovable as always, he thought.

"Gentlemen, please," Christopher repeated, finally getting

the attention of the others. "We have a difficult problem here, and we want it resolved quickly. Mr. Brody has been asked to handle whatever arrangements might become necessary. I am not going to involve myself directly in that. I'm going to leave it to you people." Christopher hesitated, taking time to look at each of the men at the table. "If this matter reaches the ears of the ambassador, the whole ballgame changes. I trust you'll see that it doesn't. Everything we've been trying to achieve in this country is at stake now. All of it, just because each of you was a bit too greedy and a bit too careless. Now you can either correct it, or you can go down the tube with it. Frankly, I don't give a damn."

Christopher stood, picked up his legal pad and loped quietly from the room, his tall, lank body looking like a reed that had withstood too much wind.

When the door closed behind him, Mallory slapped the table with the palm of one hand. "Who does that little bastard think he is, talking to us that way?"

"That 'little bastard' was just here to lay down the ground rules, the bottom line. He's the man who's giving us the chance to clean up our own mess." Brody said. "If he wasn't we'd all be busy making reservations at Leavenworth. So why don't we all just quiet down, general, and concentrate on business."

"Well, he doesn't have to talk to us that way," Wainscott said. "It's not like he never knew a little money was being made from time to time. Most of it goes to finance intelligence work. He doesn't have to be so damned pure about the whole thing. Christ, you CIA boys have been dealing in dope for years."

Brody let out a deep breath. "General, if you want to sit here and huff and puff about proper etiquette toward the military, you go right ahead. And by the time we get around to resolving this thing Bently will have made good his threat, and our friend Morris will have it all in print."

Wainscott twisted angrily in his chair, then glared across the table at Wallace. "This is your damned fault," he snapped, jabbing a finger in the air. He turned his attention to Warren. "And ours, colonel. If you had kept your damned shop secure, we wouldn't be facing this crap." He stared back at Wallace. "And if you knew what the hell your people were up to, instead of letting them run around like a bunch of whores at a Boy Scout rally, we wouldn't be sitting here now."

Brody rapped his knuckles on the table, his face pained.

"Okay, if we're through browbeating subordinates, let's stop fucking around and get down to the hard facts of life."

Wainscott fixed him with what was supposed to be a withering stare, unhappy with Brody's choice of words. Brody returned it unbothered, then continued.

He opened a folder in front of him, taking out photographs, tape cassettes and a long typewritten report. He lifted a handful of the material, then let it fall back into the folder.

"You've all seen this, so there's no sense going through it all again. Suffice to say it's painfully thorough. Right down to the name of the funeral home in Brooklyn that could be linked to some unsavory characters without too much effort."

"Sonofabitch," Mallory growled. "Where the hell do junior officers get off investigating senior staff?"

"I assure you it wasn't authorized," Wallace said, immediately regretting it when faced with Mallory's eyes.

"Look, none of that crap is relevant. And we know that Bently was never what he appeared to be. Let's just stick with what he's demanding, and what the hell we can do about it." Brody turned his attention to General Lat. "Your men, general. The major and the two sergeants."

Lat turned to face Brody. His eyes were naturally hooded, offering little more than slits from his moon-shaped face. He smiled and nodded. "Unfortunately, the major and the two sergeants were killed in battle three days ago," he said.

A dull silence ensued. *Right after you learned about the photographs,* Brody thought. "I'm sorry to hear that, general," he said. "But it does eliminate your side of the problem." He paused again, tapping a pencil on the table. "I think if you'll bear with us, we might find an equally satisfactory solution." He glanced at the others, then continued. "First, Mr. Morris."

Brody stood, walked behind his chair and placed his hands on the back, using it like a lectern. "Bently tells us he hasn't given Morris the material . . ." He paused, emphasizing the final word: ". . . *yet.*" He looked at each man before continuing. "But Mr. Morris has been in on this from the start. Even before Bently got involved. We have no way of knowing how much information he already has, or how close he is to developing it to the point of a story." Brody gave a helpless shrug. "That being the case, I don't think we have much choice. Even a speculative article would bring our operation to an indefinite halt. And we can't afford that."

"So we neutralize Morris," Wainscott said.

Brody smiled at the polite terminology. "Yes, general. We murder him." He smiled at the general's hardened expression. "But first we'll question him. He may know where Bently has stashed the originals, and I think our Mr. Canterina will be able to persuade him to tell us if he does."

"But he dies, regardless," Wallace said.

"Definitely," Brody said. He looked down at Wallace. "And I'm afraid you're going to have to help us with that, Ben." He watched Wallace twist in his chair. "Morris has probably been warned not to trust just anyone," Brody continued. "But I'm sure he's eager as hell to get what Bently has, and I think he'll gamble on trusting Bently's commanding officer in order to get it. Even Bently doesn't know you're involved. You'll have to contact Morris and explain that Bently wants you to bring him to a meeting to get the material." He shrugged helplessly again. "He'll just meet Canterina instead."

Brody watched Wallace's discomfort, pleased that he had more discomfort to offer him. "But there's a bit more, Ben. When Francesco finishes, you'll have to take Morris' body to the place Bently expects to find Canterina."

"What the hell for?" Wallace objected.

Brody held up his hand. "There are very good reasons, Ben."

"Why not let your boy, Canterina, take his body there?" Wallace's voice was insistent.

"Let's just say Canterina has a fetish about Bently," Brody said. "He won't go within a mile of any place Bently might be."

"But I'm supposed to?" Wallace snapped.

"You'll be in and out before Bently gets there, and I plan to have the area well covered by General Lat's people." Brody looked at the ARVN general and received a confirming smile.

"I still don't understand," Wallace said.

"It's very simple, Ben. Morris dies in any event. Bently too, if Morris can tell us where the material is and we can get our hands on it." He paused to smile. "Now, you told me that Bently's previous job involved locating VC supply routes inside Laos. The meeting will be near the Lao border, at Bently's request. I'm sure he wants it that way so he has an easy escape route back to his grandfather's people. But it works for us too. When Morris' body is found, we'll say Bently took him to the border to give him a story on these VC supply routes. That scenario will involve an unfortunate run-in with the VC, and subsequent torture and execution." Brody hesitated again. "We'll make it particularly gruesome so we get some good anti-VC press out of it from Morris' outraged buddies."

Heads nodded approvingly around the conference table. "Now, if Morris talks, and we locate the material, then that's it for Bently. But I doubt that will be the case."

"Why?" General Mallory demanded.

"Because I think Bently probably has the material stashed with his grandfather's people and hasn't told Morris where. If that's the case, we'll grab Bently and question him."

"Good," Mallory snapped. "I'd personally like to wire his balls to a field telephone."

"Bently won't be easy to take," Wallace interrupted. "He'll fight, and Lat's people might have to kill him. Then we're up shit's creek and whoever has the material turns it over to the press."

"Bently won't have time to fight," Brody said. "We'll have a specialist there who'll take him out with a tranquilizer gun. No fuss at all."

Wainscott tapped his fingers on the table, for attention. "And what if the material is with Sartene? We'd need a damned army to go in and take it away from that old greaseball. And we can't do that in Laos."

Brody shook his head. "We sure can't," he said. "But I think Buonaparte Sartene will bring us the material, if he has it. If he doesn't, or if Bently won't talk, we'll offer that old Corsican a choice. Find the material and deliver it, or you don't get your little boy back."

Wainscott nodded approval. "So we go Bently one better. He holds the material over our heads to get Canterina. We use the same material as the price to save his ass."

"That's basically it," Brody said.

"Two problems," Wallace interjected.

Brody watched everyone's attention rivet on the man. "What's that, Ben?" he asked.

"First, if Sartene deals for his grandson, how do we explain Bently's missing body when Morris is found?"

"Easy," Brody answered. "The VC took him for interrogation. We'll leave some of Bently's personal property behind, and a little sample blood. Nobody will question it." He continued to stare down at Wallace. "You said two things, Ben."

Wallace nodded. "Why not just give him this guy Canterina? It would be a helluva lot simpler."

"It would, indeed, and normally I'd do just that. It would take time to find a replacement, but it could be done."

"Then why not?" Wallace asked.

"Bently's ground rules are too rigid for the people upstairs. He wants Canterina, and he wants to keep the material for his future protection." He inclined his head from side to side. "It's the right way to do it. It's the way I'd do it, if I were in his shoes. Unfortunately, the people above us don't want to live with the idea of the Sartene family having that kind of leverage."

Brody let the idea sink in, then turned back to Wallace. "You think you can pull off your end?"

"I don't see why not," Wallace said. "I do think it would be a good idea if the generals and Colonel Warren took some leave time and got out of town until it's over. If anything does go wrong, the more people away from it the better."

"Good point," Brody said. He turned to Mallory and Wainscott. "You gentlemen have any problem with the idea of some R&R in Seoul?" He watched as the generals slowly shook their heads, thinking to himself that they might as well keep going if this little plan didn't work.

Brody turned to Warren. "A vacation's a good idea for you too, colonel. We can put out the same story."

"I'll be glad to get out of here," Warren said. "I've even been giving some serious thought lately to a civilian medical career."

"Well, that might not be a bad idea," Brody said. "But not until we're out of the woods on this." His eyes moved down to Wallace. "I think you and I and General Lat had better get together tomorrow to work out details," he said. "There's no point dragging our feet on this."

Mallory leaned across the table, pushing his face closer to Wallace's. "You do a good job on this, Ben, and I'll see you get a big boost toward that star you've been wanting."

Wallace smiled across at him. "I'd like that. I'd like it very much, general."

When he returned to his office, Brody dropped into his chair exhausted. Dealing with the finite minds of the military always wore him out. This time it had been even worse. He lit a cigarette and exhaled heavily, then picked up his private telephone and dialed.

When Francesco Canterina's voice came through the receiver it was like music to him. He liked dealing with professionals. There was no substitute for it.

"My friend, this is Brody. We have a go on the matter we discussed."

"Good," Francesco said. "I was hoping you'd reach that decision."

"There wasn't really much choice, was there?" Brody took another drag on the cigarette and sent a shaft of smoke across his desk. "But listen, you'll have to work with Wallace. No final action until the exact time we set. Otherwise our other fish might escape our net. You understand me?"

"Perfectly. When do you think the time will be?"

"Don't worry, my friend. It will be soon. Very soon. We'll set up your pigeon as quickly as we can."

Brody dropped the receiver back into its cradle. He eased back in his chair, wondering why the intelligence community had ever decided to become involved with heroin in the first place. It was a wonderful financial tool, he told himself. But it sure as hell escalated the level of corruption, and that made it one large pain in the ass.

Chapter 40

"You must reach him and tell him he must not go."

Molly had never heard Sartene's voice so near panic. "I'll send someone to find him immediately. But are you sure, Buonaparte?" She could hear the panic, and the fear, in her own voice as well.

"Colonel Duc just informed me. He just learned about it from General Lat. It is a trap. They are waiting there to kill him."

"I'll call you back," Molly said. She slammed the receiver down and rushed to the door of her office, screaming out Po's name as she did. There's not a chance, she told herself. Not a chance in hell of finding him.

The telephone conversation with Brody had been simple and direct. Francesco Canterina would be delivered in forty-eight hours, alive if possible, in a body bag if not. The drop would be made in the small abandoned village of Huong Hoa, which was located in Quang Tri Province, right on the Lao border, about twenty miles south of the 1954 Demarcation Line that separated North and South Viet Nam. There would be only one guard, as specified.

Peter sat in the dense forest on the outskirts of the village, marveling at Brody's ability to lie with conviction. He had arrived at the village a day early. He had telephoned Brody from Hue, then had used falsified military orders to board a short flight to the city of Quang Tri, where he had stolen a jeep and driven the final forty miles. Later that day, he had watched Wallace arrive by helicopter and supervise the placement of a canvas body bag in a small hut. Wallace's arrival and departure had taken no more than ten minutes. When he had left, Wallace took only the empty body bag with him, leaving behind the contents, along with seven ARVN snipers.

Peter let out a long breath. He had hoped Francesco's American surrogates would be sensible. But he had also anticipated the betrayal and had prepared for it. Now there would be more killing, something he had hoped to avoid.

Earlier he had watched the snipers position themselves in a concealed arc, forming a well-defined killing ground with the hut at its center.

But there were only six snipers now. The seventh lay at his feet unconscious, hands and feet bound, clear plastic tape covering his mouth. The man had been closest to Peter's position, and a quiet blow to the back of the neck had been an easy matter.

Standing now, Peter took the unconscious sniper by the shirt collar and dragged him to the well-concealed jeep, which sat fifty yards back in the bush just off the main road into the village.

Quickly, he removed a duffel bag from the rear seat, stripped the ARVN sniper, and redressed him in the uniform of a U.S. Army captain. Peter lifted the still-unconscious man into the driver's seat, looked over the ill-fitting uniform, then placed a hat on his head, adjusting the peak so it concealed his features without obstructing his vision. He then tied the man's wrists to the steering wheel, leaving just enough play to allow him to drive.

After clearing the concealing brush from the front of the jeep to expose easy access to the road, Peter slapped the sniper gently, reviving him.

At first the Vietnamese struggled against the ropes, as muffled grunts of fear came from behind the clear plastic tape that covered his mouth. Peter smiled down at him, noting his bulging eyes and sweat-filled brow. He spoke softly in Vietnamese.

"It's all right, my friend. You're just going to go for a little drive. Just straight ahead to the hut." He smiled again, removing a silencer-equipped .22 caliber High Standard pistol from his belt, and placed it against the man's temple. "If you don't I'm going to blow your brains out."

The man looked from Peter to the road, then back at Peter. A look of hope had come into his eyes.

"That's right," Peter said. "When you get out there you can

stand up and let them see you're not the American they're waiting for. But I don't think you'll want to.''

As the Vietnamese watched in terror, Peter took a STABO combat vest from the duffel bag, slipped it on, then removed one of several hand grenades that hung from it. Using one hand, he pushed the Vietnamese forward and wedged the grenade between his left buttock and the seat. He pushed the Vietnamese back and smiled.

"As long as you sit tight, the pressure will keep the grenade spoon depressed." Carefully, he reached down and pulled the pin and held it up. "But if you don't," he said, "you'll have a terrible pain in the ass."

Peter reached under the man's trembling arms and started the engine, then ordered him to depress the clutch, as he put the jeep in first gear. He stepped back and smiled again. "Drive slowly," he whispered.

The jeep rolled forward out into the road and headed toward the hut. Peter dropped back into the bush and moved on a parallel line. When the jeep reached the clearing approaching the hut, he dropped down behind a low-hanging nipa palm.

As the jeep reached the center of the clearing, Peter heard a silenced spit, and looking toward the jeep saw the feathered end of a tranquilizer dart protruding from the driver's shoulder. Within seconds the driver's body slumped to one side, and Peter dropped back behind the trunk of the palm, knowing the blast would come in three to four seconds.

He could hear the snipers jabbering excitedly just before the blast, and as the echo of the explosion was swallowed by the forest, the voices changed to shouted warnings and an uncontrolled rush back to cover.

Peter pulled back behind a row of palms, increased the distance for his circling move, then ran low in short spurts, stopping to make sure of his targets' position, then continued the circle.

He took five minutes to place himself behind the first Ranger. The equipment pack the Vietnamese wore marked him as one of General Lat's elite troops—the ARVN version of the U.S. SOG teams, the Studies and Observation Group of MACV that made regular sorties into North Viet Nam. ARVN had dubbed their teams Luc Long Dac Biet (LLDB), the South Vietnamese version of Special Forces. To the Americans, who were far from impressed with their fighting ability, they were known as "look long, duck back."

Slowly, offering as little observable movement as possible, Peter took the silencer-equipped High Standard from his belt and steadied it with both hands. The magnum-load bullet hit the Ranger in the back of the head, dropping him like a stone. Peter crouched, waiting for incoming fire, then dropped back and continued his circle. Ten yards down, two more Rangers were lying face down in a small stand of elephant grass. Too close together for their own good, Peter thought. Typical of ARVN training

Slowly again, he took a grenade from his belt, pulled the pin and lofted the grenade in a low arc, then turned and dropped back again, falling to the ground just as the grenade exploded. He glanced back over his shoulder just in time to see the bodies of two Rangers fall back to the ground. The grenade had landed between them, and exploded so quickly there had not been time even for a warning shout.

He crawled away quickly. Ahead, to his right, he saw one of the three remaining Rangers rise up and throw a grenade toward his position. Peter fired three rounds in rapid succession. The third Ranger flew back like a rag doll, the force of the bullets almost ripping his body in half.

Peter threw himself to his left and rolled. Too late. The grenade exploded, sending a shard of shrapnel into his right thigh. Almost at once, the ground around him erupted with geysers of dirt. The two remaining Rangers knew he was there now; they fired wildly, knowing the odds had suddenly decreased.

But only one of you is going to die, Peter told himself, as he crawled painfully forward, again circling their position. One of you is going to be taken alive, no matter what. And you're going to carry a message back.

The two ARVN Rangers were panicked. Reacting to their own fear, they had bunched together, back to back, each facing a direction from which they thought he would come.

Assholes, Peter thought. He was ten yards from them. Neither faced him. He was close enough to hear their rapid, high-pitched jabbering. A slight smile formed on his lips as he slowly brought the High Standard up in front of him. It was something that had always amused him about the Vietnamese. The more frightened they became, the more unsure of themselves, the louder and faster they would talk. He would have been able to hear them and pinpoint their position at ten times the distance. The High Standard jerked lightly in his hands, the muffled spit coming almost simultaneously with the impact of the bullet just above the left ear of the fifth Ranger. The ARVN soldier sat motionless for two seconds, his mouth forming a soundless circle, before he fell off to one side.

The final Ranger felt him fall and spun around in panic. His head darted back and forth, eyes wide, his entire body shaking in fear. The M-16 fell from his hand and he scrambled to retrieve it. Peter rose to his knees.

"Touch it and you cross to Yellow Springs," Peter said in Vietnamese.

The Ranger froze, his head twisting violently toward the sound of Peter's voice. His mouth was contorted, his eyes bulging from his face; he mumbled incoherently. Peter stood and limped toward him, the High Standard out in front of him. He moved slowly, watching the Ranger's eyes.

"Remain still and you live," Peter said, his voice soft and gravelly.

When Peter reached him, the Ranger bolted up, more from fear than for any planned attack. Peter's fist caught him solidly in the face, hurtling him back in an obscene cartwheel. Before he could move again, Peter was on him. The silenced barrel of the High Standard slammed against his mouth, smashing through his teeth, until it pressed against his tongue. He dropped one knee onto the Ranger's chest, paused a second to allow the man's head to clear, then clicked the pistol's safety on and off for effect. The small man's face filled with a mixture of pain and fear, the sound of the safety mechanism hitting his ears like cannonfire.

"Hands on head," Peter growled, watching as the man obeyed.

He reached out and took him by the throat with his left hand, then eased himself back, dragging the Ranger to his feet. Slowly, Peter stripped the ARVN soldier of his weapons, then stepped back, withdrawing the barrel of the pistol from his broken mouth. He spun him roughly, pointing him toward the hut, and shoved him into motion.

When they reached the hut, Peter flattened his back against the door and ordered the ARVN Ranger to open it. The door swung away and Peter pushed the Ranger inside, into the path of any booby traps that might have been laid. The only sound that came back was a sudden gasp, followed by uncontrolled retching.

Peter turned into the doorway. The ARVN Ranger was on his knees, vomiting. Peter looked past him and felt his own bile rise in his throat. There, spread-eagled on the dirt between four stakes, was the body of Joe Morris, his face twisted into a grotesque mask of pain. Morris' arms, legs and face were covered with hundreds of small knife wounds, indicating a long, slow period of torture. The final wound, which had ended his life, went from his sternum to his pubis, splaying him open like a chicken, and allowing a gray mass of intestines to spill out onto the floor beside him. Anyone who found him, Peter realized, would think he had been captured and tortured by the Viet Cong.

Peter grabbed the Ranger by the scruff of the neck and dragged him outside. The small man stood before him trembling. Peter drew a deep breath and spoke in a broken whisper.

"You go back now," he said in Vietnamese. "And you tell those who sent you that I'll be coming for them soon. And tell them that they will die as horribly as that man died."

The Ranger remained rooted to the ground, unable to move. Peter grabbed his shirt front and pushed him away, watching as the Ranger stumbled and fell, then quickly regained his feet and began running wildly down the dirt road toward the forest.

Peter reached down and felt the wound in his leg. It was superficial, but he knew it would cause him problems. He had a long way to go, through difficult terrain, before he would reach the nearest Meo village. But he would get there, and then he would return. He looked back over his shoulder at Morris' body, hidden now by the inner darkness of the hut. "Sorry, Joe," he whispered, then turned and limped toward the dense forest that lay ahead.

"I have to admit, I admire the man's balls, sending me a message like that." Brody grinned across the table. They were seated in the small restaurant where he had agreed to meet Francesco to tell him about the hunt for Pierre Sartene. Francesco did not return the smile.

"And you think he will not try to make good his threat?" Francesco said.

"He was wounded, we know that, and if he gets out of that godforsaken place alive, it will be just short of miraculous. The idea of his getting back here and doing us all in is a bit farfetched. I'm more worried about the material. I've already had Mallory, Wainscott and Warren sent Stateside."

"The Meo will be out looking for him, if they haven't found him already. They have great loyalty to Buonaparte."

"We're monitoring the Meo, and we have our own people looking. If the Meo find him before we do, they'll just save some work. But I honestly think if anyone finds anything, it's going to be a corpse."

"You also said he wouldn't get out of the ambush alive." Francesco sat back in his chair and rubbed his chin with one finger. "Now you expect the forest to do what seven of General Lat's Rangers could not."

"The forest, the North Vietnamese patrols, and our own people, who think they're hunting down a traitor. He hasn't got much going for himself against those odds, my friend."

Francesco stared at Brody for several moments. "He has Buonaparte. And he has his Corsican blood," he said at length.

Brody sat back and smiled. "Pardon my language, my friend. But you worry too much about that old greaseball. And as far as his Corsican blood goes, I'm more concerned about the training we gave him than I am about that."

"If I were you, I'd start preparing for when he gets here. We will either kill him then, or he will kill us. But he will come."

Brody laughed again. "Well, I'll believe that when I see it."

Francesco looked into Brody's eyes. The man was a fool, he told himself. And there was no point wasting words on a fool.

Buonaparte Sartene sat behind his desk, his face drawn, his eyes puffed from lack of sleep. There was a growth of beard on his face several days old, and his back no longer seemed to have the rigid, almost military stiffness that had always given him an air of defiant strength.

When the door to the study opened, he looked up at Auguste without expectation. When the smile began to form on Auguste's lips, Buonaparte's back straightened almost as though a rod had been driven along his spine, and he pushed himself up from the chair with the agility of a much younger man.

"You've heard something?" he asked.

Auguste broke into a broad smile, and his eyes filled with tears. "He is alive. The Meo have him."

Sartene fell back in his chair and exhaled deeply. "How badly is he hurt?"

"The bush took its toll, and he was wounded when they found him twenty kilometers east of Ban Phou Kheng. He came over a hundred kilometers, Buonaparte. With hardly any food or water. I can't believe it." He looked down at Sartene and saw that his eyes were also filled with tears. Auguste straightened himself. "Maybe you can shave now, and start looking human again," he snapped.

"Shut up, you old fool," Sartene said. He stood and walked around his desk and pulled Auguste to him. They embraced each other for nearly a minute, allowing the pent-up tensions to leave him. Sartene stepped back and took Auguste's shoulders between his hands. His eyes were hard now. "We must send Luc to him by plane," he said. "The Americans and Francesco's people will be looking for him among the Meo, and also here. We will have Luc bring him to the airfield at Phou Khao Kquai, and from there by car to one of our houses in Vientiane."

Sartene turned and walked to the long table that held his array of toy soldiers. He took one in his hand, then turned back abruptly to Auguste, using it to emphasize his words. His eyes were cold and black. "We will go to the house in Vientiane tonight, by boat. No one must know we have gone. Call Molly and tell her to meet us there. We must know everything that has happened in Saigon since your visit there. Tell her to take care. She is to use one of the planes from our airline. And have her alert Philippe that we will soon move against our enemies. Now all those bastards must pay. I told you we would strike quickly. And now, when Pierre is well, we shall."

Chapter 41

Buonaparte had been struck by the depth of Molly's concern for Pierre. It gave a new dimension to this woman, whom he had grown to respect in business. In some ways she now reminded him of his own wife. There was a deep strength, modified by tenderness that made the strength seem even greater. She had not seen Pierre since she had arrived at the small house in the old French quarter of Vientiane. She had reported to Buonaparte and Auguste about the developments in Saigon—things they had already learned from Pierre—the death of Morris, the involvement of Lat, Wallace and Brody in the plot to kill Pierre, and, most important, the depth of their continued support of Francesco Canterina, who was now hiding in the city. But once the business had been concluded she had prodded Sartene, almost demanding to be told the details of Pierre's injuries, suggesting that she remain in Vientiane to care for him. Sartene had declined the offer, explaining that she was needed in Saigon, but inwardly he was pleased by her concern for his grandson.

Sitting in the small living room of the house now, they waited for Pierre to join them. He had slept for the past forty-eight hours, not even waking for nourishment. The Lao physician who had treated him had assured Sartene that what remained of his injuries would heal; that the treatments administered by the Meo had purged his system of infection, and that no aftereffects would occur.

Buonaparte had visited with Pierre when he had awakened that morning, and they had discussed the events in Saigon, the death, the betrayal, the protection of Francesco. Pierre had only nodded, his eyes cold and distant, then he had kissed his grandfather, saying that he would join them downstairs shortly.

Waiting now, Molly glanced from Buonaparte to Auguste to Luc, as she nervously toyed with the cup of Chinese gunpowder tea that rested demurely on her knee. She was dressed in a pale-green *ao dai* that picked up the color of her eyes, electrifying the deep vivid emerald. She looked toward Buonaparte again, but he only smiled and nodded.

"Do you think I should go up and see if there is anything I can do to help him?" she asked.

"It's interesting to see you in the role of the concerned nurse."

Her head snapped to the doorway with the sound of his voice. Pierre's lips curved up slightly as he looked down at her. For a moment Molly could not speak. Standing there he looked battered and beaten. He had a twelve-day growth of blond beard, but beneath it she could see the insect and scorpion bites, the scratches that were only beginning to scab over. He was wearing chino slacks and a denim shirt rolled up to the elbows, and his forearms also held a labyrinth of cuts and scratches, and he supported himself with a cane. But most striking to her was the weight he had lost. His cheeks were sunken and his body, though still appearing strong and athletic, seemed almost frail to her.

She stood quickly, almost dropping her cup and saucer, her vibrant green eyes alive with the pleasure she felt. Two steps from him she stopped herself and cocked her head to one side.

"The beard suits you," she said coolly. "So does the loss of weight. Together they make you look almost intelligent." She could hear Buonaparte's soft laughter behind her, but she kept her face cool and appraising.

"I'm glad to see my recent miseries haven't softened your heart," Pierre said.

"I knew you'd be all right, Pierre. What is that saying, about the Lord looking after drunks and fools?"

He kept the smile from his lips and limped past her, lightly stroking her arm with one finger. His touch sent a surge of pleasure through her. He seated himself in a high-backed chair across from his grandfather's, as Molly took a standing position behind Buonaparte.

"We shall have to speak one day about the level of respect I receive from some members of your group, Grandpère," he said. He looked quickly toward Auguste and Luc. "I'm sorry for all the difficulty I caused you," he added.

"Your grandfather was more trouble than you, Pierre," Auguste said. "Being here with him was like living with a cranky old woman."

Pierre broke into a smile for the first time, then looked back at his grandfather. Buonaparte raised his hands, then let them fall helplessly back to his lap. Pierre thought how one day he too would like to experience a friendship like the one that existed between these two old men.

He turned back to Luc and spoke in Lao. "Your people were very good to me, my brother. I will never forget my debt to them."

Luc's face beamed pride across the room. "They did not do as well as they should have," Luc said. "You look like hell, Brother Two."

"Your region of this world is a difficult place," Pierre said. "I spent many hours wondering at your people's ability to survive it throughout all these centuries. It is even more dangerous than Molly's tongue." He added the final sentence in English.

"I'm very pleased you weren't able to kill yourself, Pierre," she said. "It would have been difficult to find someone to replace your quick wit." She placed her hand on Buonaparte's shoulder. He reached up and covered her hand with his own.

Pierre stared into his grandfather's eyes; a wordless message passed between them. Pierre nodded his agreement.

"Grandpère, there was much I wanted to say to you when I first arrived here," Pierre said. "I did not, because I decided it was better said when we were all together." He drew a long breath, then leaned forward in his chair. "As Molly pointed out before I left Saigon, I have been a fool. I chose to ignore your wisdom, but even worse, I failed to trust in your love for me. I am sorry that I showed you so little respect."

Buonaparte raised his hand. "All men are fools, Pierre. Some continue to be, because they fail to learn from their foolishness." He smiled at his grandson. "I am pleased you chose this way to tell me your feelings. You will need our help now, and it's better to have this matter removed. What do you plan to do?"

Molly watched Pierre's face. His eyes were calm, yet hard. Piercing. So much like Buonaparte's eyes. She had never noticed how much alike they were in that way, and she wondered now if they always had been, or if this was something new. Pierre leaned

back in his chair, waiting before answering his grandfather.
Molly sensed there was something false between them, something personal that had not yet been said. She wondered when it
would be.

"In two weeks, I'm going back to Saigon," Pierre answered
in Corsican. "First I want to regain my strength, and to use that
time to discuss what I plan with you and Uncle Auguste. I need
your counsel, Grandpère; I have debts to pay in Saigon. In the
meantime I would like your permission to ask a favor of my
brother, Luc, and of Molly."

Buonaparte steepled his fingers in front of his eyes. "You
have my permission, of course, Pierre. But these debts. They are
things that can be paid without you involving yourself."

Pierre nodded. "I know, Grandpere. But it would give me
pleasure to do it myself. I sent them a message with an ARVN
soldier I did not kill. It's a matter of honor to me to carry out the
promise I made them." He watched his grandfather nod his
understanding, then turned to Luc, switching languages again, as
a sign of respect. "Brother Two, I would like you to come to
Saigon with me. I need your skill."

Luc's grin filled his face. "With pleasure, my brother," he
said.

Pierre turned back to Molly, taking a sheet of notepaper from
his shirt pocket. "I have a list of names here, Molly. I would
like your man, Po, to have each of them watched closely for the
next two weeks. I'll need to know their movements, and their
habits. And any new precautions they may have taken." He
handed her the notepaper, then looked back at his grandfather
again.

"Grandpère, you once told me of this man, Faydang, who has
protected Francesco. Do you have a way of reaching him in the
north?"

Buonaparte seemed puzzled by the request, and glanced quickly
at Auguste. Auguste shrugged, equally puzzled.

"We do, Pierre," Sartene said.

"I would like you to send someone to him. I want him to
know the details of Cao's death, that it was Francesco who
betrayed her. And I want him to know about Francesco's involvement with Brody."

An expressive snort of laughter came from Auguste. "That is
brilliant, Pierre," he snapped. His eyes flashed to Buonaparte's
face, beaming with pride.

Buonaparte caught Auguste's look, and he knew what lay behind the pleasure. It pleased him as well. Perhaps the medallion was secure at last. He looked at Pierre and nodded. "It is very good, Pierre. Francesco will lose the support of the communists, and their protection."

Pierre's eyes remained hard, impassive. "Unfortunately, there are others willing to protect him. But it's a mistake they won't have a chance to make again. Very soon Francesco will be out of friends, out of surrogates, and he will have to deal with me himself."

"Francesco will be much more difficult than the others, Pierre," Auguste interjected. "Francesco will expect you to come. The others may not. And Francesco will be hard to kill, even if he is a pig."

"Auguste is right," Buonaparte added. "He will try to choose the time and place. You must make him think he is choosing it, and then spring a trap. Otherwise he will remain hidden. It would also be better to kill him from a distance. He will be very dangerous at close quarters."

Pierre stared into his grandfather's eyes. "I want him to look into my face when he dies. I want the last voice he hears to be mine." He looked past his grandfather to Molly. "I'll need one more favor. I'll need a place to stay that no one else knows about. Also clothing."

"Philippe has several places like that, Pierre," Molly said. "I can arrange something with him as soon as I return."

"No," Pierre said. "I don't want to involve anyone who is outside my family."

Molly hesitated, uncertain for the moment. "I'm not exactly family, Pierre," she said.

He looked at her softly. "Yes, you are, Molly," he said. "Yes, you are."

The noise along Le Loi Street was deafening. Jeeps and trucks vied with cars, pony cycles, motor scooters and bicycles, all blaring their horns and bells, trying to find some minute advantage in the chaotic traffic pattern. Along the graceful, tree-lined sidewalks, Vietnamese men and women moved with an equally frantic abandon, jostling each other without concern, then racing on to be jostled themselves after a few more steps, all apparently oblivious to the beauty of the flower-filled median dividers that cut the street into three separate roadways. At the curbsides peddlers hawked myriad wares, food, vegetable, fish, the smells assaulting the senses in waves, while the peddlers themselves added to the cacophony by banging large steel scissors together to accompany their singsong shouts of quality.

On the south side of the street, Pierre Sartene stood next to a shoe stall examining a pair of sandals. His beard was slightly more than a month old now, his hair longer and shaggier, and to those who passed he appeared to be one of the hundreds of merchant seamen who crowded Saigon's streets each day. He put down the pair of sandals, then picked up another. His eyes strayed across the street to the entrance of a small French restaurant, one he knew to be a favorite of Colonel Benjamin H. Q. Wallace. It was one o'clock, the time Wallace preferred to indulge himself.

A crowd of Vietnamese moved noisily past the door of the restaurant. Two men were arguing, shouting insults at each other as they moved rapidly down the street, their voices becoming louder and higher-pitched as they scurried along, almost running. The crowd kept pace, enjoying the entertainment, commenting to each other on the quality of the hurled insults. Pierre ignored the spectacle, keeping his eyes on the restaurant, waiting, watching.

The jeep carrying Wallace arrived at one-fifteen. The driver, a burly army sergeant Pierre had not seen before, waited outside. The warning had been received, he decided. And Wallace had believed it. He had never seen the man with a bodyguard before. Normally, various clerks in the office rotated as drivers. A smile came imperceptibly to his lips, then left. He turned and walked quickly down the street, to the position Luc had taken earlier.

Standing beside him at a small booth covered with various fruits, Pierre took an envelope from his pocket and handed it to Luc.

"Give me five minutes, Brother Two," Pierre said.

Inside the restaurant, Wallace sipped his martini and looked casually about the room. The place pleased him, always left him feeling a bit mellow. Even the dark brocaded wallpaper had a soothing effect. And, unlike those in most Vietnamese-run restaurants in the city, the waiters did not treat non-French-speaking customers with disdain. Wallace took another satisfying sip of the martini as the headwaiter approached his table.

"Colonel Wallace?" the headwaiter asked.

"Yes, what is it?" The thought flashed in Wallace's mind that he was about to be moved to another table. Bloody hell I will, he told himself.

The waiter held out an envelope. "This was delivered for you, sir."

Wallace took the envelope, stared at it, then back at the headwaiter. "Who brought it?" he asked.

"I never saw the gentleman before. He was Lao."

Wallace waved the man away with the envelope, then sat staring at it for a moment. A slight twitch came to his eye. Carefully, he fingered the edges and sealed portion, making sure it held no explosives. Then he took a knife from the table and slit it open. He stared at the terse message for several seconds. It read: *Your driver has been incapacitated. I await your pleasure.* It was signed: *Pierre Sartene.*

Wallace crumbled the note in his hand, then reached for his hip pocket to feel the wallet holster he carried there, and the small .25 caliber automatic it held.

Wallace signaled the headwaiter, tapping his fingers on the table as he awaited his approach. The twitch returned to his left eye.

"Would you be kind enough to have someone ask my driver to come inside?" Wallace asked. "He's sitting in a jeep, parked in front of the restaurant."

Wallace took the crumpled note and spread it out on the table before him as he waited. Goddam cheek, he told himself. Even signs it with his goddam guinea name.

The headwaiter hurried back to the table. "I'm sorry, colonel, but there is no driver and no jeep outside," he said.

"Where's your telephone?" Wallace asked.

"It has been out of order all day," the headwaiter answered.

Wallace crumpled the note again. His jaw tightened, the muscles jumping against the skin. "Is there a back door to the restaurant?" he asked.

The headwaiter's face became puzzled. "Yes, in the kitchen," he answered.

"I have to use it," Wallace said. "Show me." He pulled a ten-dollar MPC note from his pocket and laid it on the table, then stood and took the Vietnamese by the arm. "It's important," he added, glaring down into the much smaller man's face.

At the rear door, Wallace drew the small chrome-plated automatic from his back pocket and jacked a round into the chamber. He eased the door open and looked out into the cluttered alley that ran behind the building. Slowly, keeping low, he moved through the door, the automatic out in front of him.

Outside, his back close to the building, he looked up and down the alley. Nothing. There would be at least two of them, he told himself. That bastard Bently, and the Lao. His mind clicked with the possibilities. One would be in front, possibly both if they had not known about the alley. He looked up and down the alley again. Each way it ended in a side street, one only about fifty yards away, the other nearly a hundred. If no one's here now, they'll be waiting at the side street, and they'll expect me to go the shortest distance to get out, he thought. But I'll go the other way. He stepped away from the wall of the building, remaining low, and began moving down the alley.

Pierre dropped from the low roof above, his right knee slamming into Wallace's back just below the neck. Wallace fell forward; the automatic flew from his hand and clattered down the alley ahead of him. Wallace spun onto his back. Pierre stood over him, to his left, a silenced High Standard .22 caliber pistol in his hand.

Wallace's mind spun with possibilities. He was too far away for a kick, or any defensive move. He would have to talk his way out, if he could.

"Wait a minute, Bently. Just hold on." Wallace's voice was strained and he struggled to control it.

"The name is Sartene, colonel," Pierre said. His eyes were flat and cold, and did not move from Wallace's face.

"I didn't know anything about it, until after it happened. You have to believe that. Look, dammit. You're an army officer, you have to understand these things happen. Mistakes are made."

Pierre smiled at him, a cold, chilling grimace of a smile. "I'm not an officer in any army, colonel. The officer you're talking about died near the Laos border. He was killed on a mission. Another man died that same day. Do you remember him, colonel? His name was Morris. He died trying to hold his guts inside his belly. I'm sure it was very painful. You never should have helped them do that."

"Now wait a minute, Bently . . . Sartene, whoever the hell you think you are . . ."

"There's nothing more to say, colonel. The pistol is loaded with exploding bullets. I'm going to fire one into *your* belly. You won't die right away, colonel. But there won't be any chance to save you either. You'll just lie here and die the way Morris did. Slowly and in great pain."

"Wait," Wallace screamed. His voice bounced off the walls of the alley, echoing back and forth.

The sound drowned out the quiet spit as the pistol jerked in Pierre's hand. He looked down at Wallace writhing in pain on the ground, then turned and walked slowly back down the alley.

General Lat arrived home at five o'clock, stepped through the small gateway in the wall that surrounded his house and casually saluted the two ARVN privates who guarded the interior garden walkway that led to his front door.

Inside, he dropped his hat on a small circular table in the large foyer and walked on to the massive living room, where his male servant would be preparing his evening cocktail.

When he reached the living room he was surprised, then annoyed to find it empty. He spun on his heels, determined to find the fool and make his annoyance felt. He stopped abruptly. Two men blocked the doorway. A bearded European with a pistol in his hand, and a Lao with a short, black-bladed *ninja to* sword. Instinctively, Lat's hand moved toward his holster. The bearded man raised his pistol slightly, stopping him.

"Who are you?" Lat said, choosing French to be certain he was understood.

"You may speak your own language," Pierre answered in Vietnamese. "I am Pierre Sartene, the man you attempted to execute."

Lat's face cracked; the lips began to quiver. He began to speak, failed at first, then started again. "How did you get into my house?" he asked.

"Without difficulty," Pierre answered. "Your men guard just as they fight. Poorly."

"You . . . must . . . understand," Lat stuttered, stopping, then beginning again. "You must understand that I was only following the orders of your own commanders." Lat watched, his body trembling, as Luc moved across the room and stopped beside him. He was holding the *ninja to* sword in both hands, the black blade held straight up in front of his face.

"Your last words should not be a lie, general," Pierre said softly. "Are you a Buddhist?"

Lat's lips trembled; his eyes darted to the sword, then back to Pierre. "Yes," he whispered.

Luc's movements were almost too fast to see. He pivoted, bringing the sword back in the same motion, then, without any perceptible change in direction, brought it forward in a sweeping downward arc, striking Lat on the back of the neck.

Lat's head seemed to hover in the air for a moment, then toppled forward, striking the floor and rolling toward Pierre, as the headless body crumpled to the floor, the severed arteries in the neck spurting blood in a fountain of deep red.

Luc walked slowly back to the doorway, nudging the head out of his way with a foot. He smiled at Pierre.

"A fitting punishment, Brother Two. Now his soul will never leave this land of sorrow."

Brody had been shaken by the news of Wallace's death, but at first had forced himself to believe it was the work of a VC sapper, not Peter Bently. The VC, after all, had placed bounties on U.S. military personnel. Later, when the subsequent investigation had uncovered the note Wallace had left behind in the restaurant, Brody had realized he was not dealing with a random death. He had contacted Francesco Canterina by telephone to ask his advice. Upon hearing the news, Francesco had just grunted and hung up the telephone. Now he was among the missing.

Brody had remained in his office until nine o'clock. His quarters were in a villa adjacent to the embassy which housed unmarried members of the embassy staff. It too was guarded by Marine Corps personnel, but he had not wanted to make even the short trip unprotected. He had thought about telling Christopher, but had ruled it out. The chargé was best left out of the picture. It would not do well for his record if it became known he had blown the simple assignment of handling a troublesome army officer.

Fucker, he thought, sitting behind his desk now, the chair turned toward the drape-covered window. He spun the chair around violently, pulling open the middle drawer of his desk in the same motion. From the drawer, Brody took a Walther PPK automatic, fitted into an inside-the-belt-holster. The holster had been modified to carry a three-inch silencer in a separate narrow pouch. He dropped the weapon on the desk and stared down at it. Damn, he thought. You're used to being the hunter, not the goddam target. And this bastard is good. Well trained. Too damn well trained.

He jumped slightly in his chair when the telephone on his desk rang. He stared at it for a moment, deciding, then picked it up on the second ring.

"There's a Mr. Sartene on the line for you, Mr. Brody," the night switchboard operator's voice intoned. The operator repeated his name when Brody didn't answer.

"All right. Put him through." He listened to the series of clicks as the call was switched to his line. Brody could feel his heart beating in his chest; his palms were covered with sweat.

"Go ahead, Mr. Brody." The operator's voice banged in his ears.

"What can I do for you, Bently?" he heard himself say. "Oh, excuse me. It's Sartene now, isn't it?"

Pierre's voice came across the line in a soft, gravelly whisper. "I still have some materials you might be interested in having. I thought we might meet and discuss an arrangement."

"You must think I'm out of my mind," Brody snapped. "They found Wallace's body and the note you sent him, buddy boy."

"I presume, then, that they have not yet found General Lat," Pierre said.

Brody sat there stunned. "If you want to see me, why don't you drop by here?" he snapped.

Pierre's soft laughter echoed through the receiver. "I'm afraid you'll have to come to me. As you may or may not know, I kept a hotel suite at the Continental Palace under the name Bently. There's a private elevator to it. You can bring people with you to the hotel, but they cannot come up with you. The hotel is owned by my grandfather, so you can be sure people will be nearby to see that you follow these instructions. If you don't you will all be killed."

Brody snorted. "So I come alone to be killed."

"If you don't come, or if you come in force and are successful, the material will be delivered to the wire service Morris worked for, with an explanation of how and why he died, along with details about your attempt to kill me to protect Francesco Canterina. I think your own people will find you very expendable if this information falls into the wrong hands."

Brody was silent for several seconds. "You said something about an arrangement."

"A very simple one," Pierre said, his voice a near whisper. "You get the material, and people stop looking for me. I've satisfied my vendetta against my military peers who betrayed me. I view you as a technician who just did an unpleasant job.''

"And that's all you want?"

"One thing more. The same as I asked before. The whereabouts of Francesco Canterina."

"He's disappeared on me," Brody said.

"But in time you'll find him. You're my only link to him now."

Brody was silent again. "What time do you want me at the hotel?" he asked at length.

"One hour would do very nicely."

"You're very cute, Sartene. But I'll be there."

Pierre replaced the receiver and smiled across the sitting room at Luc.

"Do you think he will come, Brother Two?" Luc asked.

"He has no choice. It's unfortunate we have to do it here, but the embassy and the villa in which he lives are too well guarded. And after learning about Wallace, he would have remained in his hole for a long time."

"What was all that about Francesco?"

"Just something to make him think he would be of future value to me. Americans always like to think of themselves as necessary. As far as Francesco is concerned, my brother, we won't have to find him. He will find us."

Pierre placed an arm around Luc's shoulder and walked him into the kitchen. The stainless-steel mixing bowl was on the counter. Inside, the clear liquid reflected the overhead light. Next to the bowl were the bottles containing common household items that had gone into its making.

"I still find it hard to believe this will work," Luc said.

"It will," Pierre said. "We used it often during my explosives training. We must paint it on the tile in the foyer now. It will dry almost at once, and it will not be visible to the eye. After it does you must not go near it. When Brody arrives you are to go into the kitchen and remain there. I will be on the terrace and I will step behind one of the French doors."

"This man Brody may shoot at you from the doorway," Luc warned.

Pierre smiled at him. "As you once explained to me, the glass in the doors and all the windows is bulletproof." Pierre glanced at his watch. "Come," he said. "Philippe will not allow Brody up until it is time, but still we must hurry."

The desk clerk smiled when Brody asked for Captain Bently's suite, excused himself, and returned a few moments later with Philippe.

"Would you come with me, Mr. Brody?" Philippe said.

They walked to the center of the lobby, where Philippe stopped and turned to face the tall, squarely built American. Brody was wearing a tan cord suit, and already the sweat had begun to seep through the fabric under his arms. Philippe looked at the sweat marks and smiled.

"That is a nice suit, Mr. Brody," he said. "Is there anything else under your arms except sweat?"

Brody's jaw tightened. Philippe's thin mustache curved slightly upward with his smile, and Brody wished he could grab it and rip it from his face. "If you mean am I armed, the answer is yes."

Philippe noddded, then motioned behind himself with his head. "There is a large, rather unpleasant-looking man standing in front of the elevator behind me. You are to give him the weapon before you enter. He will return it when you come down."

"Sartene didn't say anything about a shakedown," Brody snapped.

"It is my idea, Mr. Brody. Pierre's grandfather would be very upset if anything happened to his grandson. And you would be very dead before you left the hotel. I just want to remove any temptations that might make that necessary."

Philippe was smiling at him, and Brody could feel himself stiffen with anger. Goddam greaseballs, he told himself. They're worse than the fucking Mafia back home. "Anything you say," Brody said stiffly, promising himself he would get the sonofabitch someday. Someday soon.

Inside the elevator, Brody removed a small Beretta from an ankle holster. The greaseball wasn't even smart enough to look for a backup gun, he told himself. He jacked a round into the chamber and slipped the pistol into his suitcoat pocket.

The elevator slowed and stopped. The doors opened automatically and he found himself facing a small hallway. Stepping out, he saw there were three doors, one with a suite number on it, a second with a plate identifying it, in French, as a service entrance, and a third, open now, that led to a staircase. Brody moved cautiously toward the main door. As he reached it, the service door opened, and the face of a small square oriental stared at

him. Instinctively, Brody turned to face the man, his hand
moving into his coat pocket as he did.

"You may go in, Mr. Brody," Luc said. "Monsieur Sartene
is waiting for you on the terrace."

The service door closed as quickly as it had opened, and
Brody found himself alone again, his stomach tightening into
hard knot. The little bastard had you cold, he told himself. If
they had wanted to smoke you they would have done it then.

Brody wiped his palms on his trousers, then stepped toward
the main door. Unless Sartene wants to do it himself, he thought,
Christ, I would if he had tried to set me up that way. He wiped
his hands again, then glanced back toward the service door. Still
closed. Could go in that way, but it's probably locked. He
withdrew the Beretta and pressed his back against the wall
alongside the door, then reached out with his left hand and
turned the knob. It opened. Gently, he pushed the door open
with the fingers of his left hand, then darted his head into the
opening for a quick look before withdrawing it. His mind registered a foyer, a sitting room beyond, and a man standing in the
doorway of a terrace.

"Sartene," Brody called out.

"Come in," a voice called back. "I promise you no one's
going to shoot you."

Pierre watched as Brody's large frame filled the doorway. He
held out his hands. "See," he said. "No weapons."

Brody stared across the room. Sartene was standing in the
doorway to the terrace, his body filling the one French door that
was open. Brody's hand was in his suitcoat pocket holding the
Beretta. You could shoot right through the coat and nail him, he
told himself. But there could be a half-dozen more of the
bastards inside, and how the hell do I get out of here even if
there aren't? He ran his tongue over his lips and stared harder at
the man across the room. It's Bently all right, he thought. The
beard makes him look different, and he's thinner. Probably from
the trek through the bush. Must have been hell.

"Sorry, I'm just the cautious type," Brody said.

Pierre smiled at him. "The cautious live longer. Come in.
We'll talk on the terrace. It's cooler out here."

Pierre watched as Brody stepped into the foyer, his eyes
measuring the distance between the painted and unpainted tile.
Two steps, three. Just as Brody's weight moved forward with his

fourth step, Pierre slid quickly to his left, stepping behind the closed half of the French doors.

Brody saw the movement, but could not react in time. His left foot came down on the tiles, and the area around him mushroomed with billowing flames, engulfing him.

Pierre watched from behind the glass. Even there he could feel the intensity of the flames, as the jellylike fire coated Brody's body with homemade napalm. Brody seemed to stand motionless for a brief second, then hurtled forward beating his arms at the fire that covered his body. The room echoed with his screams as he stumbled toward Pierre.

Slowly, almost casually, Pierre opened the other French door, stepping easily aside as Brody staggered blindly past him. When he reached the terrace railing, Brody turned and Pierre kicked out with his right foot. The blow caught Brody squarely in the chest, throwing him up and back. His body hurtled over the railing and plunged down into the night like a dying Roman candle.

Pierre walked to the railing and looked over, watching until Brody's body smashed into the ground. Pity, he thought. You would have enjoyed seeing that, Mr. Brody. It would have reminded you of a very patriotic Fourth of July.

Inside the room, Luc had doused the flames with a small fire extinguisher. Pierre walked quickly to his side.

"We must go, my brother. I'm afraid the authorities will want to investigate this little accident."

Luc shook his head, smiling. "It was amazing," he said. "What a wonderful weapon."

Pierre nodded. "I hope Grandpère doesn't mind the scorched walls and carpeting."

Luc threw his head back and let out a long, high-pitched laugh.

Chapter 42

Molly moved quickly along the sidewalk, the hulking Po at her side. When she reached the small outdoor café, she moved lithely between the tables, then stopped at one, leaned down and kissed Auguste on the cheek.

Auguste smiled at her as she slid into the chair across from him. "Ahh, if only I were seventy years younger," he said.

"You're not too old for me," Molly said. "And stop making believe you think you are."

"You did not come alone?" Auguste asked.

"No," she answered. "Po is on the sidewalk keeping watch."

Auguste nodded. "Many things have been happening, I see."

"Yes. Buonaparte's little boy is leaving a trail of refuse behind. Apparently the Americans trained him a bit too well."

"The Corsican blood helps too," Auguste said. He waited smiling across the table at her. "Tell me, will you marry him?"

"I told you I'm saving myself for you." Molly laughed softly then leaned forward. "Are you trying to play matchmaker?"

"It would be a good match," Auguste said.

"Interesting, at least," Molly said.

Auguste nodded slowly. "You noticed the change in him too," he said. "I don't mean the violence. Any man can be violent, especially if he's been trained for it. I mean the change in the man himself."

Molly thought of the other thing she had noticed in Vientiane an almost imperceptible sense of conflict in Pierre toward Buonaparte. Again she wondered if and when it would surface.

"Yes, I saw it in Vientiane," she said. "Especially in his

eyes. They were stronger, colder really. Except when he spoke of personal things. Then the gentleness that first attracted me to him was still there. It made me think it must have been what Buonaparte was like when he was younger.''

Auguste tapped his hand on the table, his face bright, pleased with her analysis. "In many ways that's true," he said. "But then, I never knew a man quite like that old fox. If Pierre proves to also have his grandfather's sense of justice, then we will truly have something unique." Auguste raised a finger of instruction. "But he will need someone strong close to him. Someone who loves him, who can bolster his strength at times when it will weaken.''

"Tell me, Auguste. Who did this for Buonaparte all these years?''

'In the early years, his wife. She was a strong woman. I never met her, but Buonaparte often spoke of her. I think she was much like you. I think that's why Buonaparte feels so strongly toward you, why he trusts you. Later, he had his family, his son's family. There is nothing that keeps a man's strength more firm than the need to care for people he loves.''

Molly reached across the table and covered Auguste's hand with her own. "I don't think Pierre will have difficulty finding that," she said, smiling. "We'll have to see if he's smart enough to know where to look," she added.

"He has already looked," Auguste said. "I am not a smart man. But these things I know." He removed his hand from beneath hers and withdrew an envelope from his pocket. "Now, I'm afraid, we must get on with the business of Francesco." He slid the envelope across the table and watched as she placed it in her purse.

From a rooftop across the street, Francesco studied them through field glasses. As Molly rose to leave, he motioned a slender Vietnamese to his side. The man had a jagged scar running across one cheek that looked as though it had come from a very sharp blade.

"You are to follow that woman," Francesco said. "Have people stay with her if she meets anyone. Then come and tell me at once.''

He turned his attention back to the street. Molly was moving away quickly, Po at her side. Francesco studied the supple movement of the bright-orange *ao dai* she wore, momentarily admiring her. He looked back at the café. Auguste stood to leave, and as he did, two Mua tribesmen seated a few feet away rose also. Buonaparte has his troops in the field, he told himself. But this time he has a weak flank. He will feel a need to protect his grandson, and that will make the young fool easier to find.

Two hours later, Francesco sat in a small sparsely furnished room in Cholon, one of several he had kept in the Saigon area in his constant struggle to stay out of Buonaparte's reach. The small, scarred Vietnamese had arrived moments earlier and now reported on Molly's meeting with two men.

"The woman and the large Korean were waiting outside the cathedral. In about five minutes a car stopped next to them. The woman got in the back with a European; the Korean, in front with the driver. I think the driver was Lao, but it was hard to tell. The woman gave the man in the back seat an envelope."

"What did the man in the back seat look like? The European?" Francesco prodded.

"He had hair like straw. What you call blond." The Vietnamese badly mangled the word. "And a beard, the same color."

"Where did they go?"

"To the woman's whorehouse." He spat the word out, making no attempt to hide the hatred he felt for a place where Vietnamese women served non-Vietnamese as prostitutes. "But the whorehouse is closed now. There was a sign on the door saying that repairs were being made."

"But they went inside," Francesco demanded.

The Vietnamese nodded. "And they did not leave. At least not while I was there. My men are watching, and they will tell me when that happens."

"They must especially watch for the blond man," Francesco said. "If he leaves, I must know where he goes and who he meets. If he does not leave, I must know how many others come to this house. My enemy has his people in the city, so we must be watchful for them. And when they least expect it, we must strike."

Pierre smiled as he read the letter. He was seated in Molly's apartment, just off her office. She sat across from him in a large overstuffed chair, her legs folded beneath her.

"What's in the letter?" she asked. "A bill for the damage to the hotel?"

"Some last-minute instructions from my grandfather. He's here in Saigon, probably with a small army." He handed the letter across to her, watching her as she read it.

My dear grandson,

Francesco will come for you now. This will happen sometime within the next few days. He will come at night, and he will have others with him. The others will not be so many as to be easily noticed, but enough to protect him against a trap. He will send them first, ahead of him, as we have planned. Once you have him, kill him quickly. I know your wish to face him, but he is dangerous, and will not be easily killed. He is especially good with the knife he always carries with him. I and my people will be close by, but not so close as to frighten him away.

Your Grandfather

Molly folded the note and placed it on the table beside her. "Are you going to take his advice?" she asked.

"Most of it," Pierre said.

She looked at him, her eyes narrow. "Why not all of it?"

He paused, stroking his beard absentmindedly. "Dealing with Francesco is something that goes deeper than the others," he said at length. "With the others it was pure vengeance. A vengeance for Morris and myself. With Francesco there's a more personal element involved. When I learned about my grandfather, about my father's death, and about Francesco, I knew what was expected of me, and I prepared for it. I'm a Corsican, Molly. It's something I was raised to be. I can't change that fact. And I must finish what I've been raised to do."

"And afterward?"

"First there are a pair of generals and a colonel, who are now in the United States. At the very least their past activities should be repaid. I think I owe that to Joe Morris. Then I'll go about finding my own place in the world."

"What about your grandfather? You don't plan to stay with him, to work with him within the *milieu?*"

Pierre shook his head, his eyes firm, yet sad.

"When we were in Vientiane I felt there was something you hadn't said to him, something you were holding back. Is this it?"

Pierre nodded. It was as if the gesture was easier than speaking the words aloud.

"It will hurt him deeply," Molly said.

Pierre stood and walked to the long windows and looked down into the garden. "I love him very much, Molly. I always will. I also respect him, and I understand the way he lives his life, the way he follows his own perception of morality. But I don't want my life to be a simple continuation of his. My father did that. He followed Grandpère when he was right, and he followed him when he was wrong. And in the end that decision played as great a part in his death as Francesco's greed."

Molly began to object, but Pierre raised his hand, stopping her. "I don't blame my grandfather for my father's death, Molly. For a time, Buonaparte Sartene simply chose the wrong path. It's something he told me about, something he understands and acknowledges. It was a tragic flaw in his life. It cost him his son, and it forced him to send his grandson away."

"And now his grandson will go away again." Molly's voice was only a whisper.

"Yes. But he'll understand. He's the one who taught me to be strong enough to make that choice." Pierre closed the distance between them. "When this is over, the life I choose may not be much different from his. But I won't make his life my own. I'll find my own path." He smiled down at her. "And when I do, I'd like you to be with me."

She looked down at her lap and noticed her hands were trembling. "I have great loyalty to him, Pierre, and I owe him a great deal."

"So do I, Molly," Pierre said.

She looked across at him, her vibrant green eyes soft and a little frightened. "You said you wanted me with you. As your lover or your bodyguard?" she said defensively.

"A little of each, I think. Also as my wife, if you're willing."

Molly ran her finger along the arm of her chair.

"I'm more than willing, Pierre," she said.

He reached out for her, noticing that her eyes had filled with tears.

In her bedroom he gently unfastened her dress and helped it fall away from her cream-colored shoulders. She wore nothing beneath the dress, which both pleased and surprised him. They kissed, softly, with more gentleness than passion, then she turned and walked slowly toward the bed, the surprising ampleness of her small-framed figure maintaining his attention.

He removed his clothing slowly, keeping his eyes on her, enjoying her posture as she lay on the bed, her green eyes taking in his body with a simple open pleasure.

When he came to her, they kissed and touched gently, softly exploring each other's bodies, enjoying the pleasure of the newness of it all. He kissed her neck, then ran his tongue along her shoulder and down her arm, over to her soft, flat stomach, and down along her hips to her thighs.

As he kissed her, she stroked his hair, his cheek, his ear, allowing him to enjoy her body, yet delicately guiding him by allowing him to sense the pleasure he evoked.

Her first orgasm—slow and mild—came as he kissed her body; the second—more intense—as he turned his attention to her breasts and vagina. When the time for intercourse finally arrived they joined together with abandon, losing themselves in the giving of long-awaited pleasure, their bodies thrusting against each other with the rhythm of a finely executed dance, their mouths exploring each other's face, their lungs gasping for air; denying it to themselves, until a final shuddering of breath came, and left them clinging to each other in the wetness of their own effort and pleasure.

They remained together for many minutes, idly touching each other with arms and legs. Slowly, Molly raised herself. Her hair, now in disarray, was spread across her face, and she smiled at him as if hiding behind it.

"Do you feel sufficiently weakened to repeat your marriage offer in front of witnesses?" she asked.

He shook his head. "I'm afraid my military training was too good?"

"That's a pity," Molly said. "I shall just have to try harder."

Softly, she ran her lips along his chest, exploring his body as he had hers before. He ran his hand along her neck, then allowed his eyes to wander about the room as his body concentrated on the pleasure she was giving. So many different hues of green. Her favorite color, he thought. Accentuating her eyes, emphasizing that most erotic of her features. He felt his muscles tighten, then loosen again, as pleasure seized control. She had once told him the bedroom was woman's domain. This bed, he decided, was truly her domain, and he knew he wanted to share that domain with her.

* * *

Two days passed before Francesco decided to move against
Pierre. Buonaparte's grandson had not left the house, and
from his knowledge of Carbone—who had once lived there—
Francesco knew there were no hidden exits he could have used
to escape.

He was sitting and waiting, while his grandfather's people
scoured the city—waiting for them to find him and deliver
him—and Francesco knew if he delayed longer, he might indeed
be found. If he fled, Pierre would send people after him. He was
not bound by his grandfather's agreement.

The possibility of a trap entered his head, and he weighed its
potential. First he would have to determine if, and how, the
house was protected from the outside. There had been no evidence of it that he had seen, but he knew he would have to look
again. In any event, the risk of an attack when Pierre left the
house would be too dangerous. The interior posed a more difficult question. The Lao and Korean were there with Pierre and
the woman. At least one would remain on guard throughout the
night. The ideal would be to buy the loyalty of one or both. The
risks, he decided, outweighed the possibility of success. The
same was true of luring Pierre to him. Buonaparte simply had
too many people in the city.

Finally, Francesco decided he must send out the story that he
had fled to the north, then move quickly with four of his own
people. A silent assault in the night, which would catch them off
guard while they waited to verify the report.

The plan displeased him. It forced him into a confrontation not
entirely of his own choosing. That view changed the day before
the planned attack. Shortly after seven in the evening, August
arrived at the house, remained inside for one hour, then left with
the Lao at his side. By two in the morning the Lao had not
returned.

The four Vietnamese entered the house through a rear window
at three in the morning, while Francesco waited in the garden,
hidden back among the shrubbery, his dark clothing making him
one shadow among many. He waited without movement, controlling even his breath to avoid detection. There was a silence-
equipped Browning automatic in his hand. Each of the Vietnamese
carried Sten guns, also equipped with silencers, and each had
been well trained in the north.

Five minutes passed before one of the Vietnamese—the man with the scar—returned to the garden. He moved quietly to Francesco's side and knelt. Francesco reached out and touched the barrel of his Sten gun. It was hot.

"We found the Korean downstairs and eliminated him," the Vietnamese said.

"And the others? Sartene and the woman?"

"They must be upstairs. There are no lights, no sounds. I believe they are asleep. We did not go up."

Francesco hesitated, debating whether to send the Vietnamese to do the task alone. He decided against it. He had to be sure there were no mistakes. He also wanted the pleasure of killing Buonaparte's grandson himself.

He motioned the Vietnamese ahead of him and moved toward the rear garden door through which his man had exited. The house was dark and silent, and as he reached the doorway he could see that the furniture inside had been covered with sheets. It gave the interior an eerie, almost ghostly quality.

Quietly, Francesco prepared to step inside the opened rear door. Ahead he could see the room was empty. His eyes darted back and forth, searching out any sign of movement. The movement came from behind, more like a gentle gust of wind, soundless, felt rather than heard.

The barrel of the pistol pressed against the back of his head as the hand came around, taking him by the throat.

"If you move, you die, my friend." Luc's voice, like his movements, came like the air itself.

Francesco's eyes moved to the Vietnamese ahead of him. The man turned and took the Browning from Francesco's hand.

"Do not try to reach your knife," Luc said. "Just move head slowly."

Francesco felt himself propelled forward, the hand on his throat pulling him as the barrel of the weapon pressed from behind. His heart was beating in this throat, and he fought to control his fear as his mind searched for any chance at escape.

They crossed the room, passed through a second doorway, and stopped. The room suddenly flooded with light, and Francesco found himself in the large foyer of the house. The woman stood at the foot of the stairs. Next to her was the Korean, one of the ten guns in his hands. The four Vietnamese stood ahead of him

now, slight smiles on their faces. Francesco's eyes filled with
hatred.

"Don't be too upset with your men," Molly said. "The
orders from Faydang were very clear and very difficult to refuse."

Francesco felt a sharp blow to his back that propelled him into
the center of the foyer. He turned and found the Lao, who had
left the house earlier with Auguste, smiling at him.

"My compliments," Francesco said. "You move very quietly."

Luc shrugged. "I was never far from you. The only reason
you're alive now is that Pierre wished it to be so."

Francesco turned back to Molly. "And where is my young
Corsican friend?"

"He's waiting for you upstairs. The center door along the
hallway. You'll find all the other doors are locked, as that one
will be once you enter."

Francesco felt his stomach knot; he laughed to conceal it.
"So, it will be a slow, unpleasant death," he said.

Molly stared at him, her face flat and expressionless. "You
may take your knife with you. It is far more than you would have
allowed him." She stepped back and pointed up the staircase.

Francesco moved slowly, knees weak, his stomach churning
with fear. His lips began to tremble, and he tightened them,
unwilling to show the fear he felt. He climbed the stairs slowly,
Po ahead, his body turned, the Sten gun pointed at Francesco's
chest. He glanced behind. Luc followed, pistol in hand.

At the top of the stairs he looked down the hallway, counting
the doors, then counting back, finding the one in the center of
the hall. His mind flew back to Carbone years before. It was the
insane room of his that he had heard about, the one with the
mirrored labyrinth. He paused at the door and looked back. The
others stood watching him. He turned his head to the side and
spit, then he opened the door and walked inside.

The room was bathed in the soft pink light that came from the
overhead fixtures. He was standing in a small sitting room. A
loveseat and two chairs, a small table holding a porcelain figure
of a woman, ahead the maze of mirrors, empty of any reflection
but his own fractured, fragmented image. Francesco's breath
became rapidly; he felt his body tense.

To the right of his own fragmented image, a face and shoulder
appeared, then disappeared. Francesco spun to his right, then his
left. No one.

"Interesting, isn't it?" The voice spoke in the Corsican dialect of his birth, seeming to come from everywhere.

Francesco spun in a circle, sure from the sound that Pierre was behind him. Again nothing.

"Where are you, Pierre?" Francesco's voice almost cracked with the strain.

"Within the labyrinth, waiting for you." Pierre's voice was almost a whisper, and it seemed to swirl about the small sitting room. It was everywhere and nowhere.

Francesco forced himself to laugh. "And you expect me to come and find you?"

"It's the only way out, Francesco. On the other side there is an unlocked door."

"I don't believe you." The strain was clear now, the voice cracking with the pressure he felt. "Why don't you come to me? I only have the knife." He withdrew the stiletto from his pocket and opened the double-edged blade.

"But I have no weapon, Francesco. Only the labyrinth, and the knowledge of how to pass through it." A portion of Pierre's face appeared in the mirror and disappeared again. He laughed softly. "Of course I am very capable of killing you with my hands. That is the way I prefer to kill you, Francesco. You could not face my father when you killed him, nor my stepfather when you attempted the same. And you certainly have struggled to avoid facing my grandfather. But now you must face me, if you hope to live. You see, I want to smell your fear when you die. I want to see it in your eyes. I could have had your men bring you to me days ago. But I was afraid you might resist and force them to kill you. It would have denied *me* that pleasure."

Pierre's image appeared almost whole in the mirrors, then broke apart and faded into fragments before disappearing again. Francesco jumped back instinctively, the knife tight in his hand. Pierre's laughter swirled around him. Francesco's breath came in rapid gasps; the sweat dripped from his face, and he felt bile rising in his throat. He struggled to control it.

"No. You come to me, little Pierre." Francesco heard his voice break as he shouted the words.

"I'm afraid this game is mine, Francesco." Pierre's voice was soft, swirling about the room in a gentle whisper. "Do you remember the story of the men who murdered my grandfather's sister? Do you remember how he killed the last one? I'm sure you do. It was a well-known story, one the Guerinis like to tell. Almost a legend among Corsicans, I'm told."

"I've heard it," Francesco rasped.

"Well, I'm afraid that's the death that awaits you if you choose not to cross the labyrinth. You see, I very much want our little meeting to take place. I want you very close to me when you die, very close."

Francesco's back was pressed against the door. He felt his legs trembling as he stepped forward, his breath short, his body now drenched in his own sweat. He waved the knife before him as he moved, body in a slight crouch, eyes waiting for any sign of movement. He paused before the entrance of the labyrinth. Inside, the floor and ceiling were mirrored as well. He reached out and rested his fingers on the first wall. Everywhere portions of his image reflected back. The walls were set at angles, each reflecting parts of his image, throwing them back upon each other until they seemed to fade into infinity. With each step, each movement, the images changed, becoming kaleidoscopic, the fragments breaking away from each other, then coming back together.

"No more conversation now, Francesco."

Pierre's voice seemed to come from behind him. He spun, his back smashing into the mirrored wall. He turned again, then spun back. Already the entrance to the labyrinth had disappeared.

He reached out, allowing his fingers to play on the wall to his right. To his left, part of Pierre's face and body flashed into view. Francesco slashed out with the knife, the blade striking the mirrored wall and falling from his sweating hand. He dropped down. The knife was reflected by the walls and the floor, but each time he reached for it there was nothing. A cry rose in his throat and died there. Frantically his hands raced along the mirrored floor. Then he had the knife again. He waved it in front of his body, turning slowly, the mirrors picking up on the flash of the blade, sending out streams of light that played back against each other. He stood, pressing his back against one wall. "Come, you bastard," he growled, his voice like the frightened howl of a cornered animal.

No sound came back. Slowly, he began to inch his way along the wall again, the movement stopped by another wall that sent him off again at an oblique angle. He reached out feeling with his fingers, letting them crawl ahead of him like a spider exploring uncertain ground. The fingers felt a corner where the mirrored wall cut back again. He could not see it; the repeated reflections made it invisible. Back against the wall, he felt around the corner with his hand, reaching into the unseen opening. A hand grasped his wrist, then released it. Francesco pulled back his hand and cried out. He spun away, slammed into another wall, and spun again, wildly slashing with the knife. He crashed to a halt, his back in a mirrored corner. Pierre's face came partially into view to his left; he slashed out again, this time striking something soft, something human. A gasp of pain followed the blow, and the now fragmented image of Pierre sagged slightly on his right, only inches away. Francesco brought his elbow up, again striking soft flesh. He threw his body forward, hitting another wall and spinning away, slipping, falling, then rising again and lurching ahead. Again he stumbled and fell, rolled forward and came to his knees.

His eyes widened. He was in another antechamber, different from the first. The furniture was different, the porcelain figure on the table replaced now with a slender vase. He pushed himself up and ran to the door, grabbing the doorknob, twisting it and pulling with all his weight. It would not move. It was locked. He spun around back against the door. Pierre stepped from the labyrinth, blood streaming down his arm from a slash in his shoulder.

"You lied," Francesco screamed. "You lied."

Pierre smiled at him. "Of course," he said.

Francesco jumped forward, bringing the knife across his body in a downward, slashing motion. Pierre moved easily to his left, blocking the attack and guiding the knife away with a deflecting strike of his closed left hand. Francesco stumbled toward him. Pierre struck with the heel of his right hand, an upward, driving blow that struck Francesco on the chin, then continued up, splitting the upper lip and smashing the teeth, continuing on, crushing against the nasal cartilage and bone.

Francesco staggered backward, the knife falling from his hand. Pierre moved with him in a fluid, flexible flow.

"Remember my father, and how he lay there and died for hours," he breathed.

Pierre's right hand continued its smooth flow as he spoke, moving in a rapid circular motion, then down, his hand forming a claw, ripping across Francesco's eyes.

"Remember Matthew Bently and Benito Pavlovi," he whispered.

Pierre slid to his left, turned, the left palm slamming into the side of Francesco's head, then continuing in the same circular motion before ripping down across his eyes again.

Blood streamed from Francesco's mouth, nose and eyes. He gasped for breath.

"And Lin and Morris," Pierre whispered.

The right hand flew out in a short, thrusting, open hook to Francesco's throat, then continued as he gagged for air, moving in the same flowing circle, then up and under in an open-hand slap to the groin. Francesco buckled forward as Pierre's hand closed over his testicles, pulling up and away.

"And for the Sartene family." Pierre's words were drowned out by Francesco's scream, echoing and bouncing off the walls, the sound, like the images within the labyrinth, fragmented and broken.

Francesco fell and Pierre took his wrist, twisting the arm against the movement of the fall, snapping it at the shoulder joint. Again Francesco's screams filled the room, as Pierre's right fist struck down, breaking the arm at the elbow.

Francesco slumped to the floor, still on his knees, his face pressed against the tile, blood flowing freely from every orifice. Pierre stood over him. The fighting technique he had just executed was called the *kata dan'te*, the dance of death, by the Japanese masters. There were several more moves to follow, inflicting still more pain and punishment.

Pierre stared down at the bleeding pulp of a man who had been the murderer of his father. "You bore me, Francesco," he whispered.

Reaching down, he took Francesco by the hair, ripping his head back and snapping it to one side. His neck broke with the sound of dry kindling. Pierre released him, allowing his lifeless body to flop to the ground. Weariness filled Pierre's body, and the pain he had not felt as they fought throbbed in his wounded shoulder. He staggered forward and slapped his hand against the locked door.

The door opened. Molly stood there, pale and frightened. Behind her stood Buonaparte Sartene.

Pierre stared at them for a moment, his mind needing time to accept their presence. "What had to be done here is finished," he whispered.

Pierre stepped toward his grandfather. Buonaparte studied his face, his eyes. They would talk soon, he knew. And he saw now, in Pierre's eyes, that the conversation would not be what he had hoped for over all the years.

Chapter 43

Buonaparte Sartene's bed had been placed in front of a large open window overlooking his Japanese garden. As he lay there now his breathing was slow, his mind contemplative. It was a pleasant evening, one of many in recent weeks. The pond at the garden's center shimmered peacefully with the day's dying light, and at its edges the water hyacinth and lotus blossoms sent out soft, subtle fragrances that seemed to blend into one pleasing scent. Buonaparte looked down at the garden, regretting for a moment that he would not live to see it reach perfection. But perfection in these gardens, as in so much else, he knew, took generations to achieve. The others would all leave this place soon. He understood that. The war would be lost, and with it his garden. Reclaimed by the forest it once had replaced. Perhaps that was the proper order of things after all. All things evolve, often returning to what they were.

He watched a large insect skim across the top of the pond, oblivious, like so much of the world, to what he had struggled for all his life. He shook his head weakly at the thought, then turned to the sound of soft steps coming across the room.

Auguste walked slowly toward him, his creased, wizened face showing the hint of a smile. Buonaparte watched him come. Auguste still moved spryly, and Buonaparte thought he always would, until the day God claimed him.

"Why are you grinning like an old fool?" he said as Auguste drew near.

Auguste stopped before him. "It's seeing you this way," he said. "Lying there, looking out at your fancy garden like some

438

padrone. I still remember you killing rats in a French prison. I think it suited you better."

Buonaparte shook his head in mock exasperation, until he was no longer able to keep the smile from forming on his lips. "How did it go, old friend?" he asked.

"The Americans are learning," Auguste said. "This chargé d'affaires, Christopher, sees our position clearly. He agrees that certain papers will be issued, stating that an army captain, Peter Bently, was killed in action." Auguste chuckled softly. "He even gets a medal. It's something they do automatically."

"And the documents?" Buonaparte asked.

"They remain in our care. The Americans understand that copies will be with our friends in various parts of the world, and will be released if any future actions are taken against Pierre. For Pierre's part, he must take no more actions against their people in this region. 'Forgive and forget,' I think, was the term this man Christopher used. He also gave some recent news from the United States. It was about the accidental deaths of three retired military officers who served here in Viet Nam. Mr. Christopher said he and his associates were not concerned about that."

Buonaparte nodded his head. "The Americans greatly dislike failure. But at least now Pierre is safe." He turned his head and looked out at the garden again.

Auguste hesitated, then sat on the edge of the bed. His friend's face was gray, and there were dark circles under his eyes, and the skin sagged against his cheekbones. Only the eyes were strong now. The doctor had said it would only be a matter of weeks, even days perhaps. His heart was just too weak.

"There was a letter from Pierre," Auguste finally said. "I opened it because I wanted to be sure it was nothing that would upset you."

Sartene turned back to Auguste. "You open my mail now." His voice was little more than a whisper, but the trace of the humor they had used with each other over the years was still there.

Auguste reached out and stroked his cheek.

Sartene's eyes softened as he looked up at his friend. "What does it say?" he asked. "I am not so weak that his words will kill me."

Buonaparte turned his head away. His voice was weak, and the words came slowly. "You know, I don't apologize for the way I lived my life. I lived it the way I had to live it. But there were mistakes too. And men always have to pay for their mistakes." He paused, catching his breath. "You remember how I once told you that no man can change history, but that he could choose not to be a part of something that was wrong?"

Auguste nodded his head. "I remember," he said.

"Pierre remembered also. And he was right to remember. He will not make the mistakes I made." Buonaparte looked out at the garden again. The sun was almost down now, and the pond reflected its dying light. "I was thinking of Papa Guerini before you came in," he said. "When I was very young he told me that every man lives within his own circle, and in that circle he finds the paths he can follow." He paused again, almost as though he had forgotten his next thought, then continued. "But when he goes outside that circle he is lost. For a time I was outside my circle, Auguste. And because of it I lost Jean, and now Pierre."

"You have not lost him," Auguste said. "He loves you very much." Auguste unfolded the letter. He reached out and touched Buonaparte's arm. "Here, in the letter, he writes to tell us that he and Molly have been married. They went to America to visit Madeleine and Matt, then on to Corsica, Buonaparte. They were married there. Married in the same village as you and your wife."

Buonaparte turned to his friend. "The same village?" His mind seemed to wander for the moment. "I remember that village, Auguste. What a wedding that was! Everyone was drunk and dancing. And I was so frightened I could hardly speak."

"You see," Auguste said. "Pierre does not forget you. He does not forget his heritage. Perhaps he will live there."

Buonaparte looked at him; there was a flicker of hope in his eyes. "He told me he could not live here, or in America again. But he did not say where he would go." He shook his head slowly. "But no. Even if he goes there, he still does not want to be part of us. He is a good boy, a good grandson. But he will not be part of our thing together. He has chosen his own path. I hoped it would be different, but it could not be." He began to cough, then turned his face toward Auguste. "You must take the medallion now, my friend. And then someday you must find someone who can carry on for our *milieu*."

"It will go to a Sartene," Auguste said.

Buonaparte stared at him. There was hope in his eyes again.

then it faded. "No, not a Sartene." He waved his hand weakly, then closed his eyes. "I must sleep, my friend. Now I must sleep."

Buonaparte dreamed he was strolling along the path that circled the garden. He was with Auguste, and their pace was slow, deliberate and relaxed.

"Buonaparte?" Auguste began after a time. "What of the medallion?"

"It is still in my desk, old friend. Pierre still has much to learn, but one day soon, I think, it will be offered to him. Then, if he chooses, it will be his."

Auguste looked out across the pond and smiled. Tears slowly formed in his eyes, and he kept his head turned as he brushed them away. "That's good, Buonaparte," he said. "That's very good."

The two men walked together down the path, Sartene's arm still draped around Auguste's shoulder. He was taller than his friend, and it made it seem as though Auguste was supporting him as they walked. Buonaparte knew it had been that way many times. He also knew it was how men survived. It was the only way they could survive in this world.

Epilogue

The study was dimly lit; only the desk lamp at the opposite end of the room kept everything from total darkness. The faint light played against the room itself, the bust of Napoleon, the rows of books that lined three walls, the heroic military paintings. Even the toy soldiers on the table seemed affected, appearing at times to move, to advance position in their mock battle.

Auguste sat in the leather club chair watching it all, as he had many times before. It had been a year since Buonaparte's death, but he seemed very much alive in this room. Not the same room as before, Auguste told himself, but the same objects that were so much a part of the man.

He thought of their days together. So many days. Much of it so long ago. The French prison at Marseille. The years of fighting. Mount Ventoux, Carpentras. And that small farmhouse outside Bellegarde where he saved you. Auguste rubbed the old wound on his chest. But you couldn't save him in the end. Save him from the pain he knew.

He shook his head slowly. He had not expected to outlive the man. Buonaparte had seemed so indestructible. Even when he lost, he seemed to gain more strength. But in the end there was no strength left. Only enough to endure the last bit of suffering, the final feeling of failure.

And you could offer him nothing then. Only promises. Promises that still must be kept.

The distant sound brought him back, erasing thoughts of the past. He rose quickly from his chair and hurried out of the study. He walked rapidly down the hall, then up the stairs that led to the second floor. Anyone watching him would think he was observing a much younger man. His movements were too spry, too fast for a man his age.

Outside the bedroom he eased the door open. The child's cries filled the room, and he crossed to the cradle and reached down and began stroking its small heaving chest.

"My God, what lungs you have," he cooed. "Everyone will think we are beating you."

He picked up the child and cradled it in his arms, rocking slowly, then lifting it higher so he could kiss the soft down atop its head. He crossed slowly to the window, still rocking the infant.

The door opened behind him, and Auguste turned to the sound. Pierre's large frame filled the doorway, and he looked severely at the older man and began shaking his head.

"You are going to spoil my son," he said, his voice as severe as his look.

The child stopped crying. Auguste looked from Pierre to the child, then back at Pierre. "I don't think he agrees with you," he said. "Besides, life will not spoil him. A little spoiling now can't hurt."

"Since when did you become an expert on children?" Pierre asked.

Auguste snorted. "I admit I failed with you. But a smart man learns from his failures. Now why don't you get out of here and leave us alone."

Pierre shook his head, struggling to drive away the smile that was forming on his lips. He turned to leave.

"Pierre," Auguste called softly, stopping him.

Pierre turned, questioning Auguste with his eyes.

"It is good what you have done," Auguste said.

"What, Uncle?"

Auguste held the child away from his body and stared down at it, then looked up at Pierre and smiled. "Calling the boy Buonaparte. It was a good thing."

Pierre could see the tears that had begun to form in Auguste's eyes. He nodded his head. "I hope somehow he knows."

Auguste smiled again. "He knows, Pierre. He knows."

Auguste turned back to the window and began rocking the child again. The door closed behind him. Pierre is learning, he told himself. And he has begun running his own businesses, just as Buonaparte did. And now he has all of Buonaparte's belongings. All, except one. And soon he will have that as well.

He raised the child again and kissed it. "And after him, it will be yours," he whispered.

The child let out a slight whimper, then was quiet again.

"I know. I know," Auguste whispered. "First there is much for you to learn. But Uncle Auguste is here to teach you. And after me there will be others. And it is a good place for you to learn."

He rocked the child slowly and gazed out the window. Below, the sea crashed against the rocky Corsican coast, the beauty, violence and power seeming to blend together. From the beach below, anyone looking up at the house would see only an old man, holding a small child. In no way could that watcher know what the vision truly held.

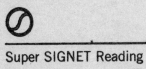

Super SIGNET Reading

Great Novels from SIGNET

*Prices slightly higher in Canada
†Not available in Canada

Buy them at your local

bookstore or use coupon

on next page for ordering.

Thrilling Fiction from SIGNET

(045

☐ **THE CHINESE SPUR by Berent Sandberg.** (122305—$2.95

☐ **FALLBACK by Peter Niesewand.** (120531—$3.95

☐ **RED SUNSET by John Stockwell.** (119126—$3.50

☐ **DEATH BY GASLIGHT by Michael Kurland.** (119150—$3.50

☐ **THE PANTHER THRONE by Tom Murphy.** (118618—$3.95

☐ **YEAR OF THE DRAGON by Robert Daley.** (118170—$3.95

☐ **THE MAN WHO WOULD NOT DIE by Thomas Page.**
(117638—$3.50

☐ **ROOFTOPS by Tom Lewis.** (117352—$2.95

*Prices slightly higher in Canada
